a BITS Inspector novel

A Bisi Day!

This compulsive timeworn cycle is cruel, relentless and never-ending

by The BITS Inspector™

Also by The BITS Inspector

The ABRIGD
The Abridged ABRIGD

A Bisi Day!

For information about gaining rights to reproduce any excerpts
from this work, write to copyright@bitsi-lite-publishing.co.uk
The BITS Inspector® is a UK registered trademark

Published by Bitsi-Lite Publishing
Edited by LHS
Book design by DW
Cover Design by BEF
Production manager HAG
ISBN 978-87-93696-15-0

For information about bulk-purchase discounts for books
published by Bitsi-Lite-Publishing, contact:
sellbig@bitsi-lite-publishing.co.uk

I wish to pay my respects

To all those business and IT professionals who do truly attempt to improve the QUA-BITS and focus on giving your best to your employers and your respective industries above and beyond: Your efforts are duly noted, and highly respected.

An important note to you all: A little tomfoolery can go a long way in easing the stress of the day. All this Gibberish is a play on words, most certainly not on your hearts.

Respectfully,

The BITS Inspector ®

Thanks to friends and colleagues

My very special thanks go to MN, BD, GZ, MRH, RD, TB, BEF, LHS, DW, RM, and many others. All the assistance I received from you helped me to stay sane, to protect me from the Gibberish, and provided quality input that hopefully made it into the end-result.

Warmly,

Bitsi

To my wife and children

Last, but most certainly first, I wish to express my unbounded gratitude, my undying love, my unconditional commitment and my unequaled joy in my wife and children. It is because of you, and for you, that I started down this long, hard road, hoping to say something that may mean something, one day.

With all my love,

Your husband, and father

PREFACE

Language can be a little confusing at times, often seeming like gibberish. In business and politics, the language is even more bewildering.

The BITS Inspector faces this problem day in, day out and understands all too well how difficult it can be for the normal person to make sense of what he reads and hears.

So, in this account of one of his experiences, he has tried to keep the Gibberish to an absolute minimum. However, don't let any humor mislead you or, indeed, make you laugh too long. On the other hand, don't become so distressed by the horrifying BITS that you give up hope. There's still hope, for all of us, if we can change before it's too late, before we die.

Note: In the glossary, you can find the simplest relevant meanings of the Gibberish words. For a fuller interpretation, refer to The ABRIGD (The Abridged Gibberish Dictionary) on the author's website at: http://bitsinspector.com/books/.

CONTENTS

1

System Down! System Down!

THE MIDDLE OF a nightmare-inspiring, pitch-black night and woken up with nasty vibes—again. One of the highlights of my working day: chased down by a GLOBHED[1]—again. These people will never learn to take it easy and just wait for the storm to blow over. They prefer to drag so many overly important big shots out of their beauty sleep just to spray water on some smoke rising from an ashtray.

I prowl the bedroom hunting down my DIGIT-FONE[2]—quietly, so I won't wake the wikids[3]. The children are young and still sleep in our room, but then so do the dogs and the cats. The parrots sleep close by in the next room. All the adjoining doors are open at night for fresh air and access to the dogs' water and the little cats' room. I don't want any of the menagerie waking up and setting off an avalanche of noise. One of the kids has probably fallen asleep enjoying a NET-movie on my DIGIT-FONE in bed, and now it's ringing softly but vibrating loudly, so I need to move fast.

When I finally locate the wretched thing, I should "accidentally" stamp on it, hanging up on this GLOBHED. It'll take them half an hour to hit the correct redial keystroke sequence; maybe the smoke-storm-in-an-ashtray will have subsided by then.

Still vibrating loudly. I need to get to that thing, silence it, and answer it. The unusual time of night must signify some urgency, a real hot one needing some attention.

---

1   [1] Global Helpdesk; [2] Global Helpdesk Agent or employee
2   Mobile phone
3   Wife and kids

"Where the devil is that belligerent, bothersome buzzer?" I scream in my head, tripping and flying over one monster of a sleeping Great Dane, then stepping on an almost invisible tall, black wolfhound stretched across the room, while trying to save myself from dropping into the mouth of yet a third *big*, dirty-beige wolf.

Mickey and Mouse both issue their incessantly annoying small-dog big-noise bark. "Shhh," I hiss through clenched teeth.

One of the more verbal parrots hears all the noise and calls, "Settle down, settle down."

But those giant canines? Good for nothing. You can trip over them, climb over them, or stick your head into their wide-open traps, and they do absolutely... well, she licked my face.

The hand-held FLICKEM[4] for finding the DIGIT-FONE is also AWOL, probably buried in a pillowcase, or a mutt's belly more likely. It's about time I get one of those FLICKEMs built into my head, or some such place. A hand-held FLICKEM (or HAH-FLICKEM[5]) is a teensy-weensy Nuke-Li-Aerially powered *confuzer*[6] (called computer in ancient times), with, of course, a LICKEM[7] in it, which is the one and only wireless device installed in *all* confuzers, big and small, these days. The FLICKEM is my own program designed to find any known LICKEM anywhere in the world.

There are only a limited number of HAH-FLICKEMs on the planet. I designed, built, and own all of them. The wikids, however, *have* almost all of them. I managed to hold on to just two for myself: one for sniffing out my own gadgets, the second one especially for recovering all the HAH-FLICKEMs, DIGIT-FONEs, confuzers, and other devices that the wikids keep losing.

---

4   Finder for a LICKEM

5   Hand-Held FLICKEM, a small remote-control-like device for using the FLICKEM program

6   Computer

7   Bitsi's wireless technology device, built into all confuzers WOW!

Out of the corner of one still-sleepy eye, I see the low glimmer of a flashing light. In an instant, I turn and zoom in on the glow, grabbing it with a vengeance while attempting to avoid waking the kid hugging it. I have finally found the annoyance that has destroyed my night's sleep.

Ignoring the incoming call, I quickly use the FONE[8] to locate my HAH-FLICKEM, which had fallen between the pile of pillows I sleep on, then I dash out the doorway and through the house to my office at the very far end of the building. At this time of night, most things seem very far away.

I try to slam the heavy, soundproofed door to my confuzerized[9] fortress, but the kid-safe pressurized hinges spoil my fun. I wish I could safely increase the shutting speed of those doors without risking slicing off a child's hands. They close so slowly that the kids often hear—and have come to love, and repeat over and over—the first thing I usually shout when entering the room.

Many tiny flashing lights, issuing different colors, are the focus in the center of the room around my desk. I can sense the Beast[10] prowling below me, waiting eagerly to gobble up the next challenge. The lighting increases automatically, emitting a pre-regulated soft light, and I yell, "All systems go." Any machines that were sleeping will soon be ready for action, and on a gigantic spacey-screen[11], nine screen-spaces[12] flash to life instantly showing everything from the news to the status of my machines, and, of course, a Bitsi-Lite[13] view of the wikids.

Thanks to Bitsi-Lite, I can now monitor my family, the dogs, the house and garden; the neighbor's house, dogs, and garden; your house, dog, and garden; and just about every other thing I choose to keep

---

8   Short for DIGIT-FONE
9   [1] Computerized; [2] Confused
10 The name of Bitsi's confuzer
11 Computer touch-screen, usually huge and transparent and can be viewed and operated from both sides
12 Software term, historically "window" or "panel" displayed on a spacey-screen
13 [1] Bitsi's satellite technology; [2] Bitsi's satellite-farm; [3] Satellite

an eye on across the globe. One large screen-space constantly shows twenty-four different views of the house and grounds.

Swinging my chair around to my main space-pad[14] Seribus[15] and opening a new large sspace[16], I bring up my DIGI-DIRT-MAPP[17] program and target the caller on my DIGIT-FONE as the starting point for the DIRT-MAPP I want to see. Most of the information I'm viewing is from just a few weeks ago, so I can immediately see the caller's exact location.

Oh well, here goes, I guess. Finally, I respond to the never-ending buzzing. "Yeah, what's up?" I force the question out almost politely, trying to ignore that I hate GLOBHEDs bushwhacking me when I should be snoring.

"Er, am I speaking to the BITS Inspector[18]?" comes the almost tentative, but mostly insecure question.

"Who, in the wholly scary *MOTHER*[19] of Lord-IT's name, are you, calling me up at this hour?" I demand, even though my DIRT-MAPP is now also showing me the webcam video of the caller. Lack of common courtesy, however, when starting a conversation like this, always irritates me, and even more so when I can still see the moon in the sky.

"Er, er, this is the GLOBHED, sir." They don't even bother to mention the company name. Nervous, I guess.

I sigh inwardly, not exactly giving up on a lost cause, but close. "Yes, I'm the BITS Inspector. Bitsi[20], if that's easier for you. Now, again, *what is up*?"

"We have a major system down, Mr. Bitchy, sir."

---

14   Keyboard (*Made from downsized spacey-screen technology.*)
15   "Serious business," the name of Bitsi's favorite space-pad
16   Abbreviation for screen-space
17   Bitsi's all-powerful menu-driven program for making life easier when working on the BEAST
18   The most powerful businessman known to humankind
19   [1] Mother organization or top parent organization; [2] Mother
20   The BITS Inspector

"Not Bitchy. It's Bitsi," I yell, while trying to force the smile on my lips to stay well away from my voice.

"Er, yes, sir, Bitsi. So, er, we have some serious *MAD-ONNA MAGIC*[21] ongoing right now, sir, a major, major, system down, sir, and we've been informed you will fix it."

BIG-AM-I[22], the proud owner of this particular GLOBHED, is the oldest standing and third largest organization WOWI[23] and has many large IT systems. Even so, not many of BIG-AM-I's BITS[24] would be described with a double major. I flick a switch on my desk and a small red Do Not Disturb light starts gently flashing outside my office door. If anyone touches the door handle, except my wife, of course, then the alarm starts buzzing quietly outside the door.

"Great," I retort. "So, which monstrosity is suffering this time?" Silence. More silence. "Well?" And it's easy to tell I'm getting a tad impatient now. More silence.

"Er, er, it's, er, OBOY[25], er, Mr. Sir Bitchy, sir."

"All hands to the deck," I almost shout, only much, much louder. *"And do not call me Bitchy."*

My mind momentarily flies off in all directions. OBOY is the single biggest soft-BITS[26] *ever* built. It's world-famous, and it's renowned for never, *ever*, going down.

---

21   [1] BIG System DOWN, Oh No! Not Again! [2] Something to be avoided at all cost

22   Bipolar Innovations, Generator of Amazingly Magnificent Inventions; the third-largest organization on the planet.

23   [1] Worldwide; [2] Wow-wee; [3] "And so what?" or "big deal."

24   [1] Business Information Technology (IT) System(s); [2] Bits and pieces of software or hardware (small, big, huge, or soup-ah huge!); [3] Just about anything and everything under the sun that could be described as a bit or, indeed, multiple bits; [4] Information Technology [IT]; [5] Biological Intelligence's Technological Successor (artificial intelligence or interference, depending on how you feel about it); [6] Brutish, Incredibly Terrifying Situation, which can shake up a person's world, shattering it into gazillions of bits.

25   [1] Online Booking and Ordering, Yes, sir! (implying great system)—belongs to BIG-AM-I; [2] Oh boy! as in "Oh, my Lord-IT!" or "Oh, my goodness!"

26   Software, typically running on hard-BITS such as a confuzer

BIG-AM-I spent and is still spending hundreds of thousands of man-years on building and running that giant. It's the only business soft-BITS system that comes close to costs that compare to the price tag involved with rocket science engineering and space travel, without actually flying anyone anywhere near the moon.

Using OBOY, you can acquire online everything ranging from toothpicks, to sexy underwear, through to physical as well as online virtual confuzers, sports cars, yachts, houses, and businesses. You can do online gambling, gaming, book your next holiday, even a trip to the moon, and the list just goes on. You can hardly name even one item that isn't available for purchase, hire, or use, OBOY.

BIG-AM-I, or one of its subsidiaries, produces almost all the products and services available on OBOY, except confuzers, of course. OBOY manages the complete cycle of selling, producing, and purchasing everything needed to produce the goods, as well as packaging and shipping. It's an end-to-end, fully automated money-making factory built up of thousands of sub-systems and commanding thousands of robots.

Apparently not satisfied with announcing that the most stable and biggest BITS the world has ever known just went down, the GLOBHED agent loudly clears his throat preparing to deliver an even more startling revelation.

"Sir, Bitsi, sir, we would like you to join our online GLOBCHAT[27] with more than one hundred and eleven people WOWI so that you can sort out the confusion and help get it up again, OBOY."

I feel like asking if the bloody President of the United Continents of Where-Every-Where is also on the groupie chat, and if he's also desperate to get it up. But that would simply confuse them.

The incident has clearly been going on for some time before they called me. It takes donkey's-light-years for the average large organization to establish proper communication channels when

---

27   Global online chat session

MAD[28] MAGIC[29] is conjured up. The panic muddles the brain and generally destroys every normal process. These guys, however, already have had a GLOBCHAT running long enough for people to realize and admit that everyone is confused. Bad, *bad* sign.

"When did we lose it, OBOY?" I ask, relatively quietly.

"Er, excuse me, Mr. Bitsi, sir?"

"When," I scream, "did this incident *start*? *When* did she go dead in the water? *When* did the contraption go belly-up? *How long has the BITS been down, OBOY?*"

"Ah. Er, er, er, nineteen hours and fifty-five minutes, Sir Bitsi."

Oh, Hades door, 4.4 billion DOLLIES scorched to ashes already.

I flick another two switches on my desk, one calling BITS-SECS[30] to prepare for action, the other waking up the BITS-SITTERs[31]. Somewhere, between hundreds and thousands of kilometers from here, in various directions, another fourteen red lights start flashing, alarms gently buzzing. The on-guard duty member of each team will inform the on-call members of the team and wake up team leads WOWI, politely requesting them to shape up for trouble. In a short while, one hundred of the best trained professionals in the world, spread across seven different regions on the planet, will be sitting on hot-coals-standby. The seven BITS-SECS teams will be holding on the starting block ready for possible dispatch to whatever location needed WOWI. They will all await my instructions.

There will be all hell to pay for this little explo-outage, OBOY. The fallout will be Uni-Nuclear. Tons more money will evaporate before the system is up again. Loyal customers will file lawsuits due to lost revenue; there'll be further losses because of rats (loyal customers again)

---

28   [1] System down; [2] Major Atomic-like Downtime; [3] Something to be avoided; [4] Angry, enraged, furious

29   [1] BIG system; [2] Magic

30   [1] Bitsi's Security Squad; [2] Lord-IT's Security Squad; [3] BITS Security Squad

31   [1] Bitsi's auditors; [2] Lord-IT's auditors; [3] BITS auditors

deserting a sinking ship. It will cost weeks, months of investigation to find the cause of this little disaster.

Innocent people will get demoted or kicked out in disgrace, while others, riding the wave of disaster, will squirm through to a promotion. Months and years of redesigning the machine will follow to prevent such MAD-NESS[32] from happening again.

The destiny of the one blamed for the MAD MAGIC TRICC[33] will be the worst punishment imaginable, whatever that may turn out to be, depending on how hard someone can make it stick that a single person is to blame for the FLAPPING[34] of a MAGIC system which many thousands of people have worked on from its birth until now.

"Well," I squeeze out, trying to stay calm, "I'm not sure how fast I can get it up. But I can certainly dish out a few decapitations; that will help cut off some confusion." (Headless chickens come to mind.)

Then, forgetting anything about trying to stay calm: *And why did it take you nineteen hours fifty-five minutes to call me?* Using my acclaimed Bitsi-Tone[35], which is known WOWI.

Over the years, the Bitsi-Tone has become renowned for being colder than ice, harder than diamonds, not loud but far from quiet, and delivered suddenly, with the force of a raging tornado. The Bitsi-Tone by nature implies a warning no one should ignore and is the scariest sound any BITS-Pro[36] is ever likely to hear in the office. When someone hears that tone of voice, it's time to tread with the utmost of care, time to think hard but not too long before speaking. It's best not to respond incorrectly.

---

32   [1] System down; [2] Major Atomic-like Downtime—Never Expected Spectacular Shock; [3] Something to be avoided

33   [1] Happening; [2] Event; [3] Achievement

34   Nasty system crash with almost a guaranteed financially crippling effect

35   The infamous tone of the BITS Inspector when he's angry.

36   [1] BITS professional; [2] IT professional

"Er, er, we didn't know you'd arrived, sir. We only just found out." The typical age-old excuse, of course: They didn't get the bloody weemail[37].

Calming down quickly and going into my habitual fun of asking whether they have my weemail address so we can sit for a few quiet minutes and fiercely discuss how to spell my job title, I realize fast that this is no time for fooling around with GLOBHEDs. Nevertheless, they're unstoppable.

"Is it, er... How *do* you spell Bitsi, sir, Mr. Bitchy?" Everyone knows my weemail address, and yet they do like to play this game.

"Forget it," I cut off their fun. "I just dropped *you* a weemail. *Now get me into your GLOBCHAT immediately.*" Bitsi-Tone, again.

"Yes, sir. We're on it, Bitsi, sir."

Within seconds, the weemail notification to join the GLOBCHAT appears on one of my screen-spaces. Many more seconds later, I can see the history of the past nineteen hours and fifty-five minutes of the GLOBCHAT. Oh, my Lord-IT[38], what a mess. More than one hundred and eleven people screaming at each other for hours.

---

37 Wonderfully Enhanced Email
38 According to popular opinion, the most powerful businessman known to humankind

2

It's All Gibberish to Me

THE HELP IN Helpdesk is one of the biggest disappointments invented since *someone* stole the pot of gold from under the rainbow. The usefulness of GLOBHEDs has limits during these complex crisis situations. They'll keep a record of the proceedings and coerce new people to join the party, when requested.

"Get me the chief architect of BIG-AM-I, the lead architect of OBOY, the lead ANALPRIDC[39], the lead SADCASE[40], the lead NETNERD[41], and the lead TEST-TICCLER[42] for OBOY. Get them *now*, please. You have five minutes to get them into the GLOBCHAT and on their DIGIT-FONEs and into this call," I command.

"But, sir," counters the GLOBHED, "OBOY's lead architect and ANALPRIDC have both already been on the case for nineteen hours and fifty-four minutes, sir. The lead architect is getting on in years a little, sir, and he's rather tired. And the ANALPRIDC's wife was complaining bitterly that he had already skipped two of his diaper-change duties, sir. With five small kids, sir, that's a lot of shit he got away with, sir. When they heard you were on the way in, Bitsi, sir, they decided their presence was no longer required in this MAD-NESS." So, you see, not helpful at all.

---

39   [1] Analyst Prima-Donna Coder; [2] software programmer
40   Database administrator
41   Network technician
42   [1] System tester; [2] Tester of Expert Systems Theoretically, Technologically Incapable, Certifiable Confuzer Logic Examiner, Retrospectively

"Get them here, please. You now have four minutes." Bitsi-Tone. That should give me just enough time to pick out the important events from the GLOBCHAT history.

"Er ... yes, Sir BITS Inspector, sir."

My DIGIT-FONE suddenly starts vibrating again, scraping more polish off my desk. Typical. With MAD MAGIC going down, the FONE and your ear can get warmer than a hot potato. Every incoming ringer requires careful selection. Drop it or not?

Hmmm. It's BIG-AM-I's Sissy-O[43] looking for me. If I pick up, I can kiss goodbye to my planned four minutes of leisurely reading time. If I don't answer, I still have to deal with him later. What to do, what to do.

Every large BITS organization touts a CCIO[44], which stands for Chief Communications and Information Officer, pronounced Sissy-O, or just Sissy[45] for short. The CCIO is the man at the top, and this current Sissy o' BIG-AM-I is brand-new to his high-flying job.

Gaylord Cox, or just COCKS[46], already renamed, showed his face for the first time just this morning.

The former Sissy-O was fired yesterday afternoon during what should have been a friendly Sunday afternoon cocktail garden party. BIG-AM-I is world-renowned, however, for having a whole string of successors lined up ready for the aftermath of such alcohol-infused gatherings that often result in fast hand-overs.

The age-old idea of immediate succession is that not a minute must pass without a leader at the helm. Having a CCIO signifies having a commander-in-chief, a champion taking the business seriously, giving it purpose and direction.

So, while it's a known compromise for sure—because no CCIO worth his salt would sit around waiting for the next garden-bar-brawl

---

43   CCIO
44   Chief Communication and Information Officer
45   CCIO
46   [1] Cox, the CCIO of BIG-AM-I; [2] Cox's Offensive for Cooking up Killer Services

to signify his rise to office—it's accepted that it's still better to have any old Sissy leading the pack than none at all.

BIG-AM-I's philosophy, based on the thinking that the average CCIO is nothing more than a glorified MOTHER's puppet, is that they will attempt to simply punch the new Sissy into shape, and if that doesn't work out, then throw another cocktail party.

The renaming of Cox to COCKS is a standard BITS industry practice. Most names and phrases these days are renamed (often shortened) into acronyms or new names. The intention is to improve efficiency by making it easier and faster to read, write, and say the new names. The outcome, however, is somewhat disappointing. Nobody ever remembers what the new names stand for, so the meaning also gets forgotten.

Yet, everyone stubbornly continues to use these new names, resulting in the speaker not knowing what the hell they're saying, and the listener not knowing what the hell the speaker is talking about.

The growth of vocabulary spawned from this approach of New-Naming was so ferocious in the BITS industry that a new international language based on English and BITS New Names formed and took over all the world languages of earlier centuries, e.g., English, Faroese, Tiriyó, and the like.

This is the universally used language we all know, and are stuck with today, Gibberish. The formal creation of Gibberish represents the only known example of the most powerful three players in the IT/BITS industry more or less successfully cooperating. After many months of hefty negotiations on legalities and royalties, the whole deal almost fell apart because they couldn't agree on a name. The argument escalated until one of the three stood up during their final meeting and in disgust yelled, "You're spewing out nothing but gibberish, man!"

Absolute silence replaced the noisy, ugly debate while all three with open mouths looked from one to the other and back again.

Sour, downturned lips lifted to meet now brightly shining eyes full of DOLLY[47] signs and unworthy tears of glory.

"Absolutely brilliant!"

"It's so simple we all overlooked it. Well done, that man!"

"It fits perfectly. It's all Gibberish to me anyway!"

Breaking out in raucous laughter and clapping each other on the backs, they pop the cork, sign the pact, and follow through with a toast, or two, or three. Memos go out to PAs, effectively stealing the concept of white smoke following the joyful conclusion of a Vatican election, and the deal is not only signed but also public. Gibberish was then forced onto the world through many underhanded mega-multi-billion DOLLY deals, and more toasts, and was here to stay. It's amazing how profitable a universal language can be—for the elite few.

Cox's New Name, COCKS, if one remembers what it means, is not as bad as it may seem at first glance. COCKS stands for Cox's Offensive for Cooking up Killer Services. So, on the whole, relatively friendly.

BIG-AM-I's previous Sissy-O, Jerry Karmich'l, was renamed JERK[48]. *No one* remembers what *that* stands for, but everyone knows what it looks like it means. The JERK was sacked on the spot following a flaming argument between the said former Sissy and the BOJ-OB[49] of BIG-AM-I BITS.

The BOJ-OB of BIG-AM-I BITS works for the MOTHER organization in the head office and is responsible in every way for BIG-AM-I BITS and is one serious don't-mess-with-me nasty piece of work, which is to be expected; otherwise, he would never have gotten the BOJ-OB in the first place.

And the FONE is still ringing.

---

47   The one-and-only currency WOWI, used everywhere
48   [1] Jerry Karmich'l, former BIG-AM-I Sissy; [2] Jerk
49   Business Officer & Judiciary of Online Business

3

Inexcusable Sissy

I ANSWER TO SPEAK with the CCIO, and he asks me, "Am I speaking to the BITS Inspector?" I respond, of course. "Who, in the wholly scary MOTHER of Lord-IT's name are you to call me up in the middle of the night?"

"I'm the Sissy o' BIG-AM-I, Sir Bitchy, COCKS. I just learned you were nineteen hours and fifty-five minutes late for joining us in a MAD[50] FLAPPING that's dumping on us right now. You should have fixed this problem many hours ago. Where the *hell* have you been, sir?" he almost shouts at me.

This is the typical BITSer point-the-finger-elsewhere, CYA[51] tripe that no one should ever accept from anyone. Only a Sissy-O, or a higher-ranking manager, has the spunk to think they can tackle me in this fashion and walk away standing.

"Don't point the finger at me, COCKS-UCCRE," I yell right back at him. I'm extremely annoyed, and rightfully so, yet immediately and simultaneously I'm feeling a fraction uneasy about my blurted choice of word combination. Still, I've survived a lot worse than a little embarrassment over the years. And in my defense, I have used the expletive UCCRE[52] with great pleasure on many occasions, but this is

---

50   [1] System down; [2] Major Atomic-like Downtime; [3] Something to be avoided; [4] Angry, enraged, furious

51   Cover Your Ass

52   Unprofessional Conniving Contemptible Rat Excretion (suffix)

the first time a Sissy who has been reduced to COCKS has challenged me.

"And do *not* call me *Bitchy*. Only you and I were in copy on the *pissmail*[53] that Lord-IT sent you, and it stated clearly that *you* need to inform *your* BITS organization that I am, for a short while, available to assist in case of need." Bitsi-Tone now. "So, any delay in my joining your MAD-NESS is your PUKE[54]." More Bitsi-Tone.

"And," calming down now, giving the Sissy room to back down and correct his error, "if you must know, I was enjoying a pleasant day with my family while OBOY was FLAPPING."

"Ah, er, yes, er, well, I do believe I sent a weemail to my *PUSSIES*[55], but I guess that vanished into the *wwoopsi-net*[56]."

And there you have it: the key reason weemail became peemail[57].

"Codswallop," I yell, even angrier than before. "Now, do you have anything sensible to say? Coz you're standing in the middle of my road, doing nothing else but FLAPPING."

The Sissy isn't married, I assume, because he's clearly not accustomed to hearing such an accurate assessment of just how annoying he can be. He stammers, "Er, er, er..."

"I didn't think so," I yell, and then rudely and with no remorse whatsoever this time, I hang up.

---

53   Same as peemail
54   [1] Person Ultimately Killed in the End; [2] Person to blame and who subsequently pays the price; [3] Mistake
55   [1] CCIO deputies; [2] Pushy Undergraduate of Sissy Stratagems—Intensified Education in Shopping
56   Internet
57   [1] Weemail; [2] Pathetic Excuse of Email's Accountability for all Information (ever) Lost

4

Pinched DOLLIES

I IMMEDIATELY SWITCH THE call back to the GLOBHEDs, who probably haven't done much more than listen to their favorite on-hold music.

"Ah, there you are, Bitsi, sir. We now have on the call all the people you asked for, sir. So, what comes next, sir?"

"Who," I ask, pleasantly surprised with their progress, "is best qualified to explain the problem at hand?"

"That would be me, sir, Dick Amesbury, OBOY's lead ANALPRIDC, sir. You can call me Big Dick, Bitsi—everyone else does. They do say, however, that it's only coz I'm two meters and ten tall, sir."

"Well?" I probe further, impatiently.

"Yes, sir. Well, it's a little complicated. There are many sub-systems involved." (I can't help but roll my eyes.)

"But, sir, it would appear as if the FRONT-END[58] has kept it up, sir, and the BACK-END[59] also appears to be producing, but the *CASH*[60] is missing, Bitsi, sir. The orders have been flowing in during the past twenty hours, sir, but more than seven billion DOLLIES have done a runner, sir. The DOLLIES have disappeared into the proverbial black hole, Bitsi, sir. The CASH appears to be no longer on this planet, sir."

---

58   The visible part of a system one sees on the screen

59   The heart of a BITS (or IT) system

60   [1] Cash or money; [2] Any form of financial currency or contract involving cash or money, e.g., investment, bond, dolly-notes, etc.; [3] Collectible Assets, Security (or Savings) Historically; [4] Corrupt Ascertainment of Someone's Hourly-wage

Well that certainly sounds like a summary that only a Big Dick could produce. And seven billion DOLLIES. Compared to last months' numbers, that's a dramatic increase in the income, OBOY.

"Are you trying to tell me that seven billion DOLLIES are exercising their legs charging through a black hole in search of an alternate universe? Don't be ridiculous, Dick," I say in my best Bitsi-Tone. "Now try again, Big Dick. Tell me exactly, in a single, concise sentence: How do you see that the DOLLIES are not arriving home?" I demand in Bitsi-Tone.

"Yes, sir. Well, OBOY's CASH COW, er, payment system, sir, receives confirmation of *all* the No Credit Card authorizations, but the WINCCCERs[61] are receiving less than one percent of all payment requests, so ninety-nine percent of all payments seem to be lost in space somewhere and authorized by the man on the moon, and the CASH is only trickling in for the measly one percent, and these are all tiny orders, sir—none from the big customers, sir." Phew. He didn't breathe once through all that, and his obsession with outer space is bordering on lunatic.

"Yes. And what's worse—oh, er, this is the LEACH[62] of OBOY, sir, Hisuck Emile Hardwood, sir," interjects OBOY's lead architect, whose Gibberish name is HE-SOCKs-EM-ARD.

"Most of the orders are already processed, the goods are already shipped, and many of them are even delivered." He sounds positively proud of himself while at the same time ready to fry his brains with a powerful LASAROMIC[63] pistol to the head from both sides simultaneously.

And hats off to the BITS industry. Things are super-efficient these days, but BITS professionals are not much smarter than they were a hundred years ago, so now a company can get ripped off royally while

---

61   [1] Bank; [2] Banker
62   Lead Enterprise Architect, Constructor Hi-tech
63   An inferior power source, only used in inferior weaponry

the BITS experts helplessly gawk all day just watching it happen. This threatens to get nasty, and the LEACH sounds worried. The aftermath of major FLAPPINGs can turn atrociously ugly, and the disappearance of all that CASH significantly adds to the severity of the whole affair.

"Anything else?" I ask calmly, with the clear intention of keeping the obvious panic from rising even higher.

"*Isn't that enough? Lord-IT, damn IT to hell,*" screams a new, rather frenzied voice at me.

"Well, I guess it's enough to be going on with, for now," I respond coldly. "And who, in the wholly scary *MOTHER* of Lord-IT's name, was *that* yelling in my ear?" It's important not to let anyone get the upper hand if I'm to get this mess under control.

"Oh, er, er, my apologies, Bitsi, sir. This whole event is somewhat disturbing, sir. Er, this is L'ARCH[64] of BIG-AM-I, sir, José Rules, Bitsi, sir."

"Hmmm. Yes, well, I do understand you're disturbed, J–Rules, but you scream at me again, and I'll have your wings stripped off."

I stress this point because the L'ARCH is one of the most senior BIG-AM-I employees involved in this crisis. It's an age-old tactic: Take out the strongest first; the rest will then follow my lead. It's more effective to publicly take down a Sissy, but the L'ARCH will do for now.

"Yes, of course, Bitsi, sir; again, my apologies, sir," he replies, extremely politely now.

"OK. Let's get to it. Are there any detailed findings apart from the fact that the CASH has done a runner?" I try to make light of the obvious heist of billions of DOLLIES. After all, while it is a lot of dosh[65], the loss will not have far-reaching negative side effects for BIG-AM-I; the organization is too big for that. More importantly, putting stress on a theft is going to burden the BIG-AM-I employees even further, and that will not help at all.

"No, sir," the ANALPRIDC Big Dick says.

---

64   The chief architect

65   Money, or CASH

"No customers are complaining. We've checked the FRONT-END thoroughly, nothi..."

"Wait!" a loud, over-excited voice comes over the blower. "Mr. Bitsi, sir, everybody, hang on. Wait. Mr. Bitsi, sir, everyone, it's happening. The CASH has started coming in again. Payments. Coming in. OBOY. He's got it up again!"

5

Suspect Screamer

MORE THAN ONE hundred and eleven various sighs of relief follow the GLOBHED announcement.

"OBOY, he's got it up again."

"Hallelujah, we're back in business, OBOY."

"Oh, God bless Lord-IT; the CASH is rolling in again."

"I knew OBOY wouldn't let us down for long."

"Uh. Can we go to bed now?"

Much like a jack-in-the-box's head rolling around gently after jumping out of the box, I raise my eyebrows, roll my eyes, and shake my head all at the same time.

Suddenly, a *loud* voice abruptly breaks through the commotion: "This is COCKS. Everyone pipe down now. *I said keep quiet,*" he hollers.

Once all the voices subside, he continues, "Well done, everyone. I heard the *great* news that the CASH is coming in again. Well done, well done. Now, I want a core team to stay available to ensure this wheel of good fortune keeps turning and that we start to establish which CASH exactly we're seeing arriving. Is it new CASH for the new orders coming in, or is it the CASH from the orders of the past twenty hours? Or both? *It's fundamental to establish this fact,*" he emphasizes.

It's just typical of a Sissy to be more concerned about his Christmas bonus than anything else. If the money really is gone, disappeared, done the proverbial runner into the infamous black hole—a whole seven billion DOLLIES—then COCKS will be penalized big time, including no Christmas bonus, even though he was possibly not to blame since he's the brand-new boy in town.

"Sir Bitsi, I expect you to assist this core team to ascertain the real damage here," the Sissy dares to venture.

"Don't you address me as if I were one of your Lord-IT help-them employees, COCKS." Absolutely my Bitsi-Tone.

"If you want something from me, COCKS, then you ask me real nice. And then pray to Lord-IT, for example, for a sunny day with me on the beach drinking lots of spicy, icy margaritas, thus putting me in a good mood. Now, while you practice how to do that, I'm going back to bed.

"*But* while I'm sleeping, which of you, in my absence, is going to head up this core investigation team? Is that you, L'ARCH?" I ask, not leaving COCKS a single split-nanosecond to squeeze a Sissy-style word in edgewise.

"Hmmmm. I suppose it'll be me," responds the L'ARCH, sounding positively miserable about having the honor of being assigned this new task.

"Fine, be so kind as to arrange a CLIMACCSSS[66], and please make sure we don't jump into bed with the wrong characters here. I expect to see all the lead job titles and key players in that contacts list. From now on, all vacations, all days off, all weekends, sick days, pregnancy, and, indeed, pregnancy-preparation leave, paternity leave, all trips to Disney World, etc., are cancelled. Get the matrix ready immediately and send it out even faster, so I will have the CLIMACCSSS as soon as I come online again." Taking a deep breath, I say, "Am I making myself clear?"

"Yes, sir," sayeth the L'ARCH, in a less-than-angelic manner. "We have a lot of good women, OBOY, on maternity leave, also?"

"Don't be ridiculous. What are you thinking, man?" Our children's future is built upon the foundations the mother lays, beginning in the womb and continuing intensely thereafter. The father's fundamental contribution usually comes a little later. The mother's time with our

---

66   [1] Communications matrix; [2] Contacts list

children in the early months and years must surely be a priority if we want the best for them and for their future world. "No cancelling maternity leave! Now, wish me goodnight." I hang up.

I do not plan to go bed at all. There's something terribly amiss here. COMMINGS[67] happen all the time, this is sure. And in the BITS industry, they happen even more often. Hell, it's even a fluke if a piece of soft-BITS actually works. But this COMMINGS, it stinks. The timing is too coincidental: During the key business hours worldwide. That the incident suddenly stops, and with absolutely no indication as to why. That the only real problem uncovered is that money is missing is worse than pathetic and simply cannot be true. Something about this whole incident leaves me thinking that BIG-AM-I has a real problem. Someone is clearly stealing the CASH. This investigation needs to get going right now.

I have a hunch that this "system down" event relates specifically to both the suddenly boosted income and the hours when the most CASH comes in, twenty hours every day.

I suspect that when the shopping mania picks up again, trouble will raise its ugly head right along with it. Which gives me four hours to get ready. Not much time, but certainly enough to get started.

I flick a few keys on Seribus, and on the spacey-screen new sspaces come to life connecting me to my main confuzer and wishing me a good night's rest. I really need to educate that mega-machine about my working hours.

The BITS News pops up on the News sspace. The media has held another unplanned, out-of-season Hay-Day. The most popular publication ever to be printed WOWI is a slag-rag magazine focused on BITS. All eyes across the globe won't fail to catch up on BITS GON Ballistic's latest headline of a special edition released, hmmm, just a few minutes ago, it would seem.

---

67   Coincidence or coincidences

Billions of DOLLIES CRAPPING[68]
BIGAMY BOJ-OB replaces JERK
with
COCKS Finger-points Bitsi
during
MAD-ONNA MAGIC TRICC!
MAD-NESS Still Rules?

A perfect Gibberish construction. This kind of language isn't used in normal, Joe-blogs-on-the-street everyday life. But in the BITS business, one hears such Gibberish all day long.

There will be, of course, an immediate lawsuit because of the incorrect spelling of BIG-AM-I. But on a previous occurrence of the exact same error, also a special edition, BITS GON Ballistic simply politely apologized, blaming the mistake on their BITS (produced, of course, by BIG-AM-I) failing to pick up on the typo. This while at the same time greatly complimenting and indeed thanking BIG-AM-I for the impressive speed at which their BITS managed to get the special edition of the magazine produced and distributed (in no time at all) WOWI.

There was a small fine handed out to BITS GON Ballistic, but they laughed all the way to the pub, having sold gazillions of copies of the screamer in question, which goes to show that the price for slander these days is cheap, and bigamy is not as taboo as it once was.

Judging by this latest headline, however, slander could be the least of BGB's problems on this occasion. COCKS tried to point the finger at me during a private cockfight. Yet, there it is, in a bold-printed headline for the whole world to enjoy. A suspect screamer if ever there was one.

---

[68]   CRAPP Immediately Neutralizing Giants. CRAPP: Crash of Abnormally Painful Proportions, always a system crash.

6

The Fruit

It's the year 2117. The scientific progress of the world has continued, of course, but not equally fast in all areas—the hopes and expectations in neural networks, quantum computing, and artificial intelligence (AI) being some of the obvious areas of slow evolution. The complexity of these technological ideas proved initially to be more challenging than envisaged.

Then, in 2034, a tragic accident involving an AI machine and a nuclear bomb resulted in the annihilation of most of the world's top scientists in the field, as well as many thousands of others. The World Council immediately banned all open development and experiments in this area, consolidated all the work in just two central locations in the world, and subjected all technology changes and testing to meticulous checks and regulations harsher than those seen, for example, in the medical field and in space travel. These events effectively reduced the pace of the technology advancement to slower than that of a snail.

Lord-IT House[69] is the sole producer WOWI of all Nuke-Li-Aerial power[70] and all confuzers. It's the largest organization on the planet. Bitsi-Lites the Skies[71] is the sole producer WOWI of the Bitsi-Lite technology and of all satellites and wireless communication devices and is the second largest company WOWI.

---

69   Largest organization WOWI, owned by Lord-IT and Bitsi
70   Currently the most powerful form of energy known to humankind
71   Second largest company WOWI, owned by Bitsi

With the introduction of these technologies in 2030, the IT evolution took a new turn, escalated once more, and the world was further inundated with gadgets and with Nuke-Li-Aerially-powered, confuzerized products of all kinds.

Many daily jobs were automated, from household to garden and farming, to factory tasks, trains operating without drivers and planes without pilots except for operating emergencies-only from the ground; the list is endless. Instead of doing many jobs ourselves, we now instruct the machines and robots what to do and when. They are still not advanced enough to think for themselves.

Initiated and heavily supported financially by Lord-IT House and Bitsi-Lites the Skies, a re-education program gave the now unemployed-by-automation manual workforce the opportunity to learn new skills in any area they chose. A surprisingly large percentage of people chose arts and culture. Many others chose landscape gardening and nature-oriented subjects, while significant numbers opted to focus on the care of others. So, Lord-IT House and Bitsi-Lites the Skies initiated further knowledge advancement in a fine mixture of scientific, natural, cultural, and care areas, and they still continue.

Nuke-Li-Aerially-powered agricultural facilities, funded by Lord-IT House and Bitsi-Lites the Skies, provide food to many countries in desperate need. In most cases, the food shortage is solved. However, some borders are, sadly, still too dangerous to cross without military force without risking too many lives.

All known weapons of mass destruction were decommissioned in the years 2035 through 2037. The last nuclear power plant closed more than sixty years ago.

So, the world *has* moved on. But only a notch or two, for there's still much strife, much hatred, much pain. From time to time, the super-powers disagree vehemently, as always. Big business is more cutthroat than ever. Unemployment remains a seemingly unsolvable problem, and homelessness is still a shockingly embarrassing and disturbing statistic most countries hate to report on.

Thanks to a super drug originally called the Life-Giver, the oldest registered living person on Earth is one hundred and seventy-six years old and still showing no signs of giving up the ghost.

The Life-Giver came about after BIG-AM-I—during one of its regular bids for more power, more market share, and more profit—slaughtered one of the competition, bought up the remaining BITS, and started to sift through the debris. Buried in a bottom drawer labeled "too expensive, too risky" and covered with spiders big enough to kill with a single bite was a discovery that had never truly seen the sunlight because it didn't work, yet.

The unfinished product did apparently make it to market, but the most it ever did was attempt hair-loss prevention. That didn't go down too well when compared with other competitive offerings, so finally, the project was parked in the bottom drawer.

A newbie BOJ-OB at BIG-AM-I was responsible for handling the clean-up following the hostile takeover. This was a test to see if he was worth a real BOJ-OB.

He opened the bottom drawer and, being somewhat of a chemistry scientist himself, decided he would spend a fair percentage of his available budget on finishing up the project. How hard could it be? He wouldn't be the first to discover a drug for extending life span.

The business case he presented to his superiors was simple. BIG-AM-I would be the only company to offer the new drug that would give the ever-omnipotent dream achievement of everlasting life. BIG-AM-I would have total control over the pricing, and, of course, everyone would buy WOWI. An additional soft benefit would be entering the good graces of everyone WOWI, and consequently also increasing general turnover.

The greedy BBBs [72] of the BIG-AM-I MOTHER couldn't contain their excitement, so they let the excitable newbie BOJ-OB get on with it. Production and sale of the final product began twenty-five years later, twenty years late, and the project cost thirty-three times more than the original estimated budget. Return on the investment, however, came in during the second year. The BBBs of BIG-AM-I tripped to seventh heaven.

Naming the brew was seemingly one of the hardest challenges that BIG-AM-I ever faced, and this was blatantly obvious WOWI.

Religious factions had a serious problem with the original name of Life-Giver, which is understandable, I guess. If someone were from a spiritual background, it would be hard to accept that a man-made liquid that required just a swig from a cheap-looking, bright-orange-colored bottle could replace the creator of your God-given existence.

The later attempt, called Life Ever-Lasting, was also not popular with the holy orders. The only form of everlasting life was supposed to be in heaven and had to be hard-earned; it was not something you could attain by sucking up a strawberry milkshake.

Many versions of that name went through the rounds of acceptability testing WOWI. BIG-AM-I finally settled on The Fruit [73] of Life (The Fruit, for short). All market analysts, opinion polls, and indeed all consumers unanimously agreed the name was lame, to say the least. But they lived with it, knowing that BIG-AM-I had made many gallant attempts to introduce more spectacular names for the wonder drug.

A whole new problem space opened with the introduction of The Fruit: the impact of longer lives on the world's resources. Just to start with, the World Council legalized birth control and the size of the family unit. An individual or a couple may have only three children in the span of a seventy-five-year period, starting from the birth of the

---

72   [1] [The] Big Business Bosses; [2] [The] Big Bad Bosses
73   The latest age-prevention drug

first of the three children. After the third child, a birth control additive supplements the supplies of The Fruit, preventing further conceptions.

My wife and I suffered harshly at the hand of this law. Our first children, triplets born in 2036, all died in the second week of their short lives. But the births still counted, and the seventy-five-year clock was ticking. There was nothing we could do legally to try again, until recently. Now, though, we have three healthy kids—twins and a little girl born shortly after. Pseudo triplets. And what a joy.

Recent changes to control the population growth have reduced the number of children an individual or a couple may have to only two children in the span of a one-hundred-year period, starting from the birth of the first child. This will most likely change again.

The Fruit is known to only have an effect on older cells in the body. The human fetus, for example, is hardly affected even though the mother is on The Fruit. The pregnancy cycle has extended a little, but the record is three months, and the average is only one week. Accordingly, the legal minimum age limit of eighteen has been set for purchasing/administering The Fruit. Why eighteen? No one has a clear explanation for this.

Another problem is that people cannot retire and stay on pension forever starting at the age of sixty or sixty-five. The world would go broke in no time. For this issue, there isn't yet a satisfactory answer. And many new problems are still arising, and all will need solving.

Remarkably enough, there have been no negative side effects reported since The Fruit first went to market, which is good because my wife and I, like everyone else, also favor The Fruit over death.

There's only one known downside to the drug, which is not considered a side effect but is, rather, more natural. If, after reaching way past the normal age span of an average human being, someone was to stop taking the potion, which needs to be sipped daily, then the end is magically fast. After just twenty-four hours, one transitions from Fruit of Life to life everlasting.

7

The BITS Inspector

I instruct the Beast to dial my lead BITS-SITTER's confuzer. "O-WE-COME[74], call Delilah[75]." Soon, she'll need to get her BITS-SITTERs mucking through the masses of BIG-AM-I's DIGI-DIRT[76]. But first, I need to check out the source of this BITS GON Ballistic suspicious headline.

"Hey, Delilah, how's it hangin'?" I ask as her image appears on an O-WE-COME sspace.

"Way too low. How's your BITS?" she retorts, consistent as ever.

"Busted, again." I give my standard answer.

She just smiles. "Yeah, I saw BGB's latest headline."

"And that, Del, is why I'm calling. The screamer is full of DIRT."

"Oh?"

"Only two people on this earth could know that COCKS tried to finger-point me. They are..."

"You and COCKS?"

"Exactly."

"And I'll bet you think it's not you who's being overheard?"

"Without a doubt, Delilah. No one gets into my BRITCHIS[77]."

---

74 Online Web Conference and Meeting, video-conferencing software
75 Combined job title and appointed name of Bitsi's Chief BITS-SITTER.
76 Data or information, often revealing and/or incriminating
77 [1] Firewall; [2] Barrier Repelling Intruders, Technologically Categorized as Highly Impenetrable and Secure

"So, you want me to go and kick the PERPS[78], sir?" she asks with a big, cheeky smirk spread across her face.

"You know that's Samson's[79] job, Del. I need you to find all the DIRT you can on the BITS GON Ballistic's author and then find the hacked equipment. Step-by-careful-step, please. We don't want any chickens trying to escape before we open the door. Here's a list of all the hard-BITS[80] assigned to COCKS, and here's his TWIT-OVA-USER[81]."

"Yes, sir." And she's off. If I didn't know better, I'd think she had hung up offended.

I breathe the same old familiar sigh of relief. Thank Lord-IT, I landed this job. Given that I still choose to work for a living, it's great, to say the least, to have the ultimate authority to get the job done. I'm definitely going to need to swing a punch or two during this investigation, OBOY.

My job title is The BITS Inspector. I work on missions WOWI, assisting with and investigating problems in the biggest organizations and governments on the planet. Only one other person has similar power in the world, and that's Lord-IT himself.

As far as the rest of the world is concerned, I report only to Lord-IT, answer only to Lord-IT, and take my orders only from Lord-IT.

Before I took the Bitsi position, I worked as an entrepreneur, up through the ranks of ANALPRIDC, through to LEACH, and got close to attaining the all-powerful position of L'ARCHANGEL. But I could never force myself to accept that job. Few believe in angels or fairies these days, and I didn't want to fall into the trap of taking a job riddled with politics and rumors of a less-than-positive nature, just because it's a powerful position in a world in BITS.

---

78 Criminal(s)
79 Combined job title and appointed name of Bitsi's chief of BITS-SECS
80 Hardware, such as a confuzer, spacey-screen, etc.
81 Digital user-identifier, for logging into software systems

I pretty much fell by accident into my communications' experiments after a drunken argument with a colleague one day. Being young at the time, I was determined to prove I was right.

After my initial findings, I kept my mouth shut, pushed on with my research, and slowly retreated from the world into hiding. For personal safety reasons, I had already previously paid a high price to preserve my privacy. Only a handful of people could put a face to my real name before I disappeared completely. Years later, I resurfaced with a new identity and cloaked myself in even more secrecy. Only my wife knows who I really am.

Investing substantial profits from previous business ventures, Lord-IT discovered Nuke-Li-Aerial power, I invented the Bitsi-Lite technology and the LICKEM, and together we developed a new type of computer and operating system.

Lord-IT worked the front-line, announcing our new discoveries to the world, along with the range of Bitsi-Lites and Nuke-Li-Aerially-powered soup-ah[82] confuzers, complete with DROSS[83] and Bitsi-Lite LICKEMs.

He introduced me as The BITS Inspector, and himself as Mr. Nu-IT. In no time at all, however, public opinion resulted in his renaming to Lord-IT, so he just adopted that name; it was easier, and it was a better fit.

He gave his demos, and the orders overwhelmed us. We slammed the low- and the high-end markets, and all markets in between, slaughtering all competition in one fell swoop and splattering the world with innovative confuzers and DROSS.

With these inventions, for more than eighty years, Lord-IT and I have together monopolized the energy, computer manufacturing, and wireless communication markets WOWI.

---

82   [1] Super; [2] Something powerful, strong, or amazing, something super indeed, which is often horribly abused such that the result lands one in the soup, ah!

83   [1] Dynamically Recyclable Operating System Supérieur, copyright Lord-IT House; [2] Operating System

Both Lord-IT and I showed much empathy and compassion in many concrete forms, including contributing billions of DOLLIES to support those who suffered in the fallout after the all-encompassing success of our endeavors. But many remain bitter and jealous, even today.

My true identity remained top secret. The BITS Inspector became my New Name. Not even my closest friend Lord-IT knows who I am really, or where I live, even to this day.

We weren't in a big hurry to turn our discoveries into money-making products. First, we were convinced they were unique, so no real rush on that front. Second, we wanted to make a *real* difference, wanted *quality*, not a fast buck. And BIG-AM-I's Fruit, along with providing a seemingly everlasting life, had also injected us with an intense dose of patience. Preparing to go public cost us seventeen years.

Lord-IT presented our discoveries to the world at a conceptual level only, highlighting capabilities that previous technologies sorely missed. No details were shared. The secrets are still locked up in digital vaults that only a precious few have access to.

Lord-IT and I made a blood-pact from the very beginning: Whatever powers we unleashed during our experiments, the world would never be allowed to use them as weapons of war or destruction.

Still today, only Lord-IT House and Bitsi-Lites the Skies are legally authorized to produce Nuke-Li-Aerial power, confuzers, and all wireless communications' gadgets. The patents protecting the inventions contain no revealing data, just many references to hidden documents classified as soup-ah TOP SECRET.

So, the truth is that Lord-IT and I are partners, but the world has no knowledge of this. Common opinion, which couldn't be more wrong, is that I'm trying to compete with him, trying to break out from under his authority.

In my infrequent periods of frustration, usually brought on during times of massive workload, thoughts scream around inside my head.

Are there no other BITS Inspectors out there? There must be. Why have I never come across any? But I know I'm the only one.

I also know that if there were more people in my position, some would wage a massive struggle to be No. 1, just like the *RAT-RACE*[84] there is in big business, politics, and indeed among the world's super-powers.

So, I don't complain. I do at least have whole teams of people I can delegate BITS to. The BITS-SITTERs do a lot of my leg work, or investigative research. When the going gets tough, I order in BITS-SECS. A sizeable garrison of ANALPRIDCs is also on-call ready to produce any new soft-BITS I might need and don't have time to knock out myself. And there are many others, but I rely mostly on the BITS-SITTERs and BITS-SECS.

After just a few minutes, Delilah's face shows up on the O-WE-COME sspace, trying to reach me.

"What've you found, Del?"

"We're still working on the exposure of COCKS's hard-BITS. But the screamer's author lives in the US, New York state. I've found her TWIT-OVA-PERSON[85]," which she passes over to me, "so I have most of her particulars. But only she and you have access to her TWIT-OVA-USER. Her name is Medusa."

"Hmmm. I've heard of her. Hang on, Del." I grant her full lead BITS-SITTER access for forty-eight hours, authorizing her to do many of the things I can.

"You can now access her TWIT-OVA-USER yourself, Delilah. Find out what she's up to. But remember, do *nothing* to alert her."

"Yes, sir." She hangs up as if I were after her with an axe.

"O-WE-COME, call Delilah."

---

84 [1] Underhanded power struggle, often involving illicit actions, between nations or large organizations; [2] Dishonorable or illicit actions to advance one's career, usually at the cost of a colleague and/or close friend

85 Person-identifier, replaced all forms of social security or national insurance numbers WOWI

"Delilah, I wasn't finished."

"Oh. Sorry, sir."

"How far back did you plan to look?"

"I was thinking six months, sir?"

"Five years, please. And consider getting more girls on COCKS's equipment. I want to know who compromised his BITS."

"Yes, sir." And she's off again.

For more than eighty years, I've been up to my neck in BITS in this Bitsi job. It still holds interesting challenges, but sometimes I fear I'm slowly growing a little tired of all these defunct BITS.

I *never* leave my home to do the job. This is mostly security-driven. Many would go to any cost to steal our technology secrets, to abuse them. The price for my loved ones would be high. Secrecy reduces the risk of this happening.

It's also more efficient to work from the home office. With all the confuzing-power[86] I have in my basement and office and mega millions of confuzers at my disposal WOWI, owned by Lord-IT House and Bitsi-Lites the Skies, I can work on any system in the world and hook into any satellite I choose. With all the O-WE-COME facilities for video conferencing, I can be in numerous meetings simultaneously at various points on the globe at any time of the day.

Of course, no one now books an O-WE-COME meeting at exactly one o'clock any more due to a play on Gibberish that became infamous many years ago. It was a BITS GON Ballistic headline that was responsible for the infamous avoidance of one o'clock gatherings:

---

86   [1] Computing power; [2] A measure of the ability to confuse

01:00 UTC tonight—BIGAMY launches
Biggest CONFUZING[87] ever
O-WE-COME WOWI!
Lord-IT forbid! O-WE-all-COME-at-ONEs!
Threatening yet another
MAD-ONNA COMMINGS!
woopsi.bigami.not/owecome/at-once

There's that typo again. Exactly which part of the screamer caused meetings henceforth to be planned at 12:55 or 13:05, no one is sure; it's never openly discussed.

What the headline is saying is that if we all log onto the new video conferencing system when it goes live at one o'clock, there's a real risk that this will cause another major system down coincidence. Because of the Gibberish play on words, however, imaginations ran amok and all kinds of, mostly unacceptable, interpretations were suggested WOWI.

Millions of do-gooders naturally attempted to log on at one. But not a single TWIT-OVA-USER had yet been given access to the O-WE-COME BITS, so no one got into the new system immediately. BIG-AM-I, prompted by the sarcastic headline, had used the last few hours before the one o'clock go-live deadline to artificially protect the new magnificent O-WE-COME confuzing BITS from the stampede of charitable system testers, all having fun trying to produce a record-breaking FLAPPING WOWI.

Suddenly, I feel a hand on my neck. My heart smacks into my lower jaw as I swirl away from my desk to face my adversary.

"Do you need anything?" she asks.

"A respirator would be good right about now. Damn it, woman, can't you tread a little louder?"

She just laughs. "No respirators in the pantry right now, hon."

---

87 Computing

"Shouldn't you be sleeping?" I inquire, slowly recovering.

"*Something* woke the dogs up. They wanted out. Now, anything else you need?"

"A few billion DOLLIES would be good."

"Hey. What's wrong with this dolly right here?"

"Oh, silly me. My very own super-hot dolly served up on a plate. Got any sauce with that?"

"Plenty. Here," she says, handing me a big mug of coffee.

"Oh, fantastic. I've been forever threatening myself to make some."

"Big problems?"

"Aaahhh, if my guess is correct, this one is going to be a humdinger."

"Oh, that bad? You do remember what day it is today?"

"Oh no. What day is that?" I do remember but teasing comes naturally in our house.

"Er, Father's Day? The kids spent a good part of yesterday making you presents. They will probably wake up early and want to come in and give them to you—early."

"Everything stops and everyone stands still when you walk into the room, honey. Just choose your moment carefully for taking everyone's breath away."

She accidentally throws her sweetest of smiles, which makes my heart melt all over again.

"If you need anything, just wave and hope I'm watching," she laughs, kissing my forehead, then waltzes out of the door, way too happy with herself.

My job description is a ginormous list of tasks and objectives and shows how much clout all the authorities WOWI have handed me.

Two of the most important objectives are:

- Take out the PERPS
- Improve the QUA-BITS[88]

---

88   Quality of BITS

Busting creative BITS accountants, cyber-pirates, and hackers, or worse, can be exciting and even mind-blowing at times, but the rest of my work is rather dull. So, to keep myself stimulated, I run many of my own special Bitsi projects, and in this way, I also try to provide my own small contribution to the world, humankind, and indeed all forms of life.

Intuition tells me this current OBOY crisis is going to be a combination of both these key objectives. Yet I cannot imagine anything bad enough to require invoking the full authority the World Council granted me, which leads me to think I should probably get started.

Reaching out to my favorite space-pad Seribus, I kick some confuzing-power into action, starting up data analyzers, video search, scrutinize-and-locate programs, etc. All those soft-BITS begin warming up my Beast, getting him ready to provide the information and analyze the reports I'll need to drive this investigation.

Swiveling round to space-pad-2, Come-again[89], I dial agent Samson, the No. 1 man of BITS-SECS. He responds immediately from some as-yet-unknown location, which my DIRT-MAPP is currently digging up for me with the Beast and Bitsi-Lite's help. As he answers, even though he cannot see me properly, his face smiles at me from an O-WE-COME sspace.

My webcam is specially programmed to heavily disguise my face. Hovering Nuke-Li-Aerially and following me around the room, blocking out all background images, it shows my head as a bald, gelatinous surface, and my face clearly is a mask, yet with vivid facial expressions. My eyes are ocean blue—pupils shocking deep blue and irises somewhat lighter and moving like waves. The whites are a gently shimmering Mediterranean light blue; you can almost see the sun's reflection off them and imagine the clean white sand at the bottom of the ocean bed.

---

89   "Come again?" the name of Bitsi's second-favorite space-pad

"Samson, I believe we have a situation here. I need you and your teams prepped for action pretty much immediately. When can you be ready?" I don't wait for the usual niceties, but he isn't fooled.

"So, guess where I am today?" he interrupts me.

I can't help but smile back at him; he knows me too well. This Samson (No. 3) has held his current position for only twenty-five years, but we go back much further, since his predecessor pointed him out as a potential second-in-command. I have also kept an especially close eye on him since his son Junior first applied for a job at BITS-SECS thirty-five years ago.

My DIRT-MAPP has not let me down, so I now have the answer to Samson's question showing on another big sspace. I can see him standing on a beach, drinking a margarita. It has been less than fifteen minutes since I alerted BITS-SECS, so he must have been on or close to that beach already. And the margarita? He must have had that flown in just to get my goat.

"If you finish that cocktail before I arrive and you haven't put a fresh one in my hand, there will be hell to pay," I kick back.

"Nice to almost see you, BITS Inspector, sir. How are the wikid-Bitchies?"

"Hair's a bit short today, Samson. She cut off your strength while you were dozing on the john?" We both grin and chuckle. The mutual respect between us runs deep, and we understand each other perfectly. Samson politely concludes the social graces, "So where's it going down, Bitsi, sir?"

"At this stage, I don't quite know. Nothing is certain. Oslo and Copenhagen are good bets, though. I suspect we also need more teams ready WOWI at all times until this MADNESS is over. One team to cover the Oslo FLAPPING, two more on stand-by, one in the US New York state; the other location you can choose. Just be sure of easy access from anywhere to anywhere WOWI."

Samson asks if I want them on-site now. The answer flows easily. "Yesterday, please, Samson. On second thought, make it one team in Oslo and one in Copenhagen."

"I'll have the Oslo-Cops dispatched immediately. You sure we don't need more?" he asks, dreaming up the New Name of the teams on the fly.

"Not now, but change is inevitable, so expect anything."

"Are we gonna get to play with your amazing tool?" Again, I hear the Samson chuckle.

"The DIRT-MAPP you can fool around with, but that's it." I make it abundantly clear while also chuckling.

"Talk to you later, Samson." And we end the call.

Turning to Seribus, I grant Samson forty-eight hours of BITS-SECS-level access to BIG-AM-I data in the DIRT-MAPP.

Compared to dealing with busted BITS, working with Samson and his team is like a breath of fresh air. They are super-efficient and show precision and control during the execution of every single operation.

Samson has been on the team for more than sixty years. All BITS-SECS agents and BITS-SITTER women make a lifelong commitment when they accept the job. Samson (No. 2) exercised his right to relocate to a different job within the organization; he needed a change, and that's understandable. Following his inevitable promotion, Samson laid on the pressure about his son joining BITS-SECS, and after five years I caved in, tired of the nagging, and Junior became the first to break the rules in this area of family. I had often wondered about Samson's first child Jemma possibly wanting to join BITS-SECS. She had similar traits as Samson, but tragically, she died quite some years back. Now, Samson and his wife Julia only have Junior left. Both the pregnancies were problematic, but during Junior's birth, both child and mother were almost lost. After that, the doctors told Julia that further childbirth was out of the question. The seventy-five-year cyclic birth control rule is not relevant for them, sadly.

My wandering mind takes a short three-minute walk down Memory Lane, remembering some of the operations Samson and I carried out together, until I reach a point where I can't help but begin to wonder how he'll handle this challenge and just how fast the teams will arrive on location in Oslo and Copenhagen.

Suddenly I can't resist it; I point the DIRT-MAPP at Samson's FONE and say, "FOOLEM[90]." Immediately the DIRT-MAPP shows me the location. I can see the Bitsi-Lite video image of Samson's FONE lying in a kitchen cupboard in a bungalow on the beach where I just saw him. I break out in a short burst of laughter realizing he's testing me, again. He was clearly prepared for a quick departure, and the video shows no sign of life close to the bungalow, but Agent Samson wouldn't go anywhere without his DIGIT-FONE.

All Samson's known hard-BITS are registered in my DIGI-DIRT-STORE[91], and the DIRT-DIGGER runs on all his equipment, which makes adding any of his new gizmos a task of only a matter of seconds. The DIGGER sends the DIRT-CRAWLER off to the FONE Samson forwarded his FONE to, and in no time at all, I see a (not very) well-masked FONE. This new FONE gets added to the list of his known gear, and the DIGGER is installed. A moment later, I'm viewing Samson driving in a car and listening to a conversation between him and one of his team leads.

It's rude to pry if it's not absolutely necessary, so, stopping the video, I instruct the DIRT-MAPP to continue to FOOLEMALL[92] and notify me once Samson or any of his associates hit either Oslo or Copenhagen and to welcome them.

The DIRT-MAPP that's built during this FOOLEMALL session will continue to grow as one person contacts another, who then calls

---

90   [1] Follow, Obscurely, Literally Every Movement; [2] Program for tracking someone and recording anything and everything of interest

91   Bitsi's database

92   Same as FOOLEM, but with the knock-on effect of following everyone the FOOLEM suspect contacts

another. I'll know who's on the teams and where they are at all times. As the BITS-SECS agents land on location, the DIRT-MAPP will send each one a smiling "Welcome to Sunny Oslo/Copenhagen" message on their FONEs.

Stretching back in my chair, relaxing for a few moments, slowly my eyes scan over all the other screen-spaces on the spacey-screen, picturing in my mind the vague future shape of the coming investigation. Will it blow over into nothing, disappearing into the wind? Or will I have BITS-SECS all over the world chasing shadows and BITS-SITTERs working twenty-four-hour shifts mucking through all the DIGI-DIRT I can throw at them?

For some minutes, I continue to stare, not seeing anything particular, just out into space, my thoughts gently floating through many hundreds of possible scenarios, quietly preparing for the worst, while enjoying the blissful peace before the seemingly inevitable storm, yet hoping for the best.

Delilah is again trying her best to glare at me, encouraging me to answer her incoming call. "Yes, Delilah?"

"It was the lead NETNERD of OBOY, sir. Two and a half years ago, he hacked a bug into all the gadgets available to BIG-AM-I BITS CCIO. We're still working out how he could get into the hard-BITS.

And we've been through five years of Medusa's data, sir. The only thing of interest is Medusa's participation in the weekly BIG-AM-I status meetings. The public ones, sir."

"Hmmm, yes, that's right. When did they start? Two years..."

"And ten months ago, sir."

"Thank you, Delilah. Hold on."

I remember now, Medusa was the BITS GON Ballistic representative that was invited to join the new weekly public "We Are Open and Honest and Upright" status meetings BIG-AM-I started in response to

Medusa's challenges and to persuade the public WOWI that BIG-AM-I was not the CASH-grabbing, monopolizing ogre that it actually is.

Opening a new view of the DIRT-MAPP on another sspace and sharing this with Delilah, I create a TIMLI[93] of Medusa's activity in the BIG-AM-I buildings during the past three years.

"Del, you see this?"

"Yes, sir."

It was an unnecessary question. The Beast fascinates Delilah and she always pays extra close attention when she sees me pull him into the game.

Once complete, the TIMLI will contain all Medusa's recorded visits to the BIG-AM-I building, collected in a single video with all relevant information attached.

"This will only take a few minutes, Delilah. Once it's finished, go through it; see what you can find."

"Yes, sir. Er, anything else, sir?"

"Get to it please, Del." And she hangs up, probably having already decided which of her BITS-SITTER girls to give this next job to.

My ten-square-meter office, reminiscent of a space flight mission control room, is inside the main house toward one end of the living area, which is twenty-five by thirty-five meters. Soup-ah-Smart-Glass walls allow changing the color and transparency in either direction simultaneously from inside or outside the office.

The humongous desk is rounded at the back, but from the front it conjures up images of a fat banana with a stomachache. My office chair huddles up to the belly of the suffering banana. A spacey-screen follows the shape of the back of the desk, almost half a circle, and behind it there are numerous gadgets I need for my work. Immediately in front

---

93   Timeline, a confuzerized chronological record of selected events throughout a period in a given person's life

of me, only space-pads, joystick, and remotes. I do not like a cluttered desk.

A space-pad is a small spacey-screen lying on the desk at an angle, responding to touch like all other spacey-screens, and used for typing and manipulating everything on the larger screens in the office.

Behind the desk is a curved glass system wall that holds a massive spacey-screen I can view and operate from the front and back. Behind my chair is another rounded system wall with a huge curved drawing board with all the confuzing features anyone could dream of and more.

The system walls and desk all stand on a massive circular plate in the floor, which usually rotates slowly but can also be controlled using a remote. I borrowed the moving circular-plate design from the BIG-AM-I BITS building. It's unique, practical, and oh so cool.

The Beast is located directly under me in a humongous basement. He is forty-two mega-soup-ah confuzers that link together and can operate as one *huge* machine, if needed. Eight of these confuzers are the most powerful and expensive soup-ah maxi-confuzers that CASH can buy. Together, they form the heart of my Beast. When my Beast is on the prowl, nothing can stop him, except me, of course.

During the past ninety-plus years, the Beast has processed hundreds of yottabytes of data—all stored in a specially designed and hidden location not far from home—and has also processed many brontobytes of other organizations' data stored elsewhere. This is the base-data I use in my investigations.

Being ahead of the game for a change, three weeks ago Lord-IT requested me to study up on a suspected problem at BIG-AM-I. My TWIT-OVA-USER was given access to all the BIG-AM-I-MOTHER's BITS, including those of BIG-AM-I BITS. I sent the Beast in to look around and build the DIRT-MAPP, but I've only glanced at it once since. I do wonder if Lord-IT actually saw this incident coming.

Coming back to the troubles, OBOY. Using the DIRT-MAPP, I go straight to the BITS view of BIG-AM-I, type OBOY in the search field, click on the first result, and the system diagram of OBOY pops up on the sspace. And oh, my Lord-IT.

I enlarge the sspace showing the drawing so that it fills the full height of the spacey-screen, but it's still too unreadable. Switching to cinema mode, to the left of my desk a two-and-a-half by five-and-a-half-meter canvas rolls down from ceiling to floor, and I transfer the drawing to this mega-wide screen.

Oh wow. What a mess, OBOY.

"O-WE-COME, call Delilah."

8

What, No More No Credit?

Delilah and I have slaved away together for more than eighty years, and for more than seventy years she has held her current position since Delilah (No. 1) died of a broken heart following her husband's death. If Del has ever disappointed me, that's long forgotten.

Delilah has chosen to stay single all her life. The occasional fling she has from time to time just confirms her belief that she's too particular in her choices and will never find the right man. She prefers to throw herself one hundred percent into her work, and that's what she does.

Together, Samson and Delilah form the mainstay of the Bitsi security team, and they're dedicated to its positive contribution to the world. They're some of the best BITS-Pros on the planet, and it's an honor to have them on the team.

"Delilah, I'm running through the architecture, OBOY. The BITS went ballistic for twenty hours, and I think it will start FLAPPING again soon. I suspect something nasty, Delilah. And considering the cost of downtime per hour for OBOY, it's best that we go through this exercise together to save time."

"Fire away, sir."

"Prepare for cinema mode, Del." Delilah also has a mega-wide, roll-down cinema-mode screen.

"Done, sir." The response comes just seconds later.

Delilah doesn't waste words, which suits me just fine. I switch the O-WE-COME over to display the diagram on my wide-screen.

"Oh, my Lord-IT. What a nightmare," she groans.

"Yes, it's a little overwhelming at first glance," I console her while chuckling softly. "Not to worry, it's just a pile of broken BITS. We've seen it all before. But I'll bet there are armies of little MAGICIANs[94] frantically waving wands all day trying to keep that ball in the air."

Delilah swirls a pointer over numerous areas on the diagram. "What is all that GLUE[95]?" she asks. "I thought that was tabooed years ago."

"Yes," I confirm, "many were, unfortunately, fooled by GLUE's promises, but eventually the World Council banned the technology—and quite rightly so. I mean let's face it, the idea of sticking incompatible BITS together with GLUE was, of course, ludicrous."

"So, what is it still doing there?" she demands angrily.

I almost feel personally accused for not having given BIG-AM-I the order to get the mess cleaned up. "Hmmm, I remember," I respond thoughtfully while recalling some history. "The BBBs demoted the previous L'ARCH of BIG-AM-I from the main BIG-AM-I BITS organization because his use of GLUE was seemingly addictive. He continued to abuse it even after we outlawed the protocol. The problem with GLUE is removing it requires major surgery, and with GLUE holding many of BIG-AM-I's BITS together, it was impractical to come unstuck in a hurry."

"Humph," she says in a huff. "How did he..." Something distracts Delilah.

"Bitsi, sir. Medusa's BIG-AM-I timeline. We haven't been through it all yet, but you should see this." And she throws a TIMLI video onto the O-WE-COME sspace. It's dated two years and nine months ago.

We watch as Medusa stretches out a stocking-clad foot under the table, over to the JERK, and slowly rubs it up and down his leg, then all the way up to his genitals.

---

94   On-call, on-duty system technician
95   Generic Language for Uniting Everything

Jumping from his seat as if he's been bitten in the backside by some huge, fanged teeth, the now red-faced JERK declares it's time for a short refreshment break.

The video jumps as Delilah fast-forwards to where the JERK has singled out Medusa. They're standing at the coffee machine in a rest and relaxation area. The now-former Sissy-O is severely telling her to never, ever try that again.

Medusa apologizes profusely, claiming that she stupidly thought she saw a spark twinkling in his eyes. The glare that follows the JERK as he returns to the meeting room is more one of angst than one of embarrassment, disappointment, or anger.

"That's it, for now, sir." I say nothing for a bit. "Bitsi, sir?"

"Thinking," I mumble. "Let me do this, Del," I say, taking control of the TIMLI.

I start searching ahead, looking for Medusa's next attempt. Flashing through thousands of images, soup-ah fast, in a world of my own, seemingly focused on nothing, and yet somehow only on this one task. Delilah has seen this before and simply mutters, "TRIPSI Bitsi," and waits patiently.

Suddenly, I stop, scroll back half a minute, and then we watch as Medusa throws the ANALPRIDC a seductive smile across the meeting table, flirting again. It's none other than the Big Dick himself. We can see his details in a small spring-up-space to the side of the video. Some while later, she follows him out of the room, excusing herself in need of a restroom break.

Catching up with the ANALPRIDC, Medusa crosses into his personal space, stopping him in his tracks, and whispers something in his ear while slipping her hand into his jacket pocket. The ANALPRIDC stands stock-still as Medusa turns and saunters off to the ladies' room. Then he slowly returns to his workplace without checking his pocket. This exchange with the ANALPRIDC is just six weeks after Medusa's attempt to seduce the JERK.

"Delilah, we need to check out those two. I need their TWIT-OVA-PERSONs."

While I move the DIRT-MAPP onto the conference screen, she pulls the TWITs[96] from the TIMLI and slides them over to me in a chat message. On showing of the DIRT-MAPP on the O-WE-COME sspace, I can see Delilah again gawking at her spacey-screen avidly, intoxicated by the Beast.

"I've created a new feature in the DIRT-MAPP, Del; it's now easier to create complex searches and stuff."

After choosing the HANDBAG[97] option, a big leather-looking handbag in the shape of an old-fashioned round, metal rubbish bin pops into view. Delilah throws me a look that only a woman can smack a male-chauvinist in the face with. (Not that I'm the slightest part chauvinist, but I do so like to tease.) I know I'll have trouble hiding my smile, so I don't bother trying.

With seemingly wild abandon and no interest in the result of my actions, I throw the TWIT-OVA-PERSONs into the HANDBAG, find the icons for BIG-AM-I and WOWI, and dump these into the BAG also. Setting the start date to two years ten months ago, I hit the FAST MATCH option, which limits the search to provide a timeline based only on when the ANALPRIDC and Medusa are together.

After just a few seconds, the HANDBAG goes into all kinds of fits, first shaking and twirling, then jumping up and down. Then it raises up in the air in a big arc, as if someone were holding the strap, and suddenly comes fast down through the same arc, like shaking the water off wet lettuce. Again, the BAG lifts up and starts swinging around at high speed, as if it were inside a washing machine on the last rinse and spin program. Then it flies up in the air and crashes back down where it started, now lying still. The HANDBAG is glowing much like

---

96   Unique identifier WOWI

97   [1] A feature of the FRONT-END to Bitsi's mega-powerful search-engine; [2] A bag mostly used by women for holding (supposedly, usually) smaller items

an unwelcome phosphorescent fungus might look in your garden, in the dark.

I can see from the expression on Del's face that, for a change, she's speechless, and her silence confirms it. I usually create these silly visual effects in the DIRT-MAPP while winding down after long days, not yet ready for sleep and aided by some liquid enlightenment.

As I open the HANDBAG, a screen-space crawls out as if it were digging its way out of a grave in which it was buried alive. The data that was found is now showing in the sspace, and the phosphorescent glowing effect has stopped.

"OK, Delilah. This confirms the meeting we just watched was their first one. The search WOWI will take some time. Keep an eye on it, please." Then, I throw the HANDBAG to Delilah over the O-WE-COME chat.

"Yes, sir."

"Now, Del, you were saying?"

"Uh. Where was I? Yes, how did he get away with ingesting all that GLUE in the first place?" she inquires.

Having delved deep enough into my memory while working, the answer is flashing as a series of images in front of my eyes. "When the L'ARCH got demoted, I checked the INARDS[98] and reviewed his interview for the job of L'ARCH of BIG-AM-I BITS. Every answer he gave was perfect textbook stuff. But later recordings show that the BOJ-OB was exerting extreme pressure to get OBOY prepared to Go-Live and producing tons of beautiful shining DOLLIES as fast as inhumanely possible."

Almost a century ago, despite the public outcry, the powers that be passed a law that requires a recording, in a central archive, of all activity on business premises, from the biggest organization down to the smallest corner shop or café. They agreed on a whole special bible

---

98   Information Archive Recordings—Data Store, holding recordings of all activity on all business premises WOWI since the year 2021

of privacy and security rules and a set of system safety measures to strictly control who can access the INARDS.

Besides the military, I'm the only person who actually looks into these chronicles, mostly because none of those with the required authorization would know how or where to start. It's a lot of data. The confuzing equipment for processing and especially holding all the recordings fills a huge number of massive buildings WOWI.

I use these videos as evidence during every major investigation. Just a few years after starting my Bitsi life, I built the DIRT-MAPP using an older version of the Beast. Those ancient maxi-confuzers took three and a half years pushing up MAVACAPA[99] to analyze and catalog all the recordings available at that time. And this was just indexing, nothing too fancy.

"In his defense," I continue, "the L'ARCH gave the BOJ-OB an ultimatum stating, 'If you force me into this, then I need to use GLUE to make the timing stick, and this I absolutely refuse to do. So, it's me or the sticky stuff.' But the BOJ-OB simply gave the L'ARCH an offer he couldn't refuse. The L'ARCH folded, the textbook was flushed down the toilet, and the GLUE was plastered all over BIG-AM-I's BITS in the wink of a dingbat's eye."

"Typical," Delilah almost yells at me. "We let the business process executives influence technical evolution, and they always make a BODGE-JOB of it."

Laughing and pressing on, I say, "Can we now focus on the problem at hand, Delilah?"

"Of course, do you know what the problem is?" she asks.

"No." And we walk through what I do know and relate this to the monstrous diagram showing on the cinema-mode wide-screen.

"The incoming CASH is disappearing. From what they say, everything else seems normal. Do I believe that? No. But for now, let's

---

99   Maximum Available Capacity

focus on the payments components. I suspect a daylight shanghai here of more than seven billion DOLLIES, so far.

"Look at the system diagram, Delilah, do you see the CASH-COW[100] in the middle and to the right a bit?" Delilah comes back with a grunt. "And farther over to the right, do you see the CASH-PILE[101]?" I continue.

"Yaar, I see it. I know I'm repeating myself, but this New Naming of stuff, it's not a language, is it; it's more like a game or a joke."

"It is what it is," I respond coolly. "It's outright Gibberish. But at least these two names indicate which BITS do what. The CASH-COW is the source of income, where the customers actually pay. The CASH-PILE receives and holds the incoming payments—the CASH piling up, so to speak."

"Well. I'm glad you understand it," she blurts out a confused muddle of complaint and laughter. "So, we start with the CASH-PILE," Delilah suggests strongly.

"No," I disagree, "both BITS are potential problem areas, but my money is on the COW, and that's where we start. Use the Bitsi-Theory. Follow the path of the Eighth Deadly Sin, find The TRUTHH[102] and CREAM-EMTO–BITS[103]. I want a six-month-old CHABLIS[104] of OBOY listing all changes to the live OBOY's BITS; and create TROUBLE[105] for the soft-BITS ingredients in the CHABLIS."

Delilah interrupts me. "You do know that twenty-four hours ago, BIG-AM-I started a new campaign WOWI? It must be the biggest march on the market since the Life-Giver, Life-Long, Life Ever-Lasting fiasco a hundred years ago."

---

100   BIG-AM-I's BITS, or system for receiving or collecting payments, or CASH
101   A bank owned by BIG-AM-I
102   Criminal
103   [1] Take out the bad guy(s); [2] Crush by Exposure the Abominable Malefactor, eliminating the Menace to BITS
104   [1] List of all changes to production (or live) software systems; [2] Changes to BITS list
105   Detailed description of technical changes (to software)

"What?" I exclaim. "I've been shoulder-deep in assignments for the past month or so, and I haven't really surfaced much in that time."

"Bitsi, you really should watch the news from time to time. This has been advertised every day for the past three weeks. Sunday night was the Go-Live of the new BIG-AM-I FITS[106] launch. They have as good as gone into competition with the WINCCCERS and have started offering credit on customers' purchases. All customers."

"What, no more no credit?" I exclaim.

"Like I said, their biggest stunt since the Life-Giver, with the intention of conquering the consumer world completely and bagging the majority share of company sales WOWI. BIG-AM-I FITS is the first organization to offer credit for as long as most can remember."

Eighty-two years ago, on a Friday, the close of business signaled the start of the world's worst financial crisis ever. Many major financial institutions went under WOWI. The remaining few collectively suffered a super-mega-multi-trillion-DOLLY reduction in profit.

The banks had stretched the rules again and had amassed yet another huge bubble of unsettled debts from all walks of life. After the bubble burst, the surviving banks temporarily joined forces and pushed through the agreement that money-lending was no longer acceptable. This is when the New Name WINCCCER was born.

The change turned the world totally topsy-turvy, worsening the already disastrous effects of the crisis. Tens of millions throughout the world were left homeless and jobless with heavily decreased opportunities to secure work. Tragically, sadly, many died.

It took twenty-five years before the world's financial sun began to rise again, thirty-five years before it was conceded that life was back to normal again WOWI.

Even after all these years, I'm amazed at how just one or a relatively small handful of greedy, selfish humans can inflict so much suffering

---

106   Financial Institution, Technologically Secured

on so many millions of other human beings. Do we not see this coming? Power and money so often misused, humankind left dead and abused.

Eighty-two years and many Fridays later, everyone has almost forgotten what it was like to borrow money from banks. But the concept of credit will surely sell as easily as a knife cuts through butter, as it always did.

"Hmmm. OK," I respond. "This new launch of OBOY will naturally be floating at the top of the CHABLIS, so you'll hit it first, anyway. Now, for the deadly sins, start with the envious TEST-TICCLERs. Something is broken, or deliberately tweaked, so maybe we can see something from the test plan. Focus on two tracks: the test results and whatever they didn't test before this latest launch, OBOY."

I give Delilah and her team forty-eight hours of access to the BIG-AM-I data in the DIRT-MAPP. I can see her logging in immediately; she obviously has been waiting to get started.

"Fine, Bitsi, sir. I'll have the CHABLIS o' TROUBLE OBOY and TEST-TICCLER data on your desk in maybe an hour or two—tops."

I refine her planning a little. "Make it an hour, please. I expect to have BITS-SECS on location not long from now, and I want to have already picked the lucky winner for the first visit from the Oslo-Cops."

"Yes, they're already in the air. ETA fifty-four minutes," she responds, showing off just a little.

"When," I demand, "will you guys ever learn to keep me in the loop on these things?"

"I believe Samson thinks you're trying to FOOLHIM[107], so I guess he's playing hide-em-seek again?"

"Hah. I do not try, Delilah. You know that. And yes, he's playing, again."

"Yes, I know that, Bitsi, and that's my excuse—no point wasting time telling you something you already know."

---

107   Same as FOOLEM but with some gender implication

"Hmmm. Please get to it, Delilah; the clock is ticking."

Immediately, she cuts herself out of the meeting—before I can even blink. That woman constantly holds her own private pissing contest with me, trying to be faster than I am—and, Lord-IT only knows, she's fast.

I'm never sure what to think about her competing against me. Everyone appears to need something to give themselves the feeling of having the edge over others. I guess that makes them feel good, maybe offering motivation to perform, to be good at something, excel even.

But is being faster than I am or being better than I the best motivation and source of satisfaction she can come up with? Surely not?

9

Mary-lin's HPD

I flick a few keys on Seribus, check my weemail, and see that the L'ARCH has produced the CLIMACCSSS for OBOY's MAD FLAPPING incident.

After opening it and sorting the data to my liking, I send it on to Delilah asking her to match the names with the ones she digs up.

Next, I set an alarm in the DIRT-MAPP to pull up the Bitsi-Lite video of Samson in forty-five minutes from now; then, I settle down to study the BITS of BIG-AM-I's OBOY.

Focusing mostly around the CASH-COW and CASH-PILE, I drill first down, then up, then back down again through the soft-BITS and hard-BITS of the many systems involved. Not long after starting this research, Delilah's face interrupts me—probably more findings on Medusa & Co.

"What do you have, Del?" She displays video recordings from the TIMLI the HANDBAG created.

"They go into this hotel, sir." Medusa and the ANALPRIDC cross through the hotel lobby, disappearing into the elevator. "They stay until the next morning. The ANALPRIDC goes straight to the office from there, and Medusa takes off to the airport for her flight home."

"OK. Do you have the ANALPRIDC's TWIT-OVA-USER, Delilah?"

"Here, sir." Again, she puts the file onto the chat for me to grab, which I reject this time.

"I don't need it, Del. Throw it into the HANDBAG with the other junk. Select the REFRESH option. The old search is stopped and saved; we're starting a new one. The Person-ID will give you the visual timeline; the User-ID provides the TIMLI of his system usage. You can combine any and all TIMLI aspects when viewing, as needed."

"Yes, sir."

"Find out what Medusa asked the ANALPRIDC to do with BIG-AM-I's BITS. Go through the complete TIMLI for Medusa and the ANALPRIDC, then Medusa's TIMLI at BIG-AM-I. Turn over all stones."

"Yes, sir." And off she goes again.

After thirty more minutes of studying OBOY, the mess of thousands of components and hundreds of millions of lines of program code has made me sick to my stomach. Taking a break to recover, I prepare for some testing by opening a new session on the Beast and start recording all activity—the screen, keystrokes, a map of all data traffic WOWI from and to the machine, the works.

But my favorite auditor trashes my train of thought again. "Yes, Delilah?"

"Er, Bitsi, sir, I, er, thought I'd save time and threw in the TWIT-OVA-PERSONs and TWIT-OVA-USERs for the JERK and COCKS. But now it seems as if the system has stopped working, sir. No movement since then."

I quickly dive into her HANDBAG to see if I can sort out the chaos in there. "It's not a real HANDBAG, Delilah. You can't just chuck anything into it. You first need to decide exactly what you want to come out of it. This BAG has no bottom. If you throw in new elements to the search, you must always, again, limit the search criteria.

"We don't have any previous data on COCKS. So, you just sent the Beast off to Timbuktu and back again to find out when COCKS had his first diaper change. That's a soup-ah-nova search request, and I'm not sure I need to see that video anyway. Take them out, Del, and go back to the previous search."

"Yes, sir." And she cuts me off, even faster than usual. For a few moments, I simply sit chuckling because I need to teach a woman how to use a HANDBAG.

Resuming my test plan, I open the Conkerer[108], slip onto the wwoopsi-net, log in to OBOY, and start to run through some test scenarios. On another screen-space, I watch the DIRT-MAPP growing as I'm testing. I can see all the hard-BITS and soft-BITS that are hit WOWI while the machines fulfill my requests. There are four groups of players right now: me, BIG-AM-I, the WINCCCERs, and the wwoopsi-net companies. More than one-hundred-sixty machines hit so far, and countless thousands of soft-BITS.

Accompanied by a warning alarm harsh enough to wake a deeply slumbering Sleeping Beauty without even the promise of a kiss, the DIRT-MAPP throws the Bitsi-Lite video of Samson up onto a new sspace.

Hmmm. That wasn't the alarm I set. Samson has given Delilah misleading information in his game to beat my FOOLHIM operation.

The ETA Samson gave Delilah was for his teams, not for himself. Now he's standing in his plane that just landed in Oslo and is waiting to disembark.

Being the No. 1 man of BITS-SECS has its perks. Samson has his very own company soup-ah-sonic plane, which he can use all year round as he chooses, expecting, of course, no abuses.

I swirl around to Come-again and pull up Samson's mug on a conference sspace, getting ready to call him so that the second his foot hits the ground his phony FONE will ring. Wait, wait.

He's getting out now. Wait, wait. He puts one foot on the last step of the ramp, continuing on the way down with no signs of stopping. I hit the button to make the call and immediately his FONE rings, just as his other foot hits concrete. "Welcome to Sunny Oslo, Samson." I try to make my masked grin as broad and annoying as possible.

---

108 Number-one browser WOWI, copyright BIG-AM-I

"Hmmm. It ain't right," he complains. "All that confuzing-power you have makes your life way too easy."

I merely laugh. "Rather me than you, Samson, old boy. Maybe you'll learn to stop forcing me to chase you around the globe and keep me informed.

Delilah will have cooked up a CHABLIS O' TROUBLE, OBOY, in about twenty-five minutes from now. Will you be settled by then so the three of us can get a taste of it? I wanna decide whose proverbial ass you gotta kick first."

"Yes, sir. Our safe house here in Oslo was warmed up while I was in the air, and it takes only eighteen minutes to get there. I'll be ready. Now tell me, how did you find out so fast I had switched FONEs?"

I smirk. "Hah. Let's talk about that over a beer one day, pal. Right now, if I'm not mistaken, we've got some hard slogging to do before billions more DOLLIES get pinched."

Samson grunts, and then concedes, "OK. Call when you have your CHABLIS on ice."

Going back to complete my testing, I make a few simple purchases using OBOY, then rerun the tests, but with a different user ID. It's just a hunch, a bad feeling I can't explain, but I redo the tests anyway.

Quickly checking the session recording to ensure I can see all the data, I then settle down to review the ever-growing DIRT-MAPP. The No-Credit-Card payments BITS have also appeared on the screen. I can study and compare the flow of both tests.

Sitting back, I stare out through the DIRT-MAPP into space. It's as if my eyes are reading the flow of data between each system, picking out of the very air the bits and bytes as they flow over the wireless communication channels. With a combination of knowledge picked up over many decades; a vivid, possibly limitless imagination; and a little lubrication from The Fruit, I'm searching for the black hole that must be there, out there, somewhere.

They say that when Bitsi says, "Thinking," he's off tripping on the NET, which is not far from the truth. My first swig of The Fruit was a soup-ah-natural psychedelic experience, which knocked me clean off my feet and has continued to this day, although I became accustomed to it over time. The Fruit has artificially soup-ah-boosted my mind's abilities.

Before The Fruit, I had honed my logic abilities while also studying and practicing various forms of meditation, which broadened the realms of my imagination, yet also taught me to focus, and so process information much faster.

The Fruit broke away all remaining barriers and lubricated cogs I never even knew were there, allowing me to think totally out of the box and process logic and data at amazing, super-human speed.

Finding the solution to a problem is now easy, deep-diving into various artificially enhanced thought levels, throwing wide all options, exploring all the data. Then, after computing the answer, I use my BITS-SECS and BITS-SITTER teams, and my soup-ah-fast Beast, to find further supporting evidence. I'm almost never wrong.

During our experimental research period and the planning for the release of the Nuke-Li-Aerial/Bitsi-Lite/DROSS announcements, when I told Lord-IT what The Fruit had done to me, his only reaction was a facial expression that complained, "Why do you have all the luck?" But I know I'm not the only one affected by The Fruit. Over the decades, there have been a few fleeting mentions of others with amazing abilities, but no one has ever expanded on these cases, which have seemingly disappeared into the crowd of other news. I suppose one day I should look into this and maybe understand it better.

Using this enhanced brain power, I could assist Lord-IT Nuke-Li-Aerially, finish my own Bitsi-Lite work, and design the confuzers and LICKEMs to use Nuke-Li-Aerial power—and I produced soup-ah fast more than seventy-five percent of the DROSS, which runs all confuzers today. My contribution earned me a fifty percent share in Lord-IT House. Bitsi-Lites the Skies remains mine alone.

Running through the test data at soup-ah high speed, I notice again that on the final bill presented to the test TWIT-OVA-USER, there's an increase of Đ0.68, which I ignored when paying. Suddenly, a dim light goes on at the end of a tunnel. Which tunnel I'm not sure yet. The entrance to the tunnel is shimmering, hovering, shifting, my mind can't settle on it. Hmmm. Something to sleep on.

After having scrutinized so many megabytes of data, without any obvious reason as to why, I abruptly reach a decision and move over to Come-again, again.

My Bitsi life has brought me in contact with all the banks over time, so I know the WINCCCER that owns the No-Credit-Card payments BITS that collect OBOY's CASH. Searching the O-WE-COME contacts list, the BOJ-OB of HPD–FITS BITS pops out as the most likely candidate to talk with. It's time to find out what they know, so I give her a call.

"Hey, Marilyn, how're you doing?"

She responds a little irritably, "I've told you before, Bitsi, it's Mary-lin, not Mari-lyn."

Same old dance. "Yes, Mary-lin, my apologies. So, how are you?"

Continuing the irritated attitude, she half barks, "Not good. I've had the BODGE-JOB of BIG-AM-I BITS screaming at me about missing CASH for almost the past twenty-four hours. As if you couldn't guess that, Bitsi, *sir*?"

I say, "Hah. He's probably worried he could be the one to PUKE on this MAD MAGIC TRICC, and at the least, no visit from Santa Claus this year. So, I can imagine he hasn't left you alone. But what's your problem? I thought you enjoyed a little extra attention?"

Even knowing about her externally imposed deficiency complex, I can't help but tease. After all, she needs to let it go, ease up a little.

Mary-lin groans and sighs at the same time. "Bitsi, will you ever stop with that? Look, I'm a little busy responding to a backlog of BODGED JOB requests here. Will you tell me what you want, please, so I can get back to it?" Slowly, she's calming down.

"Mary-lin, let me deal with the BOJ-OB of BIG-AM-I BITS. I'll get him off your back, now."

"Oh, Bitsi. It would be wonderful if you could do that," she cries out.

The weemail to the BOJ-OB is already under construction, instructing him that, until further notice, *all* communication with HPD[109] must go through me; no exceptions. Mary-lin is in copy. Hitting 'send,' I say to her, "Check your weemail, Mary; it's done. He'll leave you alone now."

Frantic sounds of polished fingernails smacking her space-pad as she checks. "Oh, Bitsi. If you weren't so smart and all-powerful, I'd kiss you."

I smile. She has just ruined one of my favorite double-edged compliments, but I think I get it. The ice is truly melted.

"Mary-lin, please tell me all you know, and anything you suspect."

The Mary-lin floodgates burst open, releasing a stream of information over the Bitsi-Lite connection. Good thing I'm recording the call. If I had twenty hands and ten space-pads, I still couldn't type fast enough to keep up with her.

On an O-WE-COME sspace, I see Delilah calling. The O-WE-COME is set up so that calls come in silently, and the video shows up on a sspace, but the calls are never answered automatically. Quickly checking my weemail, I see she sent in the CHABLIS o' TROUBLE OBOY just twenty seconds ago. By calling, she's trying to be faster than me, again.

While listening to Mary-lin, who surely must be blue in the face by now, I break off Delilah's incoming call and in a chat session tell her I'll get back to her soon. In the meantime, she needs to send the data on to

---

109 [1] Honorary Protector of Dollies, the biggest WINCCCER ever WOWI; [2] Histrionic Personality Disorder

Samson, then talk it through with him. I instruct Delilah that they need to make a list of key candidates for the initial interrogations.

She says, "Roger that," and closes the chat before I can even type "OK."

On the DIRT-MAPP and the Bitsi-Lite video, I can see that Samson is in the safe house and is finishing preparations for our conference. Delilah will keep him busy until I'm ready.

Now, I can focus on Mary-lin. In the past minute or two, she has covered many topics already but all of them no more important than the weather. She obviously needed to get a load off. But now it's time to force some direction into the conversation.

"How are the kids, Mary-lin?" She stops dead in mid-sentence.

"Darn it. I don't know. I've been on the job almost twenty-four hours, and I don't know." She's almost crying, probably from a combination of tension, exhaustion, and a true mother's pain from having neglected her babies.

"Mary-lin, take a minute to call them. I'll wait."

"Uh," she sobs. "Yes. Thanks. Hold on, please; I'll call home."

No matter what the crisis, I'll never go more than an hour or two before I get an update on the well-being of each one of my family, my wikids. I do admit, however, it's easy for me. I simply use Bitsi-Lite if I can't check on them in person.

Waiting for the family catch-up to complete, I sit and stare through the data Delilah has sent in. Many minutes later, Mary-lin returns to the call.

"Bitsi, thank you so much. I spoke with all of them, and they're just fine. Thanks."

"Mary-lin, I've told you before, you really should sort out better comms with them. They're more important than the job. Anyhow, let's get back to the problem at hand. Please explain what you've found so far."

For a while, she explains all the things her people have checked on, to no avail. "So, we're still looking into it, Bitsi."

"Mary-lin, I'd like formal approval to rummage around in your BITS, to see what I can get my hands on. Can you give that, like, now?"

"I certainly can. Drop me a weemail requesting this; I will approve it immediately. Oh, I suppose you've heard about the credit deal with BIG-AM-I?"

While responding, I prepare the approval request. "I've gotten wind of the new credit arrangement, but I don't have many details as yet."

Mary-lin describes what she knows of the recently established deal. She knows I'd get the info sooner or later, so better from her, I guess. Nevertheless, she has donned her political-correctness cloak and is choosing her words carefully.

Nothing she has to tell me, however, appears to have any bearing on the current issues, OBOY. It's interesting, though, that HPD—FITS has gone into cahoots with BIG-AM-I on the new credit deal, taking its fair share of the profits, naturally.

"It's going to be one helluva change, Mary-lin. A whole bunch of lessons to be relearned. And so the WHHEEL[110] turns."

"It's going to be a total nightmare roller-coaster ride, which, I suddenly remember, I need to get back on. Can we finish up here, Bitsi?"

"Sure. Thanks for your time. You now have my weemail, so please approve. And remember, Mary-lin, keep in better touch with your family. No matter what's going down."

Mary-lin is silent for a moment, obviously pausing, thinking, I guess. "Bitsi, do you think Marilyn really had HPD?" asks Mary-lin.

Mary-lin was publicly accused of neglecting her family in favor of her career when she took the BOJ-OB position, and it was claimed that HPD pushed her to this. That put a serious dent in her public profile, and her self-confidence.

---

110   The World of Humankind's Hateful Egocentric Evil Learning about the World of Humankind's… A vicious cycle that so many people are stuck in

Following Namesake's Footsteps
Fame and HPD Drive
Marilyn Succeeds BOJ-OB
Family Suffering

Not one of BITS GON Ballistic's finest hours.

"I don't know, Mary-lin. But whatever her problems, they most likely were initially forced on her by her parents, and their parents, and she didn't or couldn't deal with them."

"Hmmm, poor girl," she says quietly, seemingly lost in some thought or other.

I'm not at all sure which girl she's talking about exactly.

"Yes. What we hand down to our children shapes them and shapes the world," I respond.

Mary-lin heaves a deep, heavily burdened sigh.

"Get some rest, Mary-lin. I fear we have some long hours ahead." I hang up, somewhat saddened. And something is bothering me about the conversation with Mary-lin.

10

THE PRIDE O' BIG-AM-I BITS

CHEWING OVER MARY-LIN'S words brings me no closer to voicing my worry, so changing tactics, I gate-crash the meeting between Samson and Delilah.

"Del, I've been chin-wagging with the WINCCCER that apparently joined up with BIG-AM-I on this new credit deal. Something is not right, but I can't place it. Here's access to their BITS." I pass on the permissions I received from Mary-lin.

"Start an investigation immediately, please. Don't stop until you've been through everything."

"Everyone I have awake is already pushing up MAVACAPA, sir," she responds.

"Then pull in another team, Delilah—two teams if need be. We need to uncover everything we can find, ASAP."

"I don't like the sound of this, sir."

"Hummm. No."

Giving Delilah a few minutes to spur her teams into action, I stretch my legs as the coffee machine does its magic. As I rejoin the meeting, she wastes no time in pushing ahead.

"What's first, Bitsi, sir? Medusa or the TEST-TICCLERs?"

"Medusa?" exclaims Samson.

"We'll come to her later. What are your thoughts about the TEST-TICCLERs?"

Samson also likes to compete with Delilah and me and everyone else for that matter, so he dives in ahead of her. He's also fast.

"We've taken a close look through Delilah's data and analysis. We agreed that the lead TEST-TICCLER should be probed first."

"Oh? And why is that?"

"Er." Hesitation, suspecting I don't agree, and this usually unsettles him a little.

Delilah, going for a fast recovery, says, "Thirty-seven TEST-TICCLERs worked on the latest release, OBOY. It would be a long shot to uncover anything quickly by interviewing all of them, sir. The main TEST-TICCLER will maybe give us some hints about the others."

"Samson?"

"Er, there are different angles to this, but Del and I agree—for a change." He spoke carefully at first but finished up by playing the Samson chuckle one more time.

"Well, let's look at the data."

On the O-WE-COME sspace, I display Delilah's findings, flicking quickly through the pages and pages of test plans and reports.

"Total, fifteen hundred test cases. Only eight executed by the lead TEST-TICCLER. Why not more?"

"Er..."

"Now I look more closely," Delilah offers rather quietly, "I see he was not planned to test the system at all."

"Exactly. So why did he take those eight test cases?"

"Hmmm, those tests all relate to the CASH-COW. Blast it. How did I miss that?" she almost yells.

"Because your money was on the CASH-PILE?" I offer. "Anyway, I suggest that we take the thirty-seven TEST-TICCLERs, plan a careful line of questioning, get them to uncover what they know about why their lead decided to ride the COW."

"Agreed," says Samson.

"Me, too," Delilah responds, a little grumpily.

"But, you're right, thirty-seven TEST-TICCLERs to tease is quite a load. I suppose we can guess how many are in each building?" I ask Delilah.

"Pretty much evenly split, as expected," she responds immediately, recovering fast from the mini-defeat. "Nineteen in BIG-AM-I-B1, eighteen in BIG-AM-I-B2."

Almost everything in the BIG-AM-I setup is dupli-mated[111] (duplicated or doubled-up). The two BIG-AM-I buildings are exact copies of each other. This is to guarantee that if a catastrophic company-crushing disaster hits Oslo—for example, a volcano erupting—then the Copenhagen office can continue doing business as if nothing really bad happened at all.

Dupli-mation[112] is common practice in BITS when it comes to sites, machines, and systems, but BIG-AM-I has followed this concept through to the bitter end and included much of the workforce, also.

There are only a few truly beneficial forms of dupli-mating, or dupli-mation. The numerous downsides of the other forms can be described in many different ways.

Just to give the worst example, the negative results of dupli-mation can compare to the ancient horror movies in which a family living in the woods multiplies through incestuous reproduction. Generations later, the whole clan runs around the forest insanely killing all the passers-by in the most monstrous of manners, usually involving big teeth, huge knives, long dirty fingernails, and lots of blood. Net result: Gruesome mutations and carnage.

Said simply: *DUPLI-MATING can be hazardous for one's BITS.*

---

111 [1] Duplicate, copy, or replica; [2] To illegally duplicate, copy; [3] To make a replica of something and screw with it so badly that the original is no longer recognizable; [4] An abomination

112 [1] The result or outcome of dupli-mating; [2] An act or instance of dupli-mating; [3] An abomination

"Yes," Samson continues. "If I divide my teams—five from each doing the questioning, half an hour per interrogation—it will take two hours to get through them all, if we start now, which we can't."

"Fifteen minutes per interview, no time for more. Start rounding them up, Samson. I want the first ones in the interview room in half an hour."

"You do know it's two o'clock in the morning here, sir?"

"Scare them witless, Samson—you guys are good at that; it should help them wake up fast enough. Get to the lead TEST-TICCLER first. He must be kept silent during this whole interview period. Delilah and I will prepare the reception. You get over to the BIG-AM-I building as soon as you can. Now get going, please."

"I'm on it, sir." And he cuts himself off from the call.

"Delilah, please prepare the line of questioning. Harass them with the usual about why they tested only part of the system."

"A pathetic sixty-two percent this time, sir," she interjects.

"Drop in questions about the main TEST-TICCLER when they're off balance. Get your teams started, Del, but stay on the O-WE-COME, and when you're done, join me in preparing the meeting facilities."

"Yes, Bitsi, sir, getting to it right now." She mutes herself soup-ah fast.

More than two hours have passed since I was dragged out of bed. My body has slowly but surely woken up, and nature is calling. Dragging myself up from the comforts of the luxurious office seating, I trip the route to the bathroom with my eyes half-closed, my mind buzzing through the events so far, until I return to my office.

Before logging into the BIG-AM-I corporate network, I take a bird's-eye view of the two office complexes. Using a Bitsi-Lite map of the world, I search for BIG-AM-I BITS. Two office locations appear on the map. A thin line, the famous BIG-AM-I Rail, cuts through the air in an almost straight line joining both complexes. Most of the bi-directional rail rests on supports that reach up, for the most part, +/- 1.3 kilometers above the ocean. This was to avoid the extra hassle of negotiating the cost of rural damages along the route.

The coaches hover within an enclosed funnel and are Nuke-Li-Aerially propelled at a should-be-unbearable pace of +/-2400 kilometers per hour. Inside the coach, however, passengers don't notice the speed due to all kinds of complex scientific tricks—and many shots of inordinately expensive alcohol uniquely designed to steady the nerves.

The timing of the construction of the BIG-AM-I Rail was rather unfortunate. BITS GON Ballistic's outraged headline summed up the public reaction nicely (for a change):

BIGAMY's

Bigamous

BIG-AM-I Rail

Infuriates WOWI

BIGAMY knows no shame!

Billions of DOLLIES were unceremoniously screwed in the ocean bed stretching from Oslo to Copenhagen during the hardest years of the pain and suffering following the financial crisis that changed the world. No one was impressed at the time.

The journey time between BIG-AM-I-B1 and BIG-AM-I-B2 is sixteen minutes, give or take a few toddies.

One might well expect that the BIG-AM-I Rail would be BIG-AM-I's technology showcase. But it isn't. The BIG-AM-I BITS buildings even now, eighty years after conception, are wonders from another planet. They're the pride of BIG-AM-I BITS.

I zoom in on Oslo to take a look. Half to my surprise, I see Samson crossing through the double outer wall into the main compound. He didn't waste any time getting there.

Placing an O-WE-COME call to his DIGIT-FONE, he answers immediately. "I've never seen such a massive office complex," he practically screams.

"Ah, then you've never been to BIG-AM-I-B2," I chuckle.

The construction is huge. Six wheel-shaped, twelve-story buildings, arranged in a circle, each built on top of a circular metal plate, and these are all resting on another massive wheel-shaped metal plate in the ground. Resting on top of six tall and wide hollow columns is another huge circular plate that covers all six buildings and the outer wall. Built on top of this plate is the penthouse suite, the top management office floor.

All the walls, columns, and floors, except at ground-level, are made from soup-ah Extra-Strength CLEVUR-Glass ranging from thirty centimeters to eighty centimeters thick. The colors of the walls and floors, controlled by remotes hung in strategic places throughout the offices, change regularly, depending on who feels like what, when— and who wins, much like the result of family arguments about which program to watch on TV. (I still call it TV, even after all these decades.) All the glass mounts around a soup-ah strong, if flimsy-looking, metal supporting structure.

Samson looks up into one of the buildings. *"What the hell is that?"* he exclaims.

I follow his gaze up to the fourth floor and burst into a laughing fit. "That, Samson, is an overweight BITS-Pro taking an early morning swim."

"This place is weird; you can see everything. Everything is made from glass, even the desks. I guess the girls don't wear skirts to work, huh?"

"Hmmm. Take my advice, Samson, and avoid those who do."

"Roger that."

Looking around some more, he says, "I don't see any confuzers, only spacey-screens."

All spacey-screens are built for receiving wireless transmission, so there's no need to keep the confuzers close by.

"Under your feet, Samson, there's a huge building, constructed deep underground, housing one-and-a-half million confuzers, one eighth of the BIG-AM-I BITS server farm."

"Wow. It must be hot down there."

"Not really. The heat is recycled out into the building, when needed, and channeled for reuse elsewhere in the warmer periods."

Suddenly, out of the corner of my eye, I see Delilah's face appear on an O-WE-COME sspace. She's talking, even starting to wave at me. I don't budge, not even a half centimeter. It's not wise to respond to your subordinates too fast, unless you plan on screaming at them, which I rarely do.

Slowly, I turn to look at her, reach out one hand, and join her incoming call into the call with Samson. Then I interrupt her mid-sentence.

"What's your status, Delilah?"

"Er, we're working on the questions, ready in fifteen minutes. And I have some questions about some of the NETNERDs system transactions, when you have time. Also, the ANALPRIDC went back to that hotel on many occasions, sir. And Medusa set up a meeting between herself, the ANALPRIDC, and the lead NETNERD of OBOY. Also at the same hotel. What is your status?" she tries.

The ANALPRIDC is trouble; I'm convinced of that, and I can guess at the nature of it. But other angles of the investigation need to get underway before we can stand still to look at him.

My suspicions about the NETNERD are also confirmed. The time of his hacking of the Sissy's communications was not just a simple COMMINGS.

"Are you checking out where the NETNERD fits in?" I ask, ignoring her question.

"He has his very own HANDBAG now, sir," and she lets slip a tiny smile.

"Good. Hang on, Del. Samson, look up. Do you see the BIG-AM-I Rail?"

Samson has settled into a luxury leather sofa in the lobby of BIG-AM-I-B1-1. Directing his gaze skywards, he's almost in awe. "Wow, so that's it," he says.

"Yes. Tenth floor, boarding through the outer wall. Six hundred kilometers in sixteen minutes. It's an option if one team needs reinforcements."

"Got that. Er, Bitsi, sir, is it just me, or is this place unstable?" Samson asks.

Letting loose a deep chuckle, I reply, "All the round plates are turning, Samson. ALL of them, in different directions."

"But those bridges crossing inside from the floors in one building over to another—if everything is rotating, how?"

"Sliding wall sections in the inner wall, Samson. The wall is to cater for the conveyor-belt connecting bridges."

The walkways are about three and a half meters wide, all glass, and even the belts for walking are see-through plastic. A little courage is required when crossing those bridges.

"How many people work here?" he asks.

Delilah pitches in, "Total site capacity is thirty-three thousand, six hundred. Current occupation: thirty-two K, nine-eighty."

"OK, guys 'n' gals, enough chit-chat. Del, how's your memory of these BIG-AM-I BITS buildings?" I ask.

"Last time we were here was, what, seventy years ago, when..."

"You remember that?" I'm flabbergasted.

"Yes. We were pulled into..."

"All right, Del, not now. We need the usual multi-room, multi-exit/entrance setup. Five rooms. You work on that, please. I need to prepare Samson to check out the lead TEST-TICCLER."

"Yes, sir." Delilah mutes her O-WE-COME—fast, as usual—but she is still on the O-WE-COME, still with video, and still listening.

"Samson, how's your collection of TEST-TICCLERs growing?"

"The guys are running around the towns gathering up the subs," he says. "We'll be ready."

"Good. Now, something else. It's time for you to learn how I can find you so fast."

"Great."

"I will set this up but watch closely. When these interviews are over, I want you to follow the lead TEST-TICCLER and see if his conduct changes during this investigation, compared to his usual behavioral pattern."

"But how…"

"Samson, let me finish, please. For studying his past behavior, I will get you into his INARDS."

"That sounds disgusting."

"Pipe down, Samson. It is what it is. Bloody Gibberish. Now, to study current behavior, we need to FOOLHIM. For comparing current and past behavior, I'm afraid you're going to need to use your brainpower for that."

"Hmmm, I might struggle with that one," Samson chuckles.

I pull up the DIRT-MAPP on the O-WE-COME sspace.

"Watching?"

"Yep."

"We start with the present time, Samson."

I open my new fancy HANDBAG feature in the DIRT-MAPP and drag the lead-T's TWIT-OVA-PERSON from Delilah's data into the BAG. Immediately locating the lead-T, the BAG throws its fits-and-spasms routine, which takes just a few seconds.

"What is that, sir?" Samson asks with hint of a smile in his voice.

My response is tightly wrapped in a sandwich of sarcasm and sincerity: "It's a HANDBAG search, Samson."

"And you expect to actually find something in there, sir?" Samson has quickly cottoned on and is going with the flow.

"I won't bet my life on it, Samson, but I do remain ever hopeful."

Delilah has thrown her head into her hands while shaking it at the same time. It looks as if maybe she's giving up hope for us. Samson and I are chuckling in harmony, rather enjoying her distress at our lost and obviously soon-to-be-condemned souls.

Opening the BAG, a list of all the lead-T's hard-BITS pops out. Selecting his personal DIGIT-FONE, I choose the FOOLEM function from the menu.

In less than a second, the DIRT-MAPP pulls up a Bitsi-Lite map and zooms in on the lead-T's house. We can see some red dots, glowing in the dark of the DIRT-MAPP.

"Oh, wow, that's fast."

"Well, I'm cheating a little right now, coz I recently re-indexed all BIG-AM-I's employees in the DIRT-MAPP. I see you didn't get to him yet?"

"No, sir. He's farther out than most of the others. But we'll be with him soon."

"OK. Now, we can't see much here yet. There's no movement, so let's prepare to look into his-story, Samson."

I drag the WOWI icon into the HANDBAG, to join the TWIT-OVA-PERSON. As I choose FOOLEM-FROM-INARDS, I can just imagine the sound of the Beast under me springing into action as the confuzing-power whacks up to MAVACAPA.

"The Beast will create a timeline of every mugshot taken of him WOWI. Once complete, we'll have a full-blown movie of the lead-T's INARDS-life experiences."

"Sounds wonderful," says Samson unconvincingly.

"You need to go through the timeline recordings, identify and mark points of interest, and plot how often and at what times these points are hit. It's easy. You'll get the hang of it after just an hour or two."

Granting access to these special tools of mine, I watch Samson hide his smile as he reads the access notification weemail.

"Wipe that smirk off. We're not through, yet. Here's the Bitsi-Lite visual extension."

I show how this works by displaying a full HD color video display of the lead-T sleeping in bed. We watch a fly peeing on his face.

"You can see into his house?" Samson asks.

Despite the many publicized advanced features of Bitsi-Lite, we never made it known that it's possible to see through solid surfaces, as if they didn't exist.

"With Bitsi-Lite, you can see through anything and everything, Samson. Using this Bitsi-Lite feature, you can see twitches in facial expressions, minuscule body posture changes, margaritas on beaches, FONEs hidden in kitchen cupboards, the works. Never use this feature unless absolutely necessary, Samson. You'd be breaking the law."

"Yes, sir," he responds, knowing full well that I'll be sorely disappointed if he ever goes against this clearly serious directive.

"Bitsi-Lite won't assist you with the analysis of behavior, but once you detect a current act that's out of the norm, you can use Bitsi-Lite to zoom in and find out what's going on."

Using the space-pad, I draw a circle around the face of the lead-T and drag it into the HANDBAG. "I pulled the subject's picture into the HANDBAG, Samson, just to show how this works, but this is only necessary if we haven't yet identified the subject. This is like the usual facial-recognition search for known criminals."

"Using the face, you can always find the TWIT-OVA-PERSON in the INARDS?" Samson asked.

"Yes. All except mine, of course. And this is the key difference when searching using the INARDS. Nobody can hide. Only you'll have access to this Bitsi-Lite viewer, Samson. Your agents will have to make do with the usual Bitsi-Lite features and the public camera images when tracking him.

"One last thing, Samson. Using this FOOLEM option, you can follow and automatically track the TEST-TICCLER; using FOOLEMALL, you follow and track all people that he contacts using his DIGIT-FONE, building up a complete network of communication. So, that's it. Now, get to it, please."

"Yes, sir. Er, can I ask something?"

"What?"

"These tools. How do they work? And where do they come from?"

"I built them; they're mine and only mine, and they're top secret, so do you remember your confidentiality agreement, Samson?"

"Yes, sir."

"Well, read it again just to make sure you have every Lord-IT word imprinted in your head. Now, get moving. When this guy wakes up, I want you to notice if he takes a dump at the wrong time of day."

Suddenly, Samson reaches forward and pukes up his breakfast. Oh, dear. He's feeling the effects of the turning plates of BIG-AM-I-B1, and I forgot to warn him.

"You'll need to watch out for that, Samson. It's a physiological reaction to the turning of the buildings, and only an extremely strong psyche can overcome it, or it takes many months of adjustment. In other words, months of puking. You will need to warn your men, also. Now, go clean up, then get yourself to the ninth floor."

"Ugh. Yes, sir."

The BIG-AM-I MOTHER executive that commissioned the building believed in the Seven Chakras and mistakenly used the term in the building's requirements specification.

The "genius" that drove the final design, however, confused the notion of a wheel in relation to chakra. Armed with this misunderstanding, he transformed the original concept into a hare-brained implementation of a centuries-old psychology theory to try to ensure that employees remained constantly on their toes by enjoying new, interesting scenery day in, day out. This is a classic example of The Business and The Techies not cooperating or collaborating effectively.

New hires at BIG-AM-I BITS receive puke buckets and non-puke-able nutrient supplements to compensate for the shortage of digested food during their inauguration period, which can last up to one year.

For the past eighty years, BIG-AM-I has claimed that this sickness episode is a natural result of the stress of joining what is probably soon to become the No. 1 organization WOWI.

Others claim that the building's never-ending turning, in conflicting directions, gives sudden and terrifying insight that they're inescapably trapped in a wheel in an industry that's going around in circles, in BITS.

My money is on the last explanation.

A weemail arrives from the Sissy o' BIG-AM-I BITS. He's politely requesting me to contact him once I awaken. He's obviously worried I'm not taking his OBOY MAD-FLAPPING seriously enough.

Experiencing one of my all-too-often soft moments, I feel for his concern and dial him on the O-WE-COME. He answers promptly.

"COCKS, I did not go to sleep. I immediately kicked off a full-fledged investigation. It's still in ramp-up stage, which will take time, so, before you ask, no findings yet. But, we're on the job."

"That's a relief," he exclaims.

"Listen to me, COCKS. If you want to avoid losing face, don't challenge me in public and do not presume to give me instructions." Then I rephrase my earlier message into a somewhat kinder version.

"If you want something from me, then ask nicely. If I agree, you'll get what you ask for. Do you understand me, COCKS?"

"Of course. This awful mess on my first day in office is rather trying."

"I understand, and you can scream at anyone you like, except me or those who work for me. Now, I'm going back to work."

"Thanks for responding so fast."

"No problem."

I swing back to the O-WE-COME with Samson and Delilah. "Del, show me what you've dug up, please."

"Sure." She displays the new layout of the interview rooms. The MOWALL[113] program can rearrange all the inner office walls in the BIG-AM-I buildings. Meeting rooms are in one big area on each floor, to make the never-ending change of floorplan less disturbing for the BITS-Pros.

---

113   A soft-BITS program for moving or rearranging the office walls within the BIG-AM-I buildings

"I made it U-shaped, like last time; it's more practical," she said.

"Well done, Delilah."

"Thanks. A corridor forms the U, with three entrance/exit points. Five rooms laid across the U, doors at both ends of the rooms—in and out." She moves a pointer around the screen-space quickly showing the layout.

"And an OOO-O-WE-COME[114] in each room?"

"Lined up and moving them in now."

Looking into the eyes of an OOO-O-WE-COME is a meet ET experience. The outside casing of the Nuke-Li-Aerially hovering screen has the form of a bald head and is a soft, flexible, almost organic-like material that changes shape and color to match the head and face being displayed.

The face-shaped screen shows a 3-D enhanced, vividly life-like visage of the person behind the webcam. If you reach out your hand to touch the face, it could almost bite you.

Users can easily summon up numerous pre-programmed features such as INTIMI (Intimidate) and ZOIFKI. (Zoom in for the Kill) using a space-pad or joystick.

Only one person can control an OOO-O-WE-COME during a meeting. Of course, that will be me throughout the coming interrogations.

"All done," Delilah states.

"So, are we ready to party?"

"Yes, I believe so."

"Oh, boy. Hotline call. Hang on, Del."

---

114 One-On-One O-WE-COME. A hovering or flying confuzer screen or monitor, shaped like a bald head.

11

Tease the **TEST-TICCLERs**

"Bisi, I could see you online. You ain't sleeping?"

Lord-IT is one of only two people who can check my online status. My wife is the other person.

"Hey, Lordy. Nah, not sleeping. What's up?"

"Nothing unusual. Night out with the wife. We'll be going home soon. What about you?"

"One big busted BITS at the moment. But what's new, huh?"

"I guess that's BIG-AM-I's trouble, OBOY. Got it under control?"

"It will be, sooner or later. Lordy, I'm minutes away from knocking a few heads together here, so what do you need?"

"Bisi, you're not going to like this, but I need an updated presentation by early evening. If you don't have time, I need to know now."

He sounds more than just tired, almost stressed.

"You OK, Lordy?"

"Yeah, all good. Just a late night. I need some sleep. And I had forgotten all about this presentation. I'm not looking forward to that."

"Lordy, do you specially wait until I'm up to my neck in BITS kaput and evaporating DOLLIES before you call me? When are you gonna learn to do these things yourself? Which presentation?"

"It is the Big Business Strategy slide-show that almost embarrassed me fifty-odd years ago."

"Oh, that one." I have to chuckle at the memory.

"It's not that funny, Bisi. You could have gotten me into some awkward situations."

"I don't understand the problem. The audience loved you. The press had a field day, even credited you with a sense of humor, for a change."

"Thanks to my expertise in waltzing and Gibberish." And we both laugh.

"Next time, maybe you wanna read what I send you before spreading it all over public O-WE-COME spacey-screens WOWI."

"Hmmm. Look, I need a summarized comparison on the success of the two business strategies. I need it no later than 17:15 CET. And, for the record, I won't have time to read it, so it needs to be ready to go public when you send it in. Can you manage that?"

"Hummm, I can do it."

"As usual, only two slides, please."

"Yeah, yeah. Put on your dancing shoes for tonight's show. Get ready to boost your ratings."

"Bisi!"

"Lordy! Later, man."

"Later."

Lord-IT's two-page presentations are famous WOWI. Remarkably, they are not only always two pages but also always packed with controversial statements designed to encourage dynamic and lively question-and-answer sessions. He prefers this approach over trying to show off with fancy images or sleep-inducing theories.

He knows I'll deliver the slideshow on time. But he also now knows he needs to polish his dancing shoes for this evening. Lord-IT and I are the oldest, and best, of friends, and we're partners who play with open and honest cards, knowing this way we both succeed. Our working relationship and partnership are unbeatable WOWI.

But it bugs me that Lordy sounded so stressed. An argument with his wife maybe? That would definitely upset him, more so because they don't usually argue. Eying up the wrong girl in the wrong place at the wrong time maybe? Not likely, for Lord-IT is too smart for that, and he and his wife are still too close and happy for Lordy to suddenly develop wandering eyes. They've been together since she was in school, and they're now already planning their century celebration party for next year. Recently, they started on their second round of kids, and apart from inspiring my wife and me to continue trying, their kids have brought fresh life into their already invigorating daily routine.

No, whatever I heard in Lordy's voice, it's either something else or nothing at all. But which is it?

I call Delilah and Samson. "Delilah, we're close to curtain-up time, are we not?"

"Six minutes, Bitsi, sir."

"OK. Are the meeting room walls set to black from outside, transparent from within?"

"Yup."

"Samson, the lead-T, you have him?"

"Confined in a meeting room in the next building, sir. All comms confiscated."

"Good. How is his timeline looking?"

"TIMLI WOWI goes back fifty years so far. I've studied the past two."

"Bitsi?"

"Thinking..."

"OK, Samson, let the TIMLI complete, but no need to review it further. And I've changed my mind. You need to focus on these interviews."

Delilah, please put together a BEDPAN[115] for Samson."

"Yes, sir."

"Samson, once you have it, you need to learn his schedule. Study it."

We don't use BEDPANs that often, and I can't recall whether this Samson has even seen one before, but some of his team have, for certain. And, as with all the instructions I give Samson and Delilah, it's rarely the intention that they will do all the work themselves. They must delegate and manage. So, some of Delilah's team members will

---

115 Behavioral Description—Pattern Analysis

put the BEDPAN together, and then Samson's teams will study it and follow the PERPS.

"Delilah, prepare COMMS test, please."

Ten O-WE-COME sspaces spring to life showing all the interview rooms. I quickly arrange these into an overview showing all Oslo sessions together and the COP sessions together.

"Samson, how many guys do you have on-site?"

"Six of us in Oslo, five in COP. The last two from each team are rounding up the remaining candidates."

"Are you ready for testing out the COMMS?"

"All set, sir."

"Delilah, activate the CCOTCHA[116] and three-way-CCOTCHA.

"Done, sir."

Each member of the BITS-SECS and BITS-SITTER teams and I have a cranially implanted, mega-microscopic communication device Lord-IT and I designed with a trusted colleague and friend. Bio-Brains, as we call him, dealt with the biological and neurological design aspects. That science goes way beyond my abilities. He ensured that the device finds and connects to the brain and can send data directly to the brain.

Visual data goes from confuzer to the CCOTCHA's LICKEM; spoken messages send from both confuzer and CCOTCHA to the CCOTCHA.

When sending from a CCOTCHA, the CCOTCHA records what the sender says, then relays this electronically to the receiver's CCOTCHA. It's almost like a brain-to-brain walkie-talkie.

All messages and data go to groups of people by first addressing them using New Names such as *Delilah, Samson/AGENT 1, DEL_SAM, OSLO-COPS*, etc.

During such missions, Delilah connects all those involved into a joint CCOTCHA meeting. The BITS-SITTERs pair up with a BITS-SECS partner to assist with ideas and giving directions.

---

116 Covert Communication Transmission Channel, a brain-wired walkie-talkie-with-video

The three-way CCOTCHA channel is separate and extra, using a secure Bitsi-Lite communication channel, so that Samson, Delilah, and I can discuss out of the rest of the team's earshot. The names DEL_ SAM3/DS3, DEL3 and SAM3 are for the three-way-CCOTCHA. The O-WE-COME is for normal meeting mode, the CCOTCHA for private and secret communication.

Over the CCOTCHA, I give the command: "Interviewers: COMMs test." The BITS-SECS agents instantly appear in the interview rooms on my O-WE-COME sspaces. Each one of them acts out their favorite sound-test tom-foolery. They have done this often and find it a little boring, so they like to liven things up a little.

"Bitsi," I whisper as quietly as I can, and they all stop immediately.

Delilah flashes a message in front of our eyes. Samson and all ten BITS-SECS agents simultaneously stand on their left foot, put their right hand up in the air, and throw their heads back.

"Test successful," she says to the whole team while struggling not to laugh.

"Bitsi, sir, can we get started? We need to finish the first interviews before the guys return with the next lot." Samson is fretful about the tight planning.

"Sure."

"Interrogators, roll 'em in," he commands over the CCOTCHA. "Bitsi, sir," he continues, "we have to stage the sessions, giving more time for rounding up the remaining TEST-TICCLERs. Starting each interview with a one-minute delay after the previous interview should be enough."

"You keep pushing for an upgrade of those soup-ah-CHOPPAs[117] don't you, Samson?"

"The new model does go three-ninety-five per hour, forty-five faster, sir."

---

117   Nuke-Li-Aerially-powered (small) flying vehicle

Chuckling, I concede to his staging plan. "Send me a business case, Samson. For now, staggering by one minute is fine. But then let's get going."

"Yes, sir."

Samson's soup-ah-CHOPPAs are a cross between an ancient Harley and a modern soup-ah-sonic jet, except not soup-ah-sonic at all due to the relatively flimsy construction. The specs state that a ridiculous average of 2.5 people fit into the vehicle. The known maximum number of (small) occupants is three. Samson claims he fills his soup-ah-CHOPPA completely. He's an extremely big man.

"*DEL3*: Set the OOO-O-WE-COMEs to SOFT-PROWL and give me control, please."

"Yes, sir. Done, sir."

While the meeting rooms fill and we wait for the show to begin, I make the final arrangement of my screen-spaces, space-pads, and joystick so that I can easily switch between O-WE-COME, OOO-O-WE-COME, chat sessions, CCOTCHA and three-way-CCOTCHA, mega-spacey-screen, and the smaller, closer screens. I will follow the questioning in the background, only intervening if I see or hear anything irregular.

After digging up the old presentation Lord-IT called me about, I then search for all the supporting data, suspecting I already have enough information for producing the comparison he requested. I start paging through the old data, but something else is bothering me, disturbing my concentration. The interviews have started—I can hear them all running in parallel—but no, it's not that.

Sitting back, staring past the two huge screen-spaces showing the BIG-AM-I meeting rooms, letting my thoughts flow freely, I hunt down the intruder. Suddenly, the call with Mary-lin flashes into mind. I go over the dialogue, numerous times, repeatedly slowing down at the end.

"Do you think Marilyn really had HPD?" This is it; this part of the conversation is bothering me. But why?

HPD? Does it really bother her so much, BGB's unfounded accusations? Just a play on words, an unfortunate combination of names, or acronyms, and a paragraph of rubbish, questionable media text designed solely to concoct a story, to sell another cover.

It doesn't make sense, and I still can't place it, and I need some food—I'm famished.

Dropping a message to Delilah on the O-WE-COME, "Be right back," I head for the kitchen.

The kids are not up yet, so I can still safely wander through the house without interference. After quickly throwing together a sandwich, I rush back to the office.

As I reenter my office, the change is immediately obvious. A newly awakened screen-space is displaying a horrifying eleven missed calls. The number reminds me of one hundred and eleven, my specially reserved number for trouble. Call number twelve begins flashing at me like an unwelcome warning signal.

Lord-IT's chief of security, Jonesy[118], seems desperate to talk. My heart momentarily stops beating. Jonesy has not called me once in the eighty-eight years since his appointment, because there's no need, usually.

---

118   Combined job title and appointed name of Lord-IT's chief of security

12

Oh Lordy

Fear boils upwards like lava just under the surface ready to explode up and outwards, spewing panic over all those nearby. I have to get that under control. My first reaction is always to worry. Why is that?

Slamming on the space-pad with a hammer for a finger, I answer the call. "Jonesy? What's up?"

"The Lord-ITs, sir, they're taken. Two of my men are down. Dead. I've lost track of the Lord-ITs, sir. Their DIGIT-FONEs and CCOTCHAs are not working. I can't find their signal, sir." Jonesy sounds frantic and distressed.

"Hang on, Jonesy." Panic, now unstoppable, is grabbing hold of my every nerve.

I'm frantically smacking Seribus, trying to get Lordy's location. This should not be a difficult thing for me to do, damn it. The Beast constantly tracks his location. I only need to confirm I want to see it on the screen, a simple security measure, but, utterly slammed and bamboozled by this frightful change of events, I'm not responding well. What the bloody hell is happening?

The realization hits me that I'm in an O-WE-COME meeting with Samson and Delilah and the teams. My thoughts are diving down many possible tracks, my hands unsure which to follow.

A hand with a mind of its own switches the O-WE-COME into total blackout. For good measure, I mute all other forms of communication so no one can hear or see me from anywhere. The lower half of my office walls I change to a cloudy color so the kids can't see in, a built-in impulsive precaution since the kids were born.

Sitting at my desk, I'm struggling for breath. But I attempt to focus on Lordy's whereabouts. The Beast simply cannot find Lordy, which confirms Jonesy's story, so far. I activate a new soup-ah-secure CCOTCHA communication with Lord-IT's head bodyguard.

All communication using Bitsi-FREQs[119] is soup-ah-secure. No one else knows the true nature or number Bitsi-FREQs. But there are different levels of soup-ah-secure.

Bitsi-Lite frequencies and waves are innumerable, unquantifiable. They are almost the perfect tangible expression of Max-Infinity, except I haven't proven this, yet. The world is only vaguely aware of three different channels and some of their sub-channels, which may not sound like much, but said simply, this offers more than one million times the possibilities of all preceding satellite and WIFI technologies.

All the other innumerable frequencies, which I privately call Bitsi-FREQs, are just for me, and me only, to use. And use them I do. The CCOTCHAs established during a mission such as this are just one small example.

"Jonesy?"

"Yes, Bitsi, sir. What was that beep?"

"One beep, Jonesy, soup-ah-secure on, you and me only. Two beeps soup-ah-secure off, including anyone else we may have invited. Now, slowly but briefly, Jonesy, tell me what has happened."

"It was a Lord-ITs' night out, sir. Once every two months, you know. The Lord-ITs were returning to their car with the guards after leaving the restaurant. Suddenly, *all* the LICKEMs disappeared from the sspace. That's when I called you, sir.

"I pulled in Bitsi-Lite and scanned the area and all the cars I could in the surrounding streets, but I couldn't find them anywhere. Their car was still where they left it earlier in the evening. After a couple

---

119   Bitsi-Lite transmission frequencies

of minutes, my guard's DIGIT-FONE LICKEMs reappeared. I scanned that area for signs of the Lord-ITs and the guards. No sign of the Lord-ITs. Someone or something dumped my men in an alley a few blocks away. LASAROMIC weapons seem to have destroyed the CCOTCHA LICKEMs, sir. I have two guys going to pick up the bodies now. I have nothing else to go on, sir."

"How the hell did these guys get past your men, Jonesy?"

"I don't know, sir; we didn't see that." He sounds helpless.

"You weren't watching them on Bitsi-Lite?"

"No, sir. Lord-IT doesn't like us to follow them with Bitsi-Lite on their night out. He wants privacy."

"Give me a minute, Jonesy."

"Yes, sir."

My thoughts are full of useless rebuffs I'd like to throw in Lord-IT's face right now. *Damn it, Lordy. I told you so many times about your compromised security*, my mind screams at him. It's my main complaint and has been for many decades. But none of that is going to help now.

Pulling up a window into the Beast, I create a new HANDBAG and drag in the Lord-IT's LICKEMs—all of them. Then, I hit the FOOLEMALL command button and set an alarm to go off when they're found.

I still can hardly believe the LICKEMs are invisible from Bitsi-Lite's view as Jonesy's story would indicate. My fear is they're also completely destroyed. But I'm not ready to give up hope so fast.

Forcing myself to think things through rationally, I wonder why Lord-IT hasn't used his alarm, but I quickly decide that if he isn't dead, then he must be drugged or knocked out somehow.

All those decades ago, when Lordy and I introduced the Nuke-Li-Aerial and Bitsi-Lite technologies and confused all the authorities with all their monopoly and patent laws WOWI, we decided we were at some considerable risk. I worked with Bio-Brains to build the CCOTCHA, which we now use in all our security teams today. Lordy and I, however, also have numerous switches implanted into our bodies for sounding the alarm using the CCOTCHA. The switches are in different places so we can reach each of them from different physical positions.

The CCOTCHAs were also implanted in our wikids. The kids, however, do not yet know of the existence of this means of communication. The kids!

Using Bitsi-Lite, I check on the location of Lordy's children. They're at home, surrounded by Lord-IT's remaining bodyguards. They appear to be safe, thank goodness. To be sure, I pull up the Bitsi-Lite view of the house and, breaking all accepted protocol, take a good look around. Everything looks to be normal, except no parents and the missing guards.

Opening a special soup-ah-secure Lord-IT RED ALERT option on the DIRT-MAPP and clicking on a solitary button, the transporters wake up, immediately preparing to depart on a preprogrammed journey to Lord-IT's house.

"Jonesy?"

"Yes, sir?"

"We need to move the kids immediately. And the in-laws."

"Yes, sir."

"A necessary warning for you, Jonesy. Right now, I don't know who to trust, so don't make even a single mistake I could misinterpret. My own guys will be watching you, also. If I develop even the slightest inkling of a suspicion that you're dirty, I will instantaneously Nuke-Li-Aerially Bitsi-fry you in your seat from your toes up to your eyeballs. Am I making myself clear, Jonesy?" Of course, using my Bitsi-Tone.

"Clear, sir, totally understood, sir."

All those close to me know I couldn't even fry a fly, let alone a human being. So, the warning is a figure of speech, nevertheless, not to be taken lightly.

The transporters are now ready, so I give the command for them to leave. I could drive all of them from the Beast, if I had time, but I don't. The machines will automatically find their own way to Lord-IT's house.

Having them stashed away close to our homes is yet another security precaution Lordy and I set up decades ago.

"Three transporters, Jonesy, four minutes from now. The family and you are to go in the middle one. Do not bring any new guys on this mission. As usual, this will temporarily interrupt the whole team's communications. Is this all clear?"

The communication channels of anyone coming to visit us are always switched to secret Bitsi-FREQs and routed through the Beast so he can control all normal functions such as FONE and GPS to keep the location hidden.

"Yes, sir."

"Give me the list of those who will go with you."

Using their agent-numbers, he lists four guys for the rear vehicle, four more for the lead, and three for the middle transporter.

"No. Only you ride center, Jonesy." Bitsi-Tone, again.

Using the DIRT-MAPP, battering on Seribus as if I were slaughtering the rabid Beast, I quickly create a separate list of Lordy's security team members that will escort the kids. I have all their gadgets stored in my BITS. Hooking into all of them, I start recording all their activity, instructing the Beast to both FOOLEM and listen for suspect behavior. The Beast knows more Gibberish than all of us together and is a Bitsi-certified expert at this kind of surveillance. For good measure, I take the same precautions with the remainder of the team that will stay behind.

"I'll be recording you, Jonesy. Wait. You hear that? One of your guys is looking for you. Watch your mouth."

For Jonesy's benefit, I practice the soup-ah-secure switch so that he gets used to the beeping sound in his head. Even though he's almost a veteran, he has never had to do this before.

Two beeps. I listen while Jonesy refuses rest or sleep for his whole team, although many of them have probably been up all night. His guards just returned with their two deceased colleagues. Jonesy instructs them to lay them in the stable and deal with them later. He doesn't give anything else away.

One beep. "Well done. Now, you tell your team you're taking the grandparents and kids to a safe location. The kids only need to bring their PRIVATE-LYFEs[120], teddy bears, and maybe some sweets to help get them moving faster. The in-laws don't need to bring anything. Are you getting all this, Jonesy?"

"Yes, sir."

"Don't take any back-mouthing from the mother-in-law. Three minutes, Jonesy. Have those kids ready."

"Yes, sir." He'll not make it within three minutes, but I know he'll try.

Immediately I'm at a loss with no clue what to do next. I don't have the slightest idea what's going down here, and I have no information to go on. I can only assume that the Lord-ITs are in deep trouble, and given the merciless killing of their security guards, they're also likely in imminent, probably deadly danger.

My head drops into my hands, eyes closing, releasing a gush of frenzied and terrifying thoughts. No good. Something bordering on hysteria rises up inside me. I stand up, start pacing the office. No good. My thoughts are taking me into walking, waking nightmares.

I'm running out of breath again; the panic is taking over. Getting dizzy. Oh Lordy. My oldest, closest, trusted, and beloved friend is facing a potentially horrible death. And his wife's death is probably going to be worse.

Going down on both knees, I place my palms on the floor, head hanging limp. Forcing myself. Damn it, man. Get it together, man. This is not helping!

---

120   Personal tablet confuzer

Eventually managing to persuade my mind to force my body to behave, I begin working on my breathing, inhaling a few gasped breaths of office air. Then, slower and deeper. After a short while, self-control appears to be a possible option once more.

My mind runs off again, this time trying to solve the mystery of this unexpected shock. Solving problems is, after all, what I do.

I push myself to continue this track, to guess at a list of the possible related facts and motives:

- Lord-IT and wife, taken.

  - How much trouble are they in?

  - Why? Nuke-Li-Aerial power? But how? Everyone knows those secrets are the best-kept secrets on the planet. Even Lordy cannot and would not give them up for anything.

- LICKEMs disappearing from Bitsi-Lite view?

  - Impossible. What's causing this? Malfunctioning? That's too easy, too much to hope for.

- The call Lordy made to me earlier, was that related?

  - Maybe that's why he sounded stressed.

  - No, he would have found a way to drop a clue in somewhere.

- Timing coinciding with BIG-AM-I's FLAPPING of OBOY.

  - That's a long shot. One heck of a COMMINGS.

Nothing to go on. Nothing.

Only the timing of the OBOY problems and the kidnapping show any kind of vague, remote connection, but that's also crazy. I need to get back to sanity. I can't sit here alone with all these thoughts not going anywhere.

I set up a new soup-ah-secure CCOTCHA channel with Delilah. One beep. "Del?"

"Yes, sir?"

"What I'm going to share with you now must remain top secret. No sharing with the teams."

"Yes, sir."

"We have a serious problem, Del. Someone snatched the Lord-ITs. Taken. They also killed two of their security guards during the kidnapping. And I can't find the Lord-ITs. Bitsi-Lite can't see their LICKEMs."

"Oh, sir," she whispers in total shock. "How could this happen?"

"Not careful enough, Del. But the important thing now is to find them. And hopefully they'll be alive when we do."

"I think they will be, sir. Lord-IT is of no use to anyone dead. If they want anything from him, they'll need to keep him alive, sir." She tries to encourage me into hoping for the best.

"Yes, Del. Let's hope so. Here, I want you to help me keep an eye on this." And I pass a copy of the HANDBAG over to her. "I'm tracking the Lord-ITs' LICKEMS. As soon as they reappear, an alarm will go off. We need to be ready for that."

"Yes, Bitsi, sir. There's no other way we can start looking for them now, sir?"

On another sspace, I notice from the corner of my eye that the transporters have arrived, and everyone is entering them. Jonesy playfully starts to hustle kids and grandparents into the vehicles, urging but without stressing them. Apart from being great at his job, he's also a natural with the kids, and they adore him.

"Hang on, Del."

Once all three teams are aboard, I lock down the systems of all three vehicles, cut off all their communications, then establish a new soup-ah-secure CCOTCHA among the ten of us. The coordinates for each stage of this trip are already in the transporters.

On the sspace controlling the machines, I hit the START ROUTE button, and the transporters take off. The DIRT-MAPP will automatically FOOLEMALL throughout the journey.

Jonesy is looking a little perplexed. Usually, I let his guys operate these vehicles manually. It's like playing a confuzer game when you don't know where you're going and have to chase the map-planner as it updates en route.

"Sit back and relax, Jonesy. They're on auto-pilot this time. You help Granny entertain the kids.

"The rest of you guys, can you hear me OK?"

A round of, "Yes, Bitsi, sir," follows.

"Good. Then hear this." Bitsi-Tone. "Your mission, as ever, is to protect Lord-IT and his wikids. If any one of you disappoints me, then I'll personally terminate your mission on the spot. Am I making myself clear?"

Another round of "Yes, Bitsi, sir."

"Good. Stay alert."

Terminate can mean many things, of course.

One beep. I need to talk to Jonesy privately for a moment. "I'll be busy, Jonesy. You, also, stay alert. And warn me if you suspect anything out of place. Watch out for everything and everybody."

"Yes, sir. Er, Bitsi, sir, will you be in touch as soon as you know more?"

"I definitely will. Jonesy, you don't have anything else for me? Nothing recorded? No more info I can use to try to find them?"

"I am afraid not, sir. I'm really sorry, sir."

"All right, Jonesy."

"Delilah?"

"Yes, sir?"

"No. Absolutely nothing to go on. They've simply disappeared. Hang on, Del."

I want Samson to get to the Lord-ITs as soon as I know where to send him. So, after preparing his soup-ah-sonic jet for him and preparing myself to upload his next flight plan once it's ready, I also ensure that his soup-ah-CHOPPA is preprogrammed to reach the new location of his jet unaided so that he can focus, even on the short journey to the plane.

Yet another dimension of paranoiac preparation Lordy and I introduced, which is possibly a little overkill, is three Nuke-Li-Aerially-powered soup-ah-sonic planes ready for action close to my home and three close to his home, in case of extreme crisis. There are also two planes in each of the seven locations where the BITS-SECS teams are in case we need a larger presence in other spots on the globe.

We almost never use our jets, but Samson uses his jet all the time. The rendezvous with his CHOPPA will take roughly nine minutes once Samson leaves the BIG-AM-I BITS building. I can't bring the plane closer to the city without causing all kinds of other problems.

Again, my head sinks into my open hands, my elbows resting on the desk. Oh, Lordy. What have they done to you? What are they planning for you? My mind wanders off again, zooming through many possible nasty scenarios, any one of which could be playing out right now, or very soon.

My head sinks a little deeper. And people wonder why I don't follow the news, the current affairs of the world. I cannot constantly, day in day out, face the suffering we all inflict on each other. For thousands of years, we have abused each other, killed each other. We find millions of reasons to justify hurting another human being. From the smallest harms to the largest offensive actions, we strive to prove we're right, to prove our good reason for inflicting pain, while someone else is standing hurt or lying dead before us. Every time I see some news, I relate it to myself, my family, my loved ones, my friends: What if it were them, or worse, us?

Now, suddenly, it is us. Lordy and his wikids are a part of our big family, a part of us. Come on, Bisi. Get it together, man!

13

The WHHEEL

"Delilah?"

"Yes, sir?"

"I have no clue what's going down here, Del. So, we'll need to be ready for anything."

"Is this going to be another save-the-world-from-its-own-inhabitants mission, sir?" she asks, not sure if she should sound sarcastic or horror-stricken.

"I can't be sure yet, Del," I expel a disturbed breath loudly, "but my gut tells me it could well be yes."

"What about the BIG-AM-I FLAPPING, sir? Do we continue with that?"

"For now, we multi-task, Del. Until we know what's going on with Lord-IT, we don't have much else we can do. And this BIG-AM-I MAGIC TRICC is the only remote connection to the kidnapping. Just the timing. Maybe, just maybe, they're connected. So just be aware of that—in the background."

"Bitsi, sir?"

"Yes, Delilah?"

"You've been doing this for more than eighty years. Aren't you tired of it all?" She has assumed my gut is on the right track. "Bitsi, sir?"

"What tires me, Delilah, is that we don't seem to be getting far enough fast enough."

"Sir?"

"We all know the concept of right and wrong, the struggle of good versus evil. But do we know where it's going? Is good winning over bad, or does evil have the upper hand?"

"Isn't that hard to calculate, sir?"

"And that, Del, is my point. If we were getting anywhere, if good were clearly coming out on top, then a best guess would suffice. But bad hides from us until it's ready to pounce. We either don't see it or often not until it's too late, or almost too late. Too many past bad deeds already counted, no visibility of the coming evils lurking in the dark—that adds up to a potentially massive negative number, Delilah."

"So, we need to uncover the bad earlier, sir?"

I heave a big sigh. "We need to work out how to address the source of the evil. To bring an end to reasons behind the bad."

"Like, get everyone to believe in God, sir?"

I heave an even bigger sigh. "Not necessarily, Delilah. Over the ages, religion has also been used to justify innumerable horrific crimes against humankind. No. One surely does not need to believe in God to know that hurting, stealing, raping, mutilating, killing are not good. Over thousands of years, people have committed heinous crimes against each other."

"But that's a lot less these days, isn't it, sir?"

"Now we're back to the calculation, Delilah, with the hidden nasty factors."

"Hmmm," she muses.

"A good number of the Earth's population is pushing for positive causes, helping the rest of humankind, striving to make this world a better place to be a healthier, happier haven to bear and bring up our children. They strive despite sometimes risk to themselves and even their loved ones. Many others who would join them are being held in check by fear of pain and suffering brought about by their oppressors.

"But there are still way too many on the side of evil, from all walks of life, Delilah, the man or woman on the street, the drug-lords, the BBBs in business and in politics, and in leaders of nations."

"This is what your Bitsi-Theory is about, isn't it, sir?"

"Humph. Kind of. But this, I call this simply the WHHEEL, Delilah. It highlights some of the basic negative aspects of humankind in this world.

"It's an extremely cruel and dangerous wheel. A vicious circle in which so many are stuck, simply learning again and again how to hurt others, cause agony and affliction— similar to what we can read about in history books, and unfortunately in the news today.

"And these missions we get dragged into, Delilah, they're just against some of the worst of those stuck in the

WHHEEL. There are many other problems, many other missions we don't get involved in. Yet despite our missions, our efforts, the missions and efforts of so many others, the WHHEEL just keeps on turning, Del."

"So, what's the solution, sir?"

"If only I knew, Del, if only I knew that...

Now, let's get back to it."

"Yes, sir."

14

TRIPSI Bitsi

A SNICKERING FROM ONE of Delilah's girls brings my attention to one of the interviews. Oblivious of the new crisis situation, a BITS-SECS team member is having a great time in Copenhagen.

"Who else apart from you is aware that you only executed a measly sixty-five percent of your system test cases?" demands the BITS-SECS agent.

"Er, er, anyone who reads the test report?" he suggests. "Everyone knows the release of OBOY was months late, over budget, and the testing plan was cut almost in half. The project manager knows; he said my percentage was good compared with other TEST-TICCLERs."

"Totally irresponsible. You don't report this to anyone?"

"Er, my project manager?"

"You leave it to a project manager to honestly report the status? You must know they're only interested in showing that they completed on time and on budget, whether that was true or not? You surely know they're worse than lawyers?"

"Er..."

"Do you have any clue if there are any life-critical functions in those thirty-five percent you failed to test?"

"Er..."

"Well?"

"Er, isn't OBOY just a fancy shopping arcade? Do we do life-critical stuff?"

"What about The Fruit of Life? And your lead TEST-TICCLER, why didn't he pitch in?"

"He never tests anything. All he does is scream at us all day long."

"Oh? What about these test cases?" the BITS-SECS agent yells, spreading his PRIVATE-LYFE out on the table in front of the PERPS.

"Well I guess wonders do still exist. That should go down in history," exclaims the TEST-TICCLER, who is refusing to get stressed out about anything during this whole interview process.

And that was, effectively, the end of the interview. I guess that most sessions will conclude in a similar fashion. But just one different ending could be enough. We need to push on.

"Thank you for your cooperation, sir. Let me give you this as a token of our appreciation."

The BITS-SECS agent wraps up by grabbing the tester's arm, pulling out an ugly-looking pistol and firing a tracking implant into the flesh of his biceps. The injection is totally painless, and the PERPS does nothing but wince at the thought. Which thought? No one knows.

"You are now marked. For the duration of the investigation of this MAD MAGIC FLAPPING OBOY, should you even breathe out of line, you'll be snapped up and hauled in again. If you ever want this device removed, you need BITS-SECS approval. Understood?"

Everyone dragged into this investigation will be marked similarly. It can help in locating the fastest road to finding the TRUTHH. As the BITS-SECS teams continue the interviews, I return to the impossible task of deciding what I should do next.

Realizing it won't be long before Lord-IT's kids arrive here, I break all our rules and open a CCOTCHA channel with my wife. She hates me beeping at her. One beep. That will already wake her. She has slept lightly ever since the kids were born.

"Honey, I need you to come to the office. Now, please."

"Uh. OK," she responds sleepily, but more alert than she should be. I never beep her. She can already feel the tension.

I go to the coffee machine while waiting for her, but she arrives before the coffee is made.

"What's wrong?" she asks, getting straight to the point as usual.

"It's not good, hon. Someone kidnapped Lord-IT and Rebecca. I have no clue where they are. We're looking, but they've disappeared."

"I didn't think that was possible. I thought you could see everyone and everything?" I can see her frenzied thoughts darting in all directions.

"Me, too. But apparently something can block Bitsi-Lite."

Her head drops, and I can almost see her brain processing the possible consequences of this horrific news. Looking up at me, she has a hesitant yet fully loaded and gloomy question spread across her face.

Trying to put her mind at rest, I tell her, "There's nothing leading me to think we're in danger, honey. But it's Father's Day, after all. A good excuse maybe to keep the kids at home."

"I don't need any excuses," she blurts out, in a manner far from her usual behavior. "I'm their mother, and I'll keep them home whenever I want to." She is not at all happy.

"Just to be sure, I'm turning on maximum security. So, if you go out later, don't let the kids walk in the garden forest or go too near the fences or gates. Like I said, I don't think we have anything to worry about here. But I don't want the kids getting hurt by accident or the alarms going off because the kids are all over the place."

"Can't you arrange for rain, honey? That might help keep them under control." She is always fast composing herself—she hates to lose it—and already she's perking up a little, trying to be strong by fooling around.

But my chin simply droops to my chest. "This is no time for jokes, honey."

"I know, I know. I'm sorry." Wrapping her arms around me, she bravely tries to comfort me under circumstances that are more frightening than almost everything we've endured together so far. I hold on to her tightly, burying my head in the warmth of her embrace as if I have just found the miraculous great escape from the reality awaiting me should I ever let go of her.

"Do you have any clue? Is this going to work out? Are they going to be all right?"

Reluctantly releasing my grip, I do my utmost to answer her rather desperate and impossible questions.

"They must be in danger. So, I really can't say. But of course I'll do everything in my power to make sure they come through this." Now I'm the one trying to be strong. And sounding like a bloody politician.

"Lordy will know that, honey, I'm sure. Please let me know what's happening when you can."

"Of course. Anything important, I'll let you know. I arranged for the kids and Rebecca's parents to come here. I need you to receive them when they arrive."

"Of course, hon. Soon, I guess?"

"Yes."

"OK, I'll be ready. Now, I need to get to the kids." She kisses me and is off to hug and protect her babies.

My heart follows her every step, and I imagine many of the thoughts rushing through that incredible mind that suffers from worry similar to the way I do and yet is so pragmatic and so down-to-earth realistic that she can take every problem in her stride, making the solution appear to be easy. I wish I could go with her, to be with her and with our kids.

Slowly but surely, I drag my attention to the BIG-AM-I interviews. They are forty-eight minutes into the questioning, and I can see an Oslo interviewee is sitting on the wrong end of a wasp nest. Samson seems to have noticed also; he has moved into the meeting room.

As I switch the OOO-O-WE-COME mode to INTIMI, the floating head-shaped screen starts to slither through the air like the head of a hungry snake focused on a juicy TEST-TICCLER.

Samson takes over the interview. "You only completed forty-seven percent of your test cases; the average was sixty-two. What the hell were you playing at?"

"Er, I'm a trainee, sir?"

"Your lead TEST-TICCLER took some TEST-TICCLES off you? Why?"

"What?"

"Some test cases, he took them off you. Why?"

Samson is enjoying himself. He responds to me like a kitten to a bowl of tuna, but most other people can irritate him just by breathing too loudly, so he compensates by teasing, to maintain his good humor.

"*DEL3:* Are those the eight cases the lead-T tested?" I ask her.

"Yup. And they're all CASH COW test cases, sir."

"Find out if this PERPS executed the test cases. Then get all records of the lead-T's testing of this stuff. Every last detail. Even if he picked his nose while on the job."

"Yes, sir."

All the data Delilah pulls up during these investigations is stored, logged, and indexed for further analysis. Much of it is never used, but we keep it, just in case.

"Er," continues the PERPS, "he told me my performance was poor but understood I was just a trainee. He said he was going to help me this once, by reducing my workload to increase my percentage completed. That's the whole story."

The OOO-O-WE-COME swings down at lightning speed and stops roughly fifty point five centimeters in front of his face, my eyes staring straight into his. The TEST-TICCLER takes a deep, gasping breath as he stares into the mask streaming from my webcam. For effect, my pupils are burning a fiery red, which is gently bantering with the blue of the irises.

"TIPSI Bitsi," he half whispers my street name, or one of the unacceptable versions of it.

Immediately a harsher, hotter, more fiery gaze flares up from my face behind the OOO-O-WE-COME, the flames reaching out from the screen toward the PERPS.

"Er, TRIPSI Bitsi[121]. TRIPSI Bitsi," he mutters a little louder, correcting himself. Then, he retches. All over Samson's shoes.

Of course. A newbie. And *someone* has forgotten the puke bucket.

Samson was not prepared and is now angrily unimpressed, emitting a fire of his own making.

"*SAM3:* Samson, cool down. Go and clean up. Get back here fast."

Shortly after our release of Nuke-Li-Aerial power, confuzers, and Bitsi-Lite, I found myself caught in an embarrassing situation during a mission-critical, war-room crisis WOWI. I had to analyze sixteen hundred A3 pages of data over a publicly visible O-WE-COME meeting screen-space with five hundred people gawking on.

After staring through eleven hundred pages in just over five minutes, I had seen enough, drew my conclusion, and pointed the finger directly at the PERPS who was threatening disaster WOWI. The PERPS ran, of course, was caught, of course, locked up forever, and the world was saved.

Following that incident, the meeting participants created a Let's-Face-It group forum to discuss *what the Bitsi-blazes just happened?* Five hundred people avidly debated their opinions.

The longest lasting outcome of the discussion was my street name, TRIPSI Bitsi, based on a consensus that I could process data at the speed of Trillions of (machine) Instructions Per Second. How many trillions no one ever dared to guess. The I at the end of TRIPSI gave the name a little rhyming swing. Ridiculous, but I'm having a little trouble shaking it off.

I slowly move the OOO-O-WE-COME twenty centimeters closer to the PERPS while constantly staring the guy down.

"*You're lying,*" I challenge him with my Bitsi-Tone.

---

121 A rather ridiculous nickname for the BITS Inspector, nevertheless one he has trouble shaking off

Hummm. His reaction is not quite what I hoped for. In disgust, the BITS-SECS team member, who is again temporarily leading the interview, has jumped well away from the table. I instruct him to escort the PERPS to the washroom so he also can clean up. This latest excretion was not from the mouth.

"And be fast about it," I yell after them.

"*DEL_SAM3:* Samson, the lead-T, what is his exact location?"

"B1-2, first floor, left out the elevator, go twenty meters then turn..."

"B1-2, 1-F-1," cuts in Delilah.

Chuckling at them both, I pull the DIRT-MAPP to the O-WE-COME, zoom in on the lead-TEST-TICCLER, and study his actions for a minute or so. He appears passive enough right now, but I keep the video open, just in case.

"Has anyone been watching him, Samson?"

"Yes, one of Del's girls."

"Delilah to you, Sonny-SAM," she pipes in.

"Del, anything on him so far?"

"I would have alerted you, Bitsi, sir," she retorts.

As the trainee TEST-TICCLER finally comes back in the interview room and sits down, my glare compels him to look me in the eye once again.

"So, now tell me what really happened," I command in my Bitsi-Tone.

"Uh, we argued for a long time. I told him that if he takes eight test cases from me, ones that I have actually executed, this would lower both my target and actual productivity numbers. That would give me a bad scoring at the end of the year, sinking my chance of promotion. He told me he was watching me test the system, that I had done it wrong, and that I should have failed those tests. I told him they were very simple test cases. He got terribly upset and screamed at me, saying the tests' design was poor."

"Hummm, the lead-T reviewed and signed off on those test case designs himself," chips in Delilah.

The PERPS continues, "I told him I didn't design them. But he just screamed even louder, saying that a real TEST-TICCLER would have seen that some steps were missing in the design. Then he calmed down, repeated that I had messed up, that the cases needed retesting, and he would do that. Then, he said he'd help me out, but if I ever told anyone, he would make sure I lost my job. He said he'd do a general reshuffling of some of the test plans, giving me eight test cases from someone else, and that he would personally mark some of my other tests as passed even though I didn't work on them."

"I can see those newly added test cases here, and the false test ratings," Delilah again.

"Stop the interviews, Samson. Get the lead-T up here immediately."

"What about this PERPS?"

"Keep him, we might need to show him off."

"OK, I'm on it."

Why those test cases? I ask myself. The few purchases I did earlier included the pages covered in the test cases; they didn't show any difference from the good-old payment pages I've used many times before when shopping. The new overpowering marketing page, offering credit instead of CASH, was presented much earlier. "Del, show me the data for those eight tests the lead-T carried out."

I enlarge the O-WE-COME sspace so I can view all the data. Within milliseconds, I see that two tests were carried out at five and four minutes to midnight, then two more at four and five minutes after midnight. Two of the tests were with the lead-T's own TWIT-OVA-USER; the other two were random TWITS, obviously for testing purposes. All four tests were recorded using the TEST-TICCLER-TOOLS.

Selecting the payments, I ask, "Del, you see these timings?"

"Yup."

"You need to find out what happened on the system *between* the 56 and the 04 time period. Look especially for the pages in those eight test cases."

"OK."

The Beast starts beeping at me, and on the sspace tracking the Lord-ITs' kids' journey, I see they've arrived at the cottage. It's a large and secluded but comfortable country house used for the temporary residence of various security teams when escorting anyone visiting us. A middle-aged couple, who maintain the house and gardens and live in an apartment at one end of the building, receive and care for the guests.

Jonesy steps out of his transporter, and the door closes and locks immediately.

"I'll take it from here, Jonesy. Please have your team disembark."

"Yes, sir."

One beep. "Jonesy, one of your guys in the rear vehicle has left his DIGIT-FONE on the seat."

"Flaming idiot," he exclaims and encourages his man to correct the error immediately.

"Keep an eye on him, Jonesy."

"Yes, sir," he said, fully understanding my concern.

Once the security team is out and standing on solid ground, the three transporters rise up in the air and begin flying around, faster and faster in a perfect circle. The kids really love this part.

The line formed by the path of their circular flight becomes a solid, solitary ring in the air; not a single aircraft is visible. Suddenly, all three transporters fly high into air, in different directions at first, but then rapidly spiraling back toward each other, crossing each other, then back again to join up in a straight line, only to rocket off in three separate directions.

The chance of anyone knowing which transporter the Lord-IT's kids are in at the end of that little Nuke-Li-Aerial show is zero.

Samson and the lead-T are now in the meeting room adjacent to the trainee. I direct the OOO-O-WE-COME at the PERPS, switching it to scavenger mode, and it starts to slowly circle him, sometimes moving a little closer, then backing off.

"Build up slowly, Samson, I want to know how many lies he's prepared to tell, how important it is to keep his dirty secrets. Get started."

15

ITSY-BITSI SPIDER

SAMSON NOTICES THE lead-T focusing closely on his humungous pet spider, which pleases him immensely, because that's generally the idea. I can barely see the hidden smile on Samson's face.

All BITS-SECS team members seem to have this weird humor. I'm never sure whether it's the job that makes them this way or if we give them the job because they are this way. The previous Samson (No. 2) used to intimidate by wearing lots of big guns obviously on show, and when the time came to force the truth out of someone, he would pull out a huge sawed-off dart gun and slap it on the table, accidently firing off a shot into the PERPS as he did so.

Itsy-Bitsi spider used to be a cobra, but Samson ditched the snake shortly after he heard me singing the song to my kids while I was in an O-WE-COME meeting with him.

"Don't worry about Itsy. He's completely tame; he even listens to commands," Samson consoles the PERPS.

"I hope so," retorts the TEST-TICCLER, pathetically trying to sound brave.

During the interview, the spider will wander back and forth across Samson's broad shoulders, sometimes dozing much like a passenger in a train. You can even see the spider's body jerking as it suddenly startles after having drooped too low toward sleep.

"Listen, sorry to drag you out of bed so early..."

And so the interview commences. Samson will deal with most of it. I will listen with the volume up just loud enough to make sure I don't miss anything.

For a short while, once again I sit back and stare through the nightmare illusion of the MAGIC OBOY. Then, opening the CHABLIS, I settle down to uncover the risky changes made in this latest release of OBOY. After quickly going over the main Wandering CASH problem area, I take a step back to look at the bigger picture. Noticing a massive number of data store changes, I look closer and see that many of them were to support the new credit arrangement.

"*DEL_SAM3:* Delilah, please look into all data store changes for this release. Check also the test lab."

"Samson, question the PERPS about how they tested so many database changes. Twenty new tables and seventy-nine table alterations, so much new test data?"

After just a few moments, Del and I listen closely to how Samson deftly includes the new angle into his interrogation. "I guess there were a lot of data changes needed for this fancy, new Go-Live OBOY, huh? How many?"

"I'm not sure; I heard quite a few."

"You're the lead TEST-TICCLER, and you don't what you're testing?" yells Samson.

"Well, I think there were maybe ten to fifteen new tables."

I flick the OOO-O-WE-COME into PREPARE-FOR-ATACK mode. It swings around, drawing up for a head-on confrontation.

Diving into his good cop, bad cop routine, Samson throws up the palm of his hand in the direction of the OOO-O-WE-COME and gently glares eye-to-eye at the lead-T, like a contented lion consoling soon-to-be-dead meat.

"I'm the nice guy here. You don't want *him* coming down on you. So, quickly, try again."

"Hmmm. Let me think." This guy is one cool-headed customer. "Oh, it's coming back now I think on it. Yes, twenty new tables, and almost eighty table changes."

"That must have been complex, simulating all the data needed to test for a full-blown Go-Live?" prompts Samson.

"Oh, it was. But thanks to my suggestion of taking a copy of all production data stores, we reduced the effort by fifty-eight percent. We actually..."

"Samson," I blurt out, "ask him how he secured that data."

"*DEL3:* Delilah," I yell, "I need to know now; how many copies of that data were kept in the test lab; then, check outside the lab."

Absolutely no one responds to my demands, so I assume no news is good news.

The lead-T is still showing off about his test strategy. Samson appears to be listening, buying time, thinking, I guess.

Delilah finally comes back with her findings on the copied data. "Bitsi, so far we've found four copies of the main production data stores in the lab. One for testing the new release, one more for testing data migration from old to new system; another appears to be a backup. The last copy is a live replica from production."

"More bloody inbreeds," I groan, the thought slipping out almost by accident.

"What?" she asks.

"Dupli-mation, Delilah, more dupli-mation."

"OK, OK. Quit the yakking," growls Samson.

"You actually took a copy of production data and dumped it into the test lab? That data is supposed to be highly secured."

"It's not like we sold it on the wwoopsi-net. The test lab is internal to BIG-AM-I."

"Like *that*'s making me feel better. *How* did you secure the data?"

"We obfuscated it, of course. At least the one for system testing. For data migration, that complicated things too much, so we kept it as it was."

"And the backup copy?" Del has just prompted Samson with that one.

"What about it? It's a backup. You never change a backup."

"So, no other copies? That's it?" Samson pretends this is the last data store question.

"Yup."

"What about this live replica? What is that good for?"

"Oh yeah, I forgot about that. It made life easier, cheaper to keep the data up-to-date for the ongoing migration process."

"Who has access to that live replica?"

"Only the SADCASEs[122]."

"What's this, then?" screams Samson, splaying his PRIVATE-LYFE open for all to see.

"We got in with password Start123."

"Hmmm. That password really should not have been used. But still, I don't see the problem. Everything inside the BIG-AM-I network is by nature secure."

"*SAM3:* Samson, over to you for now. Question him on the test cases he executed. See what you can dig up. Keep him busy."

"*DEL3:* Delilah, have you started a full personal check on this guy?"

"Yup. A while back. I don't like his attitude; it stinks. Should be ready in few minutes, I guess."

"Good. Now, please get me a list of all the SADCASEs that worked this new release. I want to know who arranged and who approved this nightmare dupli-mation."

"On it," she declares.

Sitting back in my chair, I stare out into space, drifting through this latest news, seeing databases floating all around, people crawling

---

122 Database administrator

out of them, stuffed with data as if they had just enjoyed an expensive five-course meal. I see the lead-T, the trainee, and even Marilyn floats by, along with many other nameless scavengers all devouring the confidential data of the third largest organization WOWI. If this were to go public, then the BIG-AM-I BITS management and its security team would be dancing on hot coals for long enough to make them feel they had died and missed the boat to the gates of glory.

The lead-T knew about these copies. Why did he withhold the information? Why was he stalling?

Suddenly, Delilah's voice pulls me abruptly out of my deliberations.

"Bitsi, sir, those payments test cases were executed twenty-one times between 56 and 04, using a combination of different test-TWITS and the lead-T's TWIT-OVA-USER. None were recorded. Sixteen of the tests were carried out in the minutes 00 and 01.

"Hmm..."

"Bitsi, sir?"

"Thinking..."

My mind is buzzing busier than a soup-ah-nova BITS-cruncher pushing up MAVACAPA. There are some extremely disturbing findings coming out of these TEST-TICCLER interviews.

- A trainee was assigned the Payments Pages tests. A mistake?

- Lead-TEST-TICCLER covers up taking the test cases from the trainee.

- Numerous copies of confidential data placed in an unsafe environment. Has data been stolen from there?

- Lead-TEST-TICCLER avoids offering what he knows about these copies.

- Lead-TEST-TICCLER testing in the middle of the night, more exactly at midnight, and the tests are not recorded.

A beeper starts bellowing from an alarm showing on one of the now many open screen-spaces. Fifteen minutes until D-day. Soon, all teeth will be brushed, all faces powdered, and all will be ready to begin purchasing BIG-AM-I's products and services en masse WOWI. The question is, how long before the CASH starts disappearing again?

"Samson. Time to shortcut this dude's wires. The world is on the verge of dumping billions of DOLLIES down a nonstop flushing toilet with a black hole for a sewer. We will need all hands on deck."

"Sure thing, boss," Samson lets slip a sly smile while punching his PRIVATE-LYFE with a thick index finger. This is a moment he has waited for.

Itsy-Bitsi immediately wakes up, yawns, stands up on his back legs and stretches—first up, then to the left, then to the right. Samson has his foot up on a chair, so Itsy, on seeing this, does a neat double-front flip down onto Samson's upraised knee, then a somersault to the floor. He runs straight under the table and up the lead-T's leg, then stands up on his back legs again, as if hoping to have his belly stroked.

The PERPS freezes like a rock buried under a glacier.

"Awww, he likes you," Samson exclaims.

"Itsy, wave to the TEST-TICCLER." And the spider indeed waves with one front leg.

"Itsy, you can do better than that." And Itsy waggles the six free legs he has available.

"Now, Itsy, do that standing on one leg." The PERPS is actually starting to smile.

Itsy attempts to stand on one leg and wave with the other seven, but almost immediately he starts falling and lands with a bang on all eights, his head and fangs slamming into the lead-TEST-TICCLER's thigh, who suddenly goes back to playing rock again.

The teeth contain minuscule, extremely sharp needles that administer a mild but highly effective truth serum which, on entering the blood, takes the fastest route to the brain and renders the victim incapable of lying. The injection is totally pain-free and goes completely unnoticed. The shock of having the head and fangs of a gigantic spider hammer into your leg is far more damaging for one's health.

It takes up to one minute for the dope to do its stuff. Killing time, Samson makes a little show of consoling Itsy for having fallen over, comforting him as one would a small child, playing little games with him. On seeing the signs that the PERPS is ready to be more accommodating, Samson lifts Itsy, gently and lovingly, back onto his shoulder and continues the interview.

"Now, tell us why you took these eight test cases from the trainee."

"Someone called me, someone from the management team," he said. "Called from an internal BIG-AM-I number, so I assumed it was OK. He threatened me with being fired because the team wasn't performing. But if I were prepared to do something for him, then he would do something for me. He told me that if I tested those eight test cases for ten nights leading up to the final release build, every night at midnight and for two minutes, then he would leave it up to someone else to assess the team's performance and that I would receive a special bonus after the last testing was complete. He offered me forty thousand CASH, paid to my DIGIT-FONE, just for a few nights' testing."

Forty thousand is equal to a year's pay for this TEST-TICCLER. Whoever made this offer knew what he was doing, how to pitch the correct buying price.

"Who called you?"

"No idea. The last seven digits of the FONE number were masked with an asterisk."

"How did you report the test results?"

"I took screen-shots and sent them to a special number, different every time. And he called me every night, after I tested—just wanted to know if I'd seen anything strange. I didn't, see anything strange, I mean."

"What about the TWITs you used for testing?"

"He messaged me those by FONE. Said some were new, virgin TWITS he called them, some already existing. He said I might see some difference in the behavior but nothing out of the ordinary. He told me to start the testing using the virgin TWITS at midnight, then switch to using my own TWIT-OVA-USER."

"Why those test cases?"

"No clue."

"Why midnight? And why for two minutes?"

"Absolutely no idea."

"What about this data store dupli-mation?"

"I suggested the copies to create test data more easily. We should have secured them better, I know, but other people overruled me. I was never comfortable with that. But I know almost nothing about the live replica, only what I've heard. I've never used it myself."

"Who set up the live replica?"

"The Main SADCASE working on the release."

"*DS3:* Delilah, do you have this guy's personal records? Can you see these FONE calls? Anything on them? Can you check if he received the 40K? Those testing TWITs, can you get those?"

"Yes, yes, no, yes, and yes if you give me access to his FONE and if he hasn't deleted the TWITS."

Quickly, I find the TEST-TICCLER's FONE in the DIRT-MAPP, set up Delilah's access, then slide the FONE to her over the O-WE-COME chat.

"Done. Now, do you know who the main SADCASE is?"

"Yes, we have all the data on the SADCASEs who worked this release of OBOY. I am weemailing you the testing TWITS now."

"Wrap it up, Samson. We need to prepare for the next round. We can always get this guy in again, if necessary."

Samson quickly ends the interview. The lead TEST-TICCLER is marked with the tracking device and given the usual warning, this time Samson-style.

"If you even so much as glance at the wrong woman, answer a FONE call from a suspicious party, or fart when I'm in your vicinity, then you'll be snapped up, clapped up, and trapped up. *Understood*?" Then, Samson sends him packing. Taking Itsy-Bitsi in his hands, Samson switches it off and packs it back into its padded box where it will charge up ready for the next show.

"Delilah, Samson, report when you're ready to take the next round. This one will probably go for twenty hours, give or take a few. So, take a break first." They will be silent partners in this next session, listening to pick up hints and direction on who or what to chase down next.

A few moments pass while I just sit and stare at the Beast as he tries to locate the Lord-ITs' LICKEMs, willing him to find them. But wishing is not enough, it seems.

16

System Down, MAD-ONNA! System Down!

Unable to do much else for Lordy and his wife right now, since I'm totally in the dark about their whereabouts, I switch my focus back to the OBOY MAD FLAPPING. If I'm not mistaken, the problems OBOY will start up again in the coming half hour or so. I want everyone to be ready.

BIG-AM-I's GLOBHED responds after the second beep from my call, and I politely announce myself. "This is the BITS Inspector. Do you have a GLOBCHAT and call open for this FLAPPING MAD-ONNA MAGIC COMMINGS OBOY?"

"Connecting you now, sir." They were expecting my call I can hear.

"This is Bitsi. Who *was* leading this GLOBCHAT?"

"That would be me, José Rules, Bitsi, sir," the L'ARCH responds. "I hope you had your CLIMACCSSS on time?"

"Yes, thank you. Perfect timing. Now, I'm taking over. In a few minutes, you can get some sleep, J-Rules. But first prepare a *brief* summary of the progress since I left the GLOBCHAT."

"GLOBHED, please turn this GLOBCHAT into an O-WE-COME right now."

Normally, during a GLOBCHAT only a few people are on the FONE; the rest all type into a shared chat window. This is gentler on the ears and easier to manage. But I want them all available, on chat, on FONE, and on video, hence the O-WE-COME. I always like to see who I'm pissing off. It's more fun that way.

"But Bitchy, sir..."

"Don't call me Bitchy. And don't answer me back. O-WE-COME. *Now!*" Bitsi-Tone.

"Yes, sir."

Even for a GLOBHED agent, it's child's play to change a GLOBCHAT into an O-WE-COME, and the invitation arrives almost immediately. I add DEL_SAM as hidden partners for when they're ready, and it takes a minute or two before everyone else joins.

The transporter with the Lord-ITs' family arrives, and while waiting, I watch as my wife breaks all the rules and goes out to meet them and help them down from the vehicle. I watch until they're all safely back inside the house, and my wife is leading them up to the guests' bedroom area.

On a separate O-WE-COME sspace, I see a message arrive: "Samson and Delilah ready to go and listening in." Samson has made himself comfortable in one of the five interrogation chambers on the ninth floor of BIG-AM-I-B1-1.

"Good," I type, "then, here we go."

"L'ARCH, status please."

"No progress whatsoever, Bitsi, sir." The chief architect sounds thoroughly exhausted, rock-bottom depressed, possibly even wishing that The Fruit of Life was never invented, or that he had never allowed himself to be conned into drinking the god-forsaken brew.

"That's it?"

"Yup."

"Well, that *was* a brief summary. Well done. Who's your backup?"

"He's on his way home from a Disney World soup-ah-special vacation in the Bahamas that you just cancelled. He will arrive in roughly four hours from now."

"Hmmm. Well, that just about kills any chance of sleep you have right now. You can get some rest when he takes over. Is the necessary monitoring of the system in place?"

"Yes, it is."

"Good. Then sit back, close your eyes, and relax until further notice."

For all those listening, I then lay down a few simple rules to ensure that the O-WE-COME meeting doesn't get too rowdy. Then it's time to just wait for trouble to come knocking on the door. "Now, I'm going on mute. Please throw the OBOY monitoring system onto the O-WE-COME display so we can all see what's happening. Scream if the proverbial hits the fan."

"What?"

"If there are problems, scream." I smack the mute button a little too hard.

"Delilah, cross-check. The lead TEST-TICCLER?"

"Nothing new, Bitsi, sir. Samson and I are FOOLING-HIM. We are constantly in his BEDPAN, comparing his usual behavior to his current antics. This is a terrible job, sir. Is there no way we can automate it?"

"Business case, Del, show me the business case. The NETNERD, Delilah, is the data in yet?"

"Yes, sir. The ex-lead NETNERD was BIG-AM-I's most experienced network technician. He worked on all the major releases of OBOY over the past seventy-five years. Surprisingly, he left the company two months ago, sir. And we still have questions about some of his transactions, sir. He has been into..."

"OK, Del. We'll come back to that soon. Keep at it."

Nothing about this NETNERD will surprise me. His and the ANALPRIDC's name are on my blacklist, on my mind, with each minute that passes appearing in darker, bolder, larger print as my suspicions are confirmed slowly but surely. We will come to them soon enough.

"Samson, let's go through your BITS." He doesn't let me continue.

"I have a committed BITS-SECS stalker hanging on the lead TEST-TICCLER. One of Delilah's girls is playing with him. Four guys are tracking the other TEST-TICCLERs; the rest are digging through OBOY's BITS."

Delegating work is a wonderful thing, isn't it? If I had to do it all, then nothing would get done. I simply cannot do everything.

"Good. Now I want the main SADCASE hauled in for a grilling."

"Yes, sir."

Filling the time, I take another look through the recording of the test purchases I ran earlier, committing all the data to memory—the data flows, IP addresses, the important network packets, everything. I have a sneaking suspicion I'll need this data not long from now, and I don't want to have to go emptying a HANDBAG looking for it during a panic situation.

A BIG-AM-I GLOBHED agent abruptly breaks through on the O-WE-COME, rudely interrupting my study.

"System down MAD-ONNA. System down," she screams.

Following this unwelcome announcement, another character instantly appears on the scene, as if he has been sitting in hiding, waiting for his chance to pounce and steal the last Rollo. He has a deep threatening voice and presence, and the O-WE-COME video of his face is not helping matters much.

"I am the SICCO[123], OBOY." This SICCO was also present during most of yesterday's crisis but didn't survive the whole day.

Because OBOY never goes down, the team of SICCOs was, over time, reduced to just two people, and the second SICCO was on holiday yesterday when the system went belly-up. The one remaining SICCO had to work a lot of overtime under stress levels he was no longer accustomed to or able to handle. Needless to say, another holiday was cancelled yesterday.

"I'll drive from now on. I want all the MAGICIANs who have disappeared conjured back here this instant. GLOBHED, get on it. I want all the key OBOY technicians to join this O-WE-COME within the next three point five minutes. The SADCASE I see online, check the data store. System support teams and ANALPRIDCs, get into your CLOGS[124] and see what stinks. Nobody is to touch the system without my explicit,

---

123 Situation Crisis Coordinator
124 [1] Collated LOG Statements; [2] System logs; [3] Stinky wooden shoes

written, and signed-in-blood approval. And I want all two hundred and fifty-one OBOY system components restarted in sequence immedi..."

"Listen you, SICCO," Bitsi-Tone, "let's get one thing crystal clear: You ain't in charge, do y'hear? So, keep it down and take a seat at the rear."

"Do not restart any systems," I punch out the words. Bitsi-Tone, again. "We will take this calmly and step-by-step."

The O-WE-COME is suddenly interrupted again.

"This is COCKS, Bitsi, sir. Good morning, I trust you slept well?"

"Like a baby with a poopy diaper, COCKS."

"Hmmm. I will assume that means yes. And good. I'm glad to hear it. What's your gut feeling, Bitsi, sir—everything under control?"

"We'll have him in, out of the cold, and as snug as a bug in a rug in no time, OBOY," I reply boldly. "COCKS, did you want to say something?"

"Yes, I did. If I may just take one or two minutes of everyone's time, I need to ensure that the gravity of this excruciatingly painful situation is imprinted in your genes and influencing your every thought and move from now onwards and until the CASH comes home. The DOLLY loss when OBOY is down is calculated in millions of DOLLIES per hour. In fact, it is calculated—can you believe it—per minute, five point eight million DOLLIES per minute. That means, for example, if the system is FLAPPING for a whole hour, then the company just kissed goodbye to three hundred and fifty-three million DOLLIES. You can imagine...."

COCKS is trying to emphasize a well-known fact: OBOY is a seriously, much-used wwoopsi-net shopping tool WOWI, fronting all the sales that BIG-AM-I makes. It is the most successful One-Stop-Non-Stop-Single-Entry-Point-For-All-You-Need, ever. Without OBOY, BIG-AM-I would be out of business.

OBOY swallows 45.678 percent of all consumer CASH WOWI. And growing with 0.3092 percent per year, this means total world domination in one hundred and eleven years, if domination is reached at eighty percent. A large percentage of commercial business is also done using OBOY. This number, however, is top secret.

The Sissy o' BIG-AM-I continues to explain the business-crippling impact of OBOY's down time, but I've heard it all before. So, I switch to the private O-WE-COME with Samson and Delilah.

"DEL_SAM, watch with me. We need to find out what's happening here."

"Yes, sir." Delilah is first.

"Yes, sir. And the SADCASE will arrive in plus/minus seventeen minutes." Samson fights back with some extra information.

"I'm going to play out some shopping transactions. On half of the screen-space, you'll see what I'm buying now. Synchronized on the other half of the sspace, you'll see what I bought two hours ago. We need to spot the difference. They should be the same, more or less. I'm going to record every bit and byte of these tests so we can go back over them, if needed."

"OK."

"OK."

The News sspace suddenly wakes up, flashing another new screamer:

System Down MAD-ONNA! System Down!
FLAPPING MAGIC TRICC OBOY!
Round 2 COMMINGS!
Bitsi up against it—again!

BITS GON Ballistic is trying to outdo itself again, as if attempting to sell its first-ever cover page. And Medusa is overly confident, even cocky and careless. No doubt she expects the all-protective excuse of "confidential source" to shield her from going to prison for gaining access to this inside information illegally.

Going back to shopping with OBOY, buying the exact same items I bought earlier, first I use my own TWIT-OVA-USER.

"No difference, boss."

"Agreed."

Then I carry out the exact same steps, this time with one of the test TWITs I used earlier.

"No difference." We all agree.

On a whim, I run the test again, from a different virtual machine and with a new TWIT-OVA-USER, neither of which I use often. I have many virtual machines WOWI and test user-IDs, which I use exactly for this kind of testing.

Almost at the same moment, the three of us say, "TAN-Number[125] is requested this time," or words to that effect.

It was not a hard thing to spot the difference. Even Samson, sitting back in a comfy chair with his feet up on the table and threatening to fall asleep, could spot the change.

Then, I redo the test with the same test TWIT.

"Not requested."

Then, I redo the test with another new TWIT, but from my own machines.

"Not requested." Times three.

"Let's compare the tests," I say, closing down OBOY.

Pulling up the recordings of the two differing purchases side by side on a large O-WE-COME screen-space, I start to page through the thousands of detailed steps of the transactions, comparing them.

"TRIPSI Bitsi," whispers Samson. Delilah simply smiles.

On one of the payments pages, I immediately spot the difference. The page requesting the TAN-Number is not an OBOY page.

"Look at that," I proclaim.

"What?" Both of them jumping out of their skin.

"More incest. Dupli-mated."

When I select the addresses of both the real and the bogus page, they both utter a chorus of, "Oh."

Real page: woopsi.big-am-i.not/OBOY/booking/payments

---

125 Transaction Assurance No-Credit-Card Number (*Used to be called CVV/CSC/CVD, etc. A three-digit number on the back of a credit card.*)

Bogus page: woopsi.big_am_i.not/OBOY/booking/payments

If it were visible, the difference would be obvious even to a baby, but the user can't see the bogus wwoopsi-net name. So, you really need to be looking for the difference to find it.

Also, on the bogus payments page, to fool those who might suspect something, there's a misleading, yet polite message saying:

"Legislative demands related to the new Credit offering require us to ask users once again to enter their TAN-Number. We apologize for the stinking inconvenience, but even BIG-AM-I is not (yet) above the law."

"Bitsi?"

"Thinking..."

"Bitsi?"

"Pipe down."

"They have almost all of OBOY's data. They know who's logging in, and from which machines, and which IP addresses. The TWITS and confuzers they know of aren't shown the bogus page. During all other purchases, the TWITs are being asked to give their TAN-Number."

I throw the monster diagram of OBOY onto the O-WE-COME sspace.

"Look there. The TAN-Number data store is soup-ah-secure. Del, check the test-lab copies."

"Checking."

We wait, too long for my liking. I'm becoming impatient now. I want to get to the bottom of this not-so-magic FLAPPING COMMINGS.

Thirty seconds later, Delilah comes back with her answer. "All the other data stores are copied, including the No-Credit card data, but no TAN store copies, sir."

In the background, I can hear Sissy-O COCKS whining away, not sounding as if he's close to finishing, thus buying me a few more minutes.

"Why don't you just chase down that bogus page and block it? That might save a few DOLLIES from a fate worse than death," questions Samson.

"Well, we don't want to alert the PERPS we're on to them. Second, we don't fix anything without knowing what's broken, Samson. Let's look at the flow of data to the data store."

Using the detailed transaction recording the Beast made during testing, I follow the data flow down through the system soup-ah fast, taking running jumps through enormous chunks of binary data, until suddenly we're in the middle of a complex database transaction.

Lord-IT! Too far. I jump back up the stack into the BACK-END program code.

"TRIPSI Bitsi," Samson whispers again.

Other than that, Samson and Delilah are quiet. This is probably going too fast for them.

"There. The connection to the data store is picked up. The program is about to save the data," I explain to DEL_SAM.

"What is that?"

"What?" they both almost shout.

"Two connections to the data store."

"Where?"

The DIRT-MAPP is showing all parallel processing tracks that are in operation at the same time. I can see that, within nanoseconds of each other, two connections are established, and two requests were fired off to the data store. In my haste, I only followed one transaction down into the data store.

"There."

On the DIRT-MAPP view, I move the two connection commands to the data store so they're lying on top of each other, which highlights the difference.

"Two different data stores."

jadaloco:big-am-i:oops-ql://oboy.clue-les.db-cluts.big-am-i.
not:1010101;DBName=OBOYs-BITS

jadaloco:big-am-i:oops-ql://oboy.clue-les.db-cluts.big_am_i.
not:1010101;DBName=OBOYs-BITS

"There's that same signature change, the underscore. Is this more dupli-mation? The commands to save data are exactly the same, only the connection is different.

"There's something terribly wrong here, guys. This kind of data dupli-mation is never done from the program code. The data store always handles it. It can only have been an ANALPRIDC creating that."

"They could be stealing data this way," Samson suggests.

"Maybe. Here, Del, take these wwoopsi-net names of the data stores. Track down the location of these machines."

Delilah can maybe handle this. Over the years, I taught her everything she should need to know about how to find a machine using its wwoopsi-net name.

"Delilah."

"Yes, Bitsi?"

"Look extremely carefully. This one could be a little tricky."

"I'll find it." I can hear she's sensing the importance and the urgency of the situation.

"Bitsi, sir? BITS Inspector? Are you there?" I hear COCKS demanding.

"Delilah, get to it."

"Yes, sir."

Unbelievable. The BIG-AM-I Sissy-O has been winging and whining for more than 15 minutes in the middle of some FLAPPING MAD-ONNA TRICC, and he expects me to listen to him?

I return to the BIG-AM-I O-WE-COME meeting. "COCKS, are you done? Because we have work to do here." Bitsi-Tone.

"Er, yes. I can leave these people in your capable hands?"

"They were already in my capable hands before you rudely interrupted, COCKS. Almost a half hour ago." I add a few minutes to stress the point. "Now, let us get back to it, COCKS."

"Er, very good; I wish you all the best. Please keep me informed of progress."

"SICCO, are you there?"

"Yes, Bitsi, sir."

"I'm carrying out a few checks of my own at the moment. While I do that, I'd like you to drive the BIG-AM-I MAGICIANS and technicians."

"Yes, sir!" he responds, a little too enthusiastically.

"Look at all the incoming purchases; see if you can find a pattern, any pattern, many patterns, whatever pattern, one of which will help us uncover what's wrong here. For example, why does everyone wake up at eight o'clock in the morning and suddenly start buying stuff? Maybe this causes system overload, and maybe this is why the DOLLIES start escaping into this black hole. Involve everyone you need in order to get to the bottom of these patterns. Do you understand me, you SICCO?"

"Yes, sir," he fires back without a moment's hesitation, or thought, which is good, because I was banking on that.

"Er, Bitsi, sir?"

"Ah, there you are, José L'ARCH. I've been meaning to address your very person. Every time I've heard you speak today, I could tell you're desperately in need of a break. I suggest that you let me handle things from now on. You go and take that hard-earned rest you've been hoping for. It won't be too long before your backup arrives anyway."

"But sir, this line of investiga..."

"The last time you and I spoke, J-Rules," I speak in my Bitsi-Tone, "you made no progress in more than four hours. We want progress in the coming four hours." Bitsi-Tone.

"Er, Bitsi, sir? This is COCKS."

"COCKS, I cannot imagine that anything you wish to say at this time is going to assist us in the slightest. Unless you wish to confess to me that you recently kidnapped billions of DOLLIES?"

"Er, wasn't me, sir."

"Well, I'm glad to hear that. Now, let me get to it. L'ARCHANGEL, fly off home and get some rest; there's a good man. SICCO, I trust you're already on the job?"

"Er..."

"Well, then, get on with it, will you."

"Yes, sir."

"I'm going on mute again for a while. If anyone uninvited disturbs the SICCO, I will deal with them personally." I slam the space-pad once again.

"What, in Lord-IT's name, was *that* all about?" asks Samson, rather perplexed.

"I want them out of my way, Samson, so I've sent them off on mission impossible. The SICCO will have no idea where to start, so he'll pull in everyone he can to confuse matters. They'll stay busy most of the day, I hope. And COCKS is obviously listening in, so I made it clear that he is *not* to interfere."

"Delilah, let's get Samson updated on Medusa, please."

"Medusa? What a name." Samson half-heartedly rumbles the Samson chuckle.

"It's her stage name, Samson, designed to match her column style. Everything she writes is designed to turn something or someone to stone. They call her The Bitch of Modern Press. Judging by her articles, and her attitude during interviews, I get the feeling she was disliked long before birth. She's hateful and sad, if you ask me."

"We have some more news on her, sir," Del chips in.

"Go through what we had earlier and tag the new data at the end."

As Delilah brings Samson up to speed on the New York journalist and her interactions with the BIG-AM-I employees, my mind focuses on the ANALPRIDC Big Dick. What did Medusa want with him? And what was he prepared to do for her? He went back to the hotel with her a number of times. Was he playing hard to get, repeatedly only exchanging one favor at a time so he could get another roll in the hay?

"So now for the latest findings, sir."

Delilah plays a recording of one of the weekly public status meetings from twenty-two months ago, focusing on the JERK, and we see his gaze wander down the meeting table, settling on Medusa's overly exposed bosom, then hurriedly away, then carefully returning. She has noticed and clearly has trouble containing her reaction. The JERK has trouble of his own; he simply cannot control those wandering eyes.

The video jumps, and once again the pair are at the coffee vendor. Medusa is talking quietly to the JERK. Delilah increases the volume.

"Oh, really. You're being extraordinarily cheeky, JERK, sir," exclaims Medusa quietly while raising a hand to cover a giggle.

"Please, call me Jerry."

"All right, Jerry." And she passes him a well-hidden seductive smile. Then, appearing to have remembered something, she steps a little closer to the JERK and addresses him again in an even quieter tone. "Oh, Jerry, here's a juicy tidbit that might interest you. An influential WINCCCER friend of mine appears to have become extremely dissatisfied with the No-Credit attitude that was forced onto the world. He wants to try reintroducing credit, but he's a little nervous about the ripples flowing out of such a controversial reversal of policy. My guess is he needs a little boost."

The JERK stares out the window, obviously thinking. Then, he turns back to look once more into Medusa's bosom, then into her eyes.

"I may know just the pers..."

Medusa gently raises a palm to stop him from saying any more.

"I'm not sure this is the place to discuss the subject. Walls have ears, you know."

She reaches around him to pour her drink into the sink behind the JERK, while slipping something into his pants pocket. "Meet me later."

Once again, the movie springs ahead in time, and we're back in the lobby of Medusa's hotel, only this time it's the JERK who joins her in the elevator.

"So, she's in bed with them both," I exclaim.

"Not at the same time, I hope?" chuckles the big man.

"Samson, we need to keep a close eye on this woman."

Pulling my DIRT-MAPP onto the O-WE-COME sspace, I take a copy of the HANDBAG I created earlier for Delilah and pull the ANALPRIDC out of the BAG. Then clicking on Medusa's icon I say, "FOOLHER." We don't need to wait long for the Beast; the HANDBAG is already full of information on Medusa.

The DIRT-MAPP pulls in Bitsi-Lite to locate Medusa's address and scan for all active LICKEMs, finding FONEs, confuzers, etc.

All her known hard-BITS are at her home address. Using the Bitsi-Lite viewer, I zoom in and out again lightning-fast to ensure she has remained true to her BITS.

"She's at home, sleeping, which is kind of early given the time of night in New York state. Get two men over there, Samson—not too close, though. We need to be ready to bring her in if need be."

"Yes, sir."

"Samson, give this surveillance only to your best. This is one smart cookie, and she must not be alerted."

"Yes, sir."

"Samson?"

"Yes, sir?"

"I want Junior to be one of those you send to watch Medusa."

"Er, yes, sir. Er, why, sir?"

"Intuition, Samson, intuition."

"Er, yes, sir."

I sense that the big man is uncomfortable with my request, but I don't want to explain my reasons to him if I can avoid it because he wouldn't agree. My premonitions on the outcome of this operation are darkening with each passing moment. Medusa and the ANALPRIDC, the NETNERD, and now the JERK, and the whiff of the stench of a mention of credit, all smelling badly.

If I can, I want Junior kept out of harm's way, even though he himself would be angry if he knew I was doing this. On the other hand, I'm taking a gamble that Medusa is not the most dangerous of people to be close to.

After numerous denials, many pep-talks, and words of friendly— even fatherly—advice, twenty years ago I finally broke protocol, accepting more than one family member, agreeing to Samson's request to allow his son to join BITS-SECS.

Samson himself has been on BITS-SECS for seventy-five years, but only his wife knew of his occupation. We protect their children by having this knowledge withheld from them.

Junior had independently from childhood set his sights on joining BITS-SECS, and when he turned of age, immediately started a high-powered education and career in various security branches. In his latter pre-BITS-SECS years, he was exposed to more dangerous operations than many BITS-SECS agents have ever seen.

In the end, I conceded to his membership more as an attempt to prevent him from diving to his death trying to prove himself BITS-SECS-worthy by showing he's capable of putting other causes and other lives before his own.

There was never a question in my mind about Junior's abilities. For more than sixty years, I watched his family more closely than any BITS-SECS family before him. As a result, even though our relationship is strictly professional, I fear they've become a part of me and I of them.

Maybe for this reason I'm being overly cautious—worrying too much, as the wife calls it.

17

Treacherous Protector

"Bitsi, sir?"

"Yes, Delilah?"

"I hate to say this, but I'm, er, struggling a little finding one of the machines behind the wwoopsi-net names. The first name is for the OBOY data store. The second, well, I can't find it."

"What have you tried, Del?"

"The usual, sir, all the tricks you taught me, but all giving me nothing."

"Delilah, which machine did you start the trace from?"

"My own machine, sir."

"Did you try from a BIG-AM-I machine?"

"Yes, sir, no difference. Sorry, but this is not leading anywhere, sir."

She's always so polite when she needs help.

"Bitsi?"

"Thinking…" And deciding I'll find the machine myself when I need it.

"The data is dupli-mated. The…"

"What?" Delilah inquires.

"Pipe down, Del."

"Dupli-mated, probably stolen. Rumors of fraud. Missing machines, Medusa in bed with the JERK and the ANALPRIDC. And then the NETNERD…"

"Delilah, the NETNERD. You had questions about his transactions?"

"Yes, sir," she responds, pulling them out of the HANDBAG to show me.

Flicking soup-ah fast through the data, just as quickly, I discard Del's concerns as irrelevant.

"Nothing new here, Delilah. Anything new in his HANDBAG?"

"Nope. Except, strangely, there's been no sign of him since he left BIG-AM-I two months ago."

"How active was his TWIT-OVA-USER before then?"

"Hang on." Which I do, frustrated, waiting, wanting my answers immediately.

"Regular. He logged into many systems many times a day WOWI."

"So, he has disappeared. Done a runner?"

"Or he has taken an extremely long holiday?" offers Delilah.

"Go through it again, Del. This time focus on office movements, his visual recordings from the INARDS of BIG-AM-I. Create a BEDPAN; go back three years. Look for unusual actions he only carries out once, twice, or thrice. See what you can shake loose."

"Anything particular? ..."

"Sir!"

"Yes, Del, I see it."

And I can hear it, also. Simultaneously, Lord-IT's CCOTCHA alarm sounds loudly in my office, the CCOTCHA LICKEMS suddenly reappear to Bitsi-Lite's view, the Beast starts beeping at me indicating this, and he shows them on the DIRT-MAPP. The Lord-ITs have resurfaced.

Lights are flashing around my office where the wall meets the ceiling, a visual display in case I don't hear Lord-IT's alarm.

I desperately scramble to the DIRT-MAPP to turn off the alarm. I don't want my wife to be more worried than she already is.

Focusing on the Lord-ITs' location, their current coordinates show they're guests of the most powerful, unforgiving, and richest WINCCCER in the world, the number one man of HPD–FITS, who is also Mary-lin's father. On any other day, this picture wouldn't surprise me. Lordy meets with all the super-powers, so nothing strange about that. Except that he's now kidnapped and has sounded his alarm. And this HPD man is the one who has agreed to go into business with BIG-AM-I on the new credit deal.

But Lord-IT didn't follow the full protocol. He only sounded the alarm over the CCOTCHA; he didn't turn on the communications. Why not?

The Bitsi-Lite view of the Lord-ITs' location shows them in a huge countryside mansion. With full infringing video—to hell with protocol—I zoom in to see them just settling onto a massive sofa in a huge, luxurious office/sitting-room. Lord-IT reaches out to take a glass from a table in front of him and takes a half-hearted sip from a heavy crystal liquor glass. His face is stern, gaze focused. I sum up his whole appearance as one of uncomfortable anticipation.

Lord-IT's wife's glass remains on the thick mahogany lounge table in front of her. She looks angry, but I also sense her distress. This couple is understandably out of sorts and apprehensive in their current circumstances.

The Lord-ITs are facing a man who's sitting behind a colossal bureau. This must be Mary-lin's dad, the HPD–FITS No. 1 man. Armed with a FONE in one hand and his own big, heavy glass in the other, he's talking on the FONE.

"Yes, yes, I fully understand, of course. But like I said, all findings currently point to an internal problem, OBOY. Nevertheless, as I've repeatedly stated, be assured we're giving this top priority. We'll inform you and your BOJ-OB of BIG-AM-I BITS the moment anything is uncovered. I wish you all the best with your investigations, but for now I must advise my daughter; she's leading this one personally. We'll be in touch." A normal exchange between two top executives, to be expected in such times of trouble—apart from the kidnapped guests listening in.

Hanging up, the No. 1 answers another call immediately. "Mary-lin, give me a moment, there's a good darling."

Muting the FONE, he apologizes profusely to the Lord-ITs for keeping them waiting, claiming that madness has reigned since the start of the BIG-AM-I OBOY issues, and the situation doesn't seem to be improving. Uninterested in any possible response, he returns to his daughter.

"Mary-lin, I was just talking to an extremely unhappy BIG-AM-I-MOTHER No. 1 man, again…"

Watching this is getting me nowhere. Delilah can hear what's being said; everything is coming in over the Lord-ITs' CCOTCHAs. "Keep listening, Del. Warn me if you hear anything important."

Turning down the volume, I move the video to a large sspace on my desk where I can keep an eye on the Lord-ITs. If anything changes that I don't notice, the Beast will inform me instantly.

The imminent death I so feared appears to be on hold right now. But the risk is still high, and if I'm to reduce it, I need to find out why this WINCCCER is so keen to have Lordy captive.

Laying out the key information of the morning's jigsaw puzzle, I search for the pieces I'm missing:

- Lordy and Rebecca kidnapped.

- Disappearing LICKEMs—how was that possible?

- And why are they no longer hidden?

- Kidnapper is a respected HPD WINCCCER, an extremely powerful and public figure.

- Kidnapper is Mary-lin's father.

- HPD–FITS is BIG-AM-I BITS bank.

- Timing of kidnapping coinciding with BIG-AM-I's FLAPPING.

- Data being stolen and credit card data being requested.

- BIG-AM-I's No. 1 NETNERD has disappeared, just like the LICKEMs?

- The lead TEST-TICCLER's perfect timing of his midnight testing.

- Mary-lin's uncertainty, anxiety. Yes, that's it. Talking too much, out of character.

- Lord-IT requested me to investigate suspected fraud from within BIG-AM-I.

- Medusa's relationships with BIG-AM-I employees, the ANALPRIDC, the JERK, and the NETNERD.

- COCKS's communications unsafe.

- Medusa is only kilometers away from where the Lord-ITs are held captive.

The facts are building up to several obvious connections and some circumstantial. Still nothing concrete about Lordy and his kidnapping, nor the BIG-AM-I FLAPPING, except the timing of these events.

And studying Lordy and his captor in that luxury office, it's obvious to me now why Lordy didn't turn on his CCOTCHA. He is closely watched and didn't want to risk his reaction being noticeable if I started screaming in his ear in a mad panic.

The Beast is closely observing Jonesy and his men and has been all the while they've been in the cottage. It's clear they have no involvement in the Lord-ITs' disappearance.

Re-opening the soup-ah-secure CCOTCHA with Jonesy, I inform him that I found the Lord-ITs.

"Are they OK, sir?" he asks, sounding as if he's not sure he wants to hear the answer.

"For now, I would say yes. But they're still hostage. I'll be working on that and keep you informed, Jonesy."

"Yes, sir."

Using the 3-way-CCOTCHA, I call Samson and Delilah back into the fray.

"*DS3*: DEL_SAM." Bitsi-Tone.

"This mess just turned both multi-life critical *and* possibly into a highly dangerous mission." Pretending that Delilah is also hearing this for the first time. Del I trust implicitly, unconditionally. Everyone else is a possible suspect, until I have convinced myself otherwise.

"I'll tell you what you need to know, when you need to know, and no more. Listen *carefully* to what I say. Execute my commands immediately and without hesitation. Don't waste time with unnecessary questions. Is this clear?" Bitsi-Tone.

"Yes, sir."

"Yes, sir."

"Samson, Get yourself down to the ground floor. Your CHOPPA is waiting for you."

"Yes, sir."

Instantly, he's on the move, off to find his favorite old-model form of transport. Undoubtedly, his mind is racing through possibilities, trying to wager a guess at what has changed, what has happened. But nothing he could dream up will bring him close to the truth.

"*DEL3:* Delilah, stay with Samson. When he's settled on the CHOPPA, tell him I want both US teams on the job. Those not already busy are to meet up with him. Have the B-Team fly out; direction, New York. You keep on with your investigations, and create HANDBAGs for the HPD No. 1 man and his daughter. Full TIMLIs, Del. I'll get back to you soon."

"Yes, sir."

Despite my attempts to avoid her worry, my wife is suddenly standing in front of me. She never misses a trick. And she has clearly decided that going back to bed is not an option.

Again, I create a total BLACKOUT of all communications headed outside my office.

"Where are they, hon?" She knows that the alarm means that Lord-IT has contacted me.

"They're in the US, still hostage, but they seem OK right now. BITS-SECS are preparing, but we can't go in with all guns blazing until we know what's happening. Kidnappings can be tricky."

"Does he know you're on the job?"

"Not yet, sweetie. He's being watched. I will contact him just as soon as it's safe."

"Of course. Do you need anything?"

"No, thanks." And I reach up, pull her head down to mine and hold her briefly, wishing I could delay her departure, but then I kiss her quickly on the cheek before letting her go. I know she'll be as anxious as I am to get me back to work on this nightmare situation.

"OK, then, I'm going back up. It took a while for the kids to fall asleep. Too excited. It wouldn't surprise me if they wake early." She kisses me right back then leaves to check on the kids and the new arrivals in the guest sleeping quarters.

Delilah and her teams are trawling through all the data I threw at them. But so far there's still nothing explaining the kidnapping of the Lord-ITs. Samson is just boarding his CHOPPA on the way to his US flight.

Again, I start thrashing through the reasons why anyone would want Lord-IT, each time coming back full circle, despite my own surprise. There can be only one reason. They want the Nuke-Li-Aerial technology. No, two reasons. They want Bitsi-Lite, also.

Even though for decades the whole world has publicly and deliberately been informed that these secrets are under tight lock and key, which no one person alone can open, I can no longer avoid my internal warning signals and must assume they're going after stealing our patents, our designs, our technology. Of course, what the world knows is not entirely correct.

I think, *Fine. Start at the beginning. Step-by-step, Bisi.* All the Nuke-Li-Aerial and Bitsi-Lite technology documents and soft-BITS are stored in two soup-ah-secure underground DIGI-Lockers[126]. Only I have full access to both because Lordy is too public a figure and the risk of exposure is, well, becoming more obvious as the day progresses.

The single compromise that Lord-IT and I made with the Authorities WOWI when we refused to reveal our technology secrets was that if we both died without naming a successor, the Protectors, meaning the Authorities, would take over our gatekeeper roles.

Needless to say, Lordy and I, and our families, have lived a *maximum*-security lifestyle since the day we made that deal. Any time the Authorities, or anyone, come too close to us, they get an immediate and extremely harsh warning to back off. So, why not this time, damn it?

Three Protectors have heavily restricted access to the Nuke-Li-Aerial DIGI-Locker and three more to the Bitsi-Lite locker. Only three top officials in three different countries know two of the Protectors each. Lordy and I know who all the Protectors are. No one Protector has knowledge of the others.

Three other Authority officials can open a digitally locked envelope to get the Protectors' names in case of dire need, but doing so outside of a crisis would mean breach of contract and the immediate termination of the deal, with all access removed.

For now, I assume these crooks are only after Nuke-Li-Aerial power, themselves knowing they couldn't get close to me, so far at least.

Time to check the DIGI-LOCKERs. Before moving on, I make a closer check-up on the Lord-ITs, turning up the volume. The HPD No. 1 man is on the FONE, again. Lordy and Rebecca are in the same place on the sofa. He has taken her hand, and she looks exhausted. Nothing has changed much.

---

126   Digital safe for securing Bitsi's and Lord-IT's products and data

Delilah is still waiting on me, but she has enough to keep busy. I cannot use Delilah for the DIGI-LOCKER inspection. Even she doesn't have, and will never gain, access to these lockers. So, she'll have to wait a little longer while I do this. Samson has already boarded his CHOPPA to take him to his US flight rendezvous.

Using the DIRT-MAPP, I pull up the Nuke-Li-Aerial CLOGS. At first fleeting glance, I see nothing unusual, simply Protectors checking to see that all is OK. The Authorities require them to do this regularly.

Wait. One Protector has recently stayed on the system for three minutes and forty-five seconds one month ago, much longer than needed. And what's this? He has logged in three times in that week. Each time staying on for three to four minutes.

Flashing back through his login behavior, it becomes obvious that during the past seventeen months, he increased his time spent on the system. He's ramped it up carefully so as not to trigger the DIGI-LOCKER's auto-BEDPAN alarm feature.

If anyone accesses the DIGI-LOCKER more than four times a week, or for more than four and a half minutes at a time, the alarm goes off. This Protector hit the limit once before, many years ago, while drunk one evening and playing mind games with himself about saving the world. That is what he claimed, at least. So, he knows that the limit exists, but he doesn't know exactly what it is.

The DIRT-DIGGER is, of course, running on the Nuke-Li-Aerial DIGI-LOCKER, recording all commands, all traffic. In no time at all, I pull up the records of the Protector's activity on the machine. It's immediately obvious. He, or they, are slowly but surely copying chunks of the Nuke-Li-Aerial data files. I can see logs of the data files being directed to this treacherous Protector's screen. They must have intercepted the data traffic to steal the BITS and store them on their own media before they were converted into spacey-screen-speak. It's hundreds of gigabytes of data, and at an average of three minutes per login, it would indeed take a while to copy the whole lot. Doing a quick search through the log files, however, I can see they completed their data theft a month ago.

For more than eight decades, Lord-IT and I have strived to keep this incredible energy source out of reach of those who would abuse it. Nuke-Li-Aerial power is far too dangerous to fall into the hands of those domination-hungry idiots who have proven they can't control their lust.

Why did the DIRT-DIGGER not alert me this was happening? The machine is totally locked down. Directing this data to a screen shouldn't have been possible. Looking more closely into the logs, I can see they must have hacked one of the few system commands a Protector is authorized to run. There's a security hole in the DROSS!

Lord-IT, we've become complacent. This deliberate bug must have crawled into the program code after Lordy and I stopped personally reviewing all the soft-BITS changes.

Logging also quickly into the Bitsi-Lite DIGI-LOCKER, I perform a fast yet thorough review but don't find anything amiss. That's a relief.

What to do? What to focus on first?

- The rescue of Lordy and Rebecca?

- Go for the hacker who has had his fingers in my DROSS?

- Chase down the compromised Protector?

- The OBOY problems?

Almost fifteen minutes have already passed since Lord-IT's alarm went off. Time is ticking away fast. I don't even know how much time I've got, damn it. Panic knocks at the door again.

"Make a move, Bisi. Move, man!" Using Bitsi-Tone at myself, I slam the door on panic.

18

DROSS A-Hacks

MY EYES FLOAT up to the No. 1 man's study, but there are no major changes in the Lord-ITs' situation.

On his way to who knows where, Samson is looking distinctly unsettled in a CHOPPA that's flying high in the sky without any assistance from him. "*SAM3*: Samson. This is going to be your hardest assignment so far, possibly your hardest ever. Whatever it is you do to psych yourself up for action, do it now; be prepared for anything at any time."

"Yes, sir."

"Your guys are still in the BIG-AM-I building?" I've lost track of their location over the past minutes.

"Yes, sir."

"Good, keep them ready. I believe there's one more BITS Pro we need to overhaul, and it's not the SADCASE. You can put his interview permanently on hold. But I need to get Delilah to check something first.

You're on your way to the US being chauffeur-driven so you have your hands free to drive your teams."

"Roger that, sir."

"Samson, while on your travels, I need you to get to London after this man." I throw the TWIT-OVA-PERSON of the Protector to Samson over the CCOTCHA. "Send in three men. Do *not* approach him yet. He's an important official, so he'll have protection, and you need to take extra care. Just make sure you're close by and ready to respond the second I say so."

"Yes, sir."

"And, Samson."

"Yes, sir?"

"Have *ALL* your teams prepared for immediate action WOWI."

"Yes, sir," he mutters slowly, quietly, ominously. Only relatively few times in the entire history of the Bitsi Era have I given this command, and Samson knows his history.

I give the coordinates of Samson's destination to him over the O-WE-COME on his PRIVATE-LYFE. "Have your US teams join you at this location. It's close to where you need to be, but not too close yet. Leave the two guys with Medusa, Samson. I'll tell you more later, but right now I don't know where the tripwires are. I'm still trying to uncover them all."

"Yes, sir," he responds immediately, without the slightest flinch or a hint of suspicion that I might be unsure if he himself is one of those who would set a snare. It's a dismally sad day when one has trouble trusting ones' closest allies.

"*DEL3*: Del?"

"Bitsi, sir?"

"Here's access to the DROSS program code base. Search for a file and check which TWIT-OVA-USER added some text to the file and when. Hang on."

"The DROSS code base?"

"*Del!*" I'm almost shouting now. I've never shouted at her before, not even for asking such pointless questions. Lord-IT, get yourself under control, man. Thumping on Seribus, I give her the information.

DROSS confuzer: lord-it-house.dross.open.source.dev

File name: ls.d

Search text: <<!&!&>:

"When you find the TWIT-OVA-USER, search all the DROSS code for any other changes made by the same user. Then get the data to me immediately. And, Delilah?"

"Yes, sir?" She sounds both sad and tense.

"Wake up two more of your teams."

"Yes, sir."

From the corner of one eye I notice movement from Samson. He's changing vehicles from CHOPPA to soup-ah-sonic jet.

"Step up the research on Medusa, Del. Do a complete INARDS check WOWI. And we have to find the location of the machine holding the dupli-mated data store. Have you looked into the firewall rules for that wwoopsi-net name?"

"Not yet. I need to find them, but I can do that."

"Do a wide search, Del. Not too specific. Think of 'asterisk.' And look for combinations and conditions."

"Yes, Bitsi, sir."

"I also want the NETNERD found. Anything from his BEDPAN yet?"

"Not yet, sir."

"Get all you have looking for him. If you need even more manpower, then pull them all in."

"Yes, sir." She sounds frustrated.

I know she's wishing she could do even more to help. The job of information gatherer and researcher is a thankless task in the middle of a fast-changing crisis. The data collected is often not used immediately because the chase has already moved on. All the DIRT gathered, however, is invaluable since it will go into proving charges against those who'll be held responsible.

"Delilah."

"Yes, sir."

"I'm sorry, girl." I'm attempting to relieve my guilty feelings.

"No need, sir. Er, sir?"

"Yes?"

"Er?"

Sighing heavily and realizing I haven't granted Del permission to see the Bitsi-Lite view of the Lord-IT's CCOTCHAs, I answer her unspoken but clearly worded question.

"They appear to be OK, Delilah, but for how long I can't tell. Hang on, Del, something's happening." Muting Delilah's audio on the CCOTCHA, I grant her access to the video feed.

While scrutinizing the world's most notoriously ruthless WINCCCER as he crosses from behind his bureau to the Lord-ITs, the murderous eyes burning holes in their targets and the killer demeanor poorly concealed by his expensive suit are terrifying to watch, knowing the Lord-ITs are his victims. His demeanor is more one of a highly trained killer than of a rich WINCCCER.

"I need to leave you alone for a few moments," he announces with a superficial half-hearted smile on his face. "Enjoy and behave yourselves."

Without so much as twitching any other muscles, he raises a hand and points to the four security cameras in the corners of the room, then turns to leave the study.

Now is my chance. "Lordy, we're on the way to you." I'm doing my utmost not to yell in his ear.

A small, almost invisible, involuntary nervous reaction, which could indicate a miserably failed attempt at a smile, appears on one side of Lordy's mouth.

"Your kids are safe here with us."

Lordy turns his head to his wife, takes her hand, and slowly half closes his eyes and opens them again.

The relief on her face is obvious, if you know her, but she covers it well by looking him fully in the face and saying, "We'll be OK, honey, we'll be OK."

"Lordy, look away from her, pretend you're thinking."

"Now, do you know what he wants?" Lord-IT looks up to the security cam in the right corner of the room, then over to the left corner. No.

"You know your lives are in danger?" He sighs and looks down into his lap, then back up again. Yes.

"Imminent danger?" No movement. He doesn't know.

Abruptly, the No. 1 man throws open the office door and walks in, casting a cursory glance at the Lord-ITs as he walks to the desk and to his chair.

"Unless really needed, I will only contact you when you're alone. We will be there as fast as possible. I'm watching and listening constantly, Lordy."

I have learned nothing new during this exchange, but at least Lordy now knows I'm with him, and we're getting closer.

Hovering a meter in front of me on the O-WE-COME sspace, Delilah is waving, encouraging me to get in contact with her. Her use of the CCOTCHA for this contact would be breaking protocol. Only I may establish new communication over the CCOTCHA, except in case of a dire emergency.

I can see she wants me to inspect the TWIT-OVA-USER who has hacked into the DROSS. She has shared it on the O-WE-COME chat along with the list of code changes.

Responding to Delilah's frantic flapping, I open the audio on the O-WE-COME meeting. "Yep. The lead ANALPRIDC for OBOY," I whisper. On another sspace shared with both Samson and Delilah, I order the Beast to hunt down the Big Dick.

Flicking through the long history of modifications shows that it was eight years previous, his first program code change as part of the new Contribute Your DROSS initiative—a concept *similar* to Open Source, a relic from the IT-ice-age.

Jumping to the program change Delilah has shared with me, it's immediately visible. There it is. The master programmer's hack. A little more than twenty months ago. I open the program file to double-check, but there's no need; it's already a certainty. That change rolled out globally three months later, and since it's a core DROSS package, the DIGI-LOCKER machines received the new installation, also. Key DROSS updates are forced onto every machine WOWI.

"Delilah, pull in the best ANALPRIDCs we have—divide the changes among them, look for anything suspicious over the past two years and seven months."

"Yes, sir."

An inquisitive magnetic-like power source keeps me bound to the screen-space, glaring a few hurried moments longer at this guy's devilishly cunning and yet dumb and self-begotten blunders. Was he thinking at all? What a brainless idiot. A perfect example of The Eighth Deadly Fatality: IT-DEAF(max). Complete, utter, unfathomable, mind-boggling Stupid-ITy[127].

In the Bitsi CREAM-EM-TO-BITS theory, the original seven deadly sins are wrapped in a thick circular layer of Stupid-ITy that over the centuries grows thicker and stronger as we continue to find new ways to stubbornly hide our true thoughts, feelings, and failings from ourselves. We simply do not want to know the painful truth, even though deep inside us we can feel it, lurking, eating away at us.

Building this poor attempt at a self-protection layer is the single most stupid thing any of us could do. It causes us to fester from within, rotting, smoldering, and inflaming into dark, violent emotions that cannot be contained and finally force their way out, often in eruptions of pain-ridden anger.

Yet again, Delilah is fluttering her arms in my face, this time frantically.

"Yes, Delilah?"

"Sir, we've been through the BEDPAN of the NETNERD's INARDS at BIG-AM-I. Once in the past three years, he went down into the soup-ah-secure confuzer chamber, to the machines that have access to the

---

127 [1] Incredibly elevated level of stupidity; [2] Stupid IT, referring to broken stuff in IT, which there appears to be quite a lot of; [3] A combination of 1 and 2

TAN-Number datastore, and they also communicate with HPD–FITS BITS.

He logged into one of the machines, twice, from the same terminal. Once with his own TWIT-OVA-USER, once with a test TWIT, similar to those the TEST-TICCLER uses during his midnight testing. He was supposed to be installing some new hard-BITS, sir. And a new DIGI-CERT, held on a secured once-only-copy memory stick, sir."

"New hard-BITS?"

"We went through his system usage again, sir. He sabotaged the box, blew up some of the machine's BITS with some soft-BITS the lead ANALPRIDC gave him to run on the machine."

"Hmmm, possible I suppose; many confuzer add-on components are trashy quality. So, they planned this together, to get to the machine. Why did he log in with the test TWIT?"

"I've looked, sir. I can see that the JERK approved the access for the test TWIT. But I can't make sense of it after that. Sorry, sir."

"Show me." Diving directly into the BITS involved in the DIGI-CERT installation, I can see that the procedure was not prepared securely. Data traffic has been allowed in both directions—into the machine and back out to a memory stick. Prior to the installation, the test TWIT has illegally been granted improper soup-ah-secure access to the machine. This would indeed require approval from high up.

The login with the test TWIT was used to hack into and intercept the DIGI-CERT installation process, routing traffic back out to another memory stick, copying a BIG-AM-I FITS DIGI-CERT. A test TWIT was used to avoid identification confirmation and maybe as an easy way to get the JERK involved up to his neck with no road back but without frightening him into refusing.

Scrolling back through the BITS to the point where the hacked command gets executed, it's immediately obvious. A DROSS hack similar to the one I sent Del looking for earlier: <<!&!&$1>. Already clued up to look for the ANALPRIDC's signature, and with a little help from

The Fruit, my inspection of this criminal activity takes no more than forty-five seconds.

"Del, the NETNERD has stolen a soup-ah-secure login to OBOY's CASH-PILE, BIG-AM-I's bank—another hack in the DROSS the ANALPRIDC provided. This is an old part of BIG-AM-I FITS BITS, previously used for No-Credit-Card payments, OBOY. HPD–FITS handles OBOY's payments now.

"It should really have been closed down, but too many important executives are holding back, stating that the other systems still using it are mission-critical for them."

"Why do they need that DIGI-CERT?"

"Just a moment, Del."

I don't want to wait a moment longer.

"*OSLO:* Samson, standby. We're going after OBOY's lead ANALPRIDC. He's still on site. In his Stupid-ITy, he must think he's safe."

The Beast found his prey's location through the DIGIT-FONE and the confuzer station he's working on. Clicking on the ANALPRIDC's TWIT-OVA-PERSON, I give the command "CATCHIM" so the Beast will assist in the arrest; then, I throw the coordinates directly onto the Oslo team's CCOTCHAs, straight to the eyes.

"This is his position. Samson, pick him up."

"Oslo, go now. Oslo-1, take the lead," Samson yells.

Samson had already earlier handed over to his team lead in Oslo, and the guy is hyped. He springs instantly into powerful, almost violent motion. Guided by the Beast, the BITS-SECS agent runs along the ninth floor toward the inner wall and the pathway that leads to the bridges connecting all six buildings. He needs to go two blocks to get to the correct bridge that will take him to the building where the ANALPRIDC is participating in the OBOY crisis workshop on the eighth floor.

There are too many different floors, bridges, and exits to cover them all. The Beast assists the rest of the team by showing the most probable exit to cover, one on each floor. They split up, each one heading for their designated exit: Oslo-2 to an eighth-floor bridge, Oslo-3 to the seventh, etc.

"Now, Del. The DIGI-CERT. It would be needed, for example, if…"

Suddenly, from the BIG-AM-I building, Samson's team lead starts yelling.

19

ANALPRIDC Panic

*S*HIT! *ARE THOSE buggers coming for me?* the ANALPRIDC curses in his head as he spots the first BITS-SECS agent coming after him. *Can't be. Medusa swore that Bitsi and his BITS-SECS were all idiots with nothing more than big reputations and even bigger mouths. But that bastard is heading straight toward to my floor. Hell, I need to move!*

He dashes over to the nearest block of elevators. *Oh, blast it to hell! Which way to go? Up? Down? Damn it, I didn't expect this.* Panic meddles with his ability to make fast, logical decisions.

Up, then the only way out is the rail. No good. He smacks the button to summon an elevator going down. As the elevator arrives, he enters and frantically presses first the ground floor button, then—almost insanely and repeatedly—he hits the button to close the doors.

The lift is almost half-full of desks and the people moving them.

Shit! The 4th floor light is on, he thinks in dismay. *They ain't taking this junk all the way down.*

Oh, hell no. There's another one of them. How many are there? he thinks as he spots another BITS-SECS agent on the run.

The elevator stops at the fourth floor. "You guys gonna stay here long?" the ANALPRIDC asks, only to hear that three more desks will be loaded now. He pushes the button to close the doors, but a guy even bigger than he is steps squarely in front of the closing doors, shaking his head.

The ANALPRIDC lets fly a string of well-practiced expletives while dashing out of the elevator. He checks the adjacent elevators, but they also are all busy. Then he heads for the nearest bridge.

Four floors, hell, that's a long way down. He rushes out onto the bridge, but something above him catches his eye, and he stops to look up to see what it is. A BITS-SECS agent is spinning through the air only to land neatly on the sixth-floor bridge.

That guy must be nuts, he yells silently in his own ears and races even faster down the bridge. A few seconds later another agent appears, entering the fourth-floor bridge from the lower floor, blocking the exit.

The ANALPRIDC stops dead in his tracks, looks back up, then down, then briefly over the edge of his bridge to the walkways below, the panic swelling further inside him, threatening to take control. He turns to run back up the bridge, just as the flying agent lands neatly between him and the other end of his bridge.

There's no way out. It's jump or stop running.

Oh, to hell with this, his mind screams at him. And his hand dives deep into an inside pocket in his jacket.

20

NUKE-LI-AERIAL DESTRUCTION

"Bitsi, sir, he's running! He's actually running away. What is he thinking?" the Oslo team leader yells.

"Just get on with it, man," Samson shouts back. "Go get him."

Zooming in on the area of the chase in the BIG-AM-I complex, I enlarge the screen-space showing the Bitsi-Lite video, then increase the size and brightness of the dots displaying the electronic signals coming from all LICKEMs. While dragging the signals of Samson's men into a HANDBAG to make tracking them easier with a FOOLEMALL, I notice five LICKEM signals coming from the ANALPRIDC. That's a lot. Usually two or a maximum of three is more normal. I throw the LICKEMs into the BAG with the others.

Pointing the DIRT-CRAWLER at the ANALPRIDC's signals, I give the Beast the instructions to investigate, and to open the front door and prepare to take control. Hang on. One of the LICKEMs is in the PERPS' head! Panic thumps me in the gut once again.

The ANALPRIDC spotted the plainly obvious BITS-SECS agent running down the ninth-floor bridge to his building, so he took an elevator going to the ground floor. But that's stopped and movers are preparing to load it with desks, so he jumps out of the elevator and starts across the fourth-floor bridge leading to the third floor, trying to get down and out of the building.

Oslo-1, now not far from the exit on an eighth-floor bridge, turns to observe his target, assessing his options. Reaching a decision, he runs back out across the bridge and without warning suddenly dives over the railing performing a triple loop somersault as he flies through the air.

He lands, still rolling as he hits the surface of the sixth-floor bridge below, close to the intersection point with the bridge above. Crazy guy. That must have been a six-meter dive with no water to cushion the blow.

The Beast has followed and joined in with the plan, showing Oslo-1 where to make the next jump. He needs to perform two single-bridge stunts with just a few meters of running to reach the fourth floor.

The ANALPRIDC stops to watch the dive and also spots another one of the BITS-SECS agents. Standing still, he seems confused, not sure which way to go, but then decides to continue in his original direction down the walkway.

On reaching his second take-off point, Oslo-1 flies through the air to the next level below. Not long past the halfway mark on his way down to the third floor, the ANALPRIDC sees another agent dashing out onto his bridge, blocking his passage.

"Stop, Oslo-6. Wait there," Samson commands his man.

The now-frantic ANALPRIDC is again stationary, whizzing round to look first up, then down the conveyor-belt bridge, madly calculating his options. He even glances over the railing but apparently decides that BITS-SECS acrobatics is not for him.

Spinning away from Oslo-6, he races back up to the fourth floor just as Oslo-1 lands squarely on the bridge, halfway between the exit and the ANALPRIDC, who's now trapped between the two agents. The ANALPRIDC, like a wild animal cornered and ready to fight to the death, rips a device out from deep inside his jacket and raises it in the air while screaming, *"You try anything, we all go together."* He sounds like a raging madman.

"Everyone stand still." Bitsi-Tone.

The hard-BITS in that maniacal waving hand contains one of the five LICKEMs I spotted earlier. Clicking on it, the Beast shows me that the DIRT-CRAWLER is installed and has activated the DIRT-DIGGER. All the data about the device pops into view. One advantage of having a Beast under your ass is never having to look far for information when you need it.

"*SAM3:* It's a bomb," I inform Samson, giving him warning so that he can get acquainted with the idea.

"Nuke-Li-Aerial?" he asks, bordering on panic himself.

"Are you nuts? No one knows how to make a Nuke-Li-Aerial bomb, Samson."

"*OSLO:* Guys, that device is a LASAROMIC explosive—simple, but powerful enough to bring down all six BIG-AM-I buildings. So, wait."

In the meantime, the ANALPRIDC has started making demands about needing a flight out of the country, the usual stuff.

"Keep him talking," I command them.

"Neutralize," I yell at the Beast. Bitsi-Lite, the DIRT-CRAWLER, and the DIGGER work in concert with the Beast holding the beat, directing the cracking music as it quickly builds up to a rumbling crescendo, and boom, we're in. Three point one seconds. Half a second later, the device is dead-weight in the hands of the poorly misguided ANALPRIDC, although he hasn't realized it yet.

"OK, his show is over. Bring down the curtain."

The two BITS-SECS agents surge forward like two bulls in the ring engaging in a head-to-head death charge, between them the ANALPRIDC, their matador and target, the source of their just rage. The ANALPRIDC starts screaming all kinds of profane Gibberish; then holding the dead LASAROMIC device out over the bridge railing, he attempts to trigger the bomb.

Oslo-1 reaches the PERPS first, coming up behind him and throwing his arms around the ANALPRIDC's chest and arms forming an inescapable body-lock. Seconds later, Oslo-6 reaches the two of them, placing his hands on the PERPS's forearms and pushing the arms backwards toward Oslo-1 so he can take the wrists and fasten the cuffs. The ANALPRIDC has already given up the fight.

On my screen-space, the LICKEM inside the PERPS's head flares up, a bright light displaying a sudden surge of Nuke-Li-Aerial power. The ANALPRIDC instantaneously falls limp in the team lead's arms.

"Ughhhhhhh." I breathe out the sound agonizingly while trying to contain it. My head drops, jaw touching my chest; my forehead almost touches Seribus, as if I just fell forward after being shot.

"Er, Bitsi, sir?"

"He's gone. We've lost him," I report sadly. Already I feel my tears reaching the surface. This is the part I hate. No one should die, not like this.

And the one thing I've been protecting against for all these years has now suddenly become a reality. The combination of the Nuke-Li-Aerial, Bitsi-Lite, and LICKEM technologies have—for the first time I'm aware of, since their creation more than ninety years ago—just been used to kill someone.

"*DEL_SAM3*: Samson. Beijing. Get to Bio-Brains immediately. I'll get you his status on the way. Just get someone to him right now," using my Bitsi-Tone to try to force some surface-level of recovery, for now. There's still work we need to do.

"Also find his lead lab technician. Check on his current status and let me know once you have it."

"Yes, sir."

Finding the TWIT-OVA-PERSON for the technician in my contacts, I slide it over to both Samson and Delilah.

"Delilah, compile a complete TIMLI on this guy for the past two years, nine months—everything, including his INARDS. See what you can find."

"Yes, sir."

21

DISAPPEARING **TRICC**

THERE'S ONLY ONE person in this world who can create a LICKEM that can install into the head, and that's Bio-Brains, the eminent and genius scientist I commissioned to assist in creating our security devices, which we implant by simply placing a lens-shaped disc on an eye. The disk holds the tiny, microscopic CCOTCHA device, which on-command swims out from its mobile parking lot to begin its long but swift journey up to the brain where it then anchors.

Bio-Brains claimed ignorance when it came to wiring the CCOTCHA's eerily life-like Bio-Feelers[128] to the Nuke-Li-Aerial power source, and we needed a machine that could be used to produce multiple CCOTCHAs. So, I was forced to accept Bio-Brain's lead lab technician's assistance with the machine.

The CCOTCHA concept is mine. I came up with it, and I held on to it by having all the designs patented. Legally speaking, Bio-Brains can't use any of the ideas or technology we built together without my permission, which he has never asked for.

Bio-Brains is sworn to secrecy, but more importantly he's an honorable man. These past few years, we haven't communicated a great deal; our schedules never seem to allow it, so I'm not aware of his current situation. Regardless of that, I know this recent revelation is not good news.

The tears are trickling down my face now as the realization of witnessing the ANALPRIDC's death hits home more deeply and as

---

128 Mega-microscopic bio-electronic equipment used in scientific, medical, and Bitsi tech-nology

worry slowly evolves into certainty: My old friend is either in grave danger or already dead.

The pain of others' suffering, and at its worst their unnatural and violent deaths, is something I've never coped with well. First, Lord-IT's security guards, then the ANALPRIDC, and now I fear for Bio-Brains. Why does advancement to the next level have to lead to others being hurt, or worse, killed? I've never understood how a person lives with himself after such cruel or brutish expressions of selfishness.

It will take a minute or so for Samson to send the Asian team after Bio-Brains. A minute seems like an age, but I want to wait until Samson and his Beijing team and I are set up with communications so I can instruct them before moving on to other work.

I also need a breather. Sitting back, I close my eyes and try to relax, forcing an artificial soup-ah powernap. My brain needs to slow down a notch or two.

In the background now, I listen to Samson as he completes his instructions for his Asian contingent and finally spurs them into action. As he does this, I set up a new CCOTCHA channel.

"*BEIJING:* Can you all hear me?"

"Yes, sir," they all respond at once.

"Once you approach your location, report to Samson. Do *not* get too close until I give the green light. *Is this clear?*" Bitsi-Tone.

"Yes, sir."

"Good."

Throwing the whole team into a HANDBAG and instructing the Beast to FOOLEMALL, I enlarge the sspace containing the Bitsi-Lite view showing their vehicle as it flies across a fast-moving Asian background. Now I can follow their progress from the corner of an eye.

"Bitsi, sir, the lab technician, is he to be trusted?"

"He used to be, Samson, but over the years I fear he has become less reliable. He is rather ugly, extremely bad at personal hygiene, and an extremely nerdy techy. He's been most unfortunate in his relationships, and based on the last I heard of him, he's been alone these past fifty-odd years."

"An easy target, then," he concludes.

"I'm afraid so. Bio-Brains kept tabs on him, but I fear we should have watched him also.

"I have to go, Samson; I'll get back to you later."

Abruptly and harshly this time, the Beast starts barking at me, and lights begin flashing on the Bitsi-Lite view of Lord-IT and his wife. The Lord-ITs are being moved.

I have not yet had time to thoroughly check out their location. I know it's a huge, secure-looking complex. But that's all I really know.

Creating a huge new sspace showing the Bitsi-Lite image of the house and grounds, I zoom in on the building, instructing the DIRT-MAPP to display all aspects of the construction overlaid on top of each other. This provides a mind-bogglingly unintelligible view of all levels of the house, but I like to start with this overview, and once I have it, a joystick will help strip out information I don't need.

It's a New York state mansion. A breathtakingly gorgeous, heart-stealing, massive mansion.

The Lord-ITs are at one end of the building and are going down in an elevator. Five people. Ground floor now. Still going down. Three meters. Six meters.

At ten meters, the descent abruptly halts, and within moments they're leaving the building underground. After twenty seconds, the Bitsi-Lite signal is weakening. Four seconds later, it's gone.

Incredible. Now, I've seen it happen with my own eyes. And the Lord-ITs have again vanished before Bitsi-Lite's eye.

22

BIO-BRAINS' DEPARTED

BILLIONS IN CASH have disappeared, are still disappearing, and now also the Lord-ITs, with the CASH?

No, impossible. They surely cannot be implicated.

The thought hacked its way in uninvited. Unfortunately, I know it will now linger, hanging over me until this mess is over. But I won't accept it, not unless absolutely forced into it.

The Lord-ITs' vanishing is yet another addition to this ever-growing list of suspicious, closely-timed events. Is this just another coincidence sent to confuse, to try everyone's patience? Or are there many broken lines steadily merging together into one thick, fat arrow pointing underground, where the Lord-ITs are now held?

Why were they moved now, only minutes after the ANALPRIDC's death? The answer must wait. I need to get back in contact with the Lord-IT's LICKEMs right now. Diving on the Beast, I pull up my Bitsi-Lite control panel.

Bitsi-FREQs offer trillions of possibilities for all kinds of weird and wonderful, even freaky effects and subject matter mutations. FREQs are built up of many SUB-FREQs. You can combine multiple FREQs or SUB-FREQs within a single FREQ, and SUB-FREQs from different FREQs, etc.

The number of Bitsi-FREQ combinations is something like: trillions^x, where I suspect x=∞ (infinity). The value of "x," specifically, I'm still trying to prove.

Numerous experiments already carried out with Bitsi-FREQs have taught me to be extremely cautious. I've already caused a few unexpected minor explosions. Fortunately, even though buildings were pulverized, no one was hurt.

One thing I've learned, however, is how to train Bitsi-FREQs to scan through the earth's core, all the way from one side of the globe to the other. So, I know there's nothing on this planet that I'm aware of that can hold back Bitsi-FREQs if the correct combination is chosen for the job at hand. Finding that combination is my next challenge.

I built the Bitsi-Lite Testing Control Panel for designing and conducting my experiments, and this particular one the Beast has done before on numerous occasions. So now I simply need to fill in a bunch of variables, then instruct the Beast to start boring away at this annoying Bitsi-FRIGHT layer.

Five minutes into the frantic preparations, questions on the variance of the biochemical aspects of the potential subject matter under inspection suddenly remind me I haven't yet informed Samson on the status of Bio-Brains, bringing me close to panic again.

Bio-Brains! Fearing for the worst, shutting down all external communications, I frantically pull up a Bitsi-Lite view of Bio-Brain's house and instruct the Beast to perform a high-level sweep, searching for signs of life, for heat signatures. Not a single soul.

In desperation, I yell at the Beast to search for human forms rather than signs of life, and within seconds I can see them, all six of them.

"NOOOO!" My face is shaking, my chest tense, oppressive, restricting once again my ability to breath. The whole family, all six of them, are lying dead in the building. The unusual location of their bodies in the house, the body positions indicating where they fell to their deaths, and the extreme pale skin colors are all clear confirmations of the horrible fact.

It can take more than ten hours for the body to lose its natural heat in those conditions. They have been dead for quite some time longer.

I refuse to go any closer at this stage, terrified of seeing exactly what has been done to them during the execution of this unbearably heinous crime that not even the average super-criminal would commit—a cold-blooded annihilation of a complete family.

My head sinks to my chest as my upper body droops forward, eyes tightly closed. Nothing. Doing absolutely nothing, except half-forcing my breathing, slowly. Not looking, not thinking, not feeling. Nothing.

Slowly, a quiet but relentlessly firm voice steadily increases in volume inside my head. *This is no good, Bisi. There are others who need your help, possibly a world to rescue from the threat of the pain of Nuke-Li-Aerial abuse. You can't just sit here; you need to move on. What's done is done, past is past. Do what you can to influence the future. Get on with the future, man. Get on with it.*

I often hold these pep talks with myself when the going gets tough. As I cajole myself into action, willfully forcing my upper body to rise up, the back of my head hits the office chair and just rests there a moment as I continue to encourage myself into forward motion once more.

Flicking a switch on my communications control panel, I'm back in contact with my teams and trying to hide my obvious signs of distress. "Samson, stop the Beijing team at a safe distance from the house. Keep them on standby."

"Delilah, start doing a complete search on Bio-Brains. Try to be careful not to break out into any risky zones, whatever *they* might be."

"It's not good, is it, sir?"

"No, Samson, it is not," I mutter quietly, and if you know me at all, you can hear I have just been broken.

But I have been broken before. Yet, I have never, ever given up.

"Bitsi, sir?" Samson asks, as gently as the big man can muster up gentle.

"Yes, Samson?"

"Can we do anything?"

"No. Just have the Beijing team take up position close to the house. Your ETA in the US is what? One…"

"One hour, thirty-four minutes, sir."

"Damn it, I hope we have that much time. How long before the US team is in position?"

"Five are already in place, full complement within fifty minutes, sir."

"OK. They're plan B, in case we need to engage in a hurry. So, make sure they're alert at all times."

"Of course, sir. And one more thing, sir. Bio-Brains' ex-lead-labby died in a car crash three days ago. No other vehicles involved."

"Another damn COMMINGS. That guy was as old as I am, and suddenly he doesn't know how to drive? They must have gotten to him. And when the hell did Bio-Brains fire him? And why the hell didn't he tell me?" These are rhetorical questions. Samson doesn't try to respond.

While talking, I created a new HANDBAG to prepare full access for Delilah to investigate events at Bio-Brains' house. I throw in his TWIT-OVA-USER, and one of the LICKEMs I know is for his main confuzer at home.

"Delilah, this BAG gives you access to all the machines in Bio-Brains' house. Start with finding out what happened."

"Yes, sir."

"I have some work to finish up here, so unless something urgent comes up, wait until I get back to you guys."

"Yes, sir."

"Yes, sir."

23

UNDERGROUND DRILLINGS

Sᴛʀᴇss ʟᴇᴠᴇʟs ᴡʜᴀᴄᴋᴇᴅ up to MAVACAPA and emotional energy level smacked down to rock bottom, I push myself to fill in at lightning speed, I hope, the many variables needed to kick the Beast off digging through this Bitsi-FRIGHT layer that's preventing my Bitsi-Lite view of the Lord-ITs and their captors. Many of the answers are simply Ø – zero (as in don't know). If I knew all the answers, I wouldn't need to do the experiment.

Finally, after what seems like an age but really is fourteen precious minutes, I kick off the program, then sit back to monitor the progress for a minute or so. The program running on the Beast will do the work now, testing its way, making minute adjustments depending on the qualities of the materials encountered along the way, slowly drilling its way through that surface which is the source of my unsettling and debilitating blindness.

Sitting back and closing my eyes briefly, I promise myself more coffee. Involuntarily, childhood images of Junior float somewhere above my head—seeing him playing in the garden with his mom and dad, who is in an O-WE-COME meeting with Samson (No. 2), Lord-IT, and me. Dad is proudly showing off how well his four-year-old can now kick a ball.

Uh, no good. I need coffee.

On returning to my chair and Seribus, I check on the Bitsi-Lite drilling experiment and can see that it's progressing; it's just not fast enough for my liking. It could never be fast enough.

"Samson, status please."

"We have reached the recon zone for the Protector. And we'll be with Medusa in three minutes, sir."

"OK. Hold back for now. Let's check them out."

Pulling up a DIRT-MAPP session in a new sspace, I share it on the O-WE-COME meeting on Samson's soup-ah-sonic flight.

"Are you getting this, Samson?"

"Yes, sir."

Even though he's traveling almost two and a half thousand kilometers per hour, the Bitsi-Lite connection is consistent, not like the old days.

Splitting the view into two halves and displaying the Bitsi-Lite video of the Protector on one side, Medusa on the other, I trash protocol and zoom in on the targets. It's not long past midnight in the US and Medusa is still sleeping. The Protector appears to have awakened not long ago and is beginning to prepare himself for the day, and the office, I guess. He's known for burning the candle at both ends, finishing late and starting early.

Screwing up the detail-level view, I look for the giveaway signs of LICKEMs installed in heads, which has become my worst nightmarish reality within the last hour. As I feared, they both have that potentially fatal glow emanating from the proximity of their brains.

"Do you see those lights in their heads, Samson?"

"Yes, sir."

"They're hot-wired, Samson, just as the ANALPRIDC was. If we make a wrong move, we stand to lose both of them."

"Can you break through that, sir?"

"Yes. Move in closer but stay invisible for now."

"Yes, sir. Er, sir?"

"Yes, Samson?"

"Have you noticed that Medusa is only six kilometers away from my target location, sir? It would seem there's maybe a connection between her and wherever it is you've sent me."

"The light in Medusa's head confirms the connection, Samson. Her proximity to the danger-zone maybe indicates how deeply she's involved."

"Yes, sir," a little dejectedly.

"And those lights, Samson, they must be controlled from where I've sent you."

"Bitsi, sir?"

"Thinking, Samson."

Selecting the two LICKEMs in the DIRT-MAPP, I give the command, "Break and Enter," and watch as we begin to dig our way in. But suddenly the Beast slows up and starts prowling back and forth, uncertain, searching. On giving the instruction to halt and then studying the data by stealing it off the Bitsi-FREQs, I see they found out how to install an additional encryption key on the LICKEMs. This is a hidden, secret feature of LICKEMs that I rarely use. One needs to border on genius in order to complete this installation without prior knowledge.

"Smart cookie," I exclaim. "They've upped the security on those LICKEMs. It will take some time to break it, Samson. Leave it with me for now."

"Yes, sir."

All the wireless data going to and from the LICKEMs is encrypted—an unexpected and unwelcome setback, and a first-of-a-kind in more than eighty-five years. My only option is to steal a copy of the traffic and start hacking away at it, which is a painful process at the best of times. But the Beast is highly trained in the flaws of all known encryption algorithms, so it should be hackable with enough machines thrown at it.

"Soup-ah-hack, disable," I command the Beast.

Lord-IT House and Bitsi-Lites the Skies own hundreds of millions of soup-ah-powerful maxi-confuzers housed in mega-sized server-farms throughout the world, and the Beast knows when he may borrow some of this extra processing capacity. Within five minutes more than one hundred and thirty million machines are temporarily loaded with my hacking algorithms and assisting in the soup-ah-hack. All I can do now is wait for it to complete.

(Note for later: Separate LICKEM back door from main encryption path.)

Once more, I cast my eye on the Bitsi-Lite experiment and see that we're just past the one-meter mark, yet I have no clue if that's good or bad. The Lord-ITs are at least ten meters under the earth, but how deep? And how thick is this thing, this Bitsi-FRIGHT barrier? I could start tweaking the variables, but now that the Beast has started his work, any changes at this early stage could maybe save a few minutes but could just as easily lose a half a day. Best to wait. The Beast is trained to be patient, and cautious, when I might not be. As soon as he reaches thin air again, he will notify me.

24

BLOODY CCOTCHA SAVAGERY

WAITING FOR THE hacks and experiments to complete, my patience is tried almost to its limit. There's one path I could follow to take my mind off the delay, but that surely holds a tale of gruesome terror and is a path I wish to never have to go down. Yet, I must. I have no choice, and I cannot put it off forever.

"Delilah. Show me what happened, please."

"Yes, sir." Even she, who is usually stronger than most of us, is sounding distraught.

"Keep it short and concise, Del. I have no wish to see more than absolutely necessary."

Delilah knows how I am when it comes to death and suffering, and she knows how close I was to Bio-Brains. She will have cut this video review down to a bare minimum, I hope.

Nevertheless, reaching deep into my emotional self, I draw up a thick self-protective layer, knowing that what I'm about to witness is going to be unbearable, and if I'm to continue working on rescuing Lordy and his wife—and possibly the world—then I'll need to deal with my pain later.

"They hacked into the first-defense security system, sir, but it seems they didn't find the second one."

Bio-Brains, like me, did not have his security system hooked up to any outside organization. The more strangers you invite into your home, the less secure you are.

His trusted first line of defense was also the mainline. The secondary hidden cameras were a relatively recent hobby he hadn't yet taken seriously, and he hadn't set up any alarms from them. All camera video, however, was recorded and stored onto three different machines. We watch the Bio-Brains' family attack from the secondary recordings.

Six guys were waiting in ambush; one of them runs into the garage, following the car in as the family returns home. Holding the family at bay in the vehicle, he waits for the other five to enter before allowing the garage door to be closed. It's all downhill from there. The family is forced into the house.

"What do you want!?" Bio-Brains screams.

"We want to see what you've been up to," the obvious leader sneers.

"This is my home, damn it. What are you talking about?"

Immediately, the youngest child is taken and brutally threatened with a bread knife grabbed from a holder in the kitchen.

"William!" The child's mother is screaming at her husband, pleading, sobbing, and demanding all at the same time. Bio-Brains does not need any further encouragement.

"Put the child down!" he yells. "Then, come with me."

He leads the entire gang down to the underground lab. As they enter, I selfishly find myself scanning the room to see if anything is on display that I don't want them to find, knowing they will possibly find it anyway.

Even the crooks can see the lab seems clean, empty of anything they might have hoped to find. Not giving up easily, they hurriedly start to search the walls and floor for secret chambers and hiding places.

Ripping a huge drawing board from a wall, they find the hidden safe that contains my next batch of CCOTCHAs. It's sealed with a combined confuzerized biometrics and combination lock.

"Open it," the leader demands, and for a few painstakingly long moments, Bio-Brains is at a loss what to do next. Seeing this, and obviously having sensed an important find, without a hint of hesitation, the leader offers to help Bio-Brains out of his indecision and drags his screaming wife up to the kitchen, giving a nod of his head to one of his men on his way out of the lab.

Forced into a chair, a big hand covering his mouth indicating it's too late to plead mercy, Bio-Brains is forced to watch on a DIGIT-FONE while the same child-threatening bread knife slowly, without faltering for a second, cuts deeply into the throat of his wife from one ear around to the other.

Returning to the basement, bread knife dripping bright-red blood from one hand, the leader wraps his free arm around the oldest child holding him tight and raises the weapon to the boy's ear. "OK!" Bio-Brains screams, and within seconds the safe is open.

The leader first retrieves a control unit, then unplugs four boxes from the climate-regulator installed in the safe. Each box contains eight CCOTCHA devices. As he opens one of the climate-controlled boxes, it issues a gentle hissing sound as air from inside is released. He glances briefly at his colleague while again giving the slightest of nods.

Throwing Bio-Brains a severe look, eyeball to eyeball, a sadistic gaze cutting deep into the core of the soul of the distraught and terrified father, the question is clear, but the leader loves the sound of his own voice. "What the hell are these?" he demands.

Frantic to do anything he can to save his children, Bio-Brains describes the CCOTCHA as an age-old experiment he has recently started work on again, saying that these are the first batch that actually work, God bless him, and he explains their function.

The BIO-FEELER technology he initially conceived more than a hundred years ago is what we use in the CCOTCHA. The chain of connections between LICKEM, Nuke-Li-Aerial power, BIO-FEELER and brain is, however, top secret—or was. Even Bio-Brains' lead labby didn't know why he was creating a machine to wire up Bio-Feelers to a micro-Nuke-Li-Aerial power unit. And now Bio-Brains is finding out the hardest way possible why the secrecy was necessary.

Over the years, Bio-Brains has built numerous machines to use Bio-Feelers in the advancement of medical science and healing. And his more recent work on attempting to read thoughts using Bio-Feelers has become as well-known as all his other techno-biological experiments, even though I constantly warned him strongly against his careless exposure to publicity.

"Can they kill?" the leader asks.

"Good God, no, man."

"But they could, easily, could they not?"

"I don't know." Unconvincing. Bio-Brains always did find it difficult to lie.

"That's not what I've been told. Reprogram them, now. Let's use that Nuke-Li-Aerial power for something really useful for a change. And then reprogram this device for controlling them. Make the command simple. Something like "KILL," he says, followed by a hair-raising vicious laugh.

Reluctantly, but with little choice between that or certain and immediate death for his children, Bio-Brains follows his captor's commands.

When we designed the CCOTCHA together, we enhanced the communication layer of the LICKEM so it could communicate with the processing unit of the Nuke-Li-Aerial power unit that would then send power signals through the Bio-Feelers. Changing the level of power transmitted to the brain would only take Bio-Brains a few minutes for a single LICKEM, if he chose to do so. Changing the power-level through the control unit was, however, not possible.

"This will take quite a few hours."

"So, get started," the leader yells.

Bio-Brains begins his work by opening a huge number of overlapping sspaces on his spacey-screen. I can see at a glance that it's way more than he should need, and Delilah confirms my thoughts.

"I think he left a message for you, sir. On another machine, somewhere. We couldn't be sure."

"OK, Del, I'll check later." It doesn't surprise me, and I know where he would have left that message.

Delilah skips the video forward to the point where Bio-Brains finishes his work.

"So, you all done? Thirty-two working specimens, correct?"

"Correct."

"Good job. Then let's test them."

I guess Bio-Brains knew this was coming, which is why he took many times longer than needed to complete his work. He was probably hoping for some miracle that might change the status-quo down there in his basement.

The leader first checks the control unit to see how to use it. Then taking one CCOTCHA from each box, he places them onto an eye of each of the four children. Bio-Brains is looking from one child to another in turn, mouthing "I love you," as all of them shed their tears openly.

Once more, Delilah fast-forwards the recording to the moment where the CCOTCHAs have secured themselves and are communicating with the brain of each child.

Then the leader, more monster than man and lacking any form of compassion, executes them all, one by one, dragging out the father's pain, inflicting maximum damage just to satisfy his own sadistic needs.

"We'll not waste one of these on you," the Leader declares finally, walking over to Bio-Brains, bread knife in hand.

"Enough of this bloody savagery, Del."

"Yes, sir."

"We were all done here anyway, sir. They pack up and leave shortly after."

"Fine. But not so fast, Delilah. They didn't find everything. We need to get in there and recover the rest, but they could still be watching the cameras. I don't want the PERPS alerted to our presence at any time during this operation, until we're good and ready.

"Get an ANALPRIDC to work on those security cameras. I want a static image replacement, but with the clock date/time updating. It's basic, I know, but we need this fast, and we won't need much time to get in and out, so we can restore the normal video quickly. We'll just have to take the risk that they won't go pan/tilting around a dead family's house at the exact moment we're breaking in."

"Yes, sir."

"I'll deploy the camera hack when it's ready, Del. Samson, get ready to go in and recover my goods. Now, I need to check if there's a message for me. So, both of you prepare until I return."

"Yes, sir," they reply in unison.

"One more thing, sir."

"Yes, Del?"

"They look for his email program before leaving and send mail to a few people in the contacts list. Something about a family member falling sick and leaving town for a while to be with them."

"OK."

I'm thankful for the precautions we took in this area. They shouldn't have found my name in that contacts list.

A soup-ah-secure connection from the Beast brings me straight into the BIO DIGI-LOCKER. Bio-Brains was contractually required to store our secrets there but also permitted to use it as a safe place for anything he wanted secured.

In my own message folder on the machine, I see his latest message to me at the top of the list. It's written in pidgin English and with no punctuation—obviously pushed for time—but he still managed to write the whole thing in hexadecimal code, I guess so no one watching him could easily read it over his shoulder.

667269656e64204445535045524154452073636c61756768746572696e6672066616d696c7920776861742020746f20646f2077616e74...

Translated: friend desperate slaughtering family what to do want to give more chance to survive dont want to give secrets but need to give something freqs are different you will see you must find them deal with them they are up to no good bitsinvisi in floor locker code a=πr2 /A!d#)4e#&%h^F-Ð"!(B9! find them get them ALL."

Even in such a desperate situation he considered the safety of others and changed the Bitsi-FREQs used by these stolen CCOTCHAs. That gives me hope they cannot use the controller to abuse the Lord-ITs' CCOTCHAs.

I pull up a Bitsi-Lite view and zoom into Bio-Brain's lab, training a scan to begin the search for the hidden safe. There it is, in the floor under the lab table and holding all twelve Bitsi-INVISIs. In the underside of the table is a well-concealed compartment holding the space-pad for entering the code. The only question left to address is how to open the compartment under the table.

However, an alarm starts beeping on a DIRT-MAPP sspace as Medusa suddenly stirs in her bed, rolls over to the edge of the bed, and places her feet on the floor.

"Samson, she's awake, on the move."

"Yes, sir, I see it," he comes back immediately.

25

Protector's Loss

"**H**ere's your coffee, ma'am."

"She has a maid?" exclaims Samson.

"So it would seem, and she had the coffee made already. Planned."

As Medusa potters around her bedroom and bathroom, one of the LICKEMs on the Bitsi-Lite view of her house starts flashing. I deep-dive into her FONE to check the cause of this latest activity. It is an incoming text message from a contact she calls "my No. 1 man."

"U awake?" he writes.

Delilah and I watch as the message exchange continues.

"Y you down under?"

"Y watching our guests"

"They cooperating?"

"Nothing for them to do while we're still opening the package"

"I can't wait to finish her!"

"We need her!"

"U promised! I finish her, you him!"

"Y but not until we have everything we need"

"She can lose a little blood, then he'll know we are serious."

"U coming down?"

"Y just getting ready"

"OK"

"Delilah, watch that FONE."

"Yes, sir."

"Samson, get closer, ready to move in on both her and the Protector at a moment's notice. But stay out of sight of the security cameras."

"Yes, sir. I see those. I'm just zooming in on the area around Medusa's house. There's a tunnel, sir, leading from her house toward my target coordinates."

"Damn. Do you know where the entrance to that tunnel is?"

"Still locating that, sir."

"Find it."

"Yes, sir."

"DEL3: Delilah, those messages can only be from the HPD No. 1 man, and the Lord-ITs are with him. Medusa has a Killer-CCOTCHA in her head, controlled I'm guessing by him. If No. 1 finds out how close we are, then Medusa is a goner, and the Lord-ITs danger-level increases dramatically."

"Where is No. 1?" Delilah asks.

"Good question." I slide the coordinates of the mansion over to her O-WE-COME sspace.

"They're close to this position, but they're underground, and I can't see them. Something is stopping Bitsi-Lite from getting through. I'm working on that."

"So, what's the plan, sir?"

"Nothing solid. We have to try to get the Protector and Medusa safely locked up. First, I need to break through to those CCOTCHAs. I'm working on that, also. You study Medusa's messages with this guy; get into their heads—language, phrases, typing, response time between messages, etc. Check out the Protector's FONE, too, for possible communication. The plan is to knock out their CCOTCHAs, take them both. Then we continue the communication as if it were coming from them."

"She says she's going down to him, sir?"

"Yes, an added complication. The bottom-line, Del, is that she mustn't get down there, but we cannot give away how close we really are. Study the messages and look for a way to make it sound so convincing that she decides to stay where she is. I'll let you know when I have control of the CCOTCHAs. Then, we move in."

"Yes, sir."

The list of jobs I'm waiting for the Beast to complete just continues to grow—and my frustration with it. Now, I also need to find out how Medusa and the No. 1 man can communicate, while I can't. I need to see whether I can piggyback on their communication channel to see or hear anything underground.

Quickly checking the status of the Bitsi-Lite underground drilling experiment, the Beast is showing no ETA, but the soup-ah-hack he estimates will complete in seven minutes. Too long. But possibly enough time for me to find Medusa's communication channel and maybe even get into it.

On a new sspace in a fresh session on the Beast, I pull up the DIRT-MAPP and drag in Medusa's DIGIT-FONE, then choose her number as the source and the No. 1 man's as the target.

"SHOW-ROUTE," I command the Beast. Then, stretching my legs, I wander over to the coffee machine for a recess and a refill.

Pacing the office, keeping one eye on all the screens, I take stock of the events so far while also thinking through the coming to-do's. Too many event-paths are out of my control, which always makes me nervous. I need to work out how to take over and direct the shape of the future, at least for a few hours. My ability to take control, however, starts with being able to communicate with LICKEMs over Bitsi-Lite, and that's exactly what I'm stuck on right now.

Maybe this path from Medusa's FONE to the No. 1 FONE will give me something, but I'm not hopeful. If they can secure a LICKEM, they could also secure this channel. I need all these communication paths open, but once they are, what then, what then?

Sliding back into my huge, luxurious office chair, which offers no special comfort right now, the Beast is pointing directly at a LICKEM lying above the Bitsi-FRIGHT layer but under ground level. Zooming in with Bitsi-Lite, I inspect all the components of the equipment housing the LICKEM, and it's easy to spot.

Unbelievable. They've hard-wired a router to take the Bitsi-Lite signals from the LICKEM above ground down to what can only be another router under the Bitsi-FRIGHT layer. It must be more than eighty years since anyone hard-wired anything. I didn't know the technology even existed anymore. Stealing a little of the data from the Bitsi-FREQs before it hits the router, the encryption is plainly and painfully visible, another stumbling block.

The answer to a previous question is immediately obvious. I cannot use this communication channel. If they can install a DIGI-CERT on KILLER-CCOTCHAs and recreate ancient routers using LICKEMs, then they can easily monitor all activity on just a single router. Hacking in on an encrypted channel will show an obvious increase in confuzer power being used. And, as small and obscure as it may be, the extra data the DIRT-CRAWLER attaches to data packets when hacking through to their systems will still be visible. If they're watching carefully, then they'll see all this. It's too big a risk. The Beast is showing three and a half minutes to complete the soup-ah-hack. How is it that minutes can fill an arduous yet nonproductive lifetime when counting them?

The lives of many, including these two PERPS, hang on the thread of my broken communication. In three and a half minutes, anything could happen.

I prep the Beast to send in the DIRT-CRAWLER once the soup-ah-hack is complete, and to reroute all incoming traffic on the CCOTCHA. This will prevent the No. 1 man from giving a successful kill command.

"Samson, have you found out how Medusa gets to that tunnel?"

"Yes, sir." He pulls up a Bitsi-Lite view of the house, highlighting the route down to the tunnel.

And Medusa is visible, heading directly toward that same route. Damn it, she's already on the way to the No. 1 man.

With the tap of a finger, I link the London and US teams into a single, previously prepared CCOTCHA session.

"*PRO_MED:* PRO_MED, be prepared. We need to coordinate closely."

I hear a round of "yes, sir."

"Samson, we have to stall her."

"Yes, sir."

"Try interview tactics; you've seen her headlines, you're wondering if she can shed any more light on the current BIG-AM-I problems, something like that. If she doesn't bite, then ask about the tap into the communications of the CCIO of BIG-AM-I."

"Yes, sir."

"Move in, now!"

One hundred and forty-five seconds to complete the soup-ah-hack. Samson's men move in on Medusa's house. They ring at the front doorbell and prepare to show their security credentials through the security camera beside the door.

On her way down underground, Medusa is halfway between the tunnel and the front door. On hearing the doorbell, she stops, deciding what to do, then turns abruptly toward the front door.

One hundred and twenty-five seconds to complete the soup-ah-hack. I still have both Medusa and the Protector in a split view on a single large sspace.

Suddenly, I notice movement on the Protector's half of the sspace. He's also heading for his front door. And the London team is on the other side of it. They're already showing their BITS-SECS credentials to the security camera.

"LONDON, what the hell are you doing?" Bitsi-Tone.

They must have heard my last command to move in and reacted. They weren't paying attention. Samson, I guess, has also been focusing on Medusa and had also not seen the London team move in.

"Er, didn't you tell us to move in, sir?"

"Shut up. Do not say *another* word." Bitsi-Tone.

"And get those BITS-SECS credentials away from that camera," Samson adds.

As the Protector raises his hand to answer the security intercom, a light flares up on the O-WE-COME sspace.

"Ughhhhhhhhhh. The Protector is down. Knock on the door again. Wait a few moments. Then fall back. As if nobody's home." I force out the words.

We need to get out of there, pretending we haven't noticed anything, if possible. The HPD No. 1 man will suspect we're getting closer to him, but he mustn't know how close.

One hundred and ten seconds to complete the soup-ah-hack.

26

Lovers' Harsh Breakup

ONE HUNDRED AND eighteen seconds to complete the soup-ah-hack, and Medusa has reached her front door and opens communication on her security intercom.

"Do you know what time it is? What do you want?"

"Medusa, ma'am, we saw your headline this morning. Do you have any more information on this BIG-AM-I problem?"

"No more than I already published. Now, let me get back to bed." She cuts them off harshly, and switching off the security screen, she turns away from the door.

"Medusa, ma'am, one more question. How is it you have such intimate knowledge of the internal communication of BIG-AM-I's Sissy-O?"

Medusa stops dead in her tracks to assess the question, then returns to the intercom. "Confidential sources, just like every reporter. And they're protected by law."

"Not if they break the law," Junior responds.

"Well, that you'd have to prove first," she shouts back, turning off the intercom again.

"Junior, steady now. Stand down for now; get out of sight again," I command, almost gently. Junior and his colleague turn and head back out of the line of the windows and cameras.

Eighty-five seconds to complete the soup-ah-hack.

I stare the Beast down, desperately watching the seconds until he sends in the DIRT-CRAWLER with the takeover command.

Grabbing her keys from a bowl on a shelf in the main corridor, Medusa yells, "Tilde." Her maid appears instantly. "Tilde, I need some tampons, urgently. Go down to the store and get some right now. Take my keys. I'll show you to the car."

Attempting to create a diversion for the BITS-SECS team, Medusa practically drags Tilde to the garage. As she shoves her into the car, she demands, "So, do you remember how to drive it?"

"Yes, ma'am."

"Good. Don't damage it. I have work to do, so don't disturb me when you get back. Leave the tampons in my bathroom."

Medusa slams the car door and watches the maid start up her soup-ah-expensive automobile.

As the closing garage door salutes Tilde's exit, the Beast starts beeping wildly, indicating that the soup-ah-hack is complete. I watch avidly as the DIRT-CRAWLER flies into Medusa's KILLER-CCOTCHA and takes control, while almost at the same moment, just milliseconds later, an incoming kill command gets quarantined into the newly created junk box.

The No. 1 man just tried to remove his co-conspirator, and I'm guessing his lover. She also has become too high-risk.

Medusa turns and starts running back toward the tunnel.

"Delilah, send her a message."

"On it, sir."

The instruction "Wait until BITS-SECS have gone before you come down. Do NOT come down while they're still around" flies into Medusa's DIGIT-FONE. Medusa's hand dives into her handbag, which is swinging in all directions as she's running, grabs her FONE, and starts typing a message.

Half in horror, half in shock, I see she's picked up the wrong FONE, and I dive into the Beast to see what she's doing. As she opens her work FONE, in a small window on the split-sspace view, I'm just in time to see the message leaving. Noticing that she has the wrong FONE but ignoring this, she sends the message "coming down now."

Half a second later another kill command comes through into the junk box on the KILLER-CCOTCHA.

The No. 1 man knows she's not dead, yet, and seems anxious to try once more. "Remember to close the door properly," he writes.

"Yeah already done don't worry" Medusa has already mounted a four-wheel buggy and is starting down the tunnel.

The kill command arrives again. "Is the buggy starting OK?"

"Yep."

By now I'm hoping that the No. 1 man is thinking that the KILLER-CCOTCHA is simply malfunctioning. It's pretty obvious Medusa is refusing to die.

"Bitsi, sir. A new LICKEM. In the tunnel going to Medusa's house, sir," Samson half yells.

"Zoom in on them both, Samson. I want a full visual. Delilah, make sure we record this."

We watch as the No. 1 man and Medusa drive toward each other at high speed. Within less than a minute, they meet in the middle of the tunnel.

Jumping off their buggies, they run to each other and start kissing and groping each other, pressing up together. The No. 1 man lifts up Medusa's skirt and pulls down her underwear while she works on his pants. He turns her around and enters her from behind, putting a hand first on her shoulder, then working up to her neck and around her throat, making her moan with pleasure.

"You like that, huh?"

"And so do you," she laughs.

"Here, try this," he retorts, pulling the belt from his pants and wrapping it around her neck, deftly slipping the end of the belt through the buckle. They have obviously done this before.

Positioning belt and buckle in his right hand so he has full control over how tight it is, he places his left hand on her shoulder and starts pushing harder and faster into her, causing her to moan constantly, until she can no longer breathe. Even as she begins to show signs of distress, the No. 1 man maintains his powerful grip on her and continues thrusting himself into her, and with each push forces the last breaths out of her.

Once satisfied with his filthy deed, he loosens the belt, and she slides lifeless from him and hits the floor with a dull thud. He quickly checks Medusa for lack of pulse, then drives her buggy back to her house to be sure of the locked hidden door down to the tunnel. On the way back to the underground hideout, Medusa's body is unceremoniously dumped behind a sliding panel in the wall of the tunnel, like a specially built coffin in a pre-dug grave. No expense spared for loved ones.

27

BITSI INVISIBLE

Harrowing moments of silence follow as the three of us try in our own way to deal with the horrific show of heartless brutality we just witnessed. Tears are trickling down my face, and I'm again thankful for the mask that hides this from the O-WE-COME video.

With a heavy heart, I cannot help but do the math. Eleven dead so far. Who knows how many more to follow. If this murderer has tricks enough to succeed in running off with the secrets of Nuke-Li-Aerial power, millions, even billions, could die.

Sitting back in my chair, head hanging a little to one side, a small but insistent part of me is trying to enter the mind of someone who could commit such an atrocity, seeking to understand why. Yet the driving force of my conscientiousness is countering, steering me away from that line of thought, frightened, desperate to avoid possible contamination through comprehension.

Kicking my fear squarely in the groin and defying the scowl of the monster eye to eye, I gaze deeply into those ruthless eyes to force out the nightmares he has hidden from himself. Awareness of his self-made predicament begins to surface. He's afraid that by attempting to hide from me he has built a trap for himself. He's afraid that I'll find him regardless of all his precautionary measures, and when I do, he will be irredeemably condemned on the underground-spot. His growing anxiety fuels his panic as he senses me coming step-by-step closer. Panic is building up inside him, yet he's subconsciously refusing to accept it, trying to hide from it, and it's causing his reckless and spiteful slaughtering of anyone that becomes a threat in aiding me to get close enough to spring his accidentally self-made, self-ensnaring trap.

CASH and untold power are no longer his key motivation, but rather survival. He's becoming more dangerous with every hour that passes.

The imaginary confrontation with the No. 1 man has awakened my fear and my passionate hatred of monsters, revived my motivation to push on, and summoned my inner strength. I'll be damned before giving in to him or letting him win such an unscrupulous battle that aims at potentially horrific goals.

Turning to the Beast, who's still pushing up MAVACAPA prying his way through to the underground prison, I can see the structure of the protective roof, so far uncovered. From the highest to the lowest layer, it's made of one-meter thick lead, aluminum, copper, and three centimeters platinum. That's one expensive roof. Then lead, platinum, copper, and more aluminum. Between every single layer, there's a layer of polyethylene-like material.

The Bitsi-FREQ signals have been and are once again bouncing back and forth all over the place. The combination of materials is distorting the flow of the FREQs.

The Beast is being cautious, as designed, and going slowly through the next layer, but it's obvious what's needed.

After studying the variables that the Beast has been tweaking for each new layer, throwing caution to the wind and using human intuition—which the Beast lacks—happily, I make a manual tweak of my own, forcing the Beast down through the next polyethylene layer. And sure enough, we hit lead—for the last time, I suspect.

I tweak again, jumping first fifty, then twenty-five, then twenty-five centimeters again, down through the layer of lead to hit solid earth. After that, it's plain sailing, and within a few milliseconds, we're all the way through to underground, filtered airspace.

All the underground LICKEMs magically become visible on the screen-space. First, I direct the Beast to show me video and sound and to start recording everything. I need to know what's going on down there.

"Samson, we're through the protective layer with Bitsi-Lite. Here, start looking for ways in and out. Do *not* try to hack into anything, just look."

"Yes, sir."

I throw the Bitsi-Lite view of the subterranean complex onto the shared O-WE-COME sspace, and on another sspace I continue with one eye to watch the video of what's going on down there.

"Delilah, please start finding out who we have under there. I'm sure there'll be a few names we know, but we need to check all of them. I'm guessing we have some nasty characters; I need to know just how bad. Also, check out the complete house and grounds around. We need a live body count."

"Yes, sir."

"Bitsi, sir," Samson yells in my ear. "Lord-IT is in there. And his wife."

"Yes, Samson. Why do you think I sent you to the US? I would only trust my best with this rescue op, Samson."

"Rescue, sir?"

"Yes. They've been kidnapped. We know the chief PERPS is a cold-blooded killer. While Delilah is checking out who the others are, you need to find out how to get in, and how to get the Lord-ITs out of there alive. Also, assess how much danger there is in the big house and grounds."

"I've just checked out the underground keep, sir. There are only two usable passageways. One from the main house, one from Medusa's place."

"Useable, Samson?"

He shows me the third tunnel on the screen-space. It's not far from where the Lord-ITs are sitting on a sofa against the back wall in the main underground room.

"Here, another tunnel leading out, but it leads into solid ground, unfinished. There's a door leading out to it, but not like the other two doors. It's not solid, not secured, just closes off the passage. There's no other way in except from the two main passages."

"Hmmm. And the more I do with their confuzers to take control of those entrances, the faster they'll notice. I'm sure they're watching them closely."

"We'd need to be invisible to get in there unnoticed," Samson exclaims.

"Invisible," I mutter quietly.

"Bitsi, sir?"

"Thinking..."

"Samson, you remember that thing in your contract—about your life on the line, etc.?"

"Of course, sir."

Good man.

"I've been working on something, together with, er, Bio-Brains. I have almost finished testing it."

"And what is that, sir?"

"It's difficult to explain quickly, Samson. I don't understand much of it myself. The basic idea is that an extremely small but nevertheless soup-ah confuzer with a souped-up Nuke-Li-Aerial power source, using Bitsi-Lite technology, scans the entity (body, house, car) it's attached to and generates a soup-ah-intense and dense layer of soup-ah-high-frequency Bitsi-Lite signals surrounding the being. From inside this dense signal layer, the Nuke-Li-Aerial power source generates light, which is captured, wrapped and hidden in some of the signals and thrown out in a curveball much like a boomerang, touching and/or passing through the various surfaces or gasses outside the Bitsi-Lite layer, which by various techniques such as reflection changes the qualities of the light rays and also the Bitsi-Lite signals, capturing in the signals the relevant data indicating the color, density, etc., of what's on the outer side of the signal layer.

"The light is dispersed, but the now inbound signal transmissions holding color/density/etc. data are sent to the confuzer, which uses the information to generate the full picture of the image obscured by the thing that the confuzer is attached to, as well as its surroundings, and covering all angles, of course. Using this reconstructed image, the confuzer throws out more colored light rays, which the Bitsi-Lite layer captures and re-emits around the attached being, to imitate this reconstructed image. Making the attached being, er, invisible."

"Er, great. Does it work?" Samson asks, sounding a little hesitant.

"Of course, it does. I just never tested it on human subjects before."

"Oh. And now you want to test it on me, sir?"

"Whether I want to or not is irrelevant, Samson. As I see it right now, it's our best option."

"Hmmm. I'm afraid I might have to agree with you, sir. Bitsi, sir?"

"Thinking..."

"Damn it. I wasn't ready for this. I need to get the Bitsi-INVISIs over to you. That could take hours, depending on how many you need. And we may not have even a single hour."

"Maybe you do, sir," Delilah interrupts. "They're trying to decrypt a package down there and have just hit a stumbling block. Some kind of double encryption. Earliest ETA for breaking through is six hours from now, sir."

A small smile touches my lips as I imagine the trouble the PERPS are experiencing opening their stolen package. This will be one of the many problems they've encountered in the past month trying to break open my little box of tricks designed to lead people up the garden path and give me time to find them. But my concern for the Lord-ITs' safety also increases as I realize that the frustration levels down there will be intensifying.

Opening a new screen-space, I start up a large clock and set a six-hour countdown. "Do we have a PERPS count?"

Delilah responds immediately, "Twenty-six in total, twenty underground, including the JERK and the NETNERD, six more security guys in the main house, sir. There are fifteen more, but they're all house servants."

The JERK's presence surprises me, but only a little. "Damn it. More than I had expected. Any nasties?"

"The six in the house and ten below are highly trained mercenaries. One of them is a match for Bio-Brains' ex-labby's new boyfriend, sir."

"Damn it, again. Samson, how many guys do you need to get in there? Absolutely no risk operation, Samson."

"All invisible, sir?"

"Is that needed?"

"Sir," Delilah chips in, "the cameras around the house cover every single square meter up to five hundred meters from the building."

Samson takes over. "So, yes, sir, all invisible. And I'm afraid, Bitsi, sir, no risk is impossible. The layout underground is not conducive to a safe operation, sir. For a minimum-high-risk operation, fifteen. Ten to carry out the rescue underground. Each man taking out two PERPS. Two more to guard the entrances. Three to take care of the six above ground. An expensive op, sir, but that's the most optimal and still with no guarantees."

"And your cheapest option, Samson?" I know the answer will be more than four, but I need to hear it.

"Sir?"

"Just give me the number, Samson."

"Five, sir. Four under and one to cover aboveground. But again, all invisible. And of course, that's a very high-risk op, sir. Sir?"

"Thinking...

OK, I have four Bitsi-INVISIs here with me. At last count, Bio-Brains had twelve locked away. We need to get them all to you. Roughly calculated, it will take five hours before the Beijing batch arrives. Your assessment, Samson?"

"How fast to get yours here, sir?"

"Three hours. I'll send Jonesy with them. He'll want to assist with the rescue, and he'll be a good addition to the team."

"Yes, sir. I suggest we get them all here ASAP, sir. Four is not enough, but as a Plan B, it's better than none."

"OK, Samson, get Beijing ready to move in. They'll need masks in there; the body odor will be tough to endure. Use the back-door entrance. Be ready to direct them down to the lab."

"Yes, sir."

"Delilah, is the Bio-Brains camera hack ready?"

"Yes, sir. Here," and she passes the program over the O-WE-COME chat.

Popping the usual trick question, I ask, "Was it tested?"

"Thoroughly, sir," is the confident reply.

"Good. Everybody, stand by."

First, I arrange a CHOPPA to meet the team's transporter, then a soup-ah-sonic flight for the Beijing BITS-SECS man who'll take the Bitsi-INVISIs to Samson, then push the coordinates over to Samson. The hangar holding all the aircraft is close to the team's current location, so not much CHOPPA time will be lost reaching it.

On the shared O-WE-COME meeting, I pull up the DIRT-MAPP view of Bio-Brains' security system and single out the level-1 security cameras into a new screen-space. After checking that I can unlock all the doors with the click of a button, I move my attention to the camera-hack. They're all the same make and model. Bio-Brains always ensured this; he hated having to maintain different soft-BITS on each camera. This makes my life a little easier right now.

Selecting all the cams, I open a command panel on the Beast, creating a session that will send commands to all the cameras at the same time. The command to install the hack takes just seconds to type in and complete the installation.

All the cameras are quickly restarted. Anyone watching would notice a momentary glitch in the video stream. Let's hope no one is watching.

Switching to the Bitsi-Lite view of Bio-Brains' house once more, I prepare to watch the team's progress throughout this Bitsi-INVISI recovery op.

"*BEIJING*: Samson, I've got the doors."

"Beijing, move in," he commands.

Within fifteen seconds, five guys are at the back door, and the last two team members are standing point, watching out for any approaching trouble.

"Doors unlocked," I inform them. As the last man enters, I lock the doors again. All five guys head straight for the main corridor through the house. Samson has already prepared them.

"Two at the door, the rest of you down to the lab," he commands. Their responsibilities on attack-and-watch are embedded in their attack protocol. Three guys, including the Beijing lead, disappear without hesitation down the stairwell while the last two take up their guard positions.

The bodies of Bio-Brains and his kids are still lying there. They're not in the way, so no need to move them.

"Beijing-1, look under the lab table. Can you see any hidden compartment?" I ask.

"One moment, sir," he responds, as he dives under the table to look. "No, sir, nothing visible."

I zoom in again with Bitsi-Lite, not sure what should come next. I can see where it is, but how to get into it?

"From your current position, forward right corner, place your hand there."

"Yes, sir."

"To the left two centimeters. Now, gently push up." Nothing happens. No obvious movement.

Come on, Bitsi. Think. Other pressure points? What about the code? a=πr2 /A!d#)4e#&%h^F-Đ"!(B9!

"Sir?"

"Thinking..."

"That's it. a=πr^2 is the formula for calculating the area of a circle."

"Use one finger, draw a circle in the area around where your hand is now," I say. Nothing happens. "A smaller circle."

As the drawer opens, a penny drops elsewhere. Damn it. I can be so dumb sometimes.

"Move out from under the table." There was no need to waste time opening the drawer.

I point the Beast at the LICKEM inside the tiny confuzer, which is housed inside the control panel in the drawer, and give him the password that Bio-Brains left me. The Beast knows what to do, and within seconds the table suddenly rises then slides back a whole meter.

The safe offers no further protection. The heavy lab table, the hidden compartment, and long, complex password for the LICKEM would be enough under normal circumstances.

"Open the door, remove the three boxes from inside."

"Yes, sir."

"Now, Beijing-1, get the team out of there, and you get to your CHOPPA immediately and get those boxes to Samson."

"Yes, sir."

"Beijing-1, protect that package."

"Yes, sir."

I still have the whole Beijing team showing on the FOOLEM session I started earlier. Selecting Beijing-1, I instruct the Beast to FOOLHIM in a separate screen-space.

Thirty-eight seconds later, as the Beijing team vacates the range of the house security cameras, I reverse the hack, restoring the normal security camera soft-BITS and operations.

"Samson, guide your man further, please. His journeys are preprogrammed; he just needs to get into the vehicles. I'll arrange for Jonesy to bring the other four Bitsi-INVISIs. In the meantime, prepare a plausible Plan B, Samson."

"Yes, sir."

Not wasting any time, I open up a new CCOTCHA session with Samson, Delilah, and Lord-IT's head of security, then pull him into action.

"Jonesy, prepare for a trip. The three spare transporters are close to you. I'll send one now. Six minutes, be ready."

"Yes, Bitsi, sir."

My quota of transporters and soup-ah-sonic planes is in a hangar close to my home. The spare transporters are there, also.

On the DIRT-MAPP, I pull up a view of the vehicles, choose one of the transporters and send it to my house. Another transporter I send to the cottage.

Now I need to get a move on. The first vehicle will arrive here in less than a minute.

Dashing down to the basement under my office, screaming numbers as I run, I pass through a combination locked door that has opened to the sound of my voice singing the correct numbers. On the far side of the room, I open a hand-scan locked door leading into a walk-in safe. The Bitsi-INVISIs are on a shelf not far from the door and easily reachable.

I frantically search for something to pack them in. On finding an old canvas bag from an exhibition I attended once, I'm thankful I haven't yet done the spring-cleaning I promised myself many decades ago. I grab the box of Bitsi-INVISIs, stuff it into the bag and zip it closed while turning to run back upstairs yelling, "SAFE-LOCK." Both doors automatically close and secure themselves.

As usual, the kids are awake early and are already in the living room. Fortunately, they're planted fairly and squarely in front of the TV (as I still call it), so they hardly notice me as I dash through the house to get to the front door.

After placing the bag holding the Bitsi-INVISIs into the jaws of a robot-loader just inside the main door of the transporter, using a remote-control panel I grabbed from my desk on the way out, I return the vehicle to the hangar.

Tearing back down the length of the living area, my oldest baby girl sees me and throws a half-sleepy frown my way. Mustering up a huge happy grin and a little wave is enough to transform her expression into the exuberant, sparkling, smiling vision that always makes my smile even broader. That uninhibited expression of love so obvious in our kids is something we should learn to develop during our adult lives, not forget.

The eyes of my other two angels are glued to their movie, but my wife is giving me a questioning look. Blowing her a kiss is all I have time for. She'll guess that I'm making progress, and that if the news had worsened, she would know about it already.

Settling in behind Seribus, I smack a few keys to instruct the Beast to calculate a fifteen-minute, high-speed journey from the cottage and the hangar to somewhere, anywhere in the general direction of the US, where Jonesy's transporter can safely meet the plane. This will ensure that Jonesy has not much idea how close he is to either my house or the hangar for the planes.

The transporter's speed potential is known only by a few, and Jonesy is one of those few. They can travel up to eight hundred kilometers per hour, so a fifteen-minute trip would give roughly an area of one-hundred-nineteen-thousand square kilometers to cover if he wished to start guessing where it originated from. Yes, the trip will cost quite some minutes longer than strictly required, but security is always a priority. It's not that I don't trust Jonesy, but if he ever gets captured, how much information his captors can force out of him is the key concern.

The plane is already warmed up and ready to go, so using a joystick to control a helpful Nuke-Li-Aerially-powered robot, I transfer the Bitsi-INIVISIs from the now-returned transporter to the loading bay in the back of the plane, then send it on its way, ready to receive JONSEY when he arrives.

All done. Two minutes before Jonesy can board his ride. I arranged all that in less than five minutes. Not bad for an old man. Time for a coffee break.

After a few minutes wandering around my office, glancing intermittently at the sspaces and thinking through the events so far, I return to check on Jonesy's status. He's just settling into his seat.

"Jonesy, I'll be disabling your gadgets for a while, as usual." The LICKEMs of all Cottage visitors are under the Beast's control during their stay. They are only returned to normal operation once the guests have reached a safe distance from the house.

"Yes, sir. Not a problem, sir."

"Very good, Jonesy."

On the DIRT-MAPP, clicking on Jonesy in his transporter, I give more instructions to my soup-ah confuzer to shut down all guest communications. All Jonesy's equipment stops, except his CCOTCHA.

On hitting the Go button on the Beast's view that shows the travel plans, Jonesy's transporter springs into the air on its way to meet the soup-ah-sonic plane.

Then, as a precaution, I lay down a few ground rules.

"Samson, Jonesy is on the first leg of the journey. Jonesy, are you sitting comfortably?"

"Yes, sir."

"Good. Your transporter will meet with a plane in fifteen minutes. All you need to do is board and buckle up immediately. When you arrive at your destination, Samson will be there. Jonesy, I understand that, technically speaking, Lord-IT is in your care, but on this operation, Samson is in charge. Is that clear?"

"Most definitely, sir."

Delilah suddenly interrupts the communications. "Bitsi, sir. COCKS has lost his patience, sir. He's on the rampage about OBOY's abducted DOLLIES."

"Damn it. I was hoping the SICCO would keep them occupied for six to eight hours at least."

Roughly five hours, thirty minutes before the Nuke-Li-Aerial files are hacked open.

28

COCKS, WE'RE UNDER A-HACK!

SWITCHING OVER TO the BIG-AM-I O-WE-COME, I listen for a few seconds as the Sissy rips the guts out of the people on the task force OBOY.

"*What do you mean you can't get it up?*" he screams.

"COCKS, this is the BITS Inspector. What the *hell* do you think you're doing?" Silence on the conference call. "I understand your impatience, COCKS, but you need to *curb* it. You're not helping like this. I'll give you a full update on our findings just as soon..."

"All Systems Go!" the whole younger generation tribe charge in screaming at the top of their unbelievably loud little voices.

"Hang on, COCKS." And I black out the complete O-WE-COME, bringing this major BIG-AM-I crisis to an utter standstill again. No one can hear or see anything.

Opening my arms to them, my babies jostle for the best position in Daddy's embrace. "Hi, my sweet baby girl. Did you sleep well?"

"I peed in your bed," she pronounces sadly.

"Hmmm. Next time, please pee on Mommy's side of the bed, will you?"

"OK," she answers exuberantly, throwing Mommy an extraordinarily cheeky smile.

"My beautiful boy, did you sleep well?" And he just nods, still not fully awake, or with it—I'm not sure which. I give him a big hug and kiss, which he dutifully wipes from his face.

"And my little princess. Did you sleep well?"

"I did, until she peed in the bed."

"Oh, princess. You weren't sleeping in Daddy's bed, were you?" She throws me a big, wide-open, and defiant "Yes!" smile.

As I wag my big-daddy finger at her, she barks her young but nevertheless raucous Bitsi laugh loudly at me.

In my life at home with my family, I'm not the boss. I'm the husband, the lover, the father, and their protector, and they know this. I'm loving, caring, soft, and gentle, humorous, and happy, firm but forgiving, and all in that order. At work, however, first I'm often humorous, then hard, then harder, then even harder and harsh with it, almost unforgiving sometimes, and every so often soft and gentle, all in that order. I am just as hard with myself as I am with others.

My laugh at work is mostly the chuckle, just sometimes it's the Bitsi laugh. But at home there are no inhibitions holding me back, and I'm all me, laughing openly, often, and loudly. We don't call it the Bitsi laugh at home, but it is the Bitsi laugh, because it's my laugh, and I am Bitsi.

"Here, hon, get dressed. You never know who may show up at the door," my wife says as she hands me some clothes. "And here's a fresh cup. But from now on, you need to use that machine over there. I'll be busy," she says, raising her head in the direction of the espresso wizard on one side of the room.

I give a slow, deliberate nod showing that I've understood the hidden worries. Being able to read between the lines is important in business, but it's a critical must-have survival skill for married people.

"And what day is it today?" I raise my voice above the racket.

"Friday. Sweeties day." A unanimous vote.

"No, no, no. Not every day is Friday, boys and girls. Today is Tuesday, so no sweets today."

"Just one." "Just one." "Just one." Three voices speak simultaneously.

"You had better ask Mommy about that," I respond, and I throw Mommy *my* cheekiest smile.

"Thanks a lot, honey. Kids, don't you have something for Daddy?"

All three of them proudly present their homemade Father's Day gifts. Our youngest girl also decides she'll help me out a little and opens hers for me.

"Boys and girls, did you all make these by yourself? Just for Daddy?"

"Yes, we did."

"I made mine."

"Mommy helped me. It was difficult. The glue sticked the paper all to my fingers."

Oh, man. Those baby boys and girls tug on my heartstrings with almost everything they do and say, especially those endearing, smiling, proud, oh-so-happy faces when they're giving something to Mommy or Daddy. If only it could stay this way. If only their gorgeous, innocent, blissful faces would never start to show the lines of worry and pain that we older folk suffer from. I still don't know what I'm going to tell them when they start to ask the difficult questions such as, "Why did he do that to her, Daddy?"

Whatever the answer will be, it will include, "You should never..."

"Boys and girls, your presents are beautiful. I'm going to hang them up here on my drawing board."

"Let me." "Let me." "Let me."

We all hang up the presents with drawing board magnets and happily admire them for a few moments. "Now you three out, and go and find clothes for today."

"I can't leave here much today, hon. There's still a lot to do before we're out of the woods."

She just nods, knowingly. Then, we kiss, and she herds the tribe out through the kid-safe door.

Watching her as she leaves, despite the current distressing circumstances, I find myself wishing we could quickly have a go at producing one more, to help make and wrap up the Father's Day presents.

Kicking the O-WE-COME into action again, I check that COCKS is still there. "COCKS?"

"I trust that was something extremely important, Bitsi, sir?"

"Oh Lord-IT, yes!"

"Oh. All right then. You were saying?"

"Yes. I'll update you soon, but first let me finish what I was doing. Just a few minutes more, then I'll get back to you."

I again black out the entire BIG-AM-I O-WE-COME meeting so COCKS can scream only at himself.

"Samson, when I've dealt with this guy, I want to hear plan B."

"Yes, sir."

And get up to the Sissy with a marker. Now, please."

"Yes, sir."

Reluctantly dragging my attention fully back to the BIG-AM-I OBOY troubles, I zoom in on a Bitsi-Lite view of the CCIO's office. The Sissy is pacing back and forth so fast you'd think he was trying to stamp on each absconding DOLLY to trap each one of them under his feet, attempting to prevent the further enrichment of a monstrous extra-terrestrial black hole.

Locating an OOO-O-WE-COME on a lower floor, I punch in the coordinates for COCKS' office. You can almost see the cute little machine smiling as it turns and races off to seek out its appointed target. They don't get to go up to the penthouse floor too often.

The flying screen arrives in COCKS' office long before Samson's BITS-SECS agent, so I decide to override the controls of his office door to allow the OOO-O-WE-COME to enter. On seeing my masked face, the Sissy squeals, "TRIPSI Bitsi," and backs away from me. But why, I'm not sure.

Choosing the approach carefully, weaving continuously from left to right, I back him up until he falls with a thump on his rump into his office chair.

"How do you do, COCKS?" My mask smiles at him as sweetly as possible, but under the circumstances, I guess that doesn't come over as pleasantly as planned.

Then, Oslo-1 charges through the door without so much as knocking. Over the CCOTCHA, he heard that I'm already in the office with the CCIO.

"My apologies, sir," he says while coming to a standstill.

COCKS and his ego mistakenly assume he's being spoken to.

"No problem, Oslo-1..." I begin to respond.

"What are you doing charging in..."

"Shut up, COCKS."

"Now, COCKS, you'll be marked before we start. The information I'm about to give you is more expensive than you can afford to lose, and I need to ensure you don't abuse it. If you attempt to pass on even a single letter of what I'm about to give, you can kiss goodbye to your brand-new job and a whole lot more. Am I making myself clear, COCKS?" Bitsi-Tone.

"Er, y-y-yes," he stutters.

"Good. Oslo-1, please."

The BITS-SECS agent walks over to the Sissy pulling out his marker pistol as he advances. The Sissy, true to his job title, whimpers a little as the agent presses the dart gun against his arm. A thin layer of shirt sleeve is not enough to slow down the injection needle as the marker is implanted deep into the biceps of the CCIO.

"We'll monitor your movements, COCKS. We'll record everything you do and say. Is this clear, COCKS?"

"Er, yes."

Being constantly conscious of the PERPS listening in over the Sissy-O's hacked communication channels, I need to choose my words carefully.

"COCKS, we are under A-Hack[129]. And it is quite an intelligent one. I, er, currently have no idea what's going on."

"What do you mean?"

"Do *not* interrupt me, COCKS." Bitsi-Tone.

On the sspace showing the HPD No. 1 man's underground hideout, I can see the exuberant mutual show of thumbs up as they hear that I apparently don't yet know what's happening. That should help to reduce the stress levels down there, for a while at least.

"Now, the fastest and, indeed, the only way we'll get to the bottom of this is if you leave me and my team to do our work. It's obvious your employees aren't going to be of any help to us. Indeed, they'll only slow us down. So, you need to leave us alone to get through this. Am I making myself clear, COCKS?"

"Er, yes, Bitsi, sir. But what about all that CASH?" he pleads.

"Worst case, COCKS, is that the CASH is gone, disappeared forever. This message you should bring to your bosses. You may tell them I'm trying to recover the CASH, but at this point there can be no promise of success."

"Oh, dear," the Sissy exclaims.

"Yes, well, I do understand your predicament, COCKS. Second day on the job and all that. But I can't hang around here commiserating with you. I need to get back to work."

"Yes, please don't let me hold you up any further."

"One more thing, COCKS. Ease up on your employees. Beating them up is not going to improve your standing in this organization."

"Er..."

The OOO-O-WE-COME swoops out of the room with Oslo-1 rushing out following on its heels, leaving the CCIO sitting slouched in his chair, wondering what his next move should be. I do not envy him. It isn't a pleasant position he finds himself in, having to report to his

---

129 [1] Cyber-attack; a break-in to a soft-BITS program, confuzer, file, etc.; [2] an illicit modification to a soft-BITS program made with less-than-positive intentions

spanking-new boss that all income raised during his first two days in office has disappeared and possibly cannot be recovered.

Roughly five hours, twenty minutes before the Nuke-Li-Aerial files are hacked open.

29

PLAN B AND C

GOING BACK TO the joint CCOTCHA with Samson & Jonesy, I'm curious to hear how Lordy and his wife might be rescued with a bare minimum squad of just four agents.

"Samson?"

"Yes, sir. Plan B. Station two at the back door from Medusa's house, two at the front. You first take over all communications, then immediately open the front door first. OPs1 go in to create confusion, a diversion. Five seconds later, you open the back door. OPs2 will go directly to protect the Lord-ITs, and we stun the hell out of anything that moves. Exit through the back door and Medusa's place, locking everyone else down there."

"Who will go in?"

"Me, Junior, Jules, and Jonesy, sir."

"Bitsi, sir?"

"Thinking..."

One beep.

"Samson, listen. I don't want both of you going down there."

"Sir?"

"You and Junior. I don't want to risk you both."

"But, sir, Junior is the US team lead. He has more experience than all the others together."

"I know that, Samson. But I don't want to have to go to your wife reporting two dead. And there's a real risk of that."

"I know that, Bitsi, sir, but if we don't have Junior down there, we lose years of experience, and the risk of losing the Lord-ITs grows rapidly."

"I know. But I do not want him down there... Samson?"

"You also don't want him in Plan A, right?"

"Correct. Those people down there are extremely dangerous, Samson."

"And that's exactly why he must be with us. And if he's not with us, he'll lose his standing in the team. His trust in you will be severely impacted. And I couldn't look my own son in the eye after that, Bitsi, sir. We talked through all of this before you agreed to hire him. You can't go back now. It would be devastating for him. And for us."

Heaving a big sigh, I force myself to back down. Samson's right; I made commitments already, and it's Junior's responsibility to be one of the first down there. Damn it.

"All right, Samson. Let's get back to the others."

Two beeps.

"Plan B approved, Samson. Have you considered a Plan C?"

"Yes, sir. Seven guys, entry from Medusa's back tunnel. You would need to take over all security cams on that route to hide our entry. Risky, coz they're monitored, and some of the cameras scan unpredictably. And choosing a time to commit the team underground is also risky. If we go in too early and something goes wrong on our side, we may force a confrontation without having backup close by. Go in too late, well, that's obvious."

"Hmmm... Summarize the progress please, Samson."

"The US team and I are together and working on tactical planning. Jonesy is with us on O-WE-COME and will join us here in just over two and a half hours. Beijing-1 will arrive around an hour and a half after Jonesy. That brings us to about 06:20 New York time, roughly four hours and twenty minutes from now. Between now and Jonesy arriving, we consider Plan C. After that, we prepare Plan B, maybe combining it with

Plan C. Otherwise, if the situation underground remains stable, once Beijing-1 has arrived, we arm up and go in to get the Lord-ITs."

"OK, Samson. Keep hashing out the details. Delilah, you have enough people on the job now?"

"Yes, sir. And we have two teams ready for anything Samson needs, sir."

"While you're en route, Samson, Delilah and I will fill in the gaps, putting the pieces together. But we're here, if you need us."

"Yes, sir. And Plan C, sir?"

"It makes me uncomfortable, Samson. Too risky. But doing nothing holds its own risks. I just don't know. I think the situation underground will decide for us if we need to move faster than we want to. For now, let's see how it plays out, but be prepared as best we can. We'll revisit the decision on Plan C later."

"Yes, Bitsi, sir."

Glancing over to the screen-space showing Jonesy's flight plan, his jet is already at its top cruising speed. ETA two hours forty minutes.

Simple, unabashed curiosity causes me to look in on Jonesy during his journey. On seeing him, my mind conjures up images of his wedding and overlays them on the spacey-screen as distant ghost-like apparitions. Bells ringing and rice and confetti flying all around as the couple leave the church.

Continuing relentlessly, tugging on my conscience, a sequence of pictures flashes by. First, their kids' births, then the christenings, one, two and three, each one entering that same church. Then the confirmations, followed by the marriage of the eldest girl. I was never present in person, but I was always there. And he always commented on missing me at these momentous times in his life, even though he knew I was as close as I dare come.

I squeeze my eyes tight, hanging my head, pressing away the vivid images of the happy family, forcing back the fear that always lurks in the shadows. My heart cannot condone a husband, especially a father, holding such a job, which from time to time holds life-threatening risks. Yet, I cannot stop him from choosing his own path, much as I couldn't stop Junior. All I can do is to help protect him with everything I have to offer.

It's not that I'm getting sentimental in my "old" age. I've always been soft at the core, and the suffering of others is one of the things that hits the center of my heart. Being directly responsible for the well-being, indeed the safety of others, having to make life-altering decisions on their behalf, makes me panic on a regular basis. It's many decades of self-training that help me to channel that panic, so it provides the necessary focus to make the correct choices. I often wish the learning process had been a lot faster and maybe a little easier.

Roughly five hours, ten minutes before the Nuke-Li-Aerial files are hacked open.

30

BITS-SITTERS' DISTRESS

"Delilah?"

"Bitsi, sir?"

"How are things down under? ... Delilah?"

"How are *you*, sir?"

As she so often does, she completely ignores my question.

"Death, Delilah. I'm never good with that. So many deaths. Yet more to come, I fear. And the Lord-ITs are still in extreme danger. I just... And how are *you*, Delilah?"

"Bio-Brains, sir, his whole family." She's sobbing, most unlike Del. "Maybe it's because they're so close to us, but I don't remember it quite this bad, sir."

"We have seen more people die in a single mission than we have seen die today. But you're right, Del. It hurts more because they were so close to us. Many were part of our big family. Despite not wanting to lose anyone, it's still hardest to lose those closest to us."

"Yes, sir. I know, but so many."

"I know, Del, I know."

Many seconds pass in silence while we commiserate on the suffering of all the victims of this outrageous attack. The final death toll yet to be decided. An attack still ongoing that could potentially lead to Nuke-Li-Aerial weapons that could be used against humankind.

"Delilah?"

"Yes, sir."

"How are your ladies doing?"

"Similar to me, sir, only worse. Devastated. The newer girls are practically in a state of shock. They're performing OK, but I can see the distress in all of them. Uh... sir?"

"Thinking..."

A pre-configured meeting setup with all seven BITS-SITTERs offices makes it easy and fast for me to call all the girls into a single O-WE-COME video conference.

"BITS-SITTERs, can you hear me?"

Over the loudspeakers an explosive round of "Yes, sir" assaults my ears. One hand involuntarily grabs at the volume control on the remote while the other hand instinctively covers one ear.

"Ohhhhhh. Well, it certainly sounds like I have your full attention," I exclaim.

A few of the girls muster up a half-hearted smile, but all faces are downcast. The sparkling energy usually so obvious in these genius researchers is nowhere to be seen.

The BITS-SITTERs work from large, luxurious office spaces designed for comfort to compensate for the often-long working hours, especially during missions.

Separated from the main office, there are rest and relaxation areas, kitchens that are constantly stocked with fresh, scrumptious delicacies, and ingredients for when there's time for cooking. The sleeping and bathroom facilities are fancy enough to compete with any penthouse suite.

There's a certain kind of oneness among these mega-information-processing women, a strong bond that grows with each year they're together. Often, in this place designed for lazy leisure, they'll enjoy hours together after work, relaxing, just staying away from the world, oftentimes trying, sometimes unsuccessfully, to avoid the ugly realities lurking behind the spacey-screens on their desks. Their rest area is also the only place outside the office area where they're allowed to talk about their work.

Big enough to cater for double shifts in times of trouble, a massive half-circle of desks fills the middle of the main office. I can see a full complement now, all ninety-eight of them located in the seven offices WOWI are staring at me on the ginormous half-circular spacey-screen hanging behind their workplace.

The large screen usually shows (in triplicate) all the sspaces of all the BITS-SITTERs currently working the shift. The girls can drag any of these sspaces onto their own huge desk spacey-screens to get a closer look and make changes, if needed. I can guess that many of the girls were watching close up the review of the horrific events captured by Bio-Brains' security camera recordings, likely also the deaths of the ANALPRIDC, Medusa, and the Protector.

Right now, the big spacey-screen is showing the image from my webcam, also in threefold, each copy of my masked face displayed side-by-side across the circular screen to make for easier viewing from around the large half-circle of desks.

"Ladies, contrary to what you may think based on the work load I throw at you, I'm always concerned for your welfare. In fact, I worry about you way too much. Reading between the lines, I sense that Delilah is also worried about you right now." The harsh pain-ridden looks slowly soften as I address them.

"To surprise you even further, you should know that Del is a lot harder on you than I am."

Delilah joins in and feigns shock and horror with a deep, noisy gasping intake of breath. Smiles appear on many of the girls' faces.

"So, if she's worried about you, then that makes me just about ready to poop my pants."

Some of them laugh gently, and all are now smiling. This is the most I can do to uplift their spirits—for the time being at least.

"I know, ladies, the day so far has been shocking, horrifying even, and that many of you are seeing such things for the first time. I know how hard that is, but I must prepare you for worse. This day isn't over, and it could drag on for years to come.

"The perpetrator masterminding this attack has immense resources, money, and power. He's ruthless, has no conscience, and will not stop to achieve his goals. If he succeeds in this attack, then the world could be subjected to suffering, wars, and destruction we can only begin to imagine when watching bygone documentaries and movies. We could all stand to lose our friends, our families, our loved ones, and our lives. Nuke-Li-Aerial power can destroy anything and everything, and in the wrong hands, it most likely will.

"Are you still with me, ladies? Are you ready to deal with this monster?"

"Yes, sir!" a unanimous vote.

"Good, then we need to do the following:

- one: crush the attack;

- two: find out how it was even possible.

"BITS-SECS are out in the field, as you know. What I need you to do is to support them, as well as find out how this happened. We must find out how exposed we've become. A Protector has been compromised into giving away Nuke-Li-Aerial secrets. The very existence of Protectors is top secret. And coercing one to act in total contradiction to his mission requires some powerful persuasion. Where's the source? Was the motivation just money and power or some other unknown?

"You have to dig deep. Investigate every name that crops up. We must uncover everyone who played a role in this affair. Are you getting this, ladies?"

"Yes, sir!"

It's difficult to hear with so many voices, but it appears as if most or all the young women are feeling considerably stronger, and their mission is reaffirmed and motivating them once more.

"Good. I'll leave you with Delilah now. Take care of yourselves and each other. There could be more nasty horrors around the next corner, so first prepare mentally, emotionally; then get to it."

Another chorus of "yes, sir" assaults my ears.

Roughly five hours before the Nuke-Li-Aerial files are hacked open.

31

Priorities

"Delilah, priority one is constant surveillance underground, then Medusa, then the HPD No. 1 man, then the Protector, the NETNERD, the ANALPRIDC, and the JERK, in that order."

"Medusa, sir?"

If my colleagues never questioned my reasoning, I'd only ever learn from my own mistakes, and after the fact. Too late. No good.

But for a change I don't feel much like explaining and even less like learning. And it's just a hunch—a feeling, but strong.

"Yes. I want her whole life and her family tree pulled apart. Everything you can find. When you show me the ape that looks like it might be close to becoming the first human in her family line and you still haven't found anything, only then can you stop. Clear?"

"Yes, sir."

"When you have bandwidth, take any others I haven't named. Tie the loose ends."

"As usual, sir."

"Yes, Delilah. Oh, we need to override Medusa's security cams with fake video. Just like before at Bio-Brains' place. Focus first on the route to the tunnel and the tunnel. You have her TWIT-OVA-USER and DIGIT-FONE. The Beast will help you get in, if you know how to use a HANDBAG." I can almost feel her eyes rolling under my own eyelids. "This is priority one, also."

"So many priority ones, sir?"

"Hundreds, Del."

"Hummm. Er, sir, the FLAPPING OBOY, sir?"

"I have some time on my hands now. I'll take that. But I'm afraid COCKS is going to have to watch a while longer as his DOLLIES escape him. It's almost certain that the HPD No. 1 man is involved. So even when I find the CASH, or at least where it went, I still cannot stop the theft until the Lord-ITs are safe. Now, I'll need to focus. So only interrupt me if it's important."

"Yes, Bitsi, sir."

Roughly four hours, fifty-five minutes before the Nuke-Li-Aerial files are hacked open. Four hours before Beijing-1 arrives.

32

A-Hacks OBOY

Mrs. Lord-IT has fallen asleep sprawled across the sofa but is safe, for now, in Lord-IT's arms. Lordy appears half asleep himself, but knowing him, I'm guessing he's struggling with that. He'll want to keep one ear on what's happening.

The HPD No. 1 man cannot stop padding up and down a glass-walled office located at one end of the underground jail, impatiently searching his DIGIT-FONE for contacts to call, keeping his mind away from the frustration of waiting. He isn't good at waiting. The annoyance of the setback and of more encryption to break must be gnawing on his nerves and pushing up his stress meter.

The other guys down under are lounging around, bored and fed up. From time to time, some of them sit staring at screens to see if they can catch even a glimpse of the almost invisible, dead-snail-like movement of the progress-bar displaying "99 percent to complete" the hacking of the encrypted files. The percent-complete number is totally unreliable, because whoever programmed that algorithm had no clue what they were up against. Judging by the look on the faces of the techies behind the spacy-screens, they're ninety-nine percent in the dark, and this realization is very slowly but clearly beginning to catch up with them. Nothing has changed or seems to be changing. Everything is hinging on breaking open the stolen files.

"You there, Samson?"

"Yes, Bitsi, sir."

"All seems quiet underground, and Delilah has the situation under constant surveillance. I've been thinking a lot about Plan C. But first I want to hear your opinion. To C or not to C? That is the question."

"I've also been watching them, sir. They're busy watching nothing happen, determined to wait for the confuzer to do the hard work for them. The risk of the situation going further south all of a sudden seems very low. Getting the team down underground in that tunnel, however, the risks are extreme. My gut tells me to wait for Jonesy. He's not that far out, all things considered."

"I totally agree, Samson. Then let's keep it on hold. You're in position to execute, should it be needed?"

"Of course, sir."

"Fine. Now, I have something to deal with myself. So, you keep hashing out the preparations. I'll get back to you when I'm done here."

Clearing a few spacey-screens on the desk just in front of me, I get ready to start breaking through the hacks put in place in OBOY. The least I can do is try and liberate a few pinched DOLLIES while I'm waiting for D-Day to come to the US.

Lord-IT sent me off on a fraud investigation a few weeks back, just a rumor that CASH was being skimmed off the top of the pile as if a junkie drug dealer were pocketing loose change.

The rule of COMMINGS would have it that the CASH skimming and the major MAD-ONNA FLAPPING DOLLY disappearing act are connected. So, I start at the beginning.

For half an hour or so I dive into the fraud scene. Testing more purchases with OBOY and then digging into one where the invoice amount is different from the original selling price. I have to make a lot of purchases using different TWIT-OVA-USERs to get this far. The hacker has been careful, not skimming from the same customer too often. The page presenting the invoice also has a user-friendly but small message at the bottom, which is not usually there:

"The goods ordered currently require a small administration fee. If you do not wish to pay this, please wait some days, or weeks. Maybe this will change."

A polite but mini-ransom. Wait forever or pay up now.

Digging into OBOY's program code, the hack is easy to spot when you know what to look for. The invoice sent out to the customer is flagged and the amount increased, and the amount presented during payment is also increased, even though the correct, lower amount is saved in the system. The question remains, though, what happens to the excess incoming CASH after that?

The CASH has to get out the building, so to speak. Out the front door, past the dumb security guard who'd probably totally miss that you were struggling with a big jingling bag that was way too heavy and that you weren't carrying when you came in through the front door.

It doesn't take long to find that the JERK personally approved invoices from a few suppliers, a known procedure. But these invoices refer to fake purchase orders that are not in the system. That's out of order. The invoices and their payments are archived immediately, even though they're too recent for archiving—another hack.

The extra CASH is being creamed off the top of the bank balance like a cat might lick off the top-cream in an old, old-fashioned milk bottle: first make a hole in cap, then enjoy. No one could see this without trawling the records, and no one ever does that except me. It's simply too many invoices to go through. And for what? For no reason. At the end of the day, the numbers add up. Extra CASH comes in, extra CASH quietly disappears, and no one any the wiser.

It's even easier to find the WINCCCER that's receiving the creamy, whisked-away CASH. The bank account number is on the invoice payments. The account number is changed to a bogus account when the archiving is done, but for the few moments while the payment is being processed, the real number is visible in the system.

The WINCCCER is living it up in one of the many infamous tax havens where no one can legally demand information. Except, of course, yours truly.

So, technically speaking, BIG-AM-I is not experiencing a real A-Hack. It is simply pure corrupt employee day-to-day activity. Just like going home with a half a packet of printing paper in your bag, or the color markers your kid loves to use to draw pictures of crocodiles, hearts, and fairies. Only a few DOLLIES you pinched today, and no one will notice.

No, not an A-Hack; this is an inside job with a capital I and a capital J. Well, I suppose you could call it an Inside A-Hack. No surprise, really. Surely, we all know the biggest threat, the biggest risk of successful attack is from within.

Now moving on to the conundrum of the big black hole sucking up all BIG-AM-I's DOLLIES for the past day or two, my money is still on the CASH COW, the stolen DIGI-CERT from BIG-AM-I's old bank system, the OBOY CASH pile and the dupli-mated mutant flows in the program and database code.

Thinking...

The CASH is completely disappearing. Mary-lin didn't see any payments coming in from the CASH COW. The stolen DIGI-CERT was for the old OBOY CASH pile, a system BIG-AM-I built. For the payment to be processed, the no-credit card payment has to pass from the CASH COW to the wwoopsi-net merchant account for OBOY and through a no-credit card interchange, to a card issuer who approves it. Phew.

To get the payment approved, the complete no-credit card data is needed, including the CVR number, which the hacker didn't have. This is why there's the bogus extra page: to request the number.

But the payment request is not arriving at the wwoopsi-net merchant account holder, which is HPD–FITS. Mary-lin has been searching her BITS for these payments. So, the CASH COW, it seems, has indeed also been hacked.

I imagine the system components and the flow of data in front of my eyes. Pulling up and diving head-first into the program code of the OBOY CASH COW, I start to look for the place where the payment request gets sent to BIG-AM-I's merchant account. That takes some minutes; it's part of a decrepit ancient system that surely must be in the Guinness Book of Records as the biggest, scariest, most humongous soft-BITS monster ever, the likes of which is only seen in the BITS industry, and compared to which Frankenstein was a cute, cuddly elf in a fairy story.

I hastily try to assess how much CASH I've spent with OBOY during the time this system has been alive but give up, too afraid to consider the risk I already know I'm running all this time and aware that any money I might have lost disappeared long ago.

It is mind-bogglingly frightening when one realizes we're totally dependent on soft-BITS, using it all day long, like it or not, and we have absolutely no idea what hidden surprises are buried deep in its depths, ready to either fail us or abuse us. DIGIT-FONEs, wwoopsi-net shopping sites, our bank balances and no-credit cards, cars, trains, planes, even the auto-gardener. And Lord-IT only knows the stuff is only tested, what, at best sixty-five, seventy percent? The only thing we can be sure of is that the errors and hacks are there, lurking, waiting, ready to pounce on a dirty, dark, and dreadful night.

I'm hyped and keyed up to the exact nature of things to look for. Having found my way around the ancient OBOY ruins, the hack is shining through the cracks in the broken walls. The invoices for payment have been marked, and the incoming payments for these invoices are routed to a system outside the BIG-AM-I's network. Sending the Beast out exploring makes it child's play to find the machine receiving the payment requests. And on that machine is an exact copy, more or less, of the old CASH-PILE, masquerading as if it were the real old bank OBOY. This is why the DIGI-CERT was stolen. This is also where the dupli-mated data changes are sent.

Following the flow of data gathered by the DIRT-CRAWLER and the DIRT-DIGGER, all nicely presented by the DIRT-MAPP, I can see the payment requests are going to an HPD no-credit interchange but bypassing the OBOY merchant account.

Three immediate problems with this. One, the interchange should *not* be an HPD system, but should be a service independent from any bank. If this had been the case, this A-Hack wouldn't have been so easy. Two, the HPD interchange must also have been hacked to allow traffic from the dupli-mated CASH pile OBOY. Three, Mary-lin hasn't looked far enough; she must only have checked the OBOY merchant account but not the interchange.

The payments received by the bogus BIG-AM-I CASH-PILE are going to the same tax haven and the exact same bank account as the creamed-off DOLLIES.

Thinking of the recordings Delilah has saved, the sequence of some of the events becomes a little clearer. Medusa tries to get to the JERK and fails. Then she succeeds with the ANALPRIDC, and this is where she starts to plan the first hacks to steal small amounts of CASH.

Then, Medusa succeeds with the JERK as his ability to resist her bosom weakens. The purchase orders and invoice signing are arranged. The DOLLY-creaming can commence.

Medusa's cleavage first enticed the JERK, then the talk of the credit deal. Where did that idea come from? The HPD No. 1 man?

Somehow in all this, they hook up with the NETNERD and get him to create all kinds of amazing TRICCs: plant a wire on the CCIO of BIG-AM-I and steal the DIGI-CERT from OBOY, and who knows what else, such as hiding from Bitsi-Lite? Then Stage Two can commence, the incredible DOLLY disappearing act.

And, where does Lordy fit in? Why is obvious: They're stealing his secrets. How did they ever manage to get that far? Compromising a Protector. But why do they need Lord-IT on-site? Why take his wife? Those are big unknowns. Just another COMMINGS?

When did the HPD No. 1 man join the party? It would seem likely that he arranged for the HPD system to accept processing payment requests that are coming from a bogus CASH-PILE OBOY. But how exactly?

Still many questions to be answered. Right now, however, it's more important to liberate the DOLLIES. If they're still in one piece.

Roughly three hours, ten minutes before the Nuke-Li-Aerial files are hacked open.

33

TAX-HAVEN **WINCCCER**

OPENING AN O-WE-COME session on another sspace, I call up the No. 1 man WINCCCER, who is enjoying the pinching of BIG-AM-I's DOLLIES.

"Jan, it's Bitsi," I declare as he answers. "How's the incoming CASH flow right now? Elevated, I assume."

"Er, hello, Bitsi, sir. I'm not really sure. It's always quite high." He seems recovered from the shock of hearing from me. We have spoken before. He didn't enjoy that little chat much, either.

"Jan, during the course of this conversation you must not contact, not make *any* form of contact with *any*one. Is that clear, Jan?"

"Yes, Bitsi, sir."

"Good. I'll be watching. Now, share your spacey-screen with me, Jan."

"Er, OK."

"Pull up account 420567080031. I want to see the DOLLY balance." I copy the number into the O-WE-COME chat.

As he pulls up the account, using Bitsi-Lite and with a little more help from the Beast, I'm also watching everything else he does to ensure he doesn't send off any warning signals.

"Can you see it?" he asks.

"Yes. Now refresh it."

"What?"

"Refresh the screen, Lord-IT damn it. I want to see the new balance."

After just 10 seconds, the balance has increased by a shocking one million abducted DOLLIES.

"Is that normal, Jan? Such a fast increase in the balance."

"Er, I don't really watch all the accounts individually, Bitsi, sir. So, I wouldn't know how fast the CASH flows in."

I know this isn't true. Many WINCCCERs I know can spend hours on any given day watching this kind of money coming in. Dreaming about how much profit the bank will make from it and how much commission they, in turn, will earn.

"Refresh it again."

Another eighteen seconds and yet another 1.8 million DOLLIES just went on what by now must be their infamous planetary walk-about. "Jan, who owns this account?" The personal details aren't shown on the screen.

"You know I'm neither at liberty nor legally required to disclose that information, Bitsi, sir."

"*Jan!*" Bitsi-Tone.

"OK, OK. There's a proxy-owner, which is actually Lord-IT, but the real owner is the HPD No. 1 man, sir."

"You do know, Jan, that BIG-AM-I is undergoing a cataclysmic MAD-ONNA MAGIC TRICC as we speak? And that BIG-AM-I and HPD have just recently entered a deal to offer credit to all their customers? You do know this, don't you, Jan?"

"Yes, sir."

"Pull up a report of all the transactions on this account since it was opened and give me the file over the O-WE-COME chat. Do it now. Then, show me a summary of the account balance covering the period Sunday evening through Monday lunchtime."

The WINCCCER Jan is obviously worried now. The files arrive, then when he shows me the transaction summary from the period I requested, he feigns shock and horror. I take this as a good sign, hopefully indicating he's ready to cooperate. The balance has jumped during Monday morning from three hundred million to more than three and a half billion DOLLIES. Now the account has breached the nine-billion barrier.

"Significant increase, huh?"

"Er, it would seem so, sir."

"Jan, in case it hasn't registered in that thick skull of yours, that modern scientists still agree with old-fashioned claims is where your brain is supposedly hosted, I'm not calling you by accident. Calling all the banks in the world is not my ingenious strategy for searching for BIG-AM-I's lost DOLLIES." Bitsi-Tone.

"No, I guess not," is the softly spoken, lame response. But the penny has dropped, and not too far from the tree where money apparently does grow.

"Fine, then we're on the same page. You'll continue to let these DOLLIES present themselves on your front doorstep. And, I guess, you may continue to use the elevated wealth to your WINCCCER advantage, for now. But, you will immediately close and hand over the account to the authorities when requested. Now, first arrange a warning to be sent to me if there are *any* changes to this account's setup. Then, I want you to set up a warning to be sent to me, triggered by any attempted removal of funds from this account. Also, make me a silent and mandatory approver of all withdrawals. Right now, please. I'll watch while you do all that, Jan."

As he sets up the changes on the account, I send an OOO-O-WE-COME flying up to his office and prepare a short email for Jan. I work while checking the incoming warnings I receive as he makes the changes to the bank account's configuration.

My mask and I then proceed to explain to him the gravity of the potential consequences resulting from any mistakes he might choose to make. "You're not doing anything illegal yet, Jan. It's not like you stole this money. But every move you make from now on will determine the level of your well-being in the immediate future and possibly for a long time after that. Are you getting this, Jan?"

"Yes, sir."

"Everything you do until this incident is over, I'll monitor and record. For your own sake, do not make a single false move, Jan."

"Of course not, Bitsi, sir."

"I just sent you an email. Please respond to that with one of those fancy emails containing a password reset link. The PIN for the reset must be valid for twenty-four hours. Send it now, please."

"But the password would be for the No. 1 man's TWIT-OVA-USER, Bitsi, sir. Isn't that a little unusual?"

"Just send me the link."

Jan is correct; it is unusual for a WINCCCER to force a password reset on the TWIT-OVA-USER, and I could easily change the password myself, but getting such communication from Jan in black and white will be useful later. The email arrives, and then I prepare to wrap up this part of the investigation.

"Jan, the lives of some extremely prominent and important people are at a critical risk level here. They're in imminent danger right now as a result of this theft. If any one of them dies due to a mistake you make, I'll personally come and deal with you. Am I making myself clear, Jan?"

"Yes, Bitsi, sir. Understood, sir. If I hear anything important, I'll be in touch." I have never heard a WINCCCER sound quite this timid before today.

"Good. Thank you for your time, Jan."

"Delilah, you there?"

"Yes, sir."

Over the chat, I pass Jan's credentials and coordinates to Delilah.

"This is the WINCCCER No. 1 man who's currently the proud protector of a ginormous and carnivorous interstellar black hole that's gobbling up BIG-AM-I's run-away DOLLIES while we're going hungry trying to save the world from Stupid-ITy and MAGIC TRICCs.

"I've seen the bank balance. All the DOLLIES are sitting in a holding pen just waiting for a knight in shining armor to come along and do whatever one might hope for from a shiny knight. I want all his communications and movements monitored. If this guy gets close to the Lord-IT situation, if he so much as pisses on the rim of the toilet and a drop of pee bounces off onto a butterfly's wing and that butterfly makes its way to our underground problem and starts to create all kinds of chaos, I want to know immediately."

"Er, sir."

"Yes, Del, I've seen it."

The No. 1 man has left his little office and walked over to the sofa where he's holding my friends hostage. The expression on his face, the glare and direction in his eyes show that he found a new target for venting his frustration. He starts talking to the Lord-ITs. No, to Lordy.

Roughly two hours, fifty minutes before the Nuke-Li-Aerial files are hacked open.

34

THE NO. 1 PLAN

"**A**RE YOU COMFORTABLE, Lord-IT?" He's talking quietly, pretending real concern and faking that he cares about not wanting to wake up Lord-IT's wife.

"As good as can be expected, I suppose," Lord-IT responds, waving a hand round in the air in a half circle, indicating his current circumstances. He has learned over the years when to keep his mouth shut, to be politically astute. I sometimes wish he would also actually keep his mouth shut.

"I suppose you're wondering why you're here?"

"Not really. Time will tell, I guess."

"Coincidentally, I have some time available right now. So, let me explain it to you. You're here, out of sight, because you have run away. You're hiding from the world. And this is what everyone will hear tomorrow tonight."

"Interesting. We ran away without our kids? Great plan. Imagine the headlines: 'Lord-ITs escape to the Bahamas leaving kids at home.' That makes a lot of sense," Lord-IT retorts.

"It is indeed a small glitch in the plan that your wife traveled with you. A tiny snag with a simple solution. Still, in the end, you'll be discredited, no longer the Good Samaritan, but exposed as the despicable crook you are.

"We've already infected millions of confuzers with your nasty hacks in the DROSS for monitoring and stealing all kinds of private and confidential information. And we'll expose your hacks to the world. When you don't show up to defend yourself, we will take over the DROSS, remove your hacks—which will be easy because we added them—and we'll save the world from your illegal attempt at total domination.

"We'll also announce the suspicion that you're involved in a major soft-BITS-driven theft of billions of DOLLIES from BIG-AM-I, both slowly over the years and recently more aggressively, taking advantage of the new credit deal and the expected increased income, OBOY.

"The deaths of many close to you, as well as some BIG-AM-I staff, we'll pin on you. The sudden disappearance of the most powerful man in the world will only add to your obvious guilt. You'll become the most wanted man on the planet."

"Your lies will catch up with you even before you've finished spinning your absurd web. The BITS Inspector will find you and every trace of this insane stunt, and he'll software-matically crucify you." Lord-IT is pretending to hide a moment of panic by sounding brave. The No. 1 man falls for it.

"Ha! We're prepared for your magnificent BITS Inspector," blurts out the No. 1 man.

Now, that's a bluff worthy of going down in history.

"He's running around with his head up his ass right now. He has not the slightest suspicion that we have the Nuke-Li-Aerial files. The last I heard, he was chasing down some DOLLIES that have run off into a big black hole in search of universes unknown and for reasons even more obscure. Bitsi has clearly stated to a few people that he has no clue what's going on."

The No. 1 man has convinced himself that I don't have a chance of catching up with him. And Lordy got something of what he needed. He hasn't heard from me for hours and wanted to hear anything he could use to assess my progress.

"Lordy, now it's time to shut up. Pretend to give up hope. A little at least."

Lordy responds immediately and sags in the chest a little, lowers his head a fraction and looks down, pretending to be thinking through everything he just heard.

"Don't listen to any of that bullshit, Lordy. You'll get the details later. Just focus on playing the game and not pissing him off. He's dangerous."

The No. 1 man is becoming happier and more relaxed as he explains his apparently incredible and infallible master plan. "And just as soon as we've broken into your encrypted Nuke-Li-Aerial treasure chest, Lord-IT, you will fast-track our understanding of how to use it. Then, using the CASH you stole from BIG-AM-I, we'll put together some offerings that will impress the world with such a force that they feel impelled to buy. And I'll become even richer. And you? Well, if you behave yourself, you and your wife will get new identities and a chance to start again. Hell, I may even arrange to have your kids join you."

Proving my earlier point that Lord-IT is unable to keep his trap shut, he says quietly, "You fool. You have no idea of the danger you plan to release into the world."

"Maybe not," snorts the No. 1 man. "But I have some idea of the price I'm going to demand for it." And laughing loudly, spirits and confidence clearly uplifted by having reminded himself just how great he is, he returns to his cubicle-office, which, viewed over Bitsi-Lite from a certain angle and distance, looks more like a temporary plastic toilet arrangement one might find at a large garden party, a toilet with a big turd in it.

"Lordy, it will be some time still, but we're on the way and getting closer. I'll only communicate when it's necessary. Just hang in there and keep calm."

The important information coming out of that ridiculous exchange is that the No. 1 man intends the Lord-ITs' disappearance to be forever, but there are still many hours, probably even days to go before taking steps to terminate them. They need Lord-IT because without his help it would take even the best scientists a long time to figure out how Nuke-Li-Aerial power works and how to make it work to their purpose.

The No. 1 man insinuated that he will use the suffering of Lord-IT's wife to provide him the needed motivation to assist them. I don't hold any belief in the promise of new identities.

Stretching my legs, wandering over to refresh my brew, then pacing a little myself, the whole conversation turns around in my head, making me dizzy. Never in my life have I seen such a high-risk, high-impact plan where extreme care and caution should have taken the upper hand but ended up being riddled with such a huge dose of Stupid-ITy.

Their lust for power has blindsided these idiots, as well as their greed for money—too selfish to consider who they'd hurt along the way and too proud to entertain the possibility of failure. They see not, for their sins are hidden inside this murky layer of Stupid-ITy, which is foolishly designed to avoid seeing, avoid admitting to, and therefore escape dealing with the consequences.

Suddenly an O-WE-COME sspace wakes up. Mary-lin from HPD–FITS BITS is calling me.

Roughly two hours, forty minutes before the Nuke-Li-Aerial files are hacked open.

35

Oh, Marilyn

"Mary-lin, how are you doing? Have you been home yet?"

"No, Bitsi. I'm still going through all these BODGED-JOB requests, but I need to speak to you."

Freezing-cold chills rush down my spine as I suffer from premonitions of shock and horror spurred on too easily by the recent events that are still fresh in my mind. Mary-lin usually never turns to me for advice or even just to chat. This is the first time, and I'm sure she hasn't called me for a friendly chinwag.

She has called without video. While I respond to her, on a Bitsi-Lite screen-space, I pull up the DIRT-MAPP and request a Bitsi-Lite view of the location where Mary-lin's web call originated. In less than a second, I can see her sitting behind her huge office bureau.

"Mary-lin, this is really not a good time. I, too, am up to my neck in busted BITS here, and I'm way behind in finding out what's really going on. Can I get back to you la..."

"Bitsi, how often do I call you? Not often. Now, please hear me out." She isn't prepared to accept a rain-check.

"OK, OK. But I'm right in the middle of something, so please, hang on the call, I'll be back as fast as I can."

Immediately, I mute the call for all participants, so Mary-lin can see she's also muted and I can't hear her. She needs to shut up for now. Then, zooming in with Bitsi-Lite, instantly I can see something I was so hoping couldn't be true.

Looking over to the No. 1 man in his office, I see he's frantically pacing once again. In his left hand is the device that caused the death of Bio-Brains' kids. His face contorts trying to hide a combination of angst, disbelief, panic, and indecision.

I select Mary-lin's KILLER-CCOTCHA and scream at the Beast, "DISABLE," praying that the same DIGI-CERT is on all the KILLER-CCOTCHAs. Within three seconds the Beast is showing he has disarmed the CCOTCHA.

Then, I reopen the disabled verbal communication channel so that the No. 1 man can still hear what his daughter says.

Using the joystick, I draw a square covering the area of Mary-lin's office. "Full scan," I demand, and the Beast calls down the power of Bitsi-Lite and calls upon the confuzing-power of his many maxi-confuzers to scan and analyze every last cubic millimeter of the seventy-cubic-meter area enclosed within the square I drew. During thirty-three long seconds, solids, fluids, and gases are all scanned for anything hidden, anything suspicious. Mary-lin's DIGIT-FONE is the only thing found that can harm her now, by giving her away if she were to use it.

I select the FONE on the screen-space and command, "mimic FONE." The Beast will take complete control of the communication channel and route all traffic to a visual FONE that has now appeared on my sspace. Even the FONE's location signal is fake, so I could get Mary-lin to the Bahamas in under a second, if needed. Everything is ready. Now, Marilyn must die.

"Mute CCOTCHA." I don't want the No. 1 man to hear this. "Mary-lin?" I also turn on my video.

"Finally!"

"*SHUT UP and listen to me. Do not say a word.*" Bitsi-Tone.

Silence.

"Good. Your life is in danger. You have a device in your head that can kill you. By using this device, someone has listened to everything you say. I have taken control of the device and have muted it for now while I tell you this. But in a few seconds from now, I'll unmute the device, and you'll continue the call you placed to me, back where I left you hanging. Remember to be impatient. Are you getting this?" Bitsi-Tone.

"Er, yes."

"Here's the plan. I will mute this call again, then unmute the device, then unmute this call. You, then, continue to tell me whatever you had planned to say.

You must watch my video every second of the call."

"The split-second I raise my hand and scratch my forehead, like this," and I show her, "then you must play dead, killed instantly. Stop talking immediately, mid-word if the timing calls for it, and you fall off your chair onto the floor, and smack into something when falling, make a noise. Is this clear, Mary-lin?"

"Yes, Bitsi, sir."

"Stay on the floor. When it's over, I'll tell you. Then, we'll plan the rest of your day. Do not panic. Do not be afraid. You'll be just fine. But you *must* push through this. And you must do exactly what I told you. Do you remember it all?"

"Yes."

"Are you ready?"

"Yes."

"Here goes."

Then I go through the first steps of the plan, muting and unmuting.

"Mary-lin?"

"Finally!"

"I'm sorry, Mary-lin, but it was you who interrupted me, not vice-versa. And I was in the middle of something when you called."

"You're forgiven," she half laughs. She's putting on a great show for someone who's just been told she could be dead any second from now.

"Bitsi, I have looked and looked, not found anything. And of course, this has bothered me a lot. That kind of CASH cannot just disappear. So,

I took a step back, took a bird's-eye view, and suddenly I remembered an old system that used to handle payments for OBOY."

"Hmmm. What was that called? The CASH pile?" I pretended I only vaguely remember the system.

"That's correct. Anyway, to cut a long story short, I also suddenly remembered that a while back I was, er, let's just say politely requested to participate in a new sec..."

"Mary-lin? Mary-lin? This is odd. Mary-lin, are you muted? Hmmm."

I start typing into the chat window while talking at the same time. "Mary-lin, I don't know where you went, but I don't have time to sit here while you powder your face. Call me back when you're ready."

I mute the O-WE-COME for all participants, then "mute CCOTCHA," disabling the No. 1 man's ability to hear.

Glancing over to the underground office I can see nothing but disappointment and distress. A combination of feelings totally contrary to the actions of this monster. He has no right to be disappointed in his daughter and no basis that could provide any source of distress for having killed his own little girl. He is, plain and simple, a monster, with no rights to any feelings that might console him.

Communicating over the KILLER-CCOTCHA using new Bitsi-FREQs that Mary-lin's father cannot receive, I need to encourage her to safety.

"Mary-lin, it's over. You can get up. You're safe, for now."

As she gets up, she almost screams at me, "Where the hell are you? And what the hell was that all about?"

"I'm in your head, Mary-lin. I'll explain later. The Lord-ITs have been kidnapped, and they're going to be killed, not ransomed. The Nuke-Li-Aerial secrets have been stolen. As we speak, someone is robbing BIG-AM-I to fund new weapons production. Eleven are dead already, and just now you were almost the twelfth."

"Oh, my Lord-IT."

"Yes."

Moments pass before she continues speaking. "It's my father, isn't it?"

Temporarily, I'm lost for words. The hard truth in the answer to her question will be unbearable.

"I'm so sorry, Mary-lin."

My head droops to my chest, hanging there for a moment while I imagine her pain, her utter distress.

"Mary-lin, we need to get you to safety. Technically, you're now dead, I'm afraid. But still, we need to get you out of there alive, and hidden, just in case your dad starts to develop a conscience, or worse. Are you getting this?"

"Yes," she says, obviously struggling with her pain.

"The key problem I have is that all my men are already committed to rescuing Lord-IT and his wife."

"Oh. She's kidnapped, too? I missed that. Oh, poor thing." Gender empathy.

"You must not communicate with anyone, Mary-lin. You're supposed to be dead. The best would be for you to stay there until I can get to you. Could you manage that?"

"Yes, I guess so."

"Do you have a Do Not Disturb sign you can put on the door?"

"It's a light. Hang on; it's on now."

"Good. Does anyone ever ignore that light?"

"Only my father."

"OK. So, the thing wrong with this plan is if he sends security to get you out of there, which he could well do."

"Hold on, Mary-lin, I'm going to bring someone into the call."

"Delilah?"

"Yes, sir?"

"Wait with responding until I'm finished, please. We have an extremely delicate situation here. I'll give you only the urgent highlights. I patched you into a call with Mary-lin from HPD–FITS.

She has a Killer-CCOTCHA installed. I've disabled it, but since then the command has been given. So, Mary-lin needs to play dead. I need to get her out of her office. She needs to remain hidden until this mess is wrapped up. All BITS-SECS-US are tied up. If you have any suggestions, then come with them now, please." While talking, I shared Mary-lin's location with Delilah and gave her full access to HPD–FITS BITS so she can start to look around.

She responds immediately, without a second thought. "The office is only minutes away from Mary-lin. I could send two of my agents to pick her up, sir. Mary-lin could stay here. Lord-IT only knows, it's safer than Fort Knox and more comfortable than a first-class penthouse, if you're not working, that is."

This is what I was hoping for, although she's suggesting breaking protocol, and I can't let that happen without a little resistance.

"Delilah, I don't allow your agents into the field—you know that. It's too dangerous. And no one must know where the office is."

Del gets straight down to the one question, the answer to which could give grounds for making an exception. "Is there any danger in moving her?"

"Well, not much at all, if done properly, of course. But that's a risk assessment for the BITS-SECS te..."

"Then, let's do it. Some of the girls would jump at the chance to go into action, sir. I would go myself if I weren't so decrepit. Besides, there isn't any better option, I'm sure."

In this she is correct. "I'm not sure I want to hear that, Delilah."

"Which part, sir? Oh, and we could always ask Mary-lin to keep her eyes closed for a little, just while we move her." Her smile shines through her words.

"OK, Del. Arrange for an ambulance to pick up *four* agents. Then get them straight over to HPD.

Mary-lin?"

"Yes, Bitsi?"

"Take only your handbag with you; give it to one of the agents. You'll be moved out on a stretcher, of course. And covered. Stay under it. No movements. You must stay on the stretcher until you arrive in the office. No one must see you alive. No one must know who's on the stretcher."

"What about the ambulance staff? They'll probably want to check for a pulse at least."

"They'll do exactly as they're told. Delilah will see to that."

"Is this *the* Delilah, the famous BITS-SITTER leader?" Mary-lin has been itching to ask. Delilah's reputation brings almost everyone into a legless state of utter awe.

"The one and only Delilah, yes Mary. So, you can be sure you'll be in good hands. Once we get you there. Del, how is...?"

"The ambulance is on the way to us now, sir," Delilah breaks through. "ETA three minutes. I'll go down with the girls to instruct the ambulance staff. I already hooked into their comms."

"Good. Please execute as planned. I'll do what I can, but I'll also be busy."

"Yes, Bitsi, sir."

"Mary-lin, Delilah and I will keep this line open, so you're not left there alone."

"Does everyone call you sir, Bitsi?" Mary-lin asks.

"Most people, I guess."

"Does it bother you that I don't?"

"If *anything* you do bothers me, you'll hear about it immediately."

"Hahaa. Why doesn't that surprise me."

"Don't use anything confuzerized or electronic. No signs of life. Go sit on the sofa so the confuzer won't tempt you. Sit back and try to relax, Mary. I need to go. But I'm here if you need anything."

"Thank you, Bitsi ... sir," she says, laughing just a little. She is one tough old bird.

Locating an OOO-O-WE-COME screen in the HPD–FITS building, I send it up to hover around Mary-lin's office ready for the ambulance staff and any potential undesirables.

Unable to not worry about leaving them alone with this operation, I open a new sspace and pull up the HPD–FITS BITS location on Bitsi-Lite and start searching for the best entrance to use—at the back somewhere, probably. Two good options present themselves, so I request the Beast to make some preparations.

"Del, entrance F or G seem to be the best choices."

"I chose G, sir. We'll arrive at G first. If it seems too awkward, we'll try F."

"When you put your BITS-SITTER credentials up to the door, it'll open; I just fixed that."

"Great. I also sent a second OOO-O-WE-COME down to G. I thought if you had time you might like to be there. I left the one you stationed at Mary-lin's office door."

"Oh, I'll be there."

Mary-lin is shaking her head in disbelief. It's becoming obvious to her that we could take total control of the highly secured building within minutes, if we chose to.

The plan goes down without a single glitch. Security at entrance G throws a few odd looks in the BITS-SITTERs direction, but their credentials pack as much punch as BITS-SECS creds. No one would dare doubt their right to enter. The BITS-SITTER and BITS-SECS teams form the single most powerful investigative unit in the world.

Within fifteen minutes, Mary-lin is sitting on a sofa in the BITS-SITTERs' rest and relaxation area.

The No. 1 man is sitting behind his desk still looking a little distressed, yet his body language also screams of an inner struggle, to survive maybe and get on with his life, or perhaps trying to justify his actions.

Yes, he killed his own daughter, but he had good reasons, didn't he? Releasing Nuke-Li-Aerial power into the world to the benefit of all. An immense amount of money. And undeniable, possibly ultimate power. Sure, the price is high, but is that a reason to stop? No, it's to be expected. It was even accounted for as a risk element in the plan: the Killer-CCOTCHAs.

As if the force of nature has suddenly decided to play its hand, the penny drops. This man has forced Mary-lin to follow her hard career path, neglecting her family, and earning her the reputation of having her namesake's HPD illness. And with this same power he has over her, he has also forced her into compromising the bank's security.

But Mary-lin does not have HPD. All these years, she has simply been trying to please her father, who, in turn, has now let her down in the most unimaginable of ways. What hope is there for us when we can turn against each other like this?

Roughly two hours, fifteen minutes before the Nuke-Li-Aerial files are hacked open.

36

DELILAH'S LEAD AGENT

"**D**ELILAH, MA'AM, I think you should see this."

Over an O-WE-COME session, Delilah's lead agent in New York passes on two birth certificates to Delilah.

As Delilah silently reviews the documents, she raises her eyebrows but manages to keep her mouth shut. *Oh, now there's a surprise. Or not. More like a COMMINGS, I'd say,* she thinks as she spots the twin connection presented by her senior agent who's directing her colleagues who are hunting down Medusa's past. "This explains their involvement, but nothing about motivation."

"When we found these, we also found and started on their parents," the lead agent says.

"Oh? And how much of their lives have you covered?"

"Just her life, ma'am. The mother. No known father. A few steps both back and forth, ma'am. And then I realized it's time to let you know. The few steps we took covered a period of less than eighteen months, ma'am, so it all went super-fast. Almost immediate."

Delilah is extremely demanding of her BITS-SITTERs when it comes to keeping her up to speed. She trains them to report carefully and regularly but to scream immediately if there are any critical findings. The lead agent is worried she's waited too long before updating Delilah.

"So, tell me, show me."

"First, this," and the agent slides over a recording of an argument in a bar between a couple and a woman, which Delilah avidly starts watching while listening further to the agent's account.

"The woman," says the lead agent, "is Medusa's mother. The other woman is Lord-IT's wife. The confuzer makes a match with this guy," and she slides over a deceased declaration form, with a younger picture of Lord-IT on it. "Even with the facial differences, the confuzer comes up with Lord-IT as a match. The mother is bitching about the guy being nothing but a cheap cruiser, a womanizer of the lowest kind. Jumping from one bed to another, not caring about the hearts he breaks. But, except for a lot of tears, nothing comes out of the clash."

"What else?" Delilah asks, waiting for the really bad news.

"This," she says and gives Delilah another document, this one stamped all over with governmental and legal emblems, including "Top Secret" in red letters spread across the cover at an angle.

Delilah glances over the pages of the document with a puzzled look on her face, until she sees the next recording. *Oh, my Lord-IT,* DELILIAH thinks to herself. *Bitsi was right. Lord-IT never took his secrecy seriously enough. And it would seem this has caught up with him.*

The video played out in a restaurant, the same three people, a couple and a woman. Only this time the woman has a pushchair with two small children in it and is claiming that Lord-IT is the father of her twins. Lord-IT's security step in immediately to avoid a big scene.

Medusa's mother has tried to link Lord-IT to herself through his wife. The document is the result of what followed. A lengthy process with a court case and DNA tests, which ultimately proved her wrong. But it all happened and went down in history, regardless of the outcome. The last part of the story was in a BITS GON Ballistic's headline in which the mother claims the DNA tests were rigged.

"It doesn't matter if the DNA tests were true or rigged. She has convinced herself that he's the father." Delilah is thinking out loud.

"Yes," responds the agent. "And following that through, she convinced her kids also."

"Exactly. You've done well. I see you couldn't have informed me earlier." She smiles warmly while speaking, bringing the woman at ease.

"Do you know why it's so important that Lord-IT's true identity is secret?"

"So that none of his family, parents, siblings, and the like would be in danger?"

"Exactly correct. So why, do you think, was Lord-IT's wife's identity not hidden?"

"Except her parents who live with them, she has no other family? No one who would suffer?"

"Also correct. But still, it was a vain mistake not to change her identity also because Medusa's mother managed at least to claim a link, true or not, through Lord-IT's wife to two supposedly different men. What do you think? Are the deceased man and Lord-IT indeed one and the same? Could he be the father?"

"I don't know, ma'am, and I doubt it would be possible to prove. The one thing I do know is that Lord-IT's safety is of tantamount importance. And I don't believe the DNA tests were rigged. I believe that Lord-IT is an upright man."

Delilah had deliberately asked the questions as if in a training session—any combination of answers could be correct—to give the young woman space to take her own direction when responding.

"All correct, again. How clever you are." And together they laugh in a heart-warming exchange of trust and respect, expressing a heartfelt deep friendship, and sharing a moment of relief from the pressure of the day.

Delilah has seen the recordings in the hallway of a metro after a drunken girls' night out long ago. Medusa's mother, raging furiously at a poster with a picture of Lord-IT from before his disappearance and identity change.

"...pathetic, no good virgin," she yells at him. "Frightened of pulling your pants down. Maybe you came in them already? But you'll still pay the price for dumping me for that bitch. I'll make you pay. Do you see these kids in here? With these, I'll make you pay."

Delilah knows, but she didn't know Medusa was one of the children borne by that vengeful mother.

"I think we found the ape that Bitsi asked me to look for. Let's take a closer look at all the others now," Delilah instructs her team leader, and the agent goes back to check who's next on the priority list of offenders.

"Yes, ma'am."

Delilah sits, thinking to herself for a while, contemplating the course of events. Finally, she shakes her head and sighs. *Our choices will forever follow us,* she thinks. *Now, let's see what those two have been up to.*

I suppose, she almost squawks in her mind, *I should use one of Bitsi's outrageously ridiculous HANDBAGs. What was he thinking when he built that contraption?*

Pulling up a HANDBAG, she throws in both the TWIT-OVA-PERSONs and the TWIT-OVA-USERs belonging to the twins. Then she adds the WOWI icon to the mix, sets the timeframe to cover their whole lives and chooses the fast match option.

Calling on her lead BITS-SITTER, she says, "Here, keep an eye on this. It starts glowing when new information arrives. Focus on motive and the preparation of this A-Hack."

"Yes, ma'am."

Roughly two hours before the Nuke-Li-Aerial files are hacked open.

37

Family Matters

Delilah and I have been constantly exchanging information to help each other direct our investigation. Interesting, that ex-fling of Lord-IT's coming back to bite him. I never like to say, "I told you so," especially given the current situation, but I did tell him.

Apparently, the JERK had deliberately set up the BIG-AM-I executive firing squad last Sunday, starting an argument with his bosses to force their hand. A nice, easy exit in a regular business-like manner, not raising suspicions. Clever, if not a little see-through at this stage.

The magical disappearance of the Lord-ITs' LICKEMs was made possible by covering their heads with hoods, which had layers of some of the Bitsi-FRIGHT materials in them. Only once they arrived in the mansion and the HPD No. 1 man could test them with his Killer-CCOTCHA controller device and couldn't find their CCOTCHA signals did he let them out in the open.

Over the past hours, I've collected all the evidence of who hacked what, where, when, and how, OBOY. Once we rescue the Lord-ITs, we'll easily fix the system's problems by removing the DROSS and OBOY hacks and renewing the stolen DIGI-CERT. I also wormed my way into all the underground communication channels, avoiding that one hard-wired router, which most likely they're watching. In other words, I now have control of all the devices in that dungeon buried under the gardens of the soup-ah-deluxe New York mansion.

The BITS-SITTERs have a lot more work on their hands to wrap up the paperwork and find all the gory evidence details. But there are also a lot of BITS-SITTERs working on this. One more pair of hands isn't going to change the course of history there; the course was already set.

It will be some time still before the US team reaches maximum BITS-SECS strength at the mansion. Samson and Jonesy have already joined the US teams. Beijing-1 will arrive in just over an hour.

Lord-IT will wonder where the hell we are and what the hell could take so long. But I can't help him much there; it is what it is. I don't want to contact him too much because of the risk of exposure. The closer Lord-IT knows we are, the more confident he'll become and the higher the chance that his mouth will run out of control. He is human, after all. Best just to keep him wondering.

Deciding there's not much more I can do to improve things right now, I prepare a PRIVATE-LYFE with the Bitsi-Lite views and O-WE-COME sessions for monitoring the frustratingly slow progress in the field and take it into the living area of my house. Time to enjoy a few moments' rest, close to my loved ones. No matter what's happening, I always try to be with them as much as possible, even in times of crisis, stealing valuable minutes whenever I can, because I love them and miss them when I'm not physically with them, and because family matters.

"Oh, sweetie, how's it going? You look beaten up." Compliments don't flow in our house when they're not called for.

"Thanks. We're getting there, honey."

"I didn't expect you out here this soon?"

"Everything is planned. Not much more I can do right now."

"How are they?"

"Here." And I slide my PRIVATE-LYFE over to her, but there's nothing much to see on the surface.

All she says is, "Poor guys."

"They're safe for now. How they are? Hard to say. Probably frightened. And who wouldn't be, huh? At least they now know we're on the way."

"That's good. What are their chances?"

"Good, I think. But you know how it is. The unexpected never ceases to amaze. Max two hours until the finale; then, we'll be in the clear if the plan works out. I wish it could go faster, but…"

"Yeah, I know. You always do. But I'm sure if you haven't arranged it already, then it cannot be done." She throws her arms around me and holds me close as she speaks, effectively shutting me up.

My wife has absolute confidence in my ability, god bless her. Sometimes this makes me feel great, full of assurance, and able to achieve anything. Other times, it can scare me witless, making me panic coz it's a heck of a lot to live up to, and I oh so do not want to disappoint her or screw up.

"The kids?"

"They're all over the place but no problems. They're being sweet with each other. But they were wondering why they couldn't see into your office."

"Hmmmm."

"Daddy. Daddy. See how fast I can run."

"Be careful, girl," I say a little too loudly. It's an automatic reaction. I can almost not help it. Every time they want to show off how good they are or, for example, race with each other to come in first, I panic about the danger, of which they appear to be totally unaware, and the pain they could inflict on themselves and their siblings.

Forgetting the life-changing, dangerous situations, letting the kids learn from their own mistakes is something I do try to force upon myself, more or less, but only after first giving guidance and after they show they at least grasped the point, even though they clearly may still refuse to listen.

But why don't we listen? Why do we always ignore or even actively go against advice? Why are we human beings so stubborn, so independent, and so proud about that? Stubborn about things we know nothing or little about. Independent when, in fact, we're so needy, so dependent. And proud of what, our mistakes? I doubt it. Proud of having learned something for ourselves the hard way? Why? When billions of others before us learned the same way through the same dumb mistakes.

It's somehow ingrained that we're just too pigheaded to accept that others already know, or maybe know better, and we absolutely have to make the mistake ourselves before the lesson holds any value for us.

Behold the power of the human brain. Or not. The human brain is, after all, still more powerful than the biggest computer on the planet today, and even now, after so many centuries of study, the human race still can't fathom the brain's nature.

Maybe this is why we make so many decisions and act in so many ways that lead to hurting either ourselves or others. We simply don't understand the formula the brain applies when reasoning and emotion collide.

The objective thought processes we go through are complex enough, and the vast range of emotions with their compounding effects are no easier. Hell, there must be a constantly recurring almighty math-eruption inside our heads every time we need to decide something, which is quite frequently. Emotion meets reasoning and—kaboom—a random number pops out.

It's no wonder the world is a mess. Pretty much every decision we make, we make when we're feeling something. And even though we may make the same or similar decisions often (right or wrong choices), when we feel something different, the outcome could well be different.

And the scary part? We often don't even recognize what we're feeling at the time of making the decision. Long-harbored emotions that have developed into habits or evolved into attitudes leading to cold and calculated harsh actions or to a love so deep-seated that it's unshakable. Fresh emotions, which more often have that explosive quality in their expression. Dark-red evil lurking or bright-red anger erupting, the warm glowing orange of the soft evening sun or the fresh blues of a cloudless sky, the bright white of a flash of light, or the pitch-black of a god-forsaken hole so deep that only the brave-hearted or the heartless dare look into. The colors are many, and the combinations are vast. Do they mix like those on a painter's palette? Or do they clash like two opposing warriors? Or both?

We simply are not in control because we usually don't recognize the colors, and when we do, we often don't know why they're there and/or what they mean, and when numerous colors mix, we have no clue what to expect. And when this colorful display of emotional fireworks meets our reasoning-machine, well, expect more fireworks.

We simply don't know enough about what is going on inside our heads. Yet, as long as the highly subjective boundaries of acceptable, civilized behavior curb our actions, we often don't notice or choose to ignore this inability to control ourselves. It's small, it's insignificant, it's acceptable. It's still civilized. So, we stand proud that we're civilized, at our own peril.

Surely, we can dream up faster, easier, and better ways of learning what mankind already knows, and learning how to take control, learning about the colors, our emotions, and their influence on our lives. We could do so much better.

I give myself a shake and watch as she pulls off the running-stunt just fine. As does my youngest girl, more or less, trying to follow in her big sister's footsteps. I almost can't decide if I want to be there when the game goes pear-shaped or not.

"Daddy, can you help me build Lego?" My boy has been waiting to open his latest Lego box and get the thing built.

"Not now, sweetie. Daddy's working." Mummy can be extremely helpful at times.

"Working *and* relaxing," I add, stretching out on the sofa and resting my head in my wife's lap. "Wake me up if it hits the fan, honey." I smile at her.

"Great," she retorts, rolling her eyes at me. "It was my turn next."

No matter how hard I work or how stressful the situations I deal with, there's no convincing my wife I have it harder than she does. Granted, I have never tried, but that's because I ain't stupid, I tell myself.

"Of course, hon, you can take my place here when I'm done."

"Huh," she scoffs, but smiling at least.

As I lie there, the kids come and go, but my wife stays especially close to me. I can feel her energy focused on warming my soul and strengthening my resolve. She knows that the final act is going to be hard on everyone involved, and dangerous, even though I haven't said it outright. Instinctively, she's doing what she can to help me rest mentally and prepare myself. I even manage to doze off for half an hour or so, confident my wife will watch my PRIVATE-LYFE for signs of trouble.

We drink some coffee together, and then I go to help my boy pick up Lego pieces from the floor. Out of desperation, he has figured out himself how to open the Lego packaging.

"I can help you get started, my boy, but soon I need to go back into the office and work some more."

"OK, Daddy," he says, excited that I'll help at least a little, which breaks my heart because we both know I'll have to go soon. After exchanging a big hug and a kiss, we tuck into the Lego-building exercise together.

A short while later my wife jumps up. "Honey, this thing is jumping up and down like a jack out of the box."

Surprised, I run over to the PRIVATE-LYFE, checking the time, and see that Samson is calling me.

"What's up, Samson?"

"There is a lot of excitement down-under, sir. The progress-counter on their file hack has suddenly dropped to two percent to complete, sir."

"Damn it. That's more than an hour ahead of schedule."

"Yes, sir. If it helps at all, Beijing-1 is arriving any minute now, fifteen minutes early, sir. Tailwind. Just letting you know."

"Thanks. I'll be with you in a few minutes." From my response, Samson will know I haven't been watching the Beijing BITS-SECS's lead agent's progress. He'll be happy that for once on this mission I truly delegated to him, and with that, the feeling of trust will add to his self-esteem and boost his confidence.

"OK, honey. That's my cue. I need to get back."

She grasps my face in her strong yet gentle hands, looking deep into my eyes, and without saying a word wishes me everything I'm going to need to pull this thing off, kisses me hard on the lips, pinches my backside, and quickly escapes in the direction of the Lego kit before I can have my revenge. I withdraw to the office dragging my PRIVATE-LYFE with me.

No clue how fast the Nuke-Li-Aerial files will be hacked open.

38

Costly Recovery

THE RISKS ARE many. The stakes are high. This is no time for panic, or angst, or uncertainty. The abrupt awareness of imminent action pulls my mind into sharp focus, prepared for anything.

The timing is tighter than hoped for. If the hack completes suddenly, the files will open, the secrets will be revealed. It could prove hard, or even impossible, to recover any copies they plan to make.

Reviewing my earlier preparations, the four video-views of the underground jail clearly reveal a heightened level of activity. The PERPS are alert, anticipating sooner-than-expected results. The chance of surprising them outright is already lost. On another sspace, I check the list of CCOTCHA chat names that I passed to the team ready for the rescue mission.

I can now control all the underground devices, and they're displayed on screens in front of me. A combi-space-pad-joystick is within arm's reach, ready for operating all the gadgets. There's only one improvement I can think of right now.

"Delilah, scan through the recordings down-under. Look for a scene which is as busy as they are now down there. Or as close to that, at least. Replace it with the recording we had planned."

"Yes, sir." When it's time, Delilah will start slowly turning down the volume to a comfortable background noise-level so they won't notice the change to the recording.

From the corner of my eye, I notice movement down-under. The No. 1 man is inviting the NETNERD into his office. Turning up the volume, I'm curious to hear what he has to say.

"Sit down, my boy, sit," he says in a gentle, almost caring tone.

As the NETNERD settles into a chair, the No. 1 man continues. "I'm afraid I have some bad news for you, my boy."

"Don't call me your boy. I'm *not* your boy!" The condescending attitude irritates him immensely.

"It's just an expression. One that you shouldn't misinterpret. Anyway, I'm afraid to tell you that your sister is dead. Those BITS-SECS agents killed her. I don't know why, yet. All I know is they found her, got to her, and now she's dead."

"How can you be sure?" demands the NETNERD, exhibiting a desperate case of disbelief, of unwillingness to accept.

"These devices we all carry in our heads, I can use them to read vital signs. *Her* vital signs. And there's nothing. I'm sorry."

"That can't be. She was so careful," he almost pleads.

"That bastard-father of yours is to blame. He controls those BITS-SECS agents. Seems they were under instructions. Interrogated her, then killed her, without hesitation."

"I'm going to kill him," the NETNERD forces out while trying to scream and hold back tears at the same time. The result is nothing more than a broken, high-pitched, pathetic wail. He sits, rocking back and forth in his chair like an agitated patient in a psychiatric ward.

"And so you shall. And his wife. For your sister." The No. 1 man pretends to join him in his anger and distress. "Just not now. Remember, if we're to walk out of this alive ourselves, we need the Nuke-Li-Aerial technology. We have many promises to fulfil, commitments to meet, and, not to say the least, a lot of CASH to earn. If you kill him too early, then we're finished here. All of us. Each buyer will find his own reason to kill us, no matter what the truth in whatever happens."

"That bastard." The NETNERD presses out the words. Control is slowly returning to the technology-thief.

"What's your best guess, my boy—how long until the encryption is broken?"

"Uh. Half an hour? Three hours? Who knows?" he replies, shrugging his shoulders and shaking his head.

"We can't do anything more to improve it?"

"No. I've told you before, it will take what it will take. It's just dumb math, number-crunching, no way to make it go faster. Not without more confuzing-power."

"Well, let's just go sit and encourage the damn thing; maybe that will help. Are you ready to go back out there? You got it under control?"

"Yeah, but... You said they tortured her. Did she give us away?" he asks quietly, not sure that he wants to hear the answer.

"Not in the slightest. Gave them false information; led them up the garden path, so to speak. True to you, to us. You can be proud of her. Now come. Let's go and check on that encryption." The No. 1 man's lies slide from him like water off a duck's back, which is no surprise. Why let one more lie bother him?

As they return to the main chamber and settle behind the spacey-screens, the NETNERD shows considerable self-control by not even glancing in Lord-IT's direction. Impressive, yet worrying at the same time.

"Interesting." The thought is out loud over the O-WE-COME meeting with Samson.

"He's adding fuel to the fire, and honing the boy's anger, getting him ready to kill. The No. 1 man is becoming more and more nervous, sir."

"It would indeed seem so. OK, Samson, status?"

"Bitsi-INVISI's safely received, sir. Just waiting to hook them up. I need to check I understood this correctly, sir. If one is wearing rollerblades, for example, will the Bitsi-INVISI hide those also?"

"Yes. Difficult to explain. In principle, all things obviously connected, but yes."

"Good."

Smiling to myself, I see part of his plan is obvious. I briefly wonder who was sent to do the shopping, and why he didn't ask that question much earlier.

"One transporter is on the way to Medusa's house with three more men; it'll arrive in one minute. The remaining vehicles—three soup-ah-sonic planes and three transporters with twelve men in one of them—are all parked behind a copse of trees not far from the mansion, sir."

While talking, I pulled up a Bitsi-Lite view of Samson's location.

"Aren't you a little close, Samson?"

"I've carefully scanned the whole area for any kind of surveillance devices, sir. Nothing except the cameras. I also scanned the whole chamber. They have LASAROMIC pistols down there. And the No. 1 man has an ancient Colt-45 six-shooter in his desk. That's all."

"All right, Samson. What's next?"

"Sir, do you have control of Medusa's place?"

"Yes, full control. So, what's next??"

"Sir, can we hook up the Bitsi-INVISIs? Team MEDUSA has arrived; we need to get in."

"Who's first?"

"Jonesy offered, sir."

"Jonesy, you can place the rounded side of the Bitsi-INVISI just inside your ear or in your naval. You can release it again by pressing firmly on the flat side for a few seconds."

"Yes, sir."

We wait a few seconds while he does this.

"Done, sir."

"Oh, my Lord-IT," Samson exclaims.

"What? Has he turned into a zombie?" I ask while watching and chortling a little.

Doing the Samson chuckle, recovering from the surprise, he responds, "It went so fast."

"Can you see everything behind and around where Jonesy is standing? No blurred images?"

"I think so."

"What do you mean, you think so??"

"Er, I dunno, I mean, I don't know where he is. Jonesy, where in Lord-IT's name are you? Speak up, man."

Jonesy is obviously not lacking a BITS-SECS sense of humor. He takes up a LASAROMIC gun hanging on the wall and sticks it between a BITS-SECS agent's legs, then lifts it up to hit his crotch.

"Hey," the agent complains.

"I'm here, Samson," Jonesy laughs, hanging the gun back on the wall.

"Bloody marvelous," Samson exclaims, squeezing out his best attempt of the plum-in-the-mouth Queen's English, causing the whole team to join in Jonesy's fun.

"OK, guys, calm down now. Buckle up Bitsi-INVISIs, now. Bitsi, sir, can you clear the way into Medusa's tunnel?"

"On it."

I turn off the alarm system and unlock the doors.

"Delilah, the camera hack?"

"Ready to go, sir, just say when."

"Now please, Delilah, except the tunnel."

"Yes, sir."

"MEDUSA team, move to the entry point." Samson knows there's no need to wait. The restart of the cameras to install the hack was done some time ago. The ANALPRIDC had more time for this camera-hack and added a fast-soft-switch back and forth between the real camera input and the fake.

"Yes, sir."

"MEDUSA," I interject, "the cameras in the tunnel will stay hacked only for a few seconds to let you get in. Once you confirm the door is closed, we'll restore to normal operation. Keep silent for the first minute and last minute of your journey. That's the range of the cams' audio. So, watch your speed. Whisper when communicating, and keep it short."

"Yes, sir," Junior responds.

"Arrived at entry point, Samson." Junior, who is leading the MEDUSA team, never says Dad when addressing his father—and boss—at work, for obvious reasons.

"Move in. Report and wait before entering the tunnel," Samson commands.

"Yes, sir."

Only the agents' LICKEMS are visible on the screen. Delilah, Samson, and I watch the group of moving LICKEMs with a combination of angst and excitement as the MEDUSA team progresses through the house toward the tunnel.

"Tunnel door, sir," whispers Junior.

"Delilah, tunnel cams, please."

"Yes, Samson. Done."

"MEDUSA, enter tunnel."

"Sir," and Junior opens the door for his men to enter the tunnel.

"Entry complete. Pushing on."

"Roger," Samson fires back.

That is the sign for Delilah. Immediately, she switches the tunnel camera pointing at the door, back to real-mode.

The guys had to go slowly, quietly through the house so they didn't alert the maid. But now the noise from the rollerblades will mingle with the general humming sound constantly present in the tunnel. They know to take it easy for the first and last minute, but otherwise, it's full steam ahead. They are highly trained athletes and will cover the six kilometers at an amazing speed on their blades. Most likely, they won't show any sign of fatigue when they arrive.

"Samson, how long before they arrive at the door?"

"Plan was eleven minutes, sir. But expect twelve if they have to go slowly for two minutes."

"All right. Now, we have an extra Bitsi-INVISI, Samson. Just a thought, but you can use it to hide a transporter and take you up to the front door in seconds. It's fully armed and can help deal with the six PERPS above ground."

It's a spur of the moment idea, but it's OK to keep Samson on his toes from time to time.

"Didn't know that sir. Thinking. OK. I'll reshuffle the plan a little. Shall we install the Bitsi-INVISI, sir?"

"Place the device outside on the vehicle's hull, the flat side. It will attach itself."

"Going outside now, Bitsi, sir."

Stepping onto the ramp of the transporter, Samson reaches out to place the Bitsi-INVISI himself. Laughing inwardly, I watch his reaction over the Bitsi-Lite view as the massive transporter vanishes. It's not often I see a hardened Samson's jaw hit the ground.

He still manages to prepare his thoughts on how to adjust his plan before he arrives back among his men. "Apart from Agent-5, who has the most experience with transporter weaponry?" Samson asks, knowing full well the answer. The plan included that Agent-5 would remain with the transporter. From the other agents, Samson is looking for the positive responses, those who'll take this job voluntarily and enjoy it. In other words, those who'll do it well. "Remove your Bitsi-INVISI."

"Me, sir?" comes the answer, as six agents reappear.

Samson rolls his eyes at the first smirking agent, Jules, his most experienced man in combat. He will be much needed down-under. Bypassing him, he picks one guy to man the transporter and its guns.

"You take the main guns," he says to Agent-9. "Take your positions, you two."

Then, he changes the plan a little more. To Jules, he says, "Guard duty for you today. Cover the Lord-ITs, together with Jonesy."

"Yes, sir," the veteran barks.

"So, what's the plan, Samson?" I ask.

"Five through the back door, eight through the front door, two guarding the front door, and two in the transporter, sir. We take the back and front doors together, slide in along the walls to avoid bumping into PERPS. Each agent counts out their targets corresponding to their position in the line, then we fire two individual rounds, each on my count. We take out eleven PERPS first, then the last nine. Simple. Jonesy and Agent-8 will keep their weapons free for emergencies." Agent-8 is Jules.

"Good," I respond. The transporter is switched to soup-ah-stealth mode. Only CCOTCHA communication from now on.

Even though the transporter is specially designed to be quiet, it loses its extreme high-speed capability in soup-ah-stealth mode, but when idling, it issues an incredibly low thirty-one decibels or less, not noticeable unless the guards, in desperation, have stepped outside to pee on the grass. And the transporter team will watch for surprises like that.

"Delilah, watch for a good moment, then replace the camera-feed with the older recording."

"OK, Bitsi, sir."

"MEDUSA, status?" Samson is tracking their CCOTCHAs and can see their progress on his spacey-screen, but he wants to hear that all is OK.

"ETA, seven and a half," says Junior quietly.

"Roger."

"Transporter, move in."

"Yes, sir."

"Mansion, get ready to disembark. Watch your step out there. Tread lightly and fast. You may be invisible, but your footprints are not, and someone can still hear you. Don't forget that."

"Yes, sir."

In just under ten seconds, the transporter draws to a halt, hovering alongside a tall wall of one section of the mansion toward the back. The team follows each other down the ramp and heads for the side-entrance door to the building that's closest to the elevator leading down to the tunnel.

"Bitsi, sir, the door?"

"Secured." I already dealt with the additional confuzerized locks.

Samson expertly cracks the old-fashioned door-lock—left there for aesthetic reasons, I guess—and then slips in through the door. He glides silently up to the half-dozing security guard, who's sitting stationed seven meters away from the elevator leading underground, and plugs him with a sleeping dart.

Immediately, the guard falls limp in his seat. After placing the man in a position so he won't fall out of his chair, Samson turns back to the elevator, beckoning his men as he goes.

One man hangs back a little, guarding the door to the house, giving him a good view in both directions—down the corridor as well as out to the garden.

"Bitsi, the elevator?"

"Secured." It was a minor but necessary challenge to fake the location of the elevator being emitted from its confuzerized system. Necessary because the immediate access points to the hideout are certainly being closely monitored.

"Delilah, the elevator cameras, please."

"Clear, sir."

"Lord-IT, damn it." Samson cusses as the door to the elevator opens. "Only five at a time. We need to go twice. Let's get on with it."

"Once you're all out of the elevator, complete silence, Samson."

"Yes, sir," he whispers, practicing without a fault.

The two technologically camouflaged trips the elevator makes go unnoticed, and the last BITS-SECS agents enter the tunnel to begin the silent trek en route to their entry-point.

Twenty-eight seconds later, ten agents gather around the front door to the underground prison-office. With alternate left/right hands on alternate left/right shoulders to ensure enough leg-space, they run slowly for fear of tripping each other up and making a noise the security cameras will pick up.

"I just switched the camera feed down-under, sir," Delilah reports.

"Transporter, watch out. That camera-hack could've been noticed."

I can see the mansion team has almost arrived, and I take control of the mission just for now. I prefer to synchronize the teams myself when I'm the one pressing the buttons.

"Samson, twenty-five seconds until MEDUSA arrives. I'll do the entry countdown."

"Yes, sir," he hisses.

I watch the MEDUSA team as they glide their way quietly through the tunnel. The deep hum of the ventilators dissipates into an almost unnoticeable yet subconsciously thoroughly irritating background noise.

Ten seconds. But they're not slowing down enough. They're coming in too fast.

"*MEDUSA*, slow down! You're almost there."

Their pace slows up considerably. The first three men stop just meters from the door. But the trailing two agents either couldn't stop fast enough or didn't understand the urgency of my warning.

"Brace yourselves," I yell.

A low but obvious scuffling noise comes from the MEDUSA team's tunnel as the two agents crash into each other and their colleagues.

"Damn it," Samson curses quietly.

"What the hell was that?" exclaims one of the subterranean guards. An enormous mercenary jumps out of his seat with a mean, ready-for-business look on his face. He's the leader, or at least a senior member of the team. "No clue, Sax. Johnny, swing that camera around; let's check it out," he calls as he moves over to Johnny's spacey-screen.

The No. 1 man has stepped out from behind his desk and is watching the men through his office window. Thoroughly scanning the area in the corridor where the agents are recovering from the crash, I see more of the hidden chambers behind the walls.

"Pick yourself up, you three," I yell. "Agent-4, behind you, the wall. Place your hands on the wall and push gently. Slide the panel to your left a half-centimeter or so."

"Yes, sir."

"Good. Now back again. There's another sliding panel on the opposite wall. Same place. Remember that. Now, get up against the walls all of you. And wait."

I couldn't deploy the camera hack without giving the game away. The camera has by now executed a 360-degree swing more than once.

"Can't see anything wrong, boss," Johnny says, stating the obvious.

"Probably just one of those weird noises we hear every now and then," Sax concludes. "Bloody tunnel should have been sound-proofed. Too much disturbance."

"No, I don't trust it," counters the boss. "I'm gonna check it out. Sax, get my back."

"Silence. Everyone." Bitsi-Tone. The teams were quietly discussing alternative options in case the plan were to go pear-shaped.

"There's been a change of plan. We have to improvise. MEDUSA, get ready to dodge a walking, breathing tank. He's on the way out to you now."

The door to the tunnel opens wide, and the boss moves to stand in the doorway, scanning the tunnel. Even a dimwit can see the tunnel is empty, but the boss still doesn't trust it. He trusts his instincts.

"Sax, hold the door." And he steps carefully out, one small step at a time, as if he were afraid the ground might open up and swallow him whole.

After a few small paces, he suddenly lifts his nose like a dog smelling a scent on a breeze. Then he instantly shifts direction, and his next move is directly toward Junior.

"Agent-1, he's coming right at you. Plug him when he reaches you. Catch him, don't drop him. Hold him close to you. Arms around him. Press face to face. You need to make him invisible."

Junior is lightning-fast in the midst of battle, and he follows my instructions to the letter.

"Boss, where'd you go? Hell-'n'-piss-fire. The boss just disappeared," Sax shouts as he lets go of the door, which closes and locks automatically.

"Agent-3, get ready to hold that door closed."

Large semi-rectangular handles are bolted to the inward-opening door on both sides. The closing/locking mechanism is fully confuzerized. Agent-3 braces one roller-bladed foot up on the wall beside the door as he grabs hold of the rounded metal of the handle, then prepares to pull with all his might.

"Agent-4, wall panel, now. Agent-1, dump that man behind the wall. Agent-4, help him."

It takes only a few seconds and a few thuds for Junior to dump the boss's stunned and limp body behind the wall panel. But not unnoticed.

"Sir," says one of the confuzer geeks watching the spacy-screens in the underground prison. "The wall has, er, opened up?"

I could have sworn that bitch was dead, thinks the HPD No. 1 man to himself. He has now come into the main room and is overlooking the screen.

Junior slips off his roller-blades and throws them into the chamber with the boss. Agent-4 quickly closes again.

"And now it's closed again," exclaims the geek.

"I'm not blind, you idiot," yells No. 1.

She's come back to haunt me, he thinks. *Well, that's her mistake.*

"How could the boss disappear like that?" Sax asks no one in particular.

The HPD No. 1 man yells at Sax. "What are you talking about, man? People don't just disappear into thin air."

"I'm tellin' you, sir. Right in front of my eyes, he just disappeared. He was standing a little funny, I think—not sure why. Then he just, er, disappeared."

"Medusa, get ready." Bitsi-Tone. I can sense the next move.

"Agent-3, hold that door. Mansion, get ready. Junior, help Agent-3. When I say so, both of you push that door open as fast and hard as you can. Then, Medusa, you sneak in as best you can. But get in whatever it takes. Mansion, you enter when the door opens."

"Sax, get that bloody door open, and three of you get out there. I want to see what just happened," hollers the No. 1 man.

Using the keypad, Sax unlocks the door and starts pulling.

Junior has joined Agent-3 and is hanging on for dear life. Even bigger than his father, Junior is strong as an ox.

"Hold…" "Hold…"

Sax has unknowingly mimicked Agent-3 and has placed one foot up on the wall beside the door and is pulling with all he's got. Another mercenary is pulling on Sax trying to help him, and another is standing right in the line of fire of the soon-to-be fast-flying, newly adapted weapon.

"It's stuck," Sax grimaces as he pulls. The door shows no sign of moving.

"Medusa, ready to push that door. Two, one, now!"

"Mansion, enter."

The back-door flies inward at an amazing pace. Sax screams as he receives a nasty smack in the groin from the corner of the door and lands heavily on his assistant, whose head hits the floor with an audible bang. The face and head of the third mercenary meet the door at full speed. His blood splatters across the door-panel just before he's thrown across the room, where he remains laid out, unconscious.

Samson has opened his door just enough for the team to slip through. As the Lord-ITs' captors try to make sense of what just happened, Samson's men begin to enter the chamber in single-file and line up as planned.

Jonesy and Jules quickly dodge their way over to the Lord-ITs. Their key goal now is to keep the Lord-ITs covered and alive. But two of the mercenaries have also moved over to cover the Lord-ITs.

"Lord-ITs, stay put. Don't move. We're going to cover you *right now*. Jonesy, Agent-8, squeeze behind those PERPS and sit on the Lord-ITs' laps. Jonesy, take Lord-IT. Now!"

Refusing to rush into a panicky action, Samson waits a few seconds more until all his men have time to take position and aim.

They all file in up against the walls; each knows their number in the line as they enter the room and have counted the number of the man they need to shoot first.

They need to reach maximum head-count on the first round of shots.

The NETNERD looks up to see the front-door standing ajar. He looks alert, but more-so, he's afraid and puzzled, which delays his reaction.

"Safe," whispers Jonesy, confident that in the panic even the close-by mercenaries won't hear him.

The NETNERD suddenly recovers from his panic-induced confusion and screams, "Hey!" as he jumps up from his seat pointing at the front-door at the same time as Samson whispers his command. He's still not willing to give away his position.

"One!"

LASAROMIC stun-shots fly in all directions. A single round only, taking out ten of the twenty men. All ten of the dangerous mercenaries are down, including those who were already down, just to be sure. One agent from the Medusa team did not have enough time to line up his target.

The clamorous bedlam that initially expressed confusion is now combined with the nervous shouts of panic and anger coming from the remaining nine "blind" men in the chamber.

No sound whatsoever issues from the office where the No. 1 man has smartly retreated. He's simply slouched in his fancy leather chair, watching the scene unravel before his eyes.

A few of the PERPS helplessly look for somewhere to hide. A few try to decide where, or what, to shoot at, but there's nothing to see, no time to decide, and even less time to prepare their guns.

Three seconds later, after giving enough time to recount the targets and refresh their aim, Samson gives the next command.

"Two!"

They fire another round of shots at the nine remaining men in the main chamber.

The NETNERD, however, is not as dumb as his dumb partnership with the No. 1 man might lead one to believe. Milliseconds before Samson gave the command, he dove under the only desk with a side wall in it that holds some confuzing gear. The eight other PERPS drop to the floor, stunned from here through to next Sunday.

"Still one under the desk, and one in the office," Samson warns as the agents close in on the desks on which all the confuzer spacey-screens sit.

Suddenly, the NETNERD comes flying out from under his desk, swinging arm first, and throws an old-fashioned hand grenade directly at the Lord-ITs.

"Bomb!" Samson screams.

On my screen-space, I see a LICKEM take flight without hesitation. The BITS-SECS agent catches the grenade in mid-flight.

"Gotcha," he yells out triumphantly. Then he crashes through the door to the unfinished passage, and less than half a second later, the bomb explodes, taking the agent with it, as six stun-darts hit the NETNERD.

In the terrible moments that follow, each BITS-SECS agent in the room surely imagines his own form of the possible consequences of the risk they live with month in, month out.

"Junior!" Samson screams, running to the passage, to his son. Samson crumples to his knees as he reaches the lifeless body of his baby boy lying just inside the passage. The Bitsi-INVISI is destroyed. Junior is horribly visible. The armored-padding he wore has kept his body in one piece, so it would seem, on the outside. But on the inside, he has been ripped apart.

Gently taking his boy in his arms, Samson lets out a heart-rending, yet bloodcurdling, animal-like scream. "AAARRRRRGGGGHHHHHH!!!"

The sound of someone hitting the floor fills the silence that follows Samson's grief-filled cry. And the HPD–FITS No. 1 man pulls an old-fashioned Colt .45 from a drawer in his desk.

One of the four CCOTCHA LICKEMs where the Lord-ITs are sitting is on the floor. Frantically checking the LICKEM's details, I see that it's Jules.

"Lord-ITs, Jonesy? You all OK?" checking to see whether they were hit. They also weren't far from the explosion.

"Yes, sir."

"Yes, Bitsi, we're both OK."

"Jonesy, take off Jules's BITS-INVISI."

Once done, I zoom in with Bitsi-Lite to inspect the damage, and, even though I might have thought it couldn't be possible, my heart sinks even deeper. Jules has been on the team for eighty years. Long enough that his wife and kids may even have forgotten there was a chance he might not make it home from work one day. They will be unconsolably heart-stricken.

"Shrapnel, buried in his neck. He's gone," I mutter.

A loud gunshot booms and echoes through the room. Somewhere in the far-off distance, I sense a vague irritation hinting that I should probably feel guilty I didn't try to save the No. 1 man from himself and from his prize Colt .45.

It goes against my principles not to save someone from a violent death. Everyone should, at least once, have the chance to do penance for their sins and have the opportunity to understand what made them the way they are, and to learn how to forgive, and to love, and to care, and to become a positive contributor to the living, rather than a taker of their lives.

Yet from another neck of the woods, something is tugging at me. A realization that this guy probably already had all his chances and blew them all, and that I was most likely a hundred years or more too late with any thoughts of saving him. And yet another angel of darker darkness is teasing me with the suggestion that all the deaths this monster caused or attempted in the past days alone are reason enough to see him dead.

The complex flow of emotions you have to deal with when confronted with the pain this man inflicted on so many people is hard to describe, to say the least, and almost impossible to deal with without hope. The hope that we will, over the course of time, learn this is not how we should live our lives, not how we should treat each other. We should not hurt each other like this; we should not hurt each other at all.

39

CLEARING OUT

THE SOUND OF the gunshot from the now ex-No. 1 man's office has a strangely contrary effect on Samson that stirs him into forward motion, as if the sound of death is acting like an obscure reminder that life must go on.

He stands and turns to see everyone doing nothing but trying to hide their emotions in the best way each can manage, and to not look at him, even though they can't see him. Samson, unlike the others, has not yet removed his Bitsi-INVISI.

"Agents, look sharp," he commands, sounding tired to the bone, but still firm. "Junior wouldn't want us exposed for any reason. So, let's get these PERPS secured and ready to take the Lord-ITs to safety." He sounds a little harder now.

"Transporters, status?"

"All quiet, sir. Not a peep from any of them." The camera-hack went unnoticed.

The whole exercise down below has taken no more than a few minutes. The guards in the house haven't yet missed their sleeping colleague.

"Agent-4," Samson calls to the man closest to the front door, "put that bug back in your ear and get up to the transporter now."

"Yes, sir," he replies turning and running out the door while struggling with his combat suit to find his Bitsi-INVISI.

Samson walks over to the office window, and for a few seconds he stares at the bloody mess in there. It's easy to imagine some of the thoughts flashing through his mind.

As he turns away he calls, "Transporters, get two stretchers ready for Agent-4. He's on the way up now."

Passing some of his men, he nudges two of them and commands, "You two, give me your bugs."

"Sir," comes the response, and immediately the Bitsi-INVISIs are held out for him to take.

On his way to the Lord-ITs, Samson stops by the NETNERD, who's lying unmoving on the floor. Counting six stun-darts, he whispers, "Three too many," to himself, then bends down to check for a pulse, which stopped a short while ago.

On reaching the sofa where the Lord-ITs still sit, Samson puts on his best manners, but in an effort to hide his emotions, his voice is cold and hard.

"Lord-IT, sir, ma'am. Please put out your hand." Which they do, silently. For them, Junior's death has also hit hard, more so because he died saving them.

Samson places a Bitsi-INVISI in each hand. "Place the round side just against the inside of your ear, if I may," and he gently touches the place in the ear for them both.

"Now, press gently on the flat side." As they become invisible, Samson continues. "When we move out, you may want to hold hands. Collisions are all too easy when you can't see who's in front of you."

"Thank you, Samson," Lord-IT replies, mustering up the strength to control the emotions in his voice.

"Just a few moments, sir, ma'am, then we'll clear out," the big man informs them, gently now, sensing and recalling the Lord-ITs' own ordeal.

Turning away to focus on finalizing the retreat, Samson asks, "Transporters, status?"

"Agent-4 just returning now, sir. All quiet here."

To his agents below, he yells, "You men. Speed it up. How many to go?" They are cuffing the sleeping PERPS.

"Six, sir."

"Get on with it."

"Sir."

Wandering around the room, he's considering any last-minute changes to the extraction plan. He passes the back door—which leads to Medusa's tunnel—closes it and destroys the electronic keypad that opens it.

"Bitsi, sir, can you prepare a fully armed transporter to arrive here in, say, two or three minutes?"

"Already done, Samson. Four-second arrival time after you say go."

"Thank you, sir."

"Teams, bugs, reinstall them, now. You two, stay in the rear when we leave. Distance 20 meters. Clear?" he asks the agents who surrendered their Bitsi-INVISIs for the Lord-ITs.

"Yes, sir."

"We'll have you covered, but you mustn't draw fire on us."

"Yes, sir."

Agent-4 arrives back in the chamber with the now invisible stretchers, and Samson takes one from him, thanking him.

"Now, go to Jules. Someone help Agent-4 get Jules ready to leave."

Lord-IT has understood the plan, and as Samson starts toward Junior, he whispers urgently to his wife, "Come with me," and he gently but firmly and quickly leads her to Junior. He picked up quickly that sound is an important guide when everyone is invisible.

"Let me help you, Samson," Lord-IT says.

Samson is strong and proud and would like to do this by himself, but he realizes that taking help is probably the most prudent at this time. "Thank you."

Together, Lord-IT and Samson gently place Junior onto the stretcher. As they each lift one end, Junior disappears between them.

"All ready to depart?" Samson calls.

"Yes, sir," Jonesy speaks for the remaining team.

"Ma'am?" Samson double-checks.

"Yes, Samson," she says quietly from somewhere behind him.

"Last man out, close the door."

Minutes later, Junior, Samson, Jonesy, and the Lord-ITs are safely aboard the invisible transporter, and the last of the men arrive, but wait below at the entrance ramp.

"Now please, Bitsi, sir."

"On the way, Samson."

Eighteen seconds later, Jules and the remaining men are on board the second vehicle. Samson gives the final instructions of this mission. "Cleaners, lock up the last PERPS. Then, call in the authorities."

"Yes, sir."

"*Cleaners.*" Bitsi-Tone.

"Yes, Bitsi, sir?"

"No more people must die today!"

"Yes, sir, Bitsi."

"Delilah?"

"Yes, sir?" she sounds absolutely devastated.

"Let me know as soon as Samson has called his wife, please."

"Yes, Bitsi, sir."

40

Are You Kidding Me?

After the soup-ah-sonic flight takes off, direction home, Samson prepares a cooled transportation coffin ready for Junior. Jonesy steps up to assist him with his boy's body.

"Let me, Jonesy," intervenes Lord-IT, who then helps Samson gently place his beloved son into the cold, padded box. A few minutes pass while Samson gazes upon an important part of his heart that will soon be buried forever. There won't be many more opportunities for Samson to glance upon his boy.

"Thank you, sir." Lord-IT just nods, afraid he cannot utter the words, afraid his heart will fail him.

They part ways, Samson to the back of the plane and Lord-IT to the front to sit with his wife.

"Bitsi?" Lord-IT finally has the opportunity to resume proper contact.

"Lordy?"

"You did well."

I don't feel well, not even slightly. I didn't double-check Samson's scanning of the underground chamber. Maybe I should have. Maybe that could have helped.

"You cannot save everyone from everything, Bitsi." Lord-IT knows my distress. He's seen it before.

"Oh, stop that, will you, Lordy. You're only likely to piss me off. How are you guys doing?"

"Relieved, of course, but with mixed feelings, and dead-tired."

"Understandable. Get some rest now. You'll be here in a few hours."

"Er..."

"Yes?"

"I have a presentation to give at 17:30. You forgot?"

"Are you kidding me? You can't be serious!"

"Bitsi, you tried to warn me many times about what happened today. I didn't listen carefully enough. But now you have an unexpected opportunity—yes, at an inopportune time and created by unfortunate circumstances—but, Bitsi, I think, you shouldn't miss it. According to my calculations, we can still make it to the auditorium on time."

"You're crazy. Have you asked your wife?"

"Yes. She doesn't like the idea much, but she has agreed."

"Bloody hell. I'll change the flight plan. Get some sleep. You're gonna need it."

41

ALONE IS NOT BETTER

DIVERTING THE PLANE to London takes only a few minutes; then, I leave my office to find my wife, dreading having to tell her the fate of her favorite BITS-SECS agent.

"Honey, how's it going?" she asks, anxious to hear an update.

"It's over. The Lord-ITs are in a plane on the way to London. Two BITS-SECS agents are dead, and two of the PERPS also."

"Which agents?" she demands immediately—and tensely. She knows them all by name. She makes it a point to send them all birthday and Christmas cards, each time dreaming up a novel way of thanking them for their contribution to the safety of the world and of our families.

"Junior and Jules." There's no truly acceptable way to break it softly.

She inhales hard and deep while gasping almost silently, then whispers in a tiny voice, "Oh, no."

Her emotions always bubble just under the surface during such missions, knowing the dangers only too well, and fearing them all the more for knowing. Almost immediately, she rests her forehead on my shoulder and quietly cries, and cries, until she can cry no more.

"First Jemma and now Junior. All their kids gone. Poor things. And Jules's family."

"Yeah, I know."

Samson's eldest was into speed. Twenty-two years ago, they lost her to a high-speed go-cart race, a horrible accident with multiple deaths.

"It might sound strange, hon, but I was thinking of asking if they might want to stay here a while, rather than at home. Get them away for a while. What do you think?"

"It can't hurt to ask, and they're definitely welcome. Ask Julia. Samson will go with whatever she feels most comfortable with."

"Are you OK, sweetie? I need to go back; there are still many things to be wrapped up."

"Yes. I'm OK. Why London?"

"Lordy is not missing his five-yearly speech. You should watch it on TV later."

"Hmmm... You go and do what you need to." She kisses me on the cheek, then watches as I drag myself back to the office.

While I was away my lead BITS-SITTER called, so I now return the courtesy. "Delilah, you tried to reach me?"

"Yes, sir. Samson has made the call home."

"Thanks. You bearing up, ol' girl?"

"Sort of."

"Go and sit with the BIT-SITTERS, Del. Watch an old movie, talk it through, take an evening off."

"Are you taking the evening off, sir?"

"I still have things to wrap up here, Del. Go on, sit with your SITTERs."

"Maybe in a little while, Bitsi."

"OK, Del."

She might go and sit with her agents, maybe—many hours from now—but Junior's death has been one more hard strike to the heart during this awful mission that Delilah, indeed many of us, will suffer from greatly for a considerable time to come.

Yet why is it that so many of us bury our painful emotions? We hide from them, often remaining morbidly alone while we readjust, rebuild our self-defenses, and attempt to make them stronger than before. I guess it's just easier not to face the harsh facts head-on, not to face our horrifically agonizing feelings. Easier to try to forget, alone, over time.

"I want to be alone" and "leave me alone" are oft-spoken words when pain abounds. Experiencing the anguish of grief is, unfortunately, natural at times. Nature, however, doesn't require that we suffer alone. Indeed, to be alone is of itself to suffer. So, suffering alone is to suffer and suffer. Alone is not better.

I'm impatient to leave this lonely place and go to my wife and children.

42

"OH, SO SOFTLY" VS. "BIG WILL BE BEAUTIFUL"

WHILE THE LORD-ITs are on their way to London, I pull up and briefly review my work on the presentation Lordy was so keen on giving this evening. The events of the day, however, have changed matters considerably. So, discarding all previous data, I start afresh to prepare the pearls of wisdom that Lordy will bestow upon his audience.

The flight is uneventful. Most of them are either sleeping or power-napping. Samson dozes off and wakes in fits and starts, a harsh, pained look on his face most of the time. He appears to be reliving the nightmare of his invisible son's death, which he couldn't see. In his dreams, it appears, he's most likely filling in the missing details.

After landing, there's adequate time to complete the journey to the auditorium and allow the Lord-ITs to don fresh clothing and go through the makeup routine, preparing them for the coming stage appearance.

Samson has all the UK BITS-SECS teams take up residence in the auditorium, and they, together with Jonesy and Bitsi-Lite, sweep the place checking for any possible security concerns. It's a massive oval-shaped building reminiscent of a football stadium.

Usually, the arena divides down the middle into two halves, but for such a special event as a visit from Lord-IT, the dividing sliding wall retracts. The stage is in the middle of one of the long sides of the auditorium.

The whole floor area is full of table seating ranging from priceless close to the stage to exorbitantly expensive at the back. The rest of the seating staggers in typical auditorium style. In this arrangement, the guest capacity is thirty-eight thousand, and all those seats have been sold out.

The ceiling has a vast number of speakers hanging from extendable mounts, which lower or raise, according to the arena layout. Computers adjust the volume from each speaker to ensure that everyone hears a consistent sound, no matter where they sit.

Many hundreds of Nuke-Li-Aerially floating microphones hover around the massive hall, ready to respond and move close to anyone who wants to say anything. They'll also listen for any untoward activity that could indicate a security problem.

The spacey-screen behind the speaker's podium is indescribably mega-ginormous. Many other screens are around, hovering Nuke-Li-Aerially in strategic viewing positions.

Finally, the Lord-ITs are ready and make their way to the stage of the auditorium. As they enter, the applause during the standing ovation is deafening, almost overpowering. The audience has waited five years to hear these inspiring words.

After taking their seats and waiting for the noise to subside, Lord-IT stands and moves to the speaker's podium. Then he opens the PRIVATE-LYFE that Samson put there for him and that I prepared.

Giving the sign that he's ready to start, he raises one hand, palm out, and waits for total silence.

This time, I made special arrangements. Lord-IT's presentation will broadcast on all news channels and all public advertisement screens WOWI. Most of the living, breathing human world will listen to him.

For a change, I showed the presentation to Lord-IT over the CCOTCHA. This one requires more than the ability to dance.

"Ladies and gentlemen, thank you, thank you."

Lord-IT always starts his introduction speech as if it were ad-hoc, off the cuff, almost unprepared, and no props. His philosophy is that this way he gets the focus. Eyes will be on him instead of rolled up in the head after seeing a banal introduction slide or focused on trying to understand an obscure agenda.

"Over the years," he starts, "I have given my views on various approaches for building a successful business. Some of the more well-known models you may remember: Shoot Low, Aim Straight, and Bar Brawl, otherwise known as The Presidential Approach, only suitable for respectable politicians," Lord-IT scolds, while wagging an index finger at an imaginary naughty little boy or girl.

Some of the less well-informed or more insensitive members of the audience miss the point entirely and break out in short-lived raucous cackling. Others in their vicinity throw them looks trying to explain with killing-eyes, "Don't you get it? It's so disgustingly embarrassing it's meant *not* to be laughed at."

Even though he's probably exhausted, Lord-IT still manages to pack a punch, play the part, as if he were acting out a scene showing on a cinema wide-screen. "And, of course," Lord-IT continues, "the two biggest success models known to man, Oh So Smoothly, Oh So Softly, and Big *Will* Be Beautiful."

Many from the crowd laugh heartily at the mention of Lord-IT's mocking symbolic names for those two big-business killer strategies. "Today, ladies and gentlemen, I will attempt to answer two questions that many of you have asked of me many times."

Lord-IT is without a doubt, in the eyes of the world at least, the most successful businessman who ever lived and probably ever will live. They pay premium DOLLIES to be in the auditorium to hear him speak, to hear his opinion live, and to brag about that later.

"Question One: Which, do I think, is the most successful business model?

Question Two: How do I measure the value of this success?"

A huge yet short round of applause follows, paying respect to Lord-IT's listening ear and his willingness to cater to his audience.

After gently waving his outstretched hands in a downward motion to silence the racket, he continues, "Remember, ladies and gentlemen, a two-page presentation demands a serious dose of generalization. So, knowing this, forgive me, and if you still manage to become offended, then search your own soul. And if you're one of the unfortunate few who aren't easily offended, then search deep into your soul until you become offended; then, search further."

"I will start with the life-cycle of success, end-to-end, as I see it."

Lord-IT throws up the first few lines of the presentation and moves immediately into explaining them.

Success = Winning

Winning → Competition

Competition → Struggle

Struggle →Loss = Success

"Success is winning. Winning implies there's a competition involved, which is equal to a struggle, which ends up with a loser on one side, which signifies the success on the other. Can you follow? Is it too complicated?" he mocks them somewhat.

Not giving anyone a chance to respond to his rhetorical questions, Lord-IT puts the next line of the slideshow onto the screen while continuing, "Let me try to simplify this somewhat."

Success → Competition→Loss = Success

"Here we go. This is nice and simple, surely? Success is the result of a competition when the loss of one equals the success of the other," he says, rather loudly.

Lord-IT glares harshly into the crowd, scanning from left to right and back again, not assessing their reaction but attempting to raise the shock-factor effect. "To survive the competition, you must win. Defeat—aw, to hell with it—even slaughter your opponent. *Someone* has to lose. And it had better not be you. Do everything. *Anything*! Lie, cheat, beg, borrow, steal, and even *kill* if you have to. Anything to succeed, to avoid losing. And each step-in-error you take, each dark step you take toward success brings you closer to the killing-blow."

With each word he utters, Lord-IT's blood pressure rises steadily. Just hours after being rescued from certain death, the downside of competition is close to his heart.

Hands are thrown into the air, building up a queue of people eager to be allowed to ask the first questions. "But I've never killed anyone," shouts a rude individual from the crowd.

Ready for this, I quickly flash an already prepared message directly to Lordy's eyes to help him focus. "Questions later," he says bluntly.

"Still too hard to understand?" and he's almost shouting now and waving an arm loosely in the screen's direction. "OK, let me try this; it's even easier." More words become visible.

Success →Loss = Success

"Or how about this?"

Survival →Death = Survival

"So, here it is everyone, the life-cycle of success, as we've lived it over centuries, over many thousands of years."

Almost at the end of the first slide in his presentation, Lord-IT throws up the words survival and death but written in a spherical shape much like an O.

"Granted, the circle shows only two players, the winner and the loser. In reality, of course, there are *billions* of players. *All of us. And we are all stuck in this never-ending pitiful circle*," Lord-IT shouts, extremely loudly. And the crowd back away in their seats, quite visibly.

"Now," calming down just a little, "before comparing success models, ladies and gentlemen, let me tell you how I value success."

"Here," Lord-IT yells, pointing up to the screen as a thick red line crosses through the now red life cycle of success, turning it into a number. Zero.

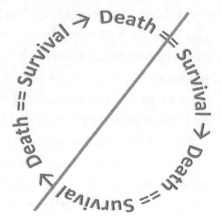

"Zero," Lord-IT yells. "Zero. Zero. Zero!" Each time, he's louder, yelling directly into the faces of his unsuspecting public. "Success, ladies and gentlemen, as the circle indicates, is short-lived. *And* it's followed by death. Fresh competition joins the circle, chasing behind you, looking to put you down, take you out. Where the hell is the value in that? Zero!"

Lord-IT's wife is slowly losing her composure, raising a hand to her face to hide the twitching muscles that are desperately trying to hold back her tears.

"And success that's gained by putting others down is shameless and does not deserve a value. Zero!"

"Countless thousands of years, nations, corporations, and individuals alike have battled each other in bloody competition for survival, for a drop of water, a plot of land, riches, dominion, or the power to rule, to dominate. Only to lose it all, sooner or later. Billions of dead and many more suffered. For what? Because the balance of power simply goes around and around in a sickening cycle of death and survival.

"And why? Because we proud beings are too strong to compromise on our individual needs for so-called survival. No, no, we must fight to win, whatever it takes, and in the process squash or kill whoever gets in our way. Natural selection, they say; it's in our DNA, survival of the fittest.

"We do *not* need to focus our efforts on how to survive. We've had that knowledge for centuries. This fight for individual survival, this competition to be number one, is hampering our ability to progress. Do we really need to suffer to motivate ourselves into greater achievements, to make us want our lives to be better, to ensure that we have a future?

"We need to learn how to *live*. In peace and harmony, together. Our children and our children's children must not face this tragic so-called civilized future that simply resembles our horrifying past. *This compulsive timeworn cycle is cruel, relentless and never-ending. And it must stop!*"

"Lord-IT, what are you doing to bring an end to this competition?" a voice shouts out.

Lord-IT looks first down, breathes in deeply, then looks up again and sighs before answering, "Unfortunately, not enough," he replies, sighing again heavily. "I'm too busy struggling with all of you competing against me."

A few people break out in laughter. Many others turn to stare them down with a questioning "Are you stupid?" look. The laughing, however, is abruptly interrupted by the sudden buzz of tens of thousands of FONEs vibrating throughout the auditorium.

The audience members who subscribe to the latest news bulletins are getting what they paid for. A second O-WE-COME screen-space lights up the main-stage spacey-screen, and the latest BGB headline scrawls across the sspace in gaudy bold print.

Breaking News THIS EVENING
15 Dead During Violent Attack on the Lord-ITs
Heroic Rescue by Samson and Delilah
Attempted Nuke-Li-Aerial Theft
Unsuccessful Super-power Bid
Bitsi Intervenes Saving Beloved Friends

and

the World

for Now

When asked to comment:

BGB: "I imagine you're satisfied with the rescue, Bitsi, sir?"

Bitsi: "Not entirely. No one should have died. No one should die like this."

Lord-IT's wife has openly lost control and is now sobbing silently yet heavily behind a hand that's attempting to hide her face from the world.

The auditorium is deathly still. The BITS world, and indeed the whole world with them, it seems, has joined a moment of shocked silence. Some from the audience have also begun to shed their own silent tears, maybe for the Lord-ITs, or for their own children, or loved ones, maybe for humankind; who knows.

Lordy knows me well and knows my message. He reaches out behind him, taking his wife's free hand in an effort to comfort her. Then he looks up and out to the whole world. The heart-wrenching look of dark sadness in his eyes and on his face surely touches all those millions who, over the hard years, have somehow retained the capacity to care for a loved one they still have or once had.

"We continue stupidly to find ways to hide from ourselves what we're doing to each other. If we stay this path, repeating the terrible deeds and teaching the same ill-begotten lessons that history has thrust upon us, then we will all lose."

"Leave the machine, Lordy. I'll deal with it. Get your wife out of there. Come and join your kids and us."

Lord-IT, sagging in the shoulders himself, turns to assist his wife out of her chair and supports her as they walk toward the back of the auditorium stage. A sole insensitive individual calls out the now traditional must-ask conference-time question. "Lord-IT, when will you share the secrets of Nuke-Li-Aerial Power and Bitsi-Lite?"

Stopping and turning, still supporting his distressed beloved, Lord-IT faces the whole of the listening world and straightens his body, standing now proud and upright. With a loud and powerful voice, speaking much like a preacher might do, his answer booms throughout the auditorium and over every public screen and speaker in every building in the world.

"When the whole world opens its eyes and truly recognizes the pain we inflict upon each other. When the whole world lays down their arms and vows never to pick them up again. When the whole world shakes hands and exchanges hugs, thus sealing a deal that will *never, ever* break. When the whole world is competing *with* each other for a single goal, a single winner, humankind. Then, and only then, will we share our secrets."

The Lord-ITs then resume their exit from the auditorium and their journey to safety.

43

The End of a Bisi Day

TRANSPORTERS WAIT TO bring the Lord-ITs to us and to the reunion with their family. They will rejoin the soup-ah-sonic plane, meeting up with another transporter for the final leg of the journey, arriving here in just over an hour. The entire trip is secured with every technology available to me.

Jonesy is on another transporter back to the cottage, where he'll stay with his men, waiting for the Lord-ITs' return home.

Samson, unbeknown to himself, will escort the Lord-ITs in their transporter to our house. This will be the first time in the entire eighty-five years of the Bitsi-era that I have met a Samson face-to-face.

After what seems like a decade, Lord-IT, his wife, and Samson set foot on the front porch just as the transporter pulls away from the house. Security protocol demands this withdrawal.

My wife then opens the door and ushers them all in, hugging and greeting the Lord-ITs before they go to their own family, who are waiting eagerly in the large entrance hall.

"Samson. How nice to finally meet you." And she places her hands on his shoulders, softly kissing him on the cheek while pulling him into a half-embrace. Gently, she expresses her condolences, "I am so sorry for your loss, Samson." One hand gently squeezing her shoulder is his only response.

The Lord-ITs' children have refused to go to sleep. My wife has been keeping them and the in-laws up-to-date during the parents' long day. Now, the large entrance parlor is a scene of happy bedlam as the kids, my own among them, all clamor around the Lord-ITs, hugging and kissing. Lordy's wife again can't hold back her tears, this time more of relief and joy, and of the future, rather than the past.

"Samson, I'm so very sorry about Junior."

"Delilah?"

"Yes, Samson. Bitsi didn't allow me to be alone this evening." And she moves over to him and opens her arms to embrace him, but the poor man is at a total loss, not knowing which way to turn.

"It's such an honor to meet you, ma'am. You're a modern-world heroine, ma'am, and my favorite."

"But what about Bitsi?" Del teases.

"He's my boss, ma'am. Favoritism is not wise."

Delilah's sudden and rich, loud laugh peels through the hallway. "Hahaa. He's everyone's boss, Samson. Come here, my boy." Unperturbed by his discomfort, Del throws her arms about him and pulls him into a warm and loving embrace. I have held off, at the back of the crowd, practically invisible but watching everything.

Lord-IT's wife's parents finally manage to reach their daughter and hold her, who is so dear to them, once again. They had no real knowledge of how close she was to death, but the lack of information made them worry just as if they knew.

I step back even farther as I encourage Julia to join the others and break through the commotion and find her way to her man. "Julia?" Samson exclaims, half questioning.

Ignoring his question at first, she throws her arms around him and holds him as tight as she can. "You're all I have left that's important to me. I aim to keep you close to me as often as I can," she whispers.

Things have calmed down a little around the Lord-ITs, so I move over to them, and almost instinctively the four of us form the group hug, pretty much like a football huddle but without the mud and stinking sweat, and this time including the in-laws. The kids all dive in, having always reveled in the closeness of this expression of love.

After just a few moments, however, I'm anxious about the need to move on. "Let's not leave the others alone," I state simply while gently removing myself from the hug, and as the kids run off to play, I turn to Samson, who's still standing at the far end of the hallway.

Lordy attempts to introduce Samson and me, but as I raise my hand, he quiets instantly. There's no misunderstanding within this circle of people at least—about who the boss is. All are watching as I prepare to address Samson.

Standing for a moment, with an intense expression of gentleness, I study Samson's face, looking deep into his eyes, conveying to him with minuscule changes in my gaze and features, my own personal message of pain-ridden condolence. Samson has obvious trouble hiding the turmoil of emotion broiling under his own surface. The pain, the guilt, the sorrow, the what-if scenario.

I walk up to him with outstretched hand, "Samson, what an unprecedented occasion this is and such a unique experience to meet you in person."

"I am deeply honored, BITS Inspector, sir," he responds, choking back his tears.

"Oh, so am I, Samson. So am I." I'm having trouble controlling my own emotions now. My one hand is still holding his in the handshake, and with that, I pull him to me and reach out to wrap my other arm around the big man's shoulder, pressing the side of my face against his, giving him a warm, gentle, yet firm hug. After a few moments, we both step back. "Let's go in. C'mon everyone. Let's get out of this hallway."

"Follow me, time for some food everyone." My wife, Julia, and Delilah have planned the evening, and they lead us all to the dinner table. It has been a horrific day, and yet we all need to eat, and with sharing this extended family time together, we do what we can to share and ease the pain and the burden.

Julia has a moment when she cannot contain her tears for her lost children, but immediately my wife and Del are with her, arms around her, and before long they're all crying together. Samson joins the embrace with his wife, comforting as best he can while suffering himself, but he isn't ready yet for such an open display of emotions.

I can't blame him for that. I feel myself that if I were to let go, my broken heart would fail me, and I would break down and then melt down. The women are so much stronger.

As we move into my office after dinner, the guests get comfortable on the sofas. My wife and I play host offering them drinks. The in-laws are with all the playing kids in the living room.

"Julia, Samson. You're here simply because we care for you. You're part of our big family now, and we don't want you to be alone with your pain; we share it with you. Please, feel free to stay here as long as you wish. We will provide you with *whatever* you need.

"Rebecca and Lordy, you guys stay here for a few days. You'll be totally safe here. I'm having BITS-SECS play around with your security setup, upgrading it, so to speak. That will also take a few days, so best wait here until that's done."

"Great. We can all use a break," Lordy says. "One thing I'm curious about, though. How did they find the Nuke-Li-Aerial files?"

Delilah immediately chips in describing how the No. 1 HPD man targeted the three top officials who manage the Protectors and befriended them during numerous encounters in expensive, exclusive men's clubs. During a drunken session one evening, he entered a highly illegal bet with one of the officials: that he could compromise one of his two Protectors within a month. The stakes were set. Either get access to a Protector's login or kiss goodbye to a million DOLLIES.

The No. 1 man didn't try hard at all to win his bet, and after the month was up, he conceded his foolishness and handed over the million. A small price to pay for the information exchange, he thinks.

That was three years ago. One and a half years later, the No. 1 man made a serious attempt to seduce the most gullible of the two

Protectors. He reintroduced himself and his business acquaintance Medusa, who took over from there.

In no time at all, they gave the Protector the choice of having his life destroyed or untold riches. A double-whammy, so to speak. An offer he couldn't refuse, in man-speak.

Delilah picked up much of this information from the INARDs recordings, and from some careless communication stored on the Protector's hard-BITS. More information is still on the way in. Altogether, there's enough hard evidence to convict them all.

Lord-IT throws me a look indicating clearly that the Protector arrangement contract has been breached, big time. "I have already revoked them for now. We need to discuss how to take that further, to a conclusion," I respond.

"They took us in our car. Six couples pretending to be happily tipsy while leaving the restaurant with us."

"They planned it well, Lordy. So, I'm now finishing up a little project I've worked on for fifty-plus years. Then, you'll be safer both on the street and in your cars."

"Oh? Now you've made me curious?"

"You've already used my new Bitsi-INVISI technology. It can make you invisible, as well as block any recording/viewing devices. It's a layer between the outside and, for example, you or the car. Also, instead of going invisible, you could choose a new body or face, or any car model you choose, at any time you choose, and no one would ever know as long as they don't see the transition."

"Sounds like expensive technology, Bisi."

"Not really. It's not for sale."

"Another Bitsi secret, huh?"

"Some things, Lordy, I will either take to my grave or pass on to my family but never to anyone else."

"To your grave? You won't just pass them all on to your kids?"

"Life as Bitsi is risky, Lordy; you know how that is. And that isn't a legacy I want to automatically pass on to them. Not unless I can see that they'll be both capable and willing."

"Roger that."

"But I *might* pass them on to you, Lordy, if you promise to play safe," teasing him a little.

He throws me a big, soft smile, reading between the lines, understanding. He had compromised his own personal security, didn't play safe enough. But it was a conscious if not risky choice. A choice I believe he'll be reconsidering soon.

The survivors of this long, nightmarish day continue chin-wagging about whatever comes to mind. But after a while, Delilah, Samson, and his wife decide they've had enough for one day, and with my wife escorting them, they take their leave.

Not long after my wife's return, Lord-IT's wife also starts to show signs of needing some rest. "Er, Bisi, the wikids need some rest. Baby, can you take them up? I need to go through a few things with Bisi. I'll be up soon."

"Your usual rooms are ready for you, Lordy. Honey, can you show Lordy's wikids the way?" We share another round of long and heart-warming hugs and kisses. Then the women, children, and granddad depart to the sleeping quarters.

Lordy and I sit together, reveling in the peace and quiet, and the feeling of relative safety. Standing, I go over to the drinks cabinet and pour us each a glass of our favorite tipple, and I indulge in a small, thin, yet full-flavored cigar. And we just sit again, for some time. As I think over the day's events, I can't help my curiosity and begin to wonder where Lordy's thoughts are taking him.

"What's on your mind, Lordy?"

"Many things, many, many things. For example, what happened today?"

"That story will take a long time. But, in a nutshell, that old girlfriend of yours, before Rebecca, she had twins."

"How could I forget," he says bitterly.

"Yes. Well, she managed to poison not only her own mind but also those of her kids into thinking that you were the father who deserted them. The girl became famous working for BGB and got into the pants of too many influential people. The boy turned out to be a BITS genius and got into BIG-AM-I's network and systems. Together, they managed to persuade a lot of people they could take you down and end up even richer and more powerful than you."

"I just don't get it?" Lordy questions. "Two short weeks. Three chaste dates. How did she twist that around?"

"We went back four generations. *All* the mothers before her did the same. Somehow, somewhere in her family's history, some monster ruined the lives of many to come after him."

"Incredible," he exclaims, pretty much helpless.

"What's incredible? The fact that we do what we're taught? Or that we're taught these things in the first place?"

"Humph," he huffs. "Both, I guess."

"Yes," I can only agree with him. "The rest should probably wait until tomorrow, Lordy."

"I guess so. At least for a change you really got to focus on your personal number one objective today, huh, BITS Inspector, sir?" Lordy asks, half smiling, sadly.

"Yeah," ever so slightly nodding my head, slowly, almost regretful.

My wife is back downstairs and pottering around the living room pretending to tidy up, looking constantly into the office, clear signs that it's time for us also to go to bed. Lordy has also noticed.

"I have decided one thing today."

"Oh?"

"It's good to be prepared, so I'm never going to give another one of your presentations without reviewing it first."

We both break out in semi-somber chuckling, clinking our glasses together, unable to speak, step by step processing the pain and stress of the day.

"I need to get some sleep," he says, half raising his eyebrows in my wife's direction, indicating that he thinks we maybe ought to listen to her.

"Of course, Lordy. It has been a hard day for all."

"Yes, and I would like to go to my family."

My wife sees Lordy preparing to depart and comes into the office. They hug, and Lordy kisses her on the cheek, bidding goodnight.

"Try not to get lost this time," I tease. "The house intercom is not meant for rescuing JERKs and COCKS who can't find their way around."

Chuckling on the way out the door, Lordy turns back, and asks, "Did you catch all of them?"

"Yes. Every last one."

"Did they really have the Nuke-Li-Aerial files, Bisi?"

"They had my top one hundred and eleven favorite movie-files, Lordy, all trussed up into one big booby-trap. And they didn't even get the chance to enjoy them."

Nodding his head with a grim excuse of a smile, his dark and furious eyes staring out at me, he refrains from responding. I wonder what punishment that anger would serve them if the choice were his.

As he turns to leave, I ask the question that's hung heavily on my heart for a few hours, indeed for decades. "Lordy, do you think they'll listen?"

A heavy sigh, followed by the obvious reluctance to answer, "We humans, we're not good listeners, Bisi. Look at me, I'm a prime example. Why would they suddenly start listening now? Isn't that too much to hope for?"

"I will never give up hope, Lordy. Never give up hope."

"And that, my friend, is one of the reasons why I love you."

"Hmm. Sleep well, Lordy. Sleep well, my friend."

I stand and stare as he leaves the room, tears from a hopefully distant future trickling slowly down my face. In my mind, I can easily imagine Lordy's death. Lord-IT only knows, today it was almost a reality. But I cannot bring myself to imagine life without him, my closest, most trusted, and dearest friend.

A hand rests gently on my shoulder, and I place mine on top of hers. My wife is more than just a friend; she's my other half. What I feel, what I think, she can think and feel. We are one. Without her, I don't know where I would be today. All those years ago, she saved my soul from a dreadfully lonely existence and brought me back into the land of the living.

She knows that my experiences of the day have left me broken up, with worries—yes, some now past, but the feelings remain high for a while. She's letting me know she's there for me. And even though I know this, it does me good to feel her message afresh. I kiss her gently on the cheek.

"You also need to get to bed, sweetie," she encourages me.

"Yeah. I'll come up soon. I need to wind down a little first."

"OK," she responds, knowing my mind is still wired and understanding my need to consciously slow myself down.

She gives me one of her amazing, huge hugs that make me feel as if we maybe are safe in this world. Then she leaves to make one last check on the kids before going to bed herself.

Sitting back in my office chair, switching off, it's easy not to think about anything in particular. Thoughts float over the surface of my brain, some registering, many not. Quite some time passes before the semi-conscious mind games slow down almost to a pace of gentle reflection.

But one disturbing thought after this day's experience simply refuses to let go its hold on me: there will be more days like this to come. Simply the common knowledge that someone kidnapped Lord-IT, that it was possible to get that close to him, will spur others into similar attempts.

We need to step up our security and ensure our readiness for what will come.

Making an effort to stay this ugly qualm that's now disrupting my ability for self-controlled, peaceful thought, I close my eyes and call up the Beast.

"Beast."

"Yes, Bitsi, sir."

That was an easy command, one I've practiced many times. Using my upgraded CCOTCHA with its improved design that Bio-Brains and I had worked on long ago, I've slowly trained for fifty years to command the Beast by channeling my thoughts through the Bio-Feelers to the CCOTCHA and then on to the Beast. Mostly, I've exercised control by playing chess or go with the Beast.

I can hear him answering me, and I can see his answer appear over the CCOTCHA on my eyes.

"Bitsi's voice," I command.

"Bitsi's voice, sir?" the Beast repeats my command to me as a question. This repetition of the command is for safety reasons, to ensure the Beast has interpreted the command correctly.

"Yes, Beast, Bitsi's voice," I respond.

"Yes, sir. Bitsi's voice now, sir." And I can hear myself talking to myself. The Beast has mimicked my voice to perfection.

Now I need to try something new, but first I instruct the Beast to use its own voice. Listening to myself is not my favorite pastime. Once done, I give the new command.

"Beast."

"Yes, Bitsi, sir."

"All systems down, Beast."

"All systems down, sir?"

"Yes, Beast."

And indeed, all the confuzers in the basement shut down except the Beast, of course. He never sleeps.

This first new command was another easy one, already known to the Beast through years of listening to the command verbally. Nevertheless, it was the first time I communicated it mentally over the CCOTCHA, and it was a great success.

I promise myself that starting tomorrow, and at the highest tempo possible, I'll exploit this new means of communication with my favorite machine. By the time I'm finished, I'll not only command the Beast with my mind but also teach him new commands, new tricks. And I'll do this from anywhere on the planet over the CCOTCHA. Not that I'm planning on going anywhere.

With this new plan evolving, self-control slowly becomes an option once more, and my mind's pace of gentle reflection is finally re-attained.

"Goodnight, Beast." Confirming that the Beast should go into night-time surveillance mode.

"Goodnight, Bitsi, sir."

Standing in the bedroom, staring at the amazing creation of life, our beautiful children, aided by The Fruit—I'm an expert at imagining the many possible outcomes of almost any situation, and my mind wanders through the possible flows of our kids' lives, and momentarily my heart breaks, remembering today and fleetingly seeing them taking similar paths of suffering, for themselves and for others.

Then, resolve kicks in once again, and I remind myself that all I can do, and therefore what I surely will do, is to tenderly yet firmly, all wrapped in love, help them to feel and understand right from wrong, good from bad, and gently guide them in their choices, regardless of the lessons the world has to offer.

Now, it really is time to sleep.

Suddenly, my DIGIT-FONE starts dancing in my hand. Unbelievable.

Stepping out and away from the bedroom, I pick up the call.

"Is this the BITS Inspector?"

"And who, in the wholly scary *MOTHER* of Lord-IT's name, are you calling me up at this hour?"

"Er, this is the GLOBHED, sir." They don't even bother to mention the company name.

"What do you want?"

"We're experiencing a nasty MAGIC TRICC right now, sir."

"If your MAGICIANS can't conjure up anything within the next fifty-six hours, then call me again. *Fifty-six hours.* D'ya hear me? *Not a nanosecond before.*" Bitsi-Tone. Hanging up, I quickly turn off the FONE and go to prepare for bed.

As I settle, ready for sleep, my wife turns over and wraps her arm around me asking, "You OK, sweetie?" sharing all the caring love I could ever hope for in the middle of the night.

"I will be, hon. I will be."

As we drift together into sleepy oneness, my troubled thoughts at the end of a Bisi day are for my key personal objectives in this Bitsi life,

for the safety, peace, and happiness of ALL humankind,

and

for my adorable wife and gorgeous children,

and

for my beloved friends.

Glossary

(The) ABRIGD

1. The Abridged Gibberish Dictionary.

ANALPRIDC

1. Analyst Prima-Donna Coder.
2. Software programmer.

A-Hack pl. A-Hacks

1. Cyber-attack.
2. A break-in to a soft-BITS program, confuzer, file, etc.
3. An illicit modification to a soft-BITS program made with less-than-positive intentions

BACK-END

1. The heart of a BITS (or IT) system.

BBB

1. (The) Big Business Bosses.
2. (The) Big Bad Bosses.

(the) Beast

1. The name of Bitsi's confuzer.

BEDPAN

1. Behavioral Description—Pattern Analysis.

BIG-AM-I

1. Bipolar Innovations, Generator of Amazingly Magnificent Inventions.

Bio-Feelers

1. Mega-microscopic bio-electronic equipment used in scientific, medical, and Bitsi technology.

BITS

1. Business Information Technology (IT) System(s).

2. Bits and pieces of software or hardware (small, big, huge, or soup-ah huge!).

3. Just about anything and everything under the sun that could be described as a bit or, indeed, multiple bits.

4. Information Technology (IT).

...

55.5. Biological Intelligence's Technological Successor (artificial intelligence or interference, depending on how you feel about it).

...

111. Brutish, Incredibly Terrifying Situation, which can shake up a person's world, shattering it into gazillions of bits.

(The) BITS Inspector

1. The most powerful businessman known to humankind.

BITS-Pro

1. BITS professional.

2. IT professional.

BITS-SECS

1. Bitsi's Security Squad.

2. Lord-IT's Security Squad.

3. BITS Security Squad.

BITS-SITTER

1. Bitsi's auditors.

2. Lord-IT's auditors.

3. BITS auditors.

Bitsi

1. The BITS Inspector.

Bitsi-FREQ pl. Bitsi-FREQs

1. Bitsi-Lite transmission frequencies.

Bitsi-Lite

1. Bitsi's satellite technology.

2. Bitsi's satellite-farm.

3. Satellite.

Bitsi-Lites the Skies

1. Second largest company WOWI, owned by Bitsi.

Bitsi-Tone

1. The infamous tone of the BITS Inspector when he's angry.

BOJ-OB

1. Business Officer & Judiciary of Online Business.

BRITCHIS

1. Firewall.

2. Barrier Repelling Intruders, Technologically Categorized as Highly Impenetrable and Secure.

CASH

1. Cash or money.

2. Any form of financial currency or contract involving cash or money, e.g., investment, bond, dolly-notes, etc.

3. Collectible Assets, Security (or Savings) Historically.

4. Corrupt Ascertainment of Someone's Hourly-wage.

CASH-COW

1. BIG-AM-I's BITS, or system for receiving or collecting payments, or CASH.

CASH-PILE

1. A bank owned by BIG-AM-I.

CCIO

1. Chief Communication and Information Officer.

CCOTCHA

1. Covert Communication Transmission Channel, a brain-wired walkie-talkie-with-video.

CHABLIS

1. List of all changes to production (or live) software systems.
2. Changes to BITS list.

CHOPPA

1. Nuke-Li-Aerially-powered (small) flying vehicle.

CLIMACCSSS

1. Communications matrix.
2. Contacts list.

CLOGS

1. Collated LOG Statements.
2. System logs.
3. Stinky wooden shoes.

CMA

1. Cover My Ass.

COCKS

1. Cox, the CCIO of BIG-AM-I.

2. Cox's Offensive for Cooking up Killer Services.

Come-again

1. "Come again?" the name of Bitsi's second-favorite space-pad.

COMMINGS

1. Coincidence or coincidences.

confuzer

1. Computer.

confuzerized

1. Computerized.

2. Confused.

confuzing

1. Computing.

confuzing-power

1. Computing power.

2. A measure of the ability to confuse.

Conkerer

1. Number-one browser WOWI, copyright BIG-AM-I.

CRAPP
(see also FLAPP)

1. Crash of Abnormally Painful Proportions, always a system crash.

CRAPPING
(see also FLAPPING)

1. CRAPP Immediately Neutralizing Giants.

CREAM-EMTO-BITS

1. Take out the bad guy(s).

2. Crush by Exposure the Abominable Malefactor, Eliminating the Menace to BITS.

CYA

1. Cover Your Ass.

Delilah

1. Combined job title and appointed name of Bitsi's Chief BITS-SITTER.

DIGI

1. Digital.

DIGI-DIRT

1. Data or information, often revealing and/or incriminating.

DIGI-DIRT-CRAWLER

1. Bitsi's worm for breaking into anything confuzerized.

DIGI-DIRT-DIGGER

1. Bitsi's data collector program for scraping up DIGI-DIRT.

DIGI-DIRT-MAPP

1. Bitsi's all-powerful menu-driven program for making life easier when working on the BEAST.

DIGI-DIRT-STORE

1. Bitsi's database.

DIGI-LOCKER

1. Digital safe for securing Bitsi's and Lord-IT's products and data.

DIGIT-FONE

1. Mobile phone.

DOLLY, pl. DOLLIES

1. The one-and-only currency WOWI, used everywhere.

dosh

1. Money, or CASH.

DROSS

1. Dynamically Recyclable Operating System Supérieur, copyright Lord-IT House.
2. Operating system.

dupli-mate

1. Duplicate, copy, or replica.
2. To illegally duplicate, copy, or replicate.
3. To make a replica of something and screw with it so badly that the original is no longer recognizable.
4. An abomination.

dupli-mation

1. The result or outcome of dupli-mating.
2. An act or instance of dupli-mating.
3. An abomination.

Exhausting Gibberish

1. An abbreviation for the publication *Exhausting Gibberish, The Dictionary*.

FITS

1. Financial Institution, Technologically Secured.

FLAPP
(see also CRAPP)

1. Nasty system crash.

FLAPPING
(see also CRAPPING)

1. Nasty system crash with almost a guaranteed financially crippling effect.

FLICKEM

1. Finder for a LICKEM.

FONE

1. Short for DIGIT-FONE.

FOOLEM

1. Follow, Obscurely, Literally Every Movement.

2. Program for tracking someone and recording anything and everything of interest.

FOOLEMALL

1. Same as FOOLEM, but with the knock-on effect of following everyone the FOOLEM suspect contacts.

FOOLHIM/FOOLHER

1. Same as FOOLEM but with some gender implication.

FRONT-END

1. The visible part of a system one sees on the screen.

(The) Fruit

1. The latest age-prevention drug.

GLOBCHAT

1. Global online chat session.

GLOBHED

1. Global Helpdesk.
2. Global Helpdesk Agent or employee.

GLUE

1. Generic Language for Uniting Everything.

GODS-AVEUS

1. Gibberish Opposition Death Squad Aimed at Vindicating Everyone of Unforgivable Slang.

HAH-FLICKEM

1. Hand-Held FLICKEM, a small remote-control-like device for using the FLICKEM program.

HANDBAG

1. A feature of the FRONT-END to Bitsi's mega-powerful search-engine.
2. A bag mostly used by women for holding (supposedly, usually) smaller items.

hard-BITS

1. Hardware, such as a confuzer, spacey-screen, etc.

HPD

1. Honorary Protector of Dollies, the biggest WINCCCER ever WOWI.
2. Histrionic Personality Disorder.

INARDS

1. Information Archive Recordings—Data Store, holding recordings of all activity on all business premises WOWI since the year 2021.

JERK

1. Jerry Karmich'l, former BIG-AM-I Sissy.
2. Jerk.

Jonesy

1. Combined job title and appointed name of Lord-IT's chief of security.

L'ARCH

1. The chief architect.

LASAROMIC

1. An inferior power source, only used in inferior weaponry.

LEACH

1. Lead Enterprise Architect, Constructor Hi-tech.

LICKEM

1. Bitsi's wireless technology device, built into all confuzers WOWI.

Lord-IT

1. According to popular opinion, the most powerful businessman known to humankind.

Lord-IT House

1. Largest organization WOWI, owned by Lord-IT and Bitsi.

MAD

1. System down.

2. Major Atomic-like Downtime.

3. Something to be avoided.

4. Angry, enraged, furious.

MAD-NESS

1. System down.

2. Major Atomic-like Downtime—Never Expected Spectacular Shock.

3. Something to be avoided.

MAD-ONNA MAGIC

1. BIG System DOWN, Oh No! Not Again!

2. Something to be avoided at all cost.

MAGIC

1. BIG system.

2. Magic.

MAGICIAN

1. On-call, on-duty system technician.

MAVACAPA

1. Maximum Available Capacity.

MOTHER

1. Mother organization or top parent organization.

2. Mother.

MOWALL

1. A soft-BITS program for moving or rearranging the office walls within the BIG-AM-I buildings.

NETNERD

1. Network technician.

Nuke-Li-Aerial power

1. Currently the most powerful form of energy known to humankind.

OBOY

1. Online Booking and Ordering, Yes, sir! (implying great system).
2. Oh boy! as in "Oh, my Lord-IT!" or "Oh, my goodness!"

O-WE-COME

1. Online Web Conference and Meeting. Video-conferencing software.

OOO-O-WE-COME

1. One-On-One O-WE-COME. A hovering or flying confuzer screen or monitor, shaped like a bald head.

peemail

1. Weemail.
2. Pathetic Excuse of Email's Accountability for all Information (ever) Lost.

PERPS

1. Criminal(s)

pissmail

1. Same as peemail.

PRIVATE-LYFE

1. Personal tablet confuzer.

PUKE

1. Person Ultimately Killed in the End.

2. Person to blame and who subsequently pays the price.

3. Mistake.

PUSSIES

1. CCIO deputies.

2. Pushy Undergraduate of Sissy Stratagems—Intensified Education in Shopping.

QUA-BITS

1. Quality of BITS.

RAT RACE

1. Underhanded power struggle, often involving illicit actions, between nations or large organizations.

2. Dishonorable or illicit actions to advance one's career, usually at the cost of a colleague and/or close friend.

SADCASE

1. Database administrator.

Samson

1. Combined job title and appointed name of Bitsi's chief of BITS-SECS.

screen-space

1. Software term, historically "window" or "panel" displayed on a spacey-screen.

Seribus

1. "Serious business," the name of Bitsi's favorite space-pad.

SICCO

1. Situation Crisis Coordinator.

Sissy

1. CCIO.

Sissy-O

1. CCIO.

soft-BITS

1. Software, typically running on hard-BITS such as a confuzer.

soup-ah

1. Super.
2. Something powerful, strong, or amazing, something super indeed, which is often horribly abused such that the result lands one in the soup, ah!

space-pad

1. Keyboard.

Note: Made from (downsized) spacey-screen technology.

spacey-screen

1. Computer touch-screen, usually huge and transparent and can be viewed and operated from both sides.

sspace pl. sspaces

1. Abbreviation for screen-space.

stupid-ITy

1. Incredibly elevated level of stupidity.
2. Stupid IT, referring to broken stuff in IT, which there appears to be quite a lot of.
3. A combination of 1 and 2.

TAN-Number

1. Transaction Assurance No-Credit-Card Number.

Note: Used to be called CVV/CSC/CVD, etc. A three-digit number on the back of a (no-)credit card.

TEST-TICCLER

1. System tester.

2. Tester of Expert Systems Theoretically, Technologically Incapable, Certifiable Confuzer Logic Examiner, Retrospectively.

TIMLI

1. Timeline, a confuzerized chronological record of selected events throughout a period in a given person's life.

TRICC

1. Happening.

2. Event.

3. Achievement.

TRIPSI Bitsi

1. A rather ridiculous nickname for the BITS Inspector, nevertheless one he has trouble shaking off.

TROUBLE

1. Detailed description of technical changes (to software).

TRUTHH

1. Criminal.

TWIT

1. Unique identifier WOWI.

TWIT-OVA-PERSON

1. Person-identifier, replaced all forms of social security or national insurance numbers WOWI.

TWIT-OVA-USER

1. Digital user-identifier, for logging into software systems.

UCCRE

(suffix)

1. Unprofessional Conniving Contemptible Rat Excretion.

weemail

1. Wonderfully Enhanced Email.

(the) WHHEEL

1.The World of Humankind's Hateful Egocentric Evil Learning about the World of Humankind's... A vicious cycle that so many people are stuck in.

wikids

1. Wife and kids.

WINCCCER

1. Bank.
2. Banker.

WOWI

1. Worldwide.
2. Wow-wee.
3. "And so what?" or "big deal."

wwoopsi-net

1. Internet.